Holy Flame Trilogy, Book 3:
Angels Among Us

C.J. Peterson

Texas Sisters Press, LLC

ISBN 978-1-952041-25-9

Published by Texas Sisters Press, LLC. Lufkin, TX U.S.A.

Texas Sisters Press, LLC.
2020

Second Edition

This book is dedicated to my loving husband and dear family who love and support me. You all mean more to me than you will ever know!! Thank you! I love you!

Also, dedicated to those brave men and women of the military, along with the firefighters/paramedics and the police officers who work night and day to keep us safe. Thank you!

A portion of the proceeds of this series will go to Airborne Angel Cadets of Texas – a non-profit group of hardworking volunteers who send care packages to our soldiers overseas. You can find them at: http://www.airborneangelcadets.com

To learn more about C.J. Peterson, you can find her online at: http://cjpetersonwrites.com

'While the stories are fiction, the journey is real!'

<u>Summary</u>

This is the third and final book in the Holy Flame Trilogy, which follows the life-changing events that surround Casey Carter (a firefighter/paramedic from Engine Company Fifteen of Denver, Colorado) and an elite, special operations unit called A.N.G.E.L. (Available to Nurture God's Eternal Love).

With help from a unique band of characters in the Outback, Casey Carter was able to work through her past. However, would it prepare her for what was to come? The battle is forming. Both sides are amassing their troops as allies align, but will there be enough remaining A.N.G.E.L.s for them to win? Without knowing the day nor the hour, will they be prepared?

What kind of battle would this be if the A.N.G.E.L.s of flesh and blood were battling against the unseen powers of darkness? This may be the deciding factor in Casey's struggle for freedom, but will the remaining A.N.G.E.L.s survive or will it be their final battle?

Revelation 12:12

[12] Therefore rejoice, ye heavens, and ye that dwell in them. Woe to the inhabiters of the earth and of the sea! For the devil is come down unto you, having great wrath, because he knoweth that he hath but a short time.

Table of Contents

Preface 1

Scenes from: THE CALL TO DUTY

(Book 1 of the Holy Flame Trilogy)

While she was in the hospital, Casey had a nightmare. It began with the smell of rancid, burnt flesh, much the same as when the man at the fire scene stumbled by her. Then, it compounded with the pungent sulfuric stench of brimstone on fire. She slowly opened her eyes to find that she was in a cold, rough catacomb structure that weighed heavily in desperation and despair. The chambers were about five feet long and two feet tall. They lined the walls of the cavern, stacked about five or six high depending on the height of the cavern at that point, and she was in the second one up from the ground.

Casey rolled over, and what she saw petrified her. Moving or breathing was the furthest things from her mind as she saw things her mind could not conceive. Fire coated the walls, but it did not consume them. There were hideous creatures walking around that were dark red, almost black in color. They had skin made of scales like a reptile. They had large wings like a bat, talons for nails, and yellowish-green eyes that darted around everywhere, searching for any sign of movement from their prey. They had fangs dripping with saliva as they scoured the scene before them, as if it were a Thanksgiving feast.

There were people walking around with only parts of their clothing still on them, some with chunks of their flesh hung off their bodies. The people walking around were in shock as they wondered around aimlessly and despondent.

She continued to scan the area the scene was almost indescribable. She was not sure she would ever be able to explain it to anyone. About thirty feet away from her was a vast, literal lake of fire. As the fire danced atop of the water, it reminded her of when someone sets a puddle of gasoline on fire. The emanation of brimstone was powerfully potent. It was suffocating to her. It overpowered any other scent, making it even difficult to breathe. Then, just when she thought she had seen it all, she noticed there were people in the lake…and they were alive! All she could do was lay there watching people reach out, grabbing others, pulling them back, deeper into the abyss. The hands had absolutely no flesh on them, yet the people were alive!

She studied the scene for a brief moment, almost mesmerized, when suddenly one of those hideous, reptile-like creatures appeared right in front of her. His tight, leather skin crinkled as he folded his arms, resting them on the side of the catacomb. He leaned down near her face. "Well, hello there," he sneered, drumming his claws on the rock.

She could not form a single thought in her head. Words were not an option. Her heart raced as she stared at him in terror. For the first time in her life she was literally scared stiff.

"Welcome, Mzzzzzz Carter," he hissed through his fangs.

She had to consciously remind herself to breathe as the saliva dripped off his sharp teeth, landing in tiny puddles less than an inch from her face.

He reached his claws out and gouged her arm, digging his claws into her skin. She closed her eyes and a scream finally escaped her mouth.

*   *   *

Casey sat there for several moments, debating it in her head. This was the biggest secret of her life. However, in order for him to understand the struggle, he needed to know.

"Whatever you decide," Mac finally said. "If you want me to, I will file it in my head and never mention it again, unless you come to me and ask to talk about it."

"Mac, it's huge."

"Talk to me. I *swear* to you. I make a *vow* to you that I will not say anything."

"If you do, so help me, I will kick your –"

He shook his head. "I won't."

She took a deep breath, before she blurted out, "Somewhere out there is a child of mine."

*   *   *

"Hey, Morgan!" Dale called out to a drop-dead gorgeous guy who got out of his car. Casey had never seen him before.

Casey watched him, stunned. "*Who* is *that*?"

"*That* is our rookie, Hunter Morgan," Dale said. "He just started this last week, you know since Tucker retired. His retirement party, by the way, is next Friday. You coming?"

She nodded, not talking her eyes off Hunter. "Actually, I probably can since 'C' shift is on."

Hunter Morgan looked to be about thirty-six or thirty-seven years old. He was six-foot-three, and had short, light brown hair that was slightly feathered on the sides and in the back, and the top was parted on the side. He also had amazing bluish-gray eyes. His tanned body, told how enjoyed his time off at the pool. Casey was sure Zoey and Bobbi Jo were already drooling over him. Unfortunately for them, it was against regulations to have relations with someone on your own shift.

"Hunter, man, come get some lunch!" Dale waved him over.

"*He's* a *rookie*?" Casey asked, making sure she heard them right.

"He's a transfer from outta Chicago," Matt explained.

*   *   *

"Man," Casey shook her head, as she nervously chuckled, "what's with you and the big questions?"

"Just curious as to what I'm dealing with here," Hunter said.

Her heart skipped a beat. "What do you mean by that?"

"Well, I don't want you jumping every time I touch you."

"Why would you be touching me at all?"

"Such paranoia!" He laughed. When he settled, he said, "Look, let's be realistic, there's an obvious attraction between us."

"Such arrogance!" Casey stood up, offended.

"No. Just honest."

Casey crossed her arms. "I don't trust you."

"But…are you attracted to me?" He looked up at her with a smile of satisfaction.

*　　*　　*

Hunter stayed where he was, not wanting to scare Casey again. He liked her a lot. She captivated him. He forced himself to keep in mind his mission, but he was struggling inside. He saw her heart, and wanted more than anything to help free her from that which was holding her heart prisoner. He wanted to be her hero.

*　　*　　*

"I've held on for you. Please don't ask me to stay. I want to live in peace with our Father. You can bet, though," he wiped the tears off her face with his thumbs, "that I'll be getting a room ready for you up there. I will *always* look out for you."

She fought to get her sobbing under control for his sake. "You always have."

"Then know that I've done my best. I've fought for you, my country, and have even won a few battles for Christ as well while I was at it. I love you, Casey."

"I love you too, Jack," she said, resting her head on his chest. She listened to his staggered breaths as his heart rate slowed.

He reached his arms around her and held her as tight as he could. He kissed her head. "I love you," he quietly cried.

"I love you too. Thank you for everything you have done for me. Please, go be at peace with our Daddy. You're free."

She heard the rhythm of his heart monitor lag as his breathing faltered. She felt desperate as she cried, "I love you, my Jumpin' Jack!"

"I love you too…Space Case," he whispered, and he was gone.

*   *   *

Chief took a moment before he continued, "While I know this is something we had to go through not more than eight months ago, I have the confidence that we will come through it stronger than ever."

Panic churned so strongly inside Casey, that she thought she was going to throw up. "Chief?" She stood up. Jesse held her arms so she couldn't go anywhere. "Chief, where's Mac?" Casey nervously asked. She did not see Mac *or* his partner Carl Warner in the room. "Where's Warner?"

"Carter," Chief shook his head. Barely able to get the words out, he said, "I'm sorry."

She gulped. "He's in the hospital, right?"

He shook his head.

"No," she whispered. Her eyes locked on Chief, she said, "This can't be! No, *he wouldn't do this to me*!"

The Colonel gestured toward them. "This is what's left of the squad."

Casey pulled a chair from the table and sat down across from Mark and the Colonel.

"You've already met Captain Mark English." The Colonel nodded toward Mark. "This is Major Derek Cruise." He nodded toward the man in the chair to his right.

Derek Cruise looked to be about thirty-nine-years-old. He was about five-foot-eleven and had blue eyes. His short, dark brown hair was mixed with gray. As he sat there, Casey noticed that he was fit, but not nearly as muscular at Mark.

He nodded toward the man on the left. "And this is Major Keith Mariano."

Keith Mariano was about thirty-seven years old. He had dark brown hair, brown eyes, a natural slight tan, and was about six-foot-two.

"Guys, as you all know, this is Casey Carter, Jack's sister," Colonel continued. The men nodded as they sat in their seats, on edge.

"What's going on, Colonel? You're dead, but you're not. Mark over there is in the same position. Are you two dead?" She asked Derek and Keith. They nodded, so she turned to the Colonel and demanded, "*Explain!*"

"In doing what we do, we need to not exist."

"That was cryptic. Mind clearing it up a bit?" she snapped. "I'm not in the mood for games."

He sighed, as he shook his head with a smile on his face. "You're amusing. I give you that."

"Colonel," she warned.

He looked up at her and said, "We aren't here. This never happened."

"Fine! Just explain!"

"We do work for the government, specifically special ops in the Air Force."

"Tell me something I *don't* know." She crossed her arms in a huff.

"We're not allowed to exist in order to do what we do. We go in and out of the law all the time. We go into places that no one should ever see. We are exposed to things that if the average person saw it, it would give them nightmares. If we told you exactly what we did, it could literally put your life in danger."

*   *   *

"While your discretion is appreciated, it's misguided here," Derek pointed out. "We're on your side. We've been protecting you for years. We just wanted you to be aware of it, so you wouldn't be paranoid if you caught sight of us."

"If you guys have been protecting me, what happened in Columbia?" Casey asked the Colonel.

"That was Marcos's assignment," he said somberly.

"Okay. And *who* is *that*?" she asked.

"Marcos was Jack's partner. He was weak from being sick, but he still wanted to pull his weight," Keith explained. "Columbia was his last assignment. He died while he was down there."
Wide-eyed, she gulped, as he continued, "When you were attacked, he was dying in his hotel room. When you called Jack, we knew something happened to him. His job was to protect you, and if something happened to you, then something had to have happened to him."

"We scrambled after we got your call," Derek continued. "We had to get Jack cleared for his leave-of-absence, and get our behinds down there to find out what happened. While Jack went to you, the rest of us looked for Marcos and found him dead in his room."

"So," she put her hand up for him to stop, "if I'm following you right, you're telling me that everywhere I ever went in the world one of you guys was following me?"

"Yes," the Colonel said. "We would trade out so one person was watching you at all times, while the rest of us were on assignments."

"So, in doing that, you probably saved me from getting hurt, with the exception of Columbia."

"Yes," Mark said.

"When did this start?" she asked.

"From the day Jack first became an A.N.G.E.L.," Mark explained.

* * *

Once again, around nine-thirty Casey got a knock on her door. "Really?" She sighed as she got up off the couch. When she pulled the curtain back, she saw Mark standing there. She slightly opened the window, and told him to go to the back.

When she opened the sliding glass door, she said, "This is getting to be a really bad habit."

"Just checking in with you," he said, sitting on the couch.

She sat in the chair near the end of the couch where he was sitting. "I'm fine. You guys don't have to hold my hand."

"The Colonel said he had a rather disturbing conversation with you at Jack's grave the other day," Mark said.

"You can't be serious! Do you guys tell each other everything?"

"When it's something as important as your relationship with God, then yes."

"Are you a Christian?"

"Yes. I found Jesus through the Colonel about ten years ago in the field. We were in Cuba at the time. We were being held prisoner in a rebel camp when I just about lost it. They tortured both of us, but got nothing. We were there for about two weeks when the Colonel sat in the shed, singing. I was furious. How could he be singing in the middle of that? He said he had a peace within him. I wanted that peace. I wanted to feel free, even though I was being held captive. Well, long story short, I accepted Jesus as my Savior in that little shed in the middle of the forest in Cuba, and haven't steered from Him since. God is a God of love, Casey."

"I don't know. While I appreciate your concern, I'm angry with Him."

"How can you be?"

She looked at him, furious. "He took everything from me!"

"He gave everything *for* you!" Mark shot back. "Jesus gave His life for you. He sacrificed just so you could be with Him in Heaven. Isn't that what you told Jack?"

"I did," she admitted. "But that was before He took Jack and Mac away."

"Casey," he rested his hand on her knee, "you're being tested. God has something really big in store for you, or He wouldn't be taking you through this test. You *are* strong. You have a tremendous heart. God loves you and knows what you are made of."

"Then He might want to check the owner's manual on me. In case you missed it, I was in the hospital, remember?"

Mark sighed, shaking his head. "I've watched you for years. I have seen you grow up and turn into this amazingly beautiful woman. You purposely go into fires to help other people. Do you understand how much courage that takes?"

"Yes."

"Think about it this way: the fires you go into are nothing compared to the fires of Hell. Jesus went down there for three days, only to come back out with –"

"I know the story," she cut him off.

"Do you understand why though?"

"Yes. I fought to trust Him for a long time. That's the part that infuriates me. I trusted Him, only to have Him rip away any security I had in this world."

"Maybe He wants you to rely solely on Him. Maybe He wants you to feel your security is in Him, and not in people. Maybe, just maybe, He wants you to fully trust Him."

"I do." She sighed. "Well, I did."

"Casey, God loves you. He really does. He wants you to trust Him again."

"How can I? I don't feel comfortable trusting anyone right now. If I get close to them, are they going to die?"

Stunned, he asked, "Where did that come from?"

"My parents? Jack? Mac? I loved all of them, and they died."

"You don't seriously think you did that, do you?"

"Sometimes I wonder," she admitted.

"Casey, maybe Mac was with you to show you something. God may yet give you another man to share your life with."

"Why? So, He can take that person away too?"

"You're reading this all wrong. Mac's time was done. Jack's time was done."

"Well, I'm kind of tired of people being done when they get close to me."

*   *   *

After lunch, they took the trail that headed out to the mountain ridge where Casey accepted the Lord as her Savior. Casey fought the flashbacks of Mac, as she scrambled down the ledge with the others.

"How are you doing?" Jesse quietly asked her as they sat down on the rock.

"Doing okay," she said, staring out at the canyon before her.

"I can see it."

"See what?"

"The memories going through your head."

"Are you two going to whisper the whole time?" Brennon scowled. "It's like you guys have a secret. Want to share?"

"Just talking." Jesse shrugged. He sat back and crossed his arms.

"Well, you two have been 'just talking' a lot lately," he pointed out.

Jesse huffed. "Jealous?"

"They're close. Get a grip, Hanson." Kim rolled her eyes.

"What's *your* problem?" he snapped at her.

"I'm just tired of you complaining about it. No one else seems to have a problem with it."

"They do too," he said. "They just don't say anything."

"Why would anyone have a problem with us being close?" Casey asked.

"Probably because we just buried your fiancé about a month ago, and you're already joined at the hip with him."

"Hanson!" Jesse snapped, almost in a yell.

Casey looked at him, appalled.

"How *dare* you!" Jesse growled.

"It's true. I dare you to say different," Brennon challenged. "Where one is, the other one is not far behind."

"Jeff and Jay are like that, but you don't accuse them of anything inappropriate," Casey pointed out.

"Hold up!" Jeff put his hands up to stop the conversation. "Jay and I *are not* gay!"

"We know that." Casey rolled her eyes, as Kim and Sally giggled. "The point is, Jesse and I are not in any way, shape, or form, romantically involved either."

"Jack made me her brother on his deathbed," Jesse explained. "We're close because of that."

"And Kara's affair had nothing to do with how close you two are, huh?" Brennon challenged.

Jesse looked like he wanted to punch Brennon. He probably would have if they were not separated by six other people and on the ridge of a mountain.

"She said it was because you were either spending time at the station or with her," Brennon said.

Jesse glared at him. "How would *you* know?"

Brennon stood in front of Jesse with his arms crossed. "*Who do you think she had the affair with?*"

Jeff and Jay immediately jumped on Jesse, who went to lunge at Brennon. There was a momentary struggle to control Jesse, before Will got up and pulled Brennon up the path to a safer spot. Kim followed them up, and together they both forced Brennon back to camp.

It wasn't until they were out of sight, that Jeff asked Casey, "Is it clear?"

She stood up and looked over the ledge. Brennon was nowhere in sight, so she nodded.

"Good." Jeff looked back down at Jesse. "We're going to let you go, and you're going to go back over there and sit on the rock so we can talk. Got it?"

Jesse didn't move. You could see the anger in his eyes. Every muscle in his body was tense.

"Jess?" Jay asked after another minute of silence.

Tommy and Sally stayed beside Casey. They hadn't breathed since Brennon's confession.

"I will *never* forgive him for that!" Jesse seethed.

"Let's talk about this, okay?" Jeff tried to calm him down. "We're going to get up, and you're going to go over and sit by Casey. Can you do that for us?"

Jess looked at Tommy, Sally, and Casey, before he turned back to Jeff and Jay and nodded. Jeff and Jay got off him, and Jesse slowly sat up.

"Jess?" Casey asked. "Can I come down?"

He nodded, so she went over to him and gave him a hug. When she hugged him, she felt the anger inside of him. Jesse and Kara were dating for almost two years before it happened.

"Come on over to the rock, okay?" Casey coaxed.

He shook his head.

"Please? We're too close to the ledge here. I'm pretty sure if Jeff and Jay didn't jump on you, that you and Brennon would have gone over the side."

Jesse stared at Casey for several tense moments before he said, "I loved her."

"I know," she nodded in understanding, "just as much as I loved Mac. That's another bond we share."

He sighed before he turned to the others, and asked, "Why would one of my brothers do this to me?"

"She did it too," Sally point out. She was furious with Kara. They had been best friends for over five years.

"But he had an option of saying no, and he *obviously* doesn't regret it." Jesse got off the ground. A combination of hurt, shock, confusion, and fury churned inside him. "Why would he do that to me?"

"Jealousy is an ugly beast," Tommy said, as he and Sally came down off the rock. "He has liked Casey since she came to the station. He was beside himself when she and Mac started courting. Then, watching the two of you bonding more and more over the last several months, becoming closer than you already were, you could see the jealousy raging inside him. I wouldn't be surprised if he got together with Kara and they planned it."

"But, we have a brother/sister relationship. Why couldn't Kara see that? I would do anything for my family."

"We know that. Brennon can be pretty persuasive though," Jeff said. "I know he planted that seed in my head too."

"About us?" Casey asked, stunned.

"Yep. There were several of us keeping an eye on you two. He was trying to get something on either one of you, to get one of you guys either fired or transferred," Jay added.

"Why would he do that?" Casey asked.

"Probably because he wanted you for himself." He shrugged. "He put it by us as the rule was being broken. Out of fairness, it was our duty to make sure the rule still held."

Casey whistled in astonishment. "Wow."

"We need to get back and figure this thing out." Jeff reminded them, "We have to go to bed sometime here in the next couple of hours, and I would rather not do it with all that rage stirring around."

"Do you think you two can have a civil conversation?" Jay asked Jesse.

"I doubt it." He shook his head. "Maybe I'll just go home."

"You can't!" Jay and Casey objected at the same time.

"You've got my house!" Jay referred to the tent.

"And you came in with me," Casey pointed out.

"Besides the fact that we'd miss your smiling face," Sally added. "Come on, stay?"

He looked at them for a moment, before he finally relented, "All right."

"We have to talk to Brennon. Think you can stay here with Casey while we do? I think we need some referees before you two get together again," Jeff said.

"Yeah," he agreed.

After they left down the path, Jesse went over and sat down on the rock. He closed his eyes as he crossed his arms. Then he stretched his legs out in front of him and took a deep breath.

"Want some company?" Casey asked.

"Yeah, come here." He patted the seat next to him. When she sat down next him, he said, "I love you like a sister."

"I know."

"While I do love you, it's not the same love I had for Kara."

"I know. I feel the same way."

"There's nothing I wouldn't do for you."

"Same here."

*   *   *

The zipper on her tent slowly opened, waking her up. It had to be about three or four in the morning.

She slowly reached into her pocket and pulled her knife out as a foot came into her tent. Her heart raced, but she did not dare move. As long as the person did not know she was aware of them, she had the upper hand.

"Case?" She heard Mark's voice as he poked his head in.

"My word! This is daring!" she whispered in shock.

"Come outside," he said, before ducking back out of the tent.

Casey scrambled out of her sleeping bag. She cautiously climbed out of her tent, looking in every direction. She didn't zip it back up, because she wanted to be able to slip back in without unzipping it.

He grabbed her wrist and pulled her to the tree line, his eyes continuously darting in every direction. He took her there, so he could see what was going on at camp without anyone seeing them.

"What's going on?" she whispered.

He didn't say anything. He just grabbed her face and kissed her. She reached up and rested her hands on his wrists as she joined him in the kiss. The passion, electricity, and excitement behind the kiss made her not want to stop.

Several minutes later, Mark took a step back. He looked at her with a lot of intensity, as he rested his hands on her face. "I'm sorry. I just couldn't hold it in any longer."

"Where did…? That was…wow," Casey stammered, as she rested against the tree to catch her breath.

He took a step forward, bending so he was eye level to her, as he said in a low voice, "I have had feelings for you for years, but you were untouchable. You were my assignment. You are not supposed to get emotionally close to your assignments. But as we got closer over the last couple of weeks, and then you hugged me today…." He sighed. "Feeling you so close to me…I'm sorry. We don't have to mention this again, if you don't –"

She cut him off by kissing him again. He ran his hands tightly down her sides to her waist, as he strongly returned the kiss. "Is this…possible?" Casey asked in between kisses.

"If we're careful…yes….There will be times…when you won't see me…maybe for weeks at a time….You think…you can handle that?" he asked in between kisses as well.

"Yes," she said…and the kiss exploded!

She wrapped her arms tightly around his neck, as he pulled her closer to him. Their bodies tingled. Their thoughts were lost in each other's kisses.

"Wow!" Casey said as she breathed heavily. She leaned against the tree to catch her breath.

He looked up at her and admitted, "I've waited for so long. Jack and I even talked about it."

"What did he say?"

"He said if circumstances were different, he would whole-heartedly approve. The problem was that you weren't to know we existed."

"And now that I do?"

He looked at her and very seriously asked, "Can you lead two different lives?"

Preface 2

Scenes from: Operation A.N.G.E.L.

(Book 2 of the Holy Flame Trilogy)

The sand was thick in the air, while the sweltering, stagnant atmosphere hung around them. Mark, Derek, and Keith were tucked into a rock cave on the side of a mountain. The sun began its descent from the sky as it neared five in the afternoon, but it didn't ease the heat. Once the sun went down, the ground would give away its heat into the air, dropping temperatures nearly thirty-five to forty degrees.

The red and tan stone of the surrounding terrain of Kirkuk, Iraq, allowed the trio to blend in with their camouflage of brown, tan, and khaki. The way the heat danced off the ground would frequently create a mirage that messed with what one saw, creating a haze that was difficult to see through once on ground level. Mark knew this could make their job that much harder.

Derek wiped the sweat off his forehead. "Man, it's hot."

A layer of dirt coated each man. When the sweat dripped off their forehead, it left long streaks on their face.

Mark sighed, as he pulled out his binoculars. "Yeah, the Colonel is enjoying camping on a cool seventy-five-degree mountainside, while we're sitting in the stifling, ninety-seven-degree, blistering heat."

Keith raised an eyebrow at Mark. "Are you jealous of the Colonel camping, or the person he's watching?"

Mark shot him a dirty look before turning back to the binoculars.

Derek looked from Mark to Keith in confusion. "Wait. What did I miss?"

Keith huffed. "You couldn't tell?"

"Tell what?"

"Shut up!" Mark snapped, as he was sandwiched between Derek and Keith.

"Man, don't you see how he looks at her?" Keith said, satisfied of the accuracy of his assessment. "They also talk...*a lot*."

"What do you mean?" Derek asked.

"They meet every night he is on and she is off and talk for hours?"

Mark narrowed his eyes. "How do *you* know?"

Keith rolled his eyes. "Did I ever tell you what I do for a living?"

"Did I ever tell you that you need to get a life?" Mark shot back.

"Is he right?" Derek asked, stunned. He did not see that one coming.

Mark shrugged it off. "She's interesting. That's all."

"Interesting?" Keith chuckled. "Is that the best you got?"

"I'm warning you."

"Come on," Derek pressed.

"Look," Mark said, innocently, "she's a sweet kid."

"*Kid*?" Keith's jaw dropped. "Open your eyes, brother! She's no kid. She's a *woman*."

Derek nudged Mark. "And a pretty one at that."

"You two can shut up now," Mark grumbled.

"Just saying. You might wanna open your eyes," Keith pointed out

* * *

Keith looked up to see the relief of four crewmen of the Blackhawk at seeing him alive. He quickly clipped himself in, and the

Blackhawks took off in the opposite direction they had come. The four Apaches flanked the Blackhawks with the F-18s overhead. When they were cleared and headed toward safety, with a tip of the wings, the F-18s broke off. The helicopters finished the journey on their own.

Lost in their own thoughts, neither Keith nor Mark said a word the entire flight. That was too close for Keith. He might have resisted this God of theirs for the last time. Seeing his life flash before his eyes when he dove for the ground may have pushed him over the edge. He and Jack were the last two holdouts of the A.N.G.E.L.s. They did what they could to support the unit, but seeing everything they had over the years made their hearts hard. When Jack came to Christ, he pleaded with Keith to listen. By that point, Keith was done with the world. His heart was jaded. He looked toward Mark who was lost in his own thoughts. Even in the midst of the chaos that ensued, he could still see the peace Mark had on his face. Mark reached in his pocket, pulled a photo out, and gently rubbed his thumb over it.

Seeing the camp in the distance, knowing they would be landing soon, Keith made a decision. He didn't want to die without God. He had been through Hell on Earth. From what he understood over the years, he would have that forever if he didn't make a decision to follow this Jesus. It was his understanding that Jesus was the one and only way to eternal safety.

Matthews rested his hand on Keith's arm. "Thanks, man."

"Anytime, brother. You would do the same."

"Anytime, anyplace," Matthews agreed. "Gotta ask," he said, as the helicopters lowered to the ground, "what unit are you guys?"

"We're A.N.G.E.L.s," Mark said as he hopped out of the helicopter. "We were never here."

"You guys are real?" He stared at him jaw-dropped and eyes wide. "I thought you were a myth! I've heard stories, but had no idea you were real."

"We were never here," Mark reiterated with a stern tone.

He nodded in understanding and appreciation. "Yes, sir."

*   *   *

Mark and Keith were quiet during their showers. It carried over to when they sat at the table, eating. Finally, Keith looked up at Mark and asked, "Who's the picture of?"

Mark raised an eyebrow. "What picture?"

"The one in your pocket. Who is it?"

"What are you talking about?"

"You were looking at a photo in the helo. Who was it?"

Mark froze for a minute, before he set down his fork. After a couple of moments, he reached in his pocket and reluctantly pulled out the photo. He glanced at it one more time before he passed it to Keith.

Keith's eyes popped. "When and where did you get this?"

Mark gave him a knowing look.

"This is recent."

"About a month after Jack passed."

"Why?"

Mark wasn't sure he could explain it. He thought of how to answer his question before he said, "She is why I'm here."

He handed the photo back to Mark, who tucked it safely into his pocket. "I don't understand," Keith said, shaking his head.

"Casey was at the station one day, and you know the crap they play on each other."

"Yeah." He chuckled. He had witnessed several of the practical jokes himself.

"She pulled one over on a couple of the guys, and the smile that lit her face…." He sighed dreamily. "I just wanted to remember what I'm giving my life for. What I'm sacrificing for."

"What's that supposed to mean?"

"John 15:13 says, *"Greater hath no love than this: to lay down one's life for one's friends."* Casey is more than a friend. She's family. When it comes to doing what we do, there is a bigger picture. It's more than just my own life at stake."

"I get that. That's why we're here…to protect freedom."

"I don't want to die, but I'm willing. However, I'm here for a greater purpose than those men we rescued today."

"Meaning?"

"The most I can do is give my life for my country," Mark said. "But, Jesus gave His life for the world – past, present, and future. I'm here to do His will."

Keith shook his head. "I don't get it. How can some guy who died thousands of years ago help me today? That doesn't make sense."

"John 3:16 and 17 says, *"For God so loved the world that He gave his one and only Son, that whoever believes in Him shall not perish but have eternal life. For God did not send His Son into the world to condemn the world, but to save the world through Him."* God sent Jesus so we, meaning you and me, can enjoy Heaven when we die. As you said earlier, we've seen the evil this world has to offer. Do you want that for all eternity?"

"Uh, no thank you. Hell on Earth for this lifetime is more than enough for me."

"Well, hate to tell you, but you're on track to face that for all eternity too."

Furrowed brow, Keith asked, "What if I don't want to?"

"Not an option. Let me explain it this way…there are two teams in play. You have to pick one or the other."

"What if I don't want to play the game?"

"It's not an option, brother." Mark shook his head. "You're already on one team. You actually have to choose to leave it to go to the other one. You're playing whether you want to or not."

Keith scoffed as he crossed his arms. "How is *that* a choice?"

"We're all born into the team headed to Hell for all eternity. God, gracious as He is, gave us another option through the blood Jesus shed on the cross. You don't have to stay on that team anymore. You can opt out and go to the other team – the team the Colonel, Derek, Jack, and I are on."

"And if I don't?"

"You'll end up in a firestorm like you set today…forever."

Keith shook his head, upset. After a long minute, he looked up at Mark. Knowing what he had to do, he asked, "How do I do that?"

A pleased smile crossed Mark's face as he said, "Matthew 7:7 says, "*Ask and it will be given to you; seek and you will find; knock and the door will be opened to you.*" All you have to do is pray and ask Jesus to be your Savior. You need to ask Him to forgive you of your sins, and to show you His purpose for your life."

"I *have* a purpose."

"Right now, your purpose is to put your life on the line for others. When are you going to do something for yourself?"

He shook his head in confusion. "I do stuff for myself all the time."

"What about your eternal security?"

Keith sighed, knowing what he meant.

xxx

"Now, don't do it just for fire insurance."

"Ha!" Keith chuckled. "That's a joke! I'm the pyromaniac of the unit. Fire doesn't bother me. On the contrary, it fascinates me. However," he held his hand up to stop Mark from interrupting, "I understand what you're saying."

"And?"

"I don't want to die at all. And, I *really* don't want to die without this Jesus of yours either."

*   *   *

"Wow." She let out a slow breath of air, remembering what Mark looked like in the woods earlier that day. He was in camouflage from head to toe. His brown eyes blended with the face paint colors of green, brown, and black, while his blond hair stood out on his six-foot frame.

Then it hit her. The dream. The kiss. The passion. Her face flushed in embarrassment as she reprimanded herself again. Mac meant the world to her. *How could she be dreaming of another man? This was too soon.* She wondered if the dream had any element of truth to it. *Did Jack and Mark ever talk about the two of them?*

*   *   *

Hunter sat down next to Casey, where she ate her lunch next to the fire pit. "Hey." He put his arm around her and asked, "So, how about a hike after lunch?"

"Um, what?" she asked, taken aback.

"Well, I think we need to talk."

She reached around and took his arm off her shoulders. "Well, I don't think we do."

"Now, why are you going to be like that? There is an obvious attraction between us. Why are you denying it?"

She shook her head in irritation. "Hunter, are you *really* going to start this again?"

"Why are you fighting it?"

"Because I don't want it."

"Sure you do." He grinned. "How could you not?"

"Could you be any more arrogant?" she snapped.

He looked at her for a minute before he leaned back in his seat, folded his arms, and tried a different tactic. He learned in working with her that she was different from most women. This made his assignment more difficult than he had anticipated. He knew people were counting on him to get certain information. He had a perfect track record, and he wasn't about to let one woman destroy that record. He had to figure out a way to get her to trust him.

*   *   *

The Colonel watched the scene from a distance. He just about spit his water out of his mouth as he laughed when he saw Casey elbow Hunter. He decided to check into him deeper when the others got back, because he reminded the Colonel of someone from his past. He knew it couldn't be him though, because that man was old enough to be Hunter's father, but could it be the sins of the father were passed down to the son?

*   *   *

Casey sighed as she soaked her legs in the waist-deep lake water. She leaned back with her arms braced behind her in the cool, refreshing water while watching the flurry of activity around her. It was nice to see the families having fun together. She appreciated watching the parents with the children the most. She missed that growing up and longed for it. She knew she would never have it though. It wasn't meant for her.

The more she reflected on the parent/child relationships around her, the more she thought about Angelina. Casey knew Angelina had what she would never have. She knew she had a set of loving parents who would take care of her for a long time. While Casey's parents did love her, they were busy and unfortunately were only around until she was eight. While she realized it wasn't by choice, it still deeply hurt her.

*   *   *

Through the next couple of days, Mark snuck into Casey's hospital room after their rescue from deep within the Colorado woodlands. He was relieved to see Casey's temperature dropping, but he was still upset with the Colonel for waiting so long.

"What's her status?" the Colonel asked when Mark walked into the hotel room.

"Her temperature is down to one-hundred-and-one-point-five. She woke up yesterday."

The Colonel studied him for a moment before he said, "I sense a little tension."

Mark pulled a soda out of the tiny refrigerator. "Not much gets by you."

The Colonel sat back in his chair and crossed his arms. "What's wrong?"

"With all due respect, you waited too long, and you know it."

He shook his head. "I don't think so."

Mark glared at him as he emptied the can of soda. Then he crushed it and tossed it into the trash can, watching it drop right in. "I beg to differ."

The Colonel cocked his head to the side as he asked, "What's going on?"

"Why didn't you bring her in sooner?" Mark demanded.

Neither Keith, nor Derek said a word. They saw the discussion coming a mile away, and didn't dare get in between the pair.

"I told you. I didn't want to risk exposing –"

"You did it anyway!" Mark cut the Colonel off.

"Because they were going the wrong way."

"Why didn't you do it the day before? You know, so she and Richter wouldn't have to be carried out of there? What? Were you going to wait until someone died?"

The Colonel leaned back in his chair with his hands behind his head. "She's fine. It turned out okay."

"I need to get out of here." Mark growled, slamming the door behind him.

He walked for over a mile before his mind even remotely slowed. While he never yelled at the Colonel, he knew his tone was disrespectful. Seeing Casey's eyes open this afternoon when he went in delighted him, while having to leave her broke his heart. *Could he have fallen for the sister of one of his best friends?*

The entire walk back to the hotel, he mulled through his mind of how it was possible. He didn't want to face the Colonel, but he knew he had to do it. Leaving things the way they were, was not an option.

The Colonel met him in the parking lot. "We need to take a drive."

Mark sighed as they walked to the truck. He didn't care where they were going, he just wanted to get 'the talk' over and done with so he could go back and rest in the hotel.

After fifteen silently tense minutes, the Colonel said, "I understand there's something going on."

"Who told you?"

"Both of them. They said you've been on edge since Kirkuk."

Mark looked over him, not sure if he would understand. "What's your motivation for getting out of the situations we seem to find ourselves in?" he asked the Colonel.

He thought for a moment. "Well, the way I look at it, if we don't then who will? The guys we pull out of trouble are the ones who need it the most…they are also the ones the country needs the most. The guys we go after are spec ops guys that are being disavowed when they are putting their lives on the line."

Mark nodded in understanding. Looking out the window, he said, "I get that, but what keeps you going?"

"I don't think about it. I just do it. I know if the situation were reversed that I would want someone coming in after me." The Colonel looked over at him for a moment, before he asked, "What's going on in your head?"

Mark sighed. "I don't know."

"Is this about Casey?"

"In more ways than one."

The Colonel narrowed his eyes for a moment before he asked, "Is there something between you two?"

"No."

"Would you like there to be?"

"I don't know."

"I see."

Mark looked over at him. "Do you?"

"I'm not as cold-hearted as I seem."

"I never said you were."

"You don't need to. I can see it in your faces when I send you guys out." The Colonel sighed in irritation. He didn't want to fight with Mark. "I don't take the missions we go on lightly. I know every time I send you out, that you potentially may not come back."

"As you said, if the situation were reversed, I would hope someone would come after me. I don't want to die, but if it came down to it, I would make that sacrifice to get them out."

"But...?" the Colonel asked, feeling there was more.

"*But*, I feel as if there's more to this life."

"Meaning?"

"Meaning…I don't know." He shook his head.

"Yes, you do."

"I honestly don't know what's going on in my head," Mark admitted. "I just know that as soon as the plane took off for Kirkuk, all I wanted was to be with Casey. I feel peace when I'm around her. When we're apart, I long to be with her with every fiber of my being. I miss her smile and laughter. I miss her lightheartedness. I miss talking to her. I guess being on edge twenty-four-seven is getting old."

The Colonel did a double-take. *Did Mark really say what he thought he said?* "Are you saying you're in love with Casey?"

"I'm *saying* that I want something more to life. I don't know. Maybe it's time to turn in the MK-23s and retire."

"You would….*what*?" The Colonel's jaw dropped. He spun the truck into the nearest parking lot and threw it into park. He turned and glared at Mark. "You're going to…what *are* you thinking?"

"I don't know."

"According to Cruise and Mariano, you've been on edge and angry."

"Because I have a lot on my mind. I can sort things out better when I am talking to Casey."

Colonel shook his head. "I don't understand."

Mark looked over at him and admitted, "That's okay. Neither do I."

*   *   *

After a minute of silence, Mark looked up at Casey as they sat in her living room one night, while the rest of the team was in Nicaragua. "This can't be easy for you – hiding us from your friends."

"It isn't, but it's worth the risk. You guys are important to me."

He looked up at her, pleasantly surprised. He was struggling to read her, whereas he used to be able to read her like a book. "Do you know I've been looking after you since you were seventeen?"

She smiled and blushed as she said, "Must feel like forever for you."

"Actually, it's been quite the opposite. To say it felt like forever implies an almost sense of torture. On the contrary, it's been a pleasure."

She glanced up at him and saw him looking back at her. She thought she might have seen something in his eyes. She decided to keep the conversation light and see where it went. "Seventeen, huh?"

"Yeah. I've watched you enjoy the work you did as a photographer and are now doing as a firefighter. While I understand the change of careers, you have a great eye as a photographer. Look at this picture for example." He got up and went to one of the landscapes on the wall. "I remember this. It was in Queensland – Burdekin Falls, I believe."

"That's right," she said, taken aback by his accuracy.

"I was on that trip with you. The other guys were on a mission for that one."

"Really? I was, what, twenty-nine?"

"Yep. Your birthday was five days before. Jack didn't want you to go, but there was no stopping you, so he sent me. He said it was because he knew I could handle myself and you, if need be. He didn't trust your guide."

"Yeah, Madison was a unique individual."

"Madison was a crook. The only reason he didn't touch you was because I threatened him within an inch of his life if he touched you or ripped you off."

Wide-eyed, her jaw dropped.

"And this one." He pointed toward another one, ignoring her reaction. "I was there for this one too. It was on the island Skopelos in Greece on the Aegean Sea, if I remember right."

"It was. How do you remember that?"

He turned and looked at her. "I told you. I've been looking after you for quite some time." He chuckled for a moment in remembrance, "Jack and I used to joke around that if you knew I existed, you and I would have made a great couple." Then he quickly added, "But you weren't supposed to know I existed."

Casey's heart skipped a beat. *So, they did talk about the two of them.* "And now that I do?" she asked.

He looked at her for a moment, before turning to another photo in the hallway. "This was the lighthouse of Dun Loaghhaire near Dublin, Ireland. You've been all over the world with one of us with you at all times."

"And now that I *do* know you exist?" Casey asked again.

He turned and looked at her. He wanted to tell her how much he admired her. He wanted to tell her how he longed to see her sparkling green eyes when they were apart, but he couldn't. He wanted to tell her that her smile lit up his heart. He couldn't say anything.

She walked over to him in the hallway. Standing in front of him, she took his hands into hers, and asked, "And now that I know you exist?"

"Can you lead two different lives?"

*   *   *

Later in the week when Casey was off-duty, she was at home watching a movie when her doorbell rang. It was two short and four long.

She sat for a minute in confusion before she slowly got off the couch. She slightly moved the curtain to see Derek, and motioned for him to go to the back door. As far as she knew, he was still down in Nicaragua with the Colonel and Keith.

She ran to the back door and opened it in time for him to come through with Mark on his heels.

"What are you doing here?" Mark asked Derek, as they went into the living room. Derek paced, as Mark sat down on the couch, on the edge of his seat.

"Have you seen or heard from the Colonel or Mariano?" Derek asked, as he anxiously paced.

To Mark, he seemed irritated and on edge, but he also detected the element of fear, and that was unusual for Derek. "They were on assignment with *you*," Mark said. "What happened?"

"We got separated. The Colonel's instructions were if we got separated to meet back here. I haven't been able to get hold of either of them. Are you sure you haven't heard from them?"

"You guys weren't supposed to check in until 2130 tonight." Mark looked at his watch. "There's still a half-hour until then."

"I tried to contact them, and no one is responding. I needed to know that you two were okay. Something happened, and I needed to know who was okay and who wasn't."

Mark furrowed his brow. "What happened?"

"Remember Hutchins? He was Naval Intelligence from several years ago."

"Yeah, but didn't he die back in ninety-nine?"

"So we think," Derek challenged.

"What does *that* mean?"

"I *saw* him."

Mark stared at him in horror. "You…no way. I saw him die."

"I swear to you. He looked like he was only about thirty-five or forty years old."

"That can't happen. He would be at least twenty years older than that by now."

"Wait a minute. Who is Hutchins?" Casey asked.

"He was Naval Intelligence," Mark explained as he got up and paced opposite Derek, rubbing the back of his neck, wracking his brain to remember details of the incident. "We were going in to pull him out from Bagdad, Iraq. He didn't make it." He stopped and looked at Derek. "Are you *sure* it was him? The age doesn't match."

"I would swear it was him."

"What did he look like?"

"He was about six-foot three, short, light-brown hair, and slate-gray eyes. A big, muscular guy, just like Hutchins."

Casey cocked her head to the side as a thought struck her. She jumped up and got on her laptop, typing in the fire department's web address. She pulled up a photo of Hunter. "Is this what he looked like?"

Mark and Derek both looked over her shoulder as she sat at the kitchen table. "Uncanny!" Mark shook his head in shock. "I never connected –"

"How could he be in Nicaragua when he works at the department?" Casey asked.

"You've been off for two days," Mark pointed out. "No one knows his schedule." He looked over to Derek and shook his head. "You don't think…?"

"No way. There is no way it's him, but he's a dead ringer."

"What happened?" Mark leaned on the chair next to Casey.

"We met with the resistance in the area, and were getting ready to make our move to pull Delgado when we were raided. We split up to give them more targets to go after. I saw several of the resistance fall, but I didn't see what happened to the Colonel or Mariano. I *did* see one of the men in the middle of the battle pull the bandanna off his face. He looked right at me." The color drained from Derek's face. He shuddered before he continued, "His eyes were gray one moment before they turned pure black. I mean completely black, like he was possessed or something."

Mark shook his head. "The heat. You had to have been dehydrated, or the heat was playing tricks on your mind."

"You're kidding, right? Does this face look I'm making something up or dehydrated? I'm a trained observer, English!" he snapped.

Casey pointed to Hunter. "And you're sure it's *this* guy?"

"It looks just like him," Derek confirmed. "Unless he has an evil twin out there, it's him."

"Hmm. You go in tomorrow, right?" Mark asked Casey. She nodded. "Let me see if I can get a hold of the Colonel or Mariano. Things may have stepped up a notch."

"What do you mean?" she asked, concerned and confused at the same time.

"We may be fighting something that will take more than one of us to protect you."

*   *   *

The humidity was beyond hot and sticky. Keith had escaped the attack on the group and found his way to a cantina in the middle of nowhere. He needed to figure out where the Colonel and Derek were. When they separated, what he saw terrified him. He saw the figure of a man inside a man. The outer shell looked like that of Hunter Morgan, Casey's coworker. The inner spirit though, was an entirely other story. He saw the evil that was within the man.

A young lady came over to his table with a tray in her hand. "You American?" She asked. She stood to maybe five foot three in a flowing skirt with a cotton top. She couldn't have been more than fifteen, so by her age, he guessed that she must have been the owner's daughter. The cantina had six tables, with Keith at one of the three under the extending roof, giving him a slight relief from the sweltering sun. The older man, who must have been the owner, stood behind the bar in the hut. He was drying glasses, keeping an eye on the young lady to make sure she was doing her job.

"Yes," Keith said.

"Drink?"

"That would be wonderful." Keith smiled. "Do you have lemonade?"

"Of course. You want?"

He nodded. "Please?"

She disappeared into the tiny hut. He watched her for only a moment when he felt it. The hair on the back of his neck stood on end. He felt someone or some*thing* watching him.

He looked around but saw nothing. The air was eerily still, and the cantina was completely silent. He looked toward the hut and saw the pair talking to each other, but he felt as if he was operating in a dream. That's when he heard it in his head. A voice that said, *"And be sure of this: I am with you always, even to the end of this age."*

He looked up toward the Heavens, and felt a feeling of peace rush over his body as the knife sliced his neck from his left to his right. As his head slowly fell to the table, he felt the warmth of his own blood as it covered the tiny table underneath him.

While his life ebbed away, he couldn't figure out why he wasn't afraid. He heard the gurgling noise that he emitted, but no words came. He thanked God for not making him feel anything. He praised Him for the peace, comfort, and numbness He provided, as Keith moved from this life to the next. He prayed for his friends – the Colonel, Derek, Mark, and Casey. His last thought was that of God standing there with His arms wide-open.

*   *   *

"I'm telling you he's dead. His...." Casey suddenly saw the vision in her mind again. She closed her eyes for a moment. Taking a deep breath, she slowly reviewed the vision in her mind before she looked back up at him. "His throat was slashed. A creature went through the café and slashed his throat. It happened too fast for Keith to react. He never saw it coming. Mark, he's dead. Derek and the Colonel could be walking into a trap!"

Mark shook his head. "A creature?"

"I saw a black figure. It was in the shape of a man, but I saw wings. Its eyes glowed. Keith was killed by something not of this world."

*   *   *

Tommy, Will, and Rob were watching television in the station. Casey was cooking dinner while she and Hunter had an intense conversation in the kitchen…once again about her.

"Why are the rules different when it comes to Carter?" Hunter challenged.

"They aren't." Will shook his head. "We respect her privacy. We don't know what every single guy here does when they are off shift. Why should we hold her to a higher standard than everyone else? Richter doesn't share everything either. It's no big deal."

"It does when we are her only family," Hunter argued.

"But you're not my keeper," Casey snapped.

She looked up to see his eyes turn completely black, and momentarily saw the black shadow of what looked like a demon from her dream standing before her, before Hunter returned to normal. She gulped. Did she push too hard? She knew she would have to tell the A.N.G.E.L.s their instincts were correct. Something about Hunter was *definitely* unnatural.

"Fine. Suit yourself," he said, and left for the weight room as if nothing happened.

Casey's heart skipped a beat when she saw his eyes and the form. She clumsily cut the vegetables until she calmed herself. She prayed in her head for strength and courage to struggle along the path that God directed her. She had a feeling of foreboding churn through her body. She knew things were coming on the horizon…bad things. She prayed she would survive them.

*   *   *

Casey, Pete, Tommy, and Marty were about twenty feet from each other and in teams of two, with three other teams from another department scattered, throughout a one-hundred-yard-long warehouse structure fire. Engine Company Fifteen's crewmembers were closer to the front of the building, when two storage tanks suddenly blew. Casey and Pete dove for the ground and covered their heads. Tommy and Marty were about twenty yards behind, and both flew through the air in opposite directions.

Casey found Tommy and comforted him as much as possible until Kim and Jesse could get there. After they got him stabilized, they cautiously maneuvered through the maze of debris from the fire.

"I'm tired," Tommy moaned.

Casey heard the helicopter and knew it was life flight for Tommy. "Hold on a little longer," she encouraged. She looked down at him and saw that his face was gray, and his body was motionless. "Tommy?"

They walked out of the building, making a beeline for the helicopter about fifty feet away.

"Tommy?" Casey gulped. When he didn't answer, she took a deep breath, focusing on securing him within the helicopter.

After they loaded him, Casey slowly took several steps back. In a silent prayer in her head, she begged for God to spare his life. She thought she heard Tommy's voice, but the noise of the helicopter's engine did its best to drown out any distinguishable noise.

"Nelson's on his way to the hospital in the ambulance," Pete said, as he walked up to Casey while the helicopter took off. "He has a broken leg."

Casey nodded, nervously biting her nails.

"He's going to be okay," Pete encouraged.

Casey shook her head, watching the helicopter turn toward the level-four hospital. "I don't know about that."

* * *

Over the next week, she did her duty. She went to Tommy's funeral, and stood by Sally the entire time, not shedding a tear. She was done with losing people. She was angry with God for taking him. Knowing Tommy would live on in the baby Sally carried was little consolation, since his baby wouldn't have the benefit of having its father around. Casey was confident that Tommy would have made a great father. It broke her heart that he died so young.

Throughout the several months following the funeral, Mark, Derek, and the Colonel tried to break through Casey's shell. She had a wall around her heart so thick that they couldn't break through no matter how hard they tried. Mark's heart broke for her, but he knew time and God would have to work on her heart together. He knew God could penetrate the hardest of hearts. He held onto the confidence that she was one of His, and he knew God didn't leave His people behind.

*　*　*

Jesse leaned on the counter next to Casey as she cooked dinner at the station as he said, "Look, I need a vacation. We had a rough year last year. Granted, this one has been a lot easier, with the exception of my personal drama and the loss of Tommy. I'm just tired, I guess. I'm tired of losing good men. I'm tired of walking into over half of the situations we walk into each day at work. I feel like I just need some time to decompress and breathe."

"All right. Let me work on it," Casey said in understanding. "What dates do you have for vacation?"

"I'm taking my four weeks of vacation, starting in two weeks."

"Will Chief let us take the same four weeks off?"

"He might let us overlap a week or two."

"Okay, let me work on it." Casey decisively nodded. He needed a vacation. He needed to relax. The more she thought about how much Jesse had been there for her, the more she wanted to make his life-long dream come true. She would go talk to Chief later, and then she would work on a flight for him and her to Australia so he could see Mount Uluru and swim in the Great Barrier Reef. She felt that was the least she could do for him.

*　*　*

Hunter had a short time to put his plan into effect. He knew Casey and Jesse were going on a two-week vacation in two weeks, and he had to find out where. He decided to tail Casey for the next couple of days to find out what he could.

He sat outside her house, but several houses down the road so he would blend into the neighborhood. Nothing looked out of place, but the hair on the back of his neck stood on end. Someone was close from the other side. He felt it when Casey was around, but this was stronger. It was an overwhelming sense of power. Under normal circumstances, he would talk to his boss about it, but he and his boss were not in agreement at that moment. His boss was a commanding and controlling woman who was used to getting what she wanted. While he respected that, he didn't agree with her assessment of the situation regarding Casey.

He sat up in his seat when he saw Casey and a man walk out of her house. So, there *was* someone else in her life. He pulled out his cell phone and took a photo of the man. He couldn't get a clear picture though; due to the sunglasses he wore and the distance. The man looked familiar to him. Deep down, something inside him told him he knew him from somewhere…another time, another place. He decided to follow them to see if he could get a better look at the man with Casey. Obviously, someone else was involved, and he would have to move to plan 'B' and take matters into his own hands. Casey's time was up.

*   *   *

As they walked away, he noticed that they were excitedly discussing what was on the paper Casey held – probably an itinerary. He needed to find out where she was going.

"Good morning. Can I help you?" Courtney asked, as she walked out of her office.

"Hello, the name's Allen Hutchins." Hunter smiled, pulling every chivalrous quality he had in his arsenal. He knew this would be a tough sell. "I need to book a vacation."

"Certainly, I have fifteen minutes before my next appointment. Please follow me," Courtney said, as she walked into her office. She looked up at him when he sat in the seat across from her "Now, where would you like to go?"

"Where are most people traveling to at this time of the year?" he asked. "This traveling thing is new to me, but I've come into some money recently, and decided I needed a vacation."

"Well, hmm, being that it's October, usually people are heading south of the equator where it's spring. For example, I just had a group of people book for Australia."

"Australia, huh?" He smiled to himself. This was almost too easy.

"Yes. The weather there is nice this time of year."

"Really?"

"Oh! Definitely! Their spring starts in the first weekend of October. The flowers are in bloom and the beaches are open once again. It's gorgeous this time of year."

"Do you have any brochures I can look at?" he asked, hoping she would leave the office so he could grab the papers from Casey's appointment.

"No need. Thanks to technology, I have the brochures right here on my computer." She smiled, turning the computer screen toward Hunter.

"I like to take things home to look at them though. I would prefer brochures." He glanced at his watch, knowing he wouldn't have much time before her next appointment.

"I would be happy to print some out for you. What are your interests?" She slid the paperwork from the previous appointment into a folder, before she rested it in her drawer to file for later. She was pleased everything from the previous appointment was all taken care of and paid for, and couldn't hide her excitement of sneaking another one in before her boyfriend arrived for lunch. She knew he would understand if she were a few minutes late. After all, the commission from another trip would benefit both of them.

Hunter took a deep breath. She was testing his patience.

"Courtney, I'm going to go for lunch." Her receptionist poked her head in. "Or do you want me to wait?"

"Don't worry about me. Warren will be here in about ten minutes. I'll be fine here with Mr. Hutchins until then."

"Okay. See you after lunch," she said, before leaving the office.

"Now, what are you mainly interested in seeing while you are in Australia?" Courtney asked, as she looked up at Hunter, who now stood as he leaned on her desk.

"I don't have time to play around anymore."

"I'm sure you don't." She looked at him, confused. Her eyes became wide, when she saw his eyes turn black as coal, and his body suddenly shifted to some creature with reddish-black skin and scales.

"We need to talk," the creature hissed.

*   *   *

"So," Jesse asked on their way to the airport, "What do you know about our fellow travelers?"

"Well, they're brothers from Texas," Casey said.

"Oh boy." He smiled. "This is going to be fun. We're going to have to translate Texan on one end and Australian on the other."

"Aw, come on, where's your sense of adventure? The brother I met seemed like a nice guy. Besides, I've got you watching my back, right?"

"Right."

With that, they drove the rest of the way to the airport, while Casey filled him in on what she knew about the brothers, Colby (Mark) and Clinton (Derek) Leighton. The cover story was that they were the only boys to oil tycoon, Bo Leighton. They moved near Denver about three months ago, due to the opening of a new branch of their business, Leighton Western Wear. After three months of hard work, they were finally confident enough to take a vacation, which was supposedly where Colby ran into Casey at the travel agency.

Casey and Jesse met the guys at the airport, and introduced each other before they headed toward security and their terminal.

*　　*　　*

"Well, lovely lady." Mark hugged her. "Hate to do this, but we have a long day tomorrow. Think you can get some rest?"

"Yep."

"That's my cue." Derek smiled, standing. "Come on over when you're ready."

Mark nodded in appreciation. "Be there in a few."

After Derek went through the doorway, Mark turned Casey around in his arms and kissed her. "I love you," he said, looking into her eyes a few moments later. "I love that I'm always on your mind. I love that you're always on your toes. I love that you respect and honor me, and everything we work for. I also love that you love me."

"I do."

He walked her over to the window. The view of the Sydney Harbour Bridge and the Sydney Opera House from Casey's room was spectacular. The water was calm outside, so the lights from the Bridge and the Opera House danced lightly on the water. The stunning view entranced Casey for several minutes, as Mark wrapped his arms around her.

"Why is your unit called A.N.G.E.L.?"

"It's an acronym that stands for: Available to Nurture God's Eternal Love. It means that we are being used by God, to show His love wherever and whenever it's needed. We are kind of God's Special Operations Unit."

"If that's the case, and I'm an A.N.G.E.L., then –"

"Then, you are being used of God. All Christians are His elite force on this planet. He put us here to do His work. Sometimes He uses His spiritual angels to provide those unexplainable miracles we receive throughout our lives, and sometimes He uses those in the physical realm. Consider them support staff. They are those who pray, playing a pivotal role in bringing power and strength to those who need it the most. There are also people who, under the direction of the Spirit, bring a special blessing to His children. They could be something as simple as giving smiles and support to someone who is in their darkest hour, or providing a meal where there is none, or even a mysterious checks or money that suddenly appears when you least expect it, but when you need it the most. The field agents are a unique breed. Some are called missionaries, who have enlisted to do His work daily at home or abroad, and some are those of us who are sent in because we can handle the worst of the worst. We do our best to retrieve and rescue those of His who are POWs for His name. Sometimes we get to them in time, sometimes we don't. But, be rest assured in the knowledge that The Lord's angels are everywhere, and He has them looking out for you."

"I see."

"You're an A.N.G.E.L., and as an A.N.G.E.L., you need to know that there is a group of special operations A.N.G.E.L.s representing each country. Though over the years, some have been battled into extinction. As you can see, our unit has been knocked down to four."

"What happens when we're gone?" she asked.

"Hopefully someone else will come along and pick up the torch. We need more soldiers for Him. That will only happen when people take a chance and talk to others about Him. Hopefully they will come along before we are gone, so we can help train them."

"It's a circle of life thing, then?"

He sighed, as he stared out the window with his arms wrapped around her. "Something like that."

"And we need the next generation to take a stand?" she asked.

"And pray that complacency won't win out over the call."

"Well said."

Mark stood behind Casey, lost in his own thoughts. He knew that with the risks they took, just like the A.N.G.E.L.s of the past, his time might be up sooner than he thought. He also knew that no reward came without risk. "Casey?"

Casey couldn't take her eyes off the serene scene before her. "Yes?"

"Will you, when this is over…will you consider marrying me?"

As soon as he asked the question, Casey spun around in his arms. She spun so fast that he took a step back. "Are you okay?" he asked, slightly taken aback.

Shock written all over her, she asked, "What did you just ask?"

When he realized it was out of surprise and not a bad reason, he took both of her hands into his, and looked into her eyes as he said, "I asked, if you, Casey Ann Carter, will marry me?"

"Are you serious?"

"In our lives, we need to take the good when we can get it. And you, my lovely lady, are one of the best things I've ever had. So yes, I'm serious. Will you marry me?"

"Yes!" She smiled in excitement. She threw her arms around his neck, and hugged him tightly. "I love you, Mark Allen English."

"Good." He chuckled. "It helps a marriage when the partners love each other."

Casey didn't say anything. In her excitement, she kissed him. After a moment, he wrapped his arms around her, and the kiss turned sensual. It lasted for several long minutes, as they relaxed in each other's arms.

Mark smiled as he reached up and tucked her hair behind her ear. "I love kissing and holding you."

"I love kissing and holding you too. Your kisses are so soft. There's so much power behind them too."

He winked at her. "Just wait until I don't have to hold back."

"Any day now," Derek called from their room.

They burst out in laughter as they held each other. "Be there in a minute!" Mark yelled to Derek, before he turned back to Casey and said, "Now, you can't wear a ring because of our cover, but would this work instead?" he asked, pulling out a gold cross necklace with a diamond in the shape of a heart in front of it. It had a tiny gold angel behind the cross, reaching around to the front with its hand holding onto the diamond.

"Yes!" Casey smiled. "I will only take it off for my shower."

"That'll work." He reached around and fixed the clasp, as it hung from her neck, kissing her neck while he was down there.

"Um, Mark, that's not…." Casey took a deep breath. "I thought you had to, um, go."

He looked up at her, with his hands on the sides of her face, and reminded her, "Just wait until I don't have to hold back."

Casey stared at him in amazement. She could not believe that this late in life, God provided her with this absolutely wonderful man. It seemed that God *was* looking out for her after all.

"On that note, sweet dreams, my little angel." He winked, before he quickly kissed her and left for his room.

Casey turned back toward the view out her window, sighing as she held the necklace. It was beautiful. It was perfect. She was so happy right then; she knew absolutely nothing would be able to ruin it.

*   *   *

When Casey woke up, a metal cord anchored to the wall shackled her feet and hands. She had a splitting headache. She felt so sick that she thought she was going to vomit.

As she rolled over, she noted that the room measured approximately fifteen feet wide by fifteen feet long. The room itself was about two stories tall with windows three feet tall and four feet wide going along the top of the outside wall of the room. Another bed occupied the room, but it was empty.

Casey rolled back over, faced the wall, and took a deep breath. She had no idea where Mark or Derek were and that petrified her. She also had no idea where *she* was, and she knew from the position she was in, it wasn't a good thing.

Two men entered the room, dragging Mark in with them. After they secured Mark to his bed, they practically dragged Casey to another room. They then set her on a chair backward and one of the guys tied her wrists and ankles around the back of the chair tightly with a rope so she couldn't move. The chair also had a headrest on it, so one of the guys flipped it back and laid her head on it before they both left the room.

A couple minutes later, a woman came in who looked to be about fifty or fifty-five years old, but very fit. She was thin, around six feet tall, had light brown, almost blond hair, and bluish-gray eyes. She pulled up a chair next to Casey. Then she sat on it backward, resting her chin on her crossed arms on the back of the chair.

"Hello, sweetie," she said to her with a thick Australian accent. Casey barely got her eyes open – her head swam. "Are ya comfy?"

"Not really," she mumbled.

"How about ya wake up a bit more, love?" Jackie smiled. "We need t' talk."

Casey struggled for a couple more minutes before she was able to pick her head up to look at her.

"There, that's better, don't ya think? Now, how 'bout you tell me a story?"

"About what?"

She got off the chair and leaned down so she was less than three inches from Casey's face. She jerked her head back by her hair, and said, "Your brother took a box of mine and I want it back. Where is it?"

"I don't know." What she said was true. At that point, Casey had no idea if the Colonel moved it or not.

Jackie took Casey's head and slammed it into the headrest, making Casey's nose bleed, before Jackie yanked Casey's head back again. "How 'bout you cooperate with me? Your friend didn't and he's not looking too good right now."

When Casey didn't say anything, Jackie picked up a syringe from the table that already had a liquid in it. She pulled up Casey's shirtsleeve and jammed the needle into her arm, emptying the stinging solution into her system. Casey gasped and gritted her teeth as she did it, but didn't yell as much as she wanted to.

"We'll just let that soak in a bit before we try again," she said, tossing the syringe onto the table behind her. Jackie then sat backward in her chair again, and rested her folded arms on the back of it. She watched Casey, impatiently drumming her long nails on the back of the chair.

Within seconds, Casey's head started spinning. "Whoa!" Casey shook her head as she fought to clear it. Things were melting together, and she saw flashes of light around the room. Casey struggled to form a complete thought of any kind.

Jackie reached up and tucked a piece of Casey's hair behind her ear. "You're a pretty one. No wonder my son liked you."

Casey looked at her in confusion. "Your son?"

"You would know him as Hunter Morgan."

Casey looked toward Heaven, and screamed in her head, *"Oh, God please help me! If she knows he is dead, I will be in more trouble than I already am!"*

* * *

After Jackie tortured Casey into unconsciousness once again, the two men came back into the room. With one holding each of her arms, they dragged Casey along with them all the way back to the room where the beds and Mark waited.

Mark rolled over and looked up when the door opened. While he was appalled at the shape Casey was in, he tried to contain himself for both of their sakes. If they knew he cared about her as strongly as he did, they would use her against him to get information.

The guys dragged her to the bed and put her down facing the wall with her back to Mark. They shackled her before leaving the room, locking the heavy metal door behind them.

Mark saw the blood soaking into her shirt. "Casey?" he asked quietly. When she didn't respond he tried again a little louder. "Casey?"

Casey tried to answer him, but her body wouldn't cooperate. She had never experienced pain like this before in her entire life. If the A.N.G.E.L.s experienced even a portion of what she just did, the admiration she already had for them jumped tenfold.

"Oh, Father." Mark looked up toward Heaven in prayer. "We need help. We are children of Yours, and we are in big trouble." He looked over at her again. With tears in his eyes, he saw the blood seep through her shirt. "Father, she doesn't deserve this. She looks…." He shook his head, unable to speak for a moment. He tried to organize his thoughts again, but gave up and spoke what was in his heart. "Father, we love You. We know You are the Almighty One. We know You are bigger than this, and more powerful than they are. Please, I beg You to help her. Please knock her out all the way, so she doesn't have to feel the pain anymore. Her screams were…." he shook his head, as Casey moaned in pain. "I'm pleading on her behalf for mercy. Have mercy on her! Please rain down Your Spirit of comfort, and give her peace and rest. Please protect her from having to go through that again. I don't think she can endure it."

He sighed as he glanced over at her. He shook his head, distraught. "Father, I love her. I love her with all my heart. Please don't make her suffer anymore. Please step in and stop this. The blood…her scream…she's losing a lot of blood, Father. Please help her."

The shackles on his hands and feet clinked as he rolled over to look at her. "I love you, Casey. I'm sorry I couldn't help you. Please forgive me?"

He wanted to go to her to comfort her. He jerked on his shackles, but they didn't budge. For fifteen minutes, he tugged and pulled with all of his might before giving up. His hands and ankles bled, but he wanted to get to her. He turned to see the blood now coating her back. He shook his head as she silently lay there for a few more minutes, when suddenly out of the corner of his eye he saw movement. He saw two shadows cast onto the wall by the moonlight through the window. He looked toward the windows at the top of the room to see two shadowy figures dangling from a rope in front of the window. "What the…?"

After a few moments, the two figures used a glasscutter, and were finally able to break through the glass. One climbed in, still attached to a rope. He swung to the window beside the one he came through and unlocked it, easily sliding it open. When he got it open, the second man came in, also attached to a rope. The first person swiftly scaled the wall, with the second closely behind him.

As soon as they both reached the bottom, they unlatched themselves and went to Mark. They picked the locks of the shackles, releasing him.

"Where's Casey?" the Colonel asked Mark.

He nodded toward the other bed. "She's over there."

"Oh my…." The Colonel shook his head, feeling sick to his stomach. "Oh, Casey."

"I don't know how much time we have until they come back." Mark rubbed his wrists. They were raw, but he was free.

Derek and the Colonel immediately picked the locks, releasing Casey from the shackles. "What's the best way to do this?" Derek asked, as he looked at her injuries. "She's unconscious…thank God."

"I've got her," Mark volunteered.

"No," the Colonel said, "you're injured too."

"But she's –"

"I know," the Colonel cut him off. "But you're not in any shape to carry her up a wall. We have to get out through *that* window in order to get out of here." He pointed up toward where the ropes dangled from the window.

Mark nodded, knowing the Colonel was right.

The Colonel gently picked her up under her arms and slid her off the bed. When she was in semi-standing position, Derek flipped her over his shoulder like a sack of potatoes.

"Let's go," Derek said, going to the ropes.

It took them several minutes to scale the wall, especially Derek. While she wasn't a heavy-weight by any means, she was still dead weight. He was also trying to be careful not to open the wounds any further.

As soon as they reached the top, Derek passed Casey to Mark, who flipped her over his shoulder. "Mark, come on. Let one of us carry her," the Colonel said.

"*I* am carrying her," Mark said adamantly. "Let's go."

"All right," the Colonel said, giving up, as he and Derek pulled the ropes back up from the room, dropping them down the outside wall. Once the ropes were in place, all three men quickly scaled the wall. When they reached the bottom, they ran into the woods located behind the warehouse where Casey and Mark were held.

"We have to hustle. As soon as they know you two are gone, they're going to start looking," the Colonel said, as they ran through the woods.

"The chopper is a mile that way." Derek pointed to the left, the direction they were already running.

As they ran, they heard gunfire in the distance. The Colonel prayed for safety for the A.N.G.E.L.s he knew were creating a distraction for their escape.

*   *   *

Casey turned toward Mark and said, "It was a woman."

"Who did that to you?"

"She was Hunter's mother."

"No way!" he said, wide-eyed. "Are you serious?"

"She wanted to know where *her* strongbox is. What's going on?"

"I think we need to get together and talk about this," Mark said, looking around for the Colonel and Derek. When he saw them by the hill that went down to the river, he whistled. Everyone in camp looked over towards them, so Mark pointed to Derek and the Colonel, and motioned for them to come into the tent.

"What's up?" the Colonel asked, as he and Derek sat down on Mark's cot across from them.

"The woman who did this to me was Hunter's mother," Casey explained.

The Colonel looked at her, wide-eyed. "Hunter? As in Morgan?"

"Don't play dumb with me!" Casey snapped. She was furious. She was still struggling with the medication, but she was livid. As soon as she snapped, everyone in camp looked up at them, stunned.

"Where'd *that* come from?" the Colonel asked.

"With all due respect, *sir*," Casey said, snidely, "I've had my back pretty much filleted. And then, just to make sure I would remember it, that woman poured hot salt water over it. I am *not* in the mood for games. She wanted the strongbox...*her* strongbox. She said Jack took it, and she wanted it back. *Where* is it and *what's* in it?"

"I can't tell you that."

Casey struggled to stand as she moved so she was eye-to-eye with the Colonel. With her hands braced on his shoulders, she demanded, "Tell me! My life, Jesse's life, Jack's life, Keith's life...as well as several other people's lives, have all been ruined, or they have been killed, because of some stupid metal box. What's in it? Why would a woman slice and dice my back because of a stupid metal box? Why would they beat the crap out of Mark because of it? While you people are used to this, I'm not. I am used to putting people back together – not running and ducking while being hunted."

"Casey, it's hidden here in the camp with us," the Colonel said calmly. "I brought it with me so it would be in our sights at all times. As far as its contents, I can't tell you. As far as that woman claiming to be the original owner, she lied – great surprise there." He rolled his eyes.

"Well, she sure *looked* like Hunter, so I *doubt* she was lying about *that*."

"I wouldn't know. I wasn't there, you were…and I trust you."

"Then tell me the truth!" she yelled. She dropped to her knees, as she shook her head and closed her eyes. She braced her arms on the ground to hold herself. The stress, mixed with the medicine, snowballed on her, knocking her to the ground.

"Come on back to the cot." Mark held his hands on her arms being careful not to touch her back. Everyone in the camp stood by the fire, watching them in shock.

Casey looked up at the Colonel with tears in her eyes as she slowly shook her head. "They almost killed us. I only want to know why."

The Colonel knelt in front of her and cupped her face in his hands. The pain in his face matched what was in her heart. "I wish I could. I wish you didn't have to go through *any* of this." He shook his head, beside himself. "If I could have taken your place, I would have. This is something we have been doing our best to keep from you. I give you my word though – swearing on your brother's grave and on all the A.N.G.E.L.s lives lost – that I *will not* let it happen again. When we get out of here, we are going under. They will *never* find you again. You're right. Enough people have been hurt or killed. We are keeping the box so it doesn't happen again. Trust me when I tell you the contents of that box could cause more death, pain, and injury than has already been inflicted. We love you. This has been killing us just as much, if not more, than it has you. I have had multiple conversations with Mark, because he blames himself for letting them get to you in the first place. Derek and I have had arguments over it. We've pointed the finger enough though. We need to be united in this. If we don't, then they'll win. We need to stand strong until we're all safe. I promised your brother to keep you safe, and I will give my life to do so. You *will* be safe. From this point on, our mission is to get you deep, keeping you hidden and safe for the rest of your days."

She stared at him in disbelief. "Is that possible?"

"Yes," he said, firmly.

She could tell by the look on his face that he would follow through with that promise.

*   *   *

"I'm gonna go tell Hawk. Keep your eyes peeled," Harper warned, and then he left the tent to his commander. Harper sat down on the log beside Hawk, and quietly told him what he saw before he went back into the tent with Marshall.

Hawk got up and went to Carson and Grant. All three immediately fanned out into the trees, going in three different directions.

Marshall nervously looked up at Harper and whispered, "English is gonna kill us if something happens t' her."

"Then we'd better not let anyone get t' her," he simply said.

After a few minutes, there was more movement. This time it was a little closer to the tent. Harper and Marshall both snapped up their heads, looking in the precise direction they saw the movement. Marshall stayed with Casey, while Harper stood. Both had their guns drawn, intently scanning the area around them.

Harper went to the table, which was about five feet from where he last saw the movement. He had his gun trained on the tree, as he said, "You might as well show yourself. You're gonna get shot if ya don't."

A moment later, a young Aboriginal man stepped out from behind the tree. He was dressed only in a pair of shorts – no shirt, no socks, no shoes. He also carried a bag of food, with a bow across his chest, and a pack with arrows on his back. He was only about five-seven, had medium-length, black, curly hair that hung just above his shoulders, and couldn't have been more than seventeen years old. As he stood there, he looked around with a grin on his face.

"Who are you?" Harper asked, as Carson, Grant, and Hawk surrounded him on three sides with their guns drawn as well.

"I'm Charlie," he simply said, with his hands loosely draped on his sides, seeming perfectly comfortable even though he currently had five guns trained on him.

"What do ya want? What are ya doing here?" Hawk demanded.

"T' help her." He nodded toward Casey. "Heard her last night. Scared da daylights outta me! She need medicine."

Hawk looked at him, studying him for a moment, before he asked, "What were ya doing all the way out here in the bush?"

"On walk-about." Charlie shrugged. "Take them all da time. Ne'er heard before what I did last night, dough. She had bad dreamtime. Fever…no?" he asked Harper.

Harper looked at Hawk to see if he should answer. Hawk nodded, so Harper nodded as well.

"High…no?" Charlie pressed.

Harper nodded again.

Charlie stood on his toes to see her better and cringed. "Can get ya something t' make dat feel better – heal faster. Got something I can get for dat fever too."

Harper looked at Hawk again for help. Hawk simply said, "You have t' understand that her other half'll kill ya with his bare hands if ya hurt her."

"I know." Charlie nodded with a smile. "I see him. He have a lotta anger in him. He should talk t' da elders. Dey help him."

"Where *exactly* is your village?" Hawk looked at him, trying to figure out what was going on.

"Jus' down da road…dat way," he said, pointing north.

"How close?" Hawk pressed.

"Day walk." Charlie shrugged. "I could get medicine for her, den go get help. We have Pete, who can help her. I also get elders for your friend. We help."

Hawk studied him for a few more minutes before he nodded. If he were willing to help Casey, knowing Mark could potentially do some serious damage to him, he would go ahead and let him do it. Besides, he had enough experience with the Aboriginals over the years to know they had medicines the military and government didn't even know existed.

*   *   *

"Dis is Ollie, George, an' Pete – our elders. And dis is Grace – me blood n' blister." He gestured toward the people with him.

Ollie looked to be about sixty or seventy years old, and was only about five-foot-five. He wore a pair of tan shorts and a white tank top – no shoes. (None of them were wearing shoes.) He kept his curly white hair short, and his white teeth stood out when he smiled.

George was about five-foot-seven, and looked to be about fifty years old. His dark hair was in curly locks, about six inches long all over, mixed with about fifty percent gray. He wore a pair of jean shorts, along with a white, green, and blue flannel patterned, button-down shirt, that was open, with a white tank top under it.

Pete was about five-nine, and looked to be only about forty years old. 'Elder' was not a word anyone would have used for him. His jet-black hair was short, and the dark eyes that all of them had, held a dancing sparkle of life. Pete wore jeans and a royal blue t-shirt.

Charlie's sister (which was what a "blood n' blister" was in Australian Strine), Grace, was very pretty. She had her black, mid-back length, curly hair, pulled back in a low-hanging ponytail. She also wore a strapless sarong tied with a rope at her waist. She was five-foot-five, and looked to be about twenty to twenty-five years old.

Hawk shook each of their hands. "Welcome."

Grace kept looking at Casey, who was asleep in the tent, while keeping a nervous eye on all of the men crawling all over the place. This was foreign to her. The idea that the men were taking care of a woman, and worse yet, that she lay there only partially dressed, was unheard of in her clan.

"Ollie an' George, are our elders," Charlie explained. "Dey need t' meet with him," he said, nodding toward Mark, who sat by Casey.

Mark looked up at the Colonel and raised an eyebrow.

"Um." The Colonel stood up and shook everyone's hand. When he got to Charlie, he asked, "Why *exactly* would they want to meet with one of my men?"

"Because his heart needs healing. Dey da one's dat'll fix it, like da medicine fix her back…yes?" Charlie asked.

The Colonel looked at the unconventional band that was before him, trying to assess what everyone's function would be. "And the other two? Who are they here for?"

"Oh! Pete knows recipes better den me. He and his dad, Buri, are da most smart about dat type of stuff. He make better tea den me."

The Colonel nodded toward Grace. "And her?"

"She help Pete. It more proper for da women t' take care of da women," he explained.

"I see." The Colonel nodded in understanding. "That makes sense. Um," the Colonel ran everything through his head one more time before he asked, "And what *specifically* are they gonna do with English to heal his heart?"

"Dey take him t' dreamtime."

*   *   *

"She need dreamtime," Ollie insisted. "She healed on outside. Now need t' heal inside."

lxv

George nodded, looking into Casey's eyes. "Da soul is torn and scarred."

"We kind of need t' keep these guys moving," Hawk spoke up. "I don't know if we can wait three more days. I don't know what the outside world looks like right now."

George looked at him very sternly, and said, "Her core needs t' be healed before her body. Dat more important. It takes as long as it takes."

Hawk shook his head in frustration. While he trusted these people, time was precious. He was responsible for the A.N.G.E.L.s in his care.

George grabbed Hawk's wrist, and brought him to Casey, as Mark stood to the side with his arm around her. "Look at her eyes." George pointed to her face as he said, "Her core is being held prisoner. She *needs* dreamtime. She *need* it *now*."

Hawk looked at her, almost studying her, before he finally nodded in approval.

"Just so you know, we're all going too," the Colonel said, standing from where he sat around the fire.

Ollie shook his head. "She needs t' do dis on her own."

"We're going," the Colonel said firmly. "We *will not* let her out of our sight again. Come on, Cruise," he said to Derek, who nodded in response as he stood. "He's going," the Colonel said, pointing to Derek. "He's going," he said, pointing to Mark. "I'm going. And he's going," the Colonel said, pointing to Hawk. "The rest of you will hold down the fort."

Grace grabbed Casey's hand. "I go too."

Ollie sighed in frustration, shaking his head. "Right-oh. Let's go."

*　*　*

"She's one of His!" The angel stood up with authority in his voice as they were in the hut, in Casey's 'dreamtime.' "Her heart and soul are His!"

"Ahhhh, but her core isssss mine," the demon said, holding up a key. "This issss the key to her core. She won't give it up…and neither will I. It'ssss locked, forever." It reached up and touched the side of her face as it hissed, "Isn't it, precioussss?"

Casey stared at the demo in horror as she watched its face transform into Jackie's right in front of her eyes. "Yessss, another wonderful day," Jackie cackled. Her face and body were Jackie, but her voice was that of the demon. "Her core wasss mine before, but thisss sssealed it. Your precioussssss A.N.G.E.L.ssss failed." She glared at the angel. As she did, she transformed back into the demon. "They failed…and sssss did you. Shhhe'sssss mine!" it hissed.

"No! Let her go!" the angel demanded.

Suddenly, Casey turned to see the man from Columbia on the other side of her from the demon. He reached over and touched her face. She couldn't go anywhere. She was trapped.

Just when she didn't think it could get any worse, as Casey trembled in terror, Jackie appeared by a sink. She poured salt into the bowl of water. As she walked over, she let out a foul, sinister laugh. She snapped her fingers, and the contents of the bowl in her hand instantly turned into fire. Jackie continued to laugh as she slowly walked toward her.

 The closer she came, the more Casey looked around for a way to get out of this horrific nightmare, only to see the man from Columbia run his fingers down her arm. He kissed her shoulder and then looked up at her, laughing an evil laugh as well. The mocking laughter filled the hut, coming out from every corner. It was almost deafening.

Casey thought she was going to lose it as she stared at the demon. It reached up and rubbed it hand on the side of her face with a malicious look in its eyes. "You're mine, precioussss!" it hissed, and then let out a heinous laugh that blended with the other two.

Casey screamed in pure terror. She looked up toward the sky and shouted, "Father! By the blood of Jesus, I beg you to release me from this. What is…." It was a struggle to breathe, as the snake tightened its grip on her, almost completely cutting off her air. "What is free in Christ…is free indeed!" She gasped for air before she collapsed.

Mark looked up at the angel, who nodded toward him. He called for Derek and the Colonel to come in, and together they stood in front of the door of the tent with a righteous anger, their arms crossed, blocking anyone from leaving. No one was getting out until this was over.

"You can't *do* anything!" the demon hissed. "She'sssss mine! I won!"

The angel glanced at the Colonel, Derek, and Mark, and then to Jack and Mac, who collectively prayed for strength for the angel.

As they prayed aloud, the angel stood taller. He glared at the trio who surrounded his charge, and said, "What is free in Christ is free indeed. *Release her immediately*!"

"No!" The demon stood up, as Jackie and the other man slowly moved away to the safety of the other side of the fire. They moved as far away from the angel as they could get in the little hut. The demon stayed its ground while it glared at the angel.

"In the name of the Almighty One, I demand that you release her!" the angel shouted.

A smile slowly formed on the demon's face as it stood up and said, "I'll releasssse her, but *I ssstill* hold the key." It dangled the key in front of it, on its talon, as it walked through the fire with the other two. As soon as it was on the other side, the snake disappeared, and Casey fell to the ground, unable to move. She was finally able to get the precious air she needed.

The angel nodded toward the Colonel, Mark, and Derek, who went to Casey. While Derek placed one of his hands on her forehead and one on her stomach, Mark was on the other side of her, placing one of his hands over her eyes, and then placed his other hand over her heart. The Colonel took both of his hands and cupped her head, spreading his fingers as he wrapped them from the side to the back of her head, so her entire head was covered with all of their hands.

When they were in place, they all three prayed in a language Casey didn't understand. As she lay there, her body shook worse than it was already.

When they prayed, the angel suddenly began to glow. He pulled his sword out of the sheath. It was glowing as well…almost singing.

The demon, Jackie, and the man from Columbia stared at the angel in wide-eyed horror. They knew what was going on in the little hut, and that they were in deep trouble. The demon narrowed its eyes at the angel. Casey belonged to them!

"Give me the key!" the angel demanded with such authority in his voice, that it shook the tiny hut. "She is His – *heart, mind, body, soul…and core*. She has asked for it. The penalty has been paid."

"Never! Thissss wassss my masssterpiece." The demon leapt across the fire, landing on the angel, and a struggle immediately ensued between the angel and the demon.

Mark glanced up at the battle going on before him, and then closed his eyes and soaked in the glory of the Lord that had rained down on them in a steady flow. As he, the Colonel, and Derek continued to pray, Mac, Jack, and Casey's parents disappeared…leaving only them, Jackie, the man from Columbia, the angel, the demon, and Casey in the tiny hut.

It was a strange and unique place for a battle, but the stakes were high, so they were going to do their best. As they continued to pray, the angel got stronger, overpowering the demon. Both were bloody. Both gave it their all, not holding anything back.

As the prayers of the trio got stronger, the band of three men shook as well. The battle became more intense. The angel glowed brighter and brighter, until suddenly he shoved the demon across the hut. The demon slammed into the wall, separating the man from Columbia and Jackie. They both looked down at him in horror, trembling in fear, before they looked back toward the angel.

The angel hovered off the ground, glowing so brightly that they had to shield their eyes to look at him. His clothes were as white as snow, and his wounds were instantly healed, as he reared his sword back.

The demon wasn't going to give up though. It scrambled to its feet, just in time to see the angel swing his arms forward with his sword glowing, heading directly toward them! The sword held so much of God's glory that the instant it made contact with the trio, it sliced them through the middle, disintegrating them on contact.

As soon as the angel's arms swung through, his feet touched the ground and he lowered his sword, keeping his hands on it, exhausted. He slowly replaced the sword into the sheath, as he waited a few moments, watching the ash descend to the ground on the other side of the fire.

When it settled, he walked through the fire to the other side and crouched on the ground. He brushed some dust out of the way before he found what he was looking for. He picked up the key, and brought it back through the fire to where the guys prayed over Casey. Then he knelt down, and placed it gently into her hand, securely fastening it within her fingers.

As he held her hand, he looked up toward her face and confidently said, "What is free in Christ is free indeed."

"Is it finished?" Mark asked, looking up at the angel.

He nodded as he stood. Then he looked down at the powerful men of prayer and faith, and said, "Well done, my little A.N.G.E.L.s. Keep up the good work." With that, he flew straight into the air until he was out of sight.

They watched until they couldn't see him anymore, before all three looked down at Casey.

"She done now," Ollie said, as he and George sat cross-legged on the other side of the fire.

At that point, Grace sat where Jack and Mac had sat. She nodded in agreement.

The guys took their hands off Casey, as they looked down at her. She couldn't move. She couldn't talk. It took everything she had to stay somewhat conscious enough to hear and feel everything.

Mark took a moment before he reached down and scooped her up into his arms. He lovingly looked down at her as he said, "It's finished. Just rest, my love. We're here. You're safe. Just rest."

*   *   *

Jackie sat in her room looking in her vanity mirror. She glanced down at her desk in front of her to see the angel necklace of Casey's. She took it off her when Casey passed out.

Jackie reached down and clasped it in her hand, as she hissed, transforming into the demon. "You may have won that battle, but *I* shall win the war. You may have defeated the few, but we are legion…we are many. Shhhhe isssss mine. Do you hear me? Shhhe issss mine!" The demon laughed a heinous laugh, as it placed the necklace around his neck. "She is sssssstill mine."

<u>Chapter 1</u>

God's Grace

Victoria Stanton and her partner, Shawn O'Brien, hid behind a boulder that lazily rested on the sandy beach, with their hearts pounding out of control. Under normal circumstances, the serene scene of the moonlight dancing off the waves of the Waterfront in Cairns would serenade them in a romantic moment from a passionate love story. The breeze coming off the salt water would add to the surroundings, creating an ambiance that ignited many a moment between lovers. However, this moment was something reminiscent of nightmares.

Over the years as an A.N.G.E.L., God graced them with numerous glimpses of His boundless love and mercy, but what they saw on that day was something beyond unnatural. She looked to be that of a woman in her late fifties, and under normal circumstances they wouldn't have thought twice about her, but the form inside of her sent chills down their spine. The tall, thin frame of this beautiful woman would normally send out the comfort of a woman who had lived her life, and would guide other women through the trials life threw at them, but the form inside the woman marred and mangled anything that got in its way, creating an enigma of unmistakable significance. She was the queen bee of a swarm of evil that had only one thought on their mind: to annihilate the A.N.G.E.L.s. If they succeeded, it would create a void in the world that would allow evil to have a stronghold on the inhabitants of the planet it would never release. It was up to the A.N.G.E.L.s to keep the balance of power in check.

The pair were the lookout for the American A.N.G.E.L.s while they went in to rescue two of their crewmembers. This situation was not abnormal, since A.N.G.E.L.s from the various units had crossed paths over the years in regards to missions, but this one was different. This one made the hair on the back of their necks stand on end, as a paralyzing terror surged through their bodies. They had never seen or felt anything of this magnitude before, and to know that it was in their backyard, horrified them beyond words. *How could something have formed and functioned of this immense size and they not know?*

"We need t' get to Hawk and warn him," Victoria whispered in the dim moonlight.

Shawn nodded in response. He wanted to stay as silent as possible. He adored his partner, Victoria, and admired her skill over the years. She could take a man even of Mark English's size down in a matter of seconds, and it brought a sense of pride to know she was his love.

Victoria gulped. Her heart skipped a beat when she heard a stick crack about fifty feet away. She didn't want to die. She and Shawn had formally begun a relationship only a couple of months ago, and the last thing she wanted to do was lose him…or worse yet, the thought of him having to watch her die broke her heart. She didn't want to imagine the pain either scenario would cause them.

Shawn rested his hands on her shoulders and whispered, "I love you with all my heart. You are a source of strength for me." Her body shook under his hands. He knew it would take a miracle of God to pull them from the impending doom that surrounded them.

They used themselves as a distraction so the other four A.N.G.E.L.s could get away. The pair heard the alarm in the voices of those within the warehouse, and instantly knew those inside realized their prisoners had escaped. Shawn sent a couple rounds through the front window, to pull the attention away from the back of the warehouse where he knew the others were making their escape.

Several large men ran out of the concrete hive, making a beeline in their direction. Even though the floodlights were a good hundred yards away, they watched in alarm as the tall fair-haired woman's eyes shifted to pure black as she shouted orders.

Their hearts skipped a beat. At that moment, they knew. Time momentarily stopped for the two A.N.G.E.L.s as their eyes were opened to what was around them. They saw the true form of not only the demon, but also of the legion that possessed her followers.

They bolted for the boat they stashed as a get-away vehicle. It was nestled in the Cairns Wharf, tucked away from any prying eyes. They made it to the waterfront before they heard those in pursuit closing in on them. While the distance to their escape was not far, it felt like a thousand miles to the fleeing pair.

"We need to run," Victoria whispered in response.

Shawn nodded as he looked at the blond-haired beauty before him. Her expressions did not give away a hint of how lethal she could be. She was a walking weapon. Deadly, and a steel core that could freeze even the hottest area in The Outback if she put her mind to it, but now she looked like a scared child. "You have to be strong. We will make it."

"I love you," she whispered, resting her hand on his strong jawline. His reddish-blond hair complemented the freckles that danced across his nose. Only the A.N.G.E.L.s, and those he worked with in the military, knew the man before her had killed many men during his lifetime, even though he did it from one to two hundred yards away in order to help others escape. He was the best marksman of the Australian A.N.G.E.L.s, yet he had a heart of gold. He would do anything for anyone who needed him – that included giving his life.

"You go," he said. "Get the boat ready."

She shook her head in alarm. "I can't leave you."

"You have to. I'll distract them while you run. I want you to run as fast as those gorgeous legs of yours will carry you. Don't look back. Get to Hawk and tell him. He *has* to know."

"What will happen to you?"

"Don't worry about me. I will either meet you in Heaven or in the Outback."

She looked at him blankly for a moment as their reality sunk in. He was going to sacrifice his life to get her to safety. "I can't let you do it."

He grabbed her face as he held it close to his. "You have to. Only one of us will have a chance. We won't be able to make it out together. They *will* get us if we try. Go down Wharf Street until it crosses Spence Street. Turn right. Spence Street dead ends into the wharf. Get out of there as fast as you can and don't look back. Do you hear me? Don't look back."

She heard him, but she shook her head as she felt the color drain from her face. *What was he saying?* If she did that, then she knew she would never see him on this planet alive again. "You're not fighting flesh and blood."

"I know what they are."

"You won't survive."

"But *you* will," he said. "Don't argue with me about this."

Victoria leaned forward and kissed him with every ounce of love she had for him. She knew the kiss would have to last them a lifetime. She prayed she would be wrong, and that God would protect them as He often did in the past, but there was a feeling of foreboding that churned deep inside her.

He returned the kiss with the love he had for her. He knew what he was doing. He would protect Victoria with everything in his power. He would start as soon as he saw the first one in his site until that was no longer an option. Then he would step into the line of fire. He had to give her enough time to get to the wharf and escape.

"I love you. Now go," he said, feeling the pit in his stomach wanting to take over his emotions, but he forced it back down.

"I love you too…with all of my heart. May God have mercy on you, my love."

"God will have mercy one way or another. I am one of His. He will either call me home, or allow me to see those beautiful blue eyes of yours once again here on Earth. May He keep you safe."

"A prayer from both of our lips to God's ears," Victoria whispered.

They held each other one last time, before Victoria looked around the rock to make sure her way was clear. Not seeing any movement, she bolted toward the road, knowing Spence Street was but a few precious blocks away. If she had to, she would cut through Marlin Parade to get to the dock.

As she ran, she heard the distinct pop of Shawn's rifle, and knew the firefight had begun behind her. The stride of her long legs covered the ground before her, as she felt she might have made a mistake leaving Shawn. She remembered his words, *"Get out of there as fast as you can and don't look back. Do you hear me? Don't look back."*

Massive rounds of gunfire erupted from where she left Shawn. Her stomach lurched when the barrage of gunfire came to an abrupt halt. Tears stung her eyes and her heart skipped a beat. She turned down Spence Street. She knew her lover was sitting in the peace and comfort of The Lord, but how could he leave her there by herself to continue the fight without him?

The wharf. It was in her sights when a horrific sting pierced the back of her right thigh, and another bit into her left shoulder. She fell to the ground and skid about five feet, with sand splattering into her face. She spit it out and wiped off her face as she pushed up and ran, creating a cloud of dust around her. The wharf was less than five feet away. She didn't look back. She didn't want to know how close they were to her.

Her feet thumped across the wood of the wharf as adrenaline surged through her body, carrying her further than she would be able to go on her own. With each step, visions of her life flashed before her eyes. God had protected her and granted her many exciting adventures that allowed her to save numerous lives in His name throughout the years. He allowed her to be a part of plans that helped His children out of situations they would not otherwise escape from. She was part of an elite force for not only her government, but, most importantly, for The King of Kings and Lords of Lords. She took pride in the work He granted her over the years.

Another capsule of searing heat grazed her head. She dropped off the wharf into the water. A peace enveloped her at hearing God's words clear in her mind, *"Before I formed you in the womb I knew you, before you were born I set you apart. You have done well My good and faithful servant. Come home."*

* * *

Casey saw it all. She had no idea if it was real or not, but it felt as strong as the dream she had of Keith, and that turned out to be real. She had to let the others know, but her body didn't want to cooperate. She pushed until her eyes flew open and she gasped. "They're gone!" Then, just as quickly, her eyes closed and her head dropped to the side while she lay in Mark's arms, unconscious once again.

"Who's gone?" Mark knelt on the ground with her in his arms. When she didn't respond, he scooped her back up in his arms and picked up his pace. He wanted to get her back to camp.

The Colonel had to practically run to catch up with Mark. "She'll be okay, brother, slow down a bit, eh?"

"She'll be okay now, but will she be able to weather the incoming storm?"

"What storm?"

Mark stopped short, spinning toward the Colonel. "You and I both know it's coming. It gets bigger day by day. They're coming for us. I know we can handle it, but is she ready for it?"

"She will be. Trust us to get her ready. Trust God. He hasn't let us down yet. I don't think He's going to start now."

"From your lips to God's ears."

*   *   *

As the small band walked back into camp, the A.N.G.E.L.s who stayed behind anxiously stood from where they sat around the fire.

"What happened to her?" Harper ran to meet them when he realized Mark was carrying Casey…and worse yet, that she wasn't moving.

"She just sleeping," Ollie assured him. "No worries, she'll be apples."

"Meanwhile, we're hungry," Hawk said, while the scent of the stew cooking on the fire wafted past him. "How 'bout getting us some tucker?"

Harper looked up at his commander, baffled and confused. Casey was unconscious, her hair was dripping with sweat, and no one seemed to have a problem with it.

"No worries," George said, almost reading his thoughts. "Grace look after her."

Grace immediately headed over to the tent, with Mark on her heels still carrying Casey. When they went in, Mark laid Casey down on the cot and covered her so she wouldn't get cold from the chilly spring air. "She's sweating," he remarked.

Grace brought over a bowl of cool water and a washcloth. "I do. You eat. Been a couple days."

"A couple of days?" he asked, eyes wide. "It only seemed like hours."

"More than a couple of hours…it two an' half days."

"Really?"

"Yes. Now eat or I get Hawk."

He smiled as he stood to leave. "No need. I'll go eat. Take care of her for me, will ya?"

"Of course. Dat why I here."

He leaned down and kissed Casey's cheek before he left. He didn't want to leave her, but he knew Grace would take care of her.

Derek sat down on a log by the fire with the others, while Carson and Grant disbursed the food to those who returned. "Wow! That was wild!" Derek said.

"We were getting worried," Carson said, relieved to see them. "It's been almost three days."

Hawk raised an eyebrow at him. "Dinkum?"

"'Strewth!" Harper agreed, on edge. "Then you come back carrying her in your arms acting like everything is perfectly fine."

"No worries. She in good hands," Ollie assured him.

"Where are Pete and Charlie?" George asked, noticing they were not around.

"Something came up at your village. They came and got Pete, saying something about friends of his coming on a boat," Grant said. "Sorry, didn't get it all, but Charlie went w' him"

"He showed me how t' make some of those 'recipes' of his before he left," Harper added.

"You showed the others, right?" Hawk asked.

"Does Jack Newton swim in circles?"

"Good onya!" Hawk patted his shoulder. "I knew you were a good bloke."

George took a bite of his bread. "Pete good too."

"Yeah, his blood's worth bottling," Harper agreed.

After a few minutes Hawk asked, "So, have we heard anything from the others lately?"

Carson nodded. "Yep. Fletcher flew in yesterday. He was only here for a couple hours before he flew back out."

"What did he say?"

"Well," Carson started, as he sat on the ground, resting his elbow on his knee while he stirred the stew with his other hand, "They know about Hunter Morgan. They've identified the body."

"Do they know what happened?"

"They're pegging it a suicide."

"What about our other friends?"

"They're still chasing their tails t' find out what happened t' them." Carson nodded toward the American A.N.G.E.L.s.

"Have we heard from Stanton and O'Brien yet?" Hawk asked.

"No. Not yet." Carson shook his head. "Not since that night, but we're keeping an eye out for them. You'll be happy to know that Parker and Peters are home and hosed."

"Good," Hawk said, relieved. Hawk took a moment to dwell on the men and women who worked for him. He was concerned about not hearing from Stanton and O'Brien, but he knew they were in God's hands, and he had to trust that God would take care of them. "Find out where they are. I want to know. If they are on another assignment, that's fine, but something doesn't feel right. We should have heard something by now."

"Yes, sir."

"Make it a top priority."

"Yes, sir," Carson said, getting up, going to the tent to radio Fletcher.

The A.N.G.E.L.s throughout the world did a lot of work over the years, and many were lost in battle. Only the Aussies had their full crew of ten. While there were some narrow escapes, they hadn't lost one in over thirty years. Hawk prayed that streak was still intact.

* * *

While the others talked by the fire, Grace wiped Casey down, quietly humming an Aboriginal song her mum sung to her as a young child. As she did, she thought through the horrible visions she saw in the hut. While she never got used to it, the insight she often gained boggled her mind. What goes on during dreamtime forces people to take a good, hard look at their life, enabling them to see things from a different perspective.

Casey's dreamtime was different from anything Grace ever experienced prior to that point. The man in white was strong and powerful. The authority he spoke with was not his own. She wanted to know more. She wanted to know why, with the angel speaking in the name of 'The Almighty One,' the demon was forced to release the girl. And, how would three men praying, create such a power behind the sword, that made it so strong it allowed the angel to disintegrate the trio on contact. It was a comfort to her to know the words from praying hearts held so much power.

She made a decision right there to ask one of the three men from America about it after dinner. She knew she would have to be clever in how she did it though – she didn't want anything to seem improper or inappropriate in the eyes of George and Ollie. This, however, was something she had to do. She *had* to know.

* * *

"We need t' work on getting you people out of here," Hawk said to the Colonel, as he ate his beef stew, damper bread, and water – his mind working overtime.

The Colonel shook his head. "Not until she's up to good health. If we have to fight or run, I want her healthy. We're safer here to get her strength up, than we would be out in the real world. We're also going to have to do more in-depth training with her. I want her to be able to defend herself."

Hawk nodded in understanding. "You're gonna want big n' burly o'er there healthy too, yeah?"

Mark narrowed his eyes at Hawk regarding his new nickname. He had worked with these men for years, but this was the first time they actually called him 'big n' burly.'

The Colonel nodded. "That would be preferred."

"How come I've been granted a nickname all of the sudden?" Mark asked, using his bread to sop what was left of his stew. "I'm not used to having that type of nickname. It's kind of a slam."

"We're not used t' you being hulked up with us either," Harper pointed out.

"We understand why, though. Ya got a valid reason," Marshall interjected. "She's a beauty."

"Thanks…I think." Mark wasn't sure if he followed the conversation. He struggled as they pulled more Aussie lingo than normal. He had to guess at over half of the conversation.

Carson saw the confusion on his face, so in order to set his mind at ease, he said, "No worries, it's all good."

"You need us here?" Ollie asked. "We go?"

"If you guys could have Grace watch her 'til the morning, we'd appreciate it. That way English can get some rest." Hawk glanced over at Mark. "I think he feels more comfortable with Grace watching her than the other guys."

"Only because she's a woman," Mark clarified. "Casey and I both have full confidence in you guys, but –"

Harper held up his hand, cutting off Mark. "We get it. No worries."

"Will that work?" Hawk asked.

Ollie nodded in agreement. "We leave in da morning."

The Colonel rested his hand on Ollie's shoulder. "Please accept our sincere thanks and appreciation to you and your clan for your help. You guys have done a lot for us, and we're strangers to you. We appreciate it."

Ollie's white teeth glowed in the firelight with a peaceful smile, as he said, "We knew you coming. We just waiting."

Derek furrowed his brow in confusion. "You knew we were coming?"

"Yes."

"How?"

"Had dream 'bout it couple days before. Is normal." Ollie waved Derek off. "We just needed t' wait."

"I see."

"Well, guys," Mark said, as he stood from the log by the fire, handing his empty bowl and tin cup to Carson. "I'm still tired. I'm gonna hit the hay. Anyone mind if I sleep on the cot next to Casey?"

The Colonel refilled his own bowl as he said, "I would *appreciate* it if you slept on the cot next to Casey. Then I know she's being looked after."

"You guys can sleep in my tent if you want to," Mark offered Ollie and George. "Not as comfy as your bed at home, I'm sure, but it's a roof over your head."

"We do. Thank you," Ollie said in appreciation.

"Thank you all," Mark said. "There is no way I can repay you for everything you have done for me and Casey."

"With da work you do, debt already paid," Ollie said, knowingly.

"What do you mean by that?"

Ollie thought for a minute about how to word his statement before he said, "Your dreamtime, Casey's dreamtime, and da visions we had in our own dreamtime, showed us your true missions."

Hawk's heart skipped a beat, but he tried to play it off until he knew more. "Don't know what ya mean, mate."

"It's okay. We know," Ollie assured them, trying to set the men at ease.

All the men sitting around the fire froze. They wondered how much these strange little men knew about them and their work over the years. If they even knew a portion of it, it could paint a target on them that could put their entire clan in danger.

"No worries," George said, reading their faces. "Just Ollie and me know. We not tell. Secret safe."

"Just how much *do* ya know?" Hawk challenged.

George and Ollie glanced at each other, before they looked each man steadily in the eyes. Ollie said, in probably the clearest he had yet to speak since his arrival, "Your actions as A.N.G.E.L.s are known. We admire your hearts and valor. Your missions are never easy, but with your faith and prays, you reach many. While you may not win all da battles, you *will* win da war. Your side is stronger den *anyding* da enemy can give."

The men stared at him, stunned. They didn't know what to say.

"What...how...?" Mark sat back down in shock.

Ollie chuckled, tickled by their reactions. "No worries."

"Are you followers of Christ?" Derek bluntly asked. He was tired of the cryptic messages. He wanted the bottom line.

Ollie nodded. "Drough Pete, we know. He bring back many stories so we test."

"And?" Derek pushed.

"George and I are, yes. Not many know."

Derek nodded, satisfied with his answer. If their clan mates knew, they might have difficulty within their clan, or at the very least be taken down from the status of elder. As long as their secret was kept, they could lead the clan with God's guidance.

The group sat there quietly for a few more minutes, before Mark got up and went to the tent. He didn't understand what was going on, but that was nothing new. He only knew what he needed to know – nothing more, nothing less. All he was required to do was obey and follow the orders passed down to him, whether they were from the Colonel or from God. The two were never in contradiction, so he always knew he was working with the right people. He thanked The Lord for the opportunities God gave him over the years.

When Mark walked into the tent, Grace looked up from washing Casey. She finished Casey's legs and was in the process of washing her arms. She kept Casey's sarong on and only washed what was exposed.

"You ok?" Grace asked in concern. He looked exhausted.

"Just tired," he said, sitting down on the cot. "How's she doing?"

"Okay." She glanced toward Ollie and George to make sure they were distracted, before she turned toward Mark and asked, "Can I talk?"

"To me?"

"Yes. Is okay, yes?"

"Yeah, sure. Why wouldn't it be?"

"Not proper."

Mark watched her for a moment, as she nervously glanced at where the men sat around the fire, and then turned back to him. He crossed his arms, studying her. "What do you need to ask me?"

She was slightly taken aback by the way he asked the question. It was as if he knew she specifically needed to talk to him.

"In da dreamtime, Casey's?"

"Yeah."

"Dat man was powerful, no?"

"Yes."

"His words, dey hold power, no?"

"Yes." Mark nodded, praying silently for clarity and direction. He was having a hard time following her questions. As important as this conversation was, he wanted to make sure he understood her words.

She looked down, thinking for a moment. *Oh, how she wished Pete was there to help her talk to him. If he was there though, she wouldn't have the opportunity to ask at all.* She glanced back toward the men around the fire before she looked back to Mark and asked, "Dat man glowed. He was stronger, no?"

"Yes."

"You dree helped, no?"

"Yes."

"Why he stronger den da other one? Why da ugly one let her go at just his words? Why power with your prays?"

Mark took a deep breath, praying for the right answers. "Angels have power – they get it from God, the Almighty One. They get stronger, though, when the saints are down on their knees in prayer, taking the authority granted to them by Jesus' death and resurrection on the cross."

"He no dead, no more?" she asked, confused.

Mark was tired and in pain, but this was important so he pushed himself. "The simplest way I can explain this is to spell it out. So, bear with me, this could take a while."

She nodded in understanding. At this point, she didn't even care if George or Ollie saw her, she needed to know. She needed to understand what happened in that hut, and she knew this man would help her.

Mark sat her down and explained what is known as 'the ABC's of Christianity.' He explained what happened regarding Adam and Eve's sin, and how that sin created the reason Christ needed to come in the first place. When they disobeyed God, it created a break in the communication between God and man.

Then, he rolled it into the birth, life, crucifixion, and resurrection of Jesus. Once the communication was broken, the only way to God was through a blood sacrifice. It had to be a sacrifice of a perfect lamb, One who did not have a spot or blemish. In order to fix the communication, there had to be bloodshed. Since Jesus was the only perfect 'Man,' it was only by His blood that the communication could be restored. He shared John 3:16 – *"For God so loved the world, that He gave His one and only Son, that whosoever believes in Him shall not perish, but have eternal life."* And also, Romans 6:23 – *"For the wages of sin is death, but the gift of God is eternal life through Jesus Christ, our Lord."*

Afterward, he ended with Christ's second coming in Revelation. He used First Thessalonians 4:16 – *"For the Lord Himself will come down from Heaven, with a commanding shout, with the voice of the Archangel, and with the trumpet call of God. And the dead in Christ will rise first."*

While this information was new to her, it made complete sense. She felt bad it took Mark hours of the precious sleep she knew he needed, but she was grateful he explained it. She was so excited about the story, that it took all she had to wait and finish listening before she jumped at the chance to pray, asking Jesus for forgiveness of her sins, and to accept His gift of Salvation.

As they talked and prayed, the men around the fire felt the Spirit swirling around them, and one-by-one they began to pray. They prayed for courage, strength, power, and for the Spirit to rain down on their little group. While they prayed, they realized what was happening less than twenty feet from them, and prayed for Grace. By the time Grace and Mark were on their knees in prayer, the men had wandered into the tent, and were laying their hands on Grace's head and shoulders, praying for her and her new life with Christ.

<u>Chapter 2</u>

No Regrets

"Mmmm," Casey groaned, as she struggled to wake the next morning.

"Casey?" Mark looked over from his cot. He was in a cot on one side of her, while Grace was in a cot on the other side.

"Yeah."

He sat up and made his way over to Casey's side. Running his fingers through her hair, he knelt on the ground and asked, "Can you actually *open* those gorgeous green eyes of yours?"

She slept hard – harder than she had ever slept in her life to date. "Um, gimme a minute." Casey took a few more minutes before her eyes fluttered open.

"There ya go." Mark smiled. "We were worried about you." While Mark was still in a lot of pain from his broken bones, he was trying to hide it for her sake. He didn't want her to know how much pain he was in. The broken bones in his body were not healing fast enough for him, much to his dismay.

"What is the phrase they use here in The Outback? Um, oh yeah, no worries, mate," Casey said, as she yawned and stretched. When she did, she felt something in her hand. "What's this?"

Inside her fist was a small, delicate key made of solid gold. It resembled a key one would see used for locks on a treasure chest or an old strongbox. When she held it up to look at it, Mark smiled, shaking his head.

"What is this to?" Casey asked.

"That is the key to your core," Mark explained. "You remember your dreamtime, right?"

She looked at him in wide-eyed terror as her heart raced. *"That was real?"*

"Yes. All of it was real."

She glanced from him, to the key, and back again. Then she asked, "What am I going to do with it? I can't let that demon get it again."

"Hmmm." Mark looked around the tent, while Casey slowly sat up on her cot, swinging her feet down to the solid ground.

After a few minutes of searching, he found a bolt of twine in the corner they used to set up the camp. He cut a piece about a foot and a half in length, and then unbraided the ropes until there was only one strand. He left the remaining portions on the table, while he knelt in front of her and explained, "If you put it on here, you can wear it around your neck so you always know where it is."

"But that didn't work very well with my angel necklace."

"Hmm." He sat down on her cot as he contemplated what to do with the valuable key. After a minute he shrugged, and asked, "What do you want to do with it? It's *your* key."

Casey looked the fragile key as it rested in her hand. There was no one on earth she wanted to trust it to. Deep down she wished the angel kept it and passed it on to Jesus, but he didn't and he must have had a reason, so now it was in her hands. The more she looked at it, the more she dwelt on the events in the tiny hut. It had to have been real. She was holding the key in her hand.

Casey sighed. "I'll have to put it around my neck. I really don't have any other option right now."

"All right."

Mark held the string while she nervously slid the key on it. The fight for the precious key was a rough one, so she knew she had to protect it with her life – her innermost core depended on it.

Mark reached around and tied it, pulling her hair through in the back when he finished. Then he sighed, shaking his head as he looked at her. "Still beautiful."

Casey reached up and touched his face. Mark's strength and faith amazed her. She looked into his tender eyes and said, "The prayers in the hut. They were of someone who was well-grounded, and who knew the power they held."

"Prayers hold more power than people give them credit," Mark explained. "God hears His children. Prayer also helps strengthen The Lord's angels, allowing them to carry out their work."

"I see," she said, admiring the key dangling around her neck. She wrapped her hand around the key before she asked, "The angel called you guys his little A.N.G.E.L.s. Why?"

"We've been working closely with him for a long time. He's an Archangel. All of our assignments don't come directly from the government of the United States – some are from God."

"Really? He still does that? I mean…I know He did in Bible times, but now?"

"In a manner of speaking. It's not like the ground shakes around us and this mysterious voice comes from Heaven," he explained. "The Spirit tells us. There are men and women held captive all over this world due to their faith. Some are held literally. Some are held spiritually like you were. Sometimes we get to them, and are able to rescue them, but sometimes we don't make it on time. In a lot of those situations though, the only way we would have known where they were is through the leading of the Spirit. Sometimes it's not something that dramatic. Sometimes it's getting down on our knees in prayer after being woken-up in the middle of the night. Sometimes it's sending cash in the mail to a family, or leaving a bag of groceries on their front step. It's not something I completely understand, but it's something I know I need to do. There are A.N.G.E.L.s all over the world who do this kind of stuff."

"How do they know, though?"

"How did the Colonel and Derek know where we were?"

She looked at him, not sure how to answer. She never thought of how they found them, she was just grateful they did.

He rested his hand on her leg as he calmly said, "We don't always understand. Our job is to follow. If we weren't here, Charlie wouldn't have stumbled into the camp. If he didn't, then Grace wouldn't have come and had to help you. If you didn't have to go through what you went through, you wouldn't have had to go into dreamtime, and she wouldn't have seen what she did. If she didn't, then she wouldn't have asked the questions she did last night. And if she didn't ask those questions, then she wouldn't know today that she was a daughter of The King. She wouldn't have Jesus as her Savior. Make sense?"

She nodded as she ran through the steps in her mind again. "In a weird twisted way, yes."

He took her hand into his as he continued, "Let me try it again. If Derek and the Colonel hadn't rescued us, then you would have died in that place – I'm sure of it. They started hard, and torture tends to get rougher, not easier. If they didn't pull us, then you wouldn't have come here. If we didn't come here, Charlie wouldn't have heard your screams and stumbled on our camp. If he didn't come here, he wouldn't have brought Ollie and George. If he didn't bring them, you wouldn't have gone into dreamtime. If you didn't go into dreamtime, then your core would still belong to that demon. If the angel didn't win, then the key to your core would still be in the demon's possession. Since all those events occurred, though, *you* are the one now holding the key. Make sense?"

Casey thought about it for a moment before she nodded. "So, what you're trying to tell me is that God works in mysterious ways. And that even though it looks *really* bad, I need to have confidence that it's being done for a reason."

"Not to say that your torture was a good thing by any means, but what Satan intended for evil, God used for good. Grace can attest to that."

Casey looked over at Grace. She was sleeping peacefully. She knew it was due to the Spirit. She was happy for Grace, and knew she would be a strong witness for Him. In her clan, Grace might be limited on how she would go about spreading God's word, but knowing her the way Casey had come to know her over the last several days, she had the confidence Grace would find a way to do it. She was a strong woman. She often worked outside of the box when it came to taking care of Casey. She had the utmost confidence Grace would figure out a way to get the message of Christ to her clan mates. Casey prayed that she would be able to talk to Grace someday to find out how she was doing, and be able to see what God did in her life.

"So, does that answer your questions my beautiful, hopefully someday soon, bride-to-be?" he asked, bringing Casey back to their reality in the Outback.

Casey had to smile at that one. "Yes."

"Good. Now that brings me to another problem."

She looked at him, nervously. Whenever he shifted from lighthearted to serious that quickly, it concerned her. "Uh-oh."

He took both of her hands into his as he said, "Being in the situation we were in, and the ones I am sure are going to follow, I need to warn you that we've already been in some situations, where: a) we've crossed modesty lines, and b) where our lives were in danger. Now, in my life I try to have the least amount of regrets as possible. There have been many times over the last year, with the last couple of weeks being the strongest, where I have regretted not having you as my wife. Yes, we are together, but to know you are not my wife, that our lives aren't one, is a regret of mine. I wouldn't do myself any justice if I didn't ask you to think about how soon you would like to get married. I'm not saying tomorrow. I'm only asking you to think about it, so I know what day to look forward to, where I know I will be able to sleep with you in my arms, and hold you all night long. So, I know from what point on I can have the privilege of your face being the last one I see at night, and the first one I see in the morning. I love you, Casey. I have loved you for years. While we've only been together a little over a year, I have known you most of your life. So, would you at least do me a favor and think about it?"

Casey nodded, unable to say anything. The beauty in his words and heart amazed her.

"Now, I know we are in the middle of the Outback and that we have some work ahead of us before we get out, but if you would keep those thoughts in your mind and let me know what you think sometime soon, I would appreciate it."

Casey hugged him. She loved him so much and didn't want to let him go.

He chuckled. "I take that as a yes?"

Casey nodded as the tears formed in her eyes. "I love you."

"I love you too. I only want to love, protect, and honor you for the rest of our lives."

She sat back, wiping away the tears that escaped. "When?"

He looked at her in confusion. "That's what I asked you to think about."

"No. When? How soon? I don't want to die without you being my husband. I want to feel you holding me as I sleep, knowing you are praying for me. I want to know that wherever we are, together or apart, that you're my husband. I want to know that if you go on another mission and have to leave me behind for a little while, that when you come back, I can wrap my arms around you and never let you go. I want to –"

He cut her off with a passionate kiss. She didn't care that the guys were fanned-out in various areas around camp, some not more than ten-to-twenty feet from them. She didn't even care that Grace was sleeping in a cot right beside them. All she cared about, at that moment, was the man God gave her, and the future God had in store for them.

* * *

Later that morning, Casey and Mark talked to the Colonel and Hawk about their decision to get married as soon as possible. George, Ollie, and Grace were sitting by the fire eating breakfast with them as well.

Mark and Casey explained that they wanted more than anything to be joined together as one man and one woman, forever. Life was short – their lifestyle more than proved that. They knew they were never guaranteed a tomorrow. They wanted to be joined before too many more days slipped past them.

Grace said she would take care of Casey's wedding attire and flowers, while Ollie and George fought over who was going to do the ceremony. George finally won because his English was better.

After that was decided, Ollie and George instructed Hawk and the Colonel on what to go over with Mark and Casey in the way of pre-marital counseling until they would return a week later. Mark and Casey were to look deep into their lives, and discuss the various aspects of married life…and they meant everything. From children, to lifestyle, to their dreams and desires, to even the way they spent money. Granted, they already discussed most of that over the last year on some of those long nights where he was watching her, but with a third-party there it would be different. They might catch something Mark and Casey missed.

Later, everyone said good-bye to their Aboriginal friends, and they left off for their village. When they were gone, Hawk and the Colonel sat Mark and Casey down with the rest of the guys in camp. They were excited about the news of the marriage, but then they went on to more serious matters.

"Now, we have some work ahead of us, mates," Hawk started. "We gotta train this one." He nodded toward Casey. Then he added, nodding toward Mark, "And get that one back in shape. They're gonna be leaving us as soon as English is healed, so we have t' work fast."

Casey raised her hand. "What do you mean by train me?"

"I want to be sure you know what you're doing. I know Jack did some training with you and laid a good foundation, but we are talking major hiding here. You need to know what to do in the event that we get separated," the Colonel explained. "I want to have the confidence of knowing you will know what to do if something happens to the person watching you."

"Basically, you don't want a repeat of the last situation?" Carson asked.

"They were taken by surprise. English's abilities have never been in question. They have always been exemplary, but –"

"*But* that brought about a major security issue," Mark finished the Colonel's statement in full understanding. "She's working with us now. She needs to know."

The Colonel nodded in response.

"Needs to know *what*?" Casey asked, as she nervously looked from one guy to the next. With everything she had seen, heard, and had happened to her over the last year, she wasn't sure if she *wanted* to know.

"Know how to survive the worst, endure the merciless, persist in the face of evil, and carry on when you are depleted," Derek explained.

"While Carter taught you some, you need t' go deeper," Carson added.

Seeing her shifting nervously, Marshall clarified, "Now, we know you're a smart one, and we have the utmost confidence in you.

We're just gonna improve and enhance the skills Carter already instilled in you."

Harper continued, "We're gonna push you to your limits, so you know just how much further you *can* go."

"We're gonna help you t' run on instinct. You're gonna be able t' assess a situation and react with split-second accuracy," Grant finished.

"Sooooo," she looked at them nervously, "this is going to be a form of boot camp for me?"

The Colonel rested his hand on her shoulder to comfort her. "Don't look at it as bad. We're going to prepare, teach, guide, and educate you on the finer points of survival. You will work as one of us. You will be able to not only fight your way out of tough situations, but also you will learn how to avoid them even occurring."

"I don't want to kill anybody," Casey said. "I was trained to help and repair, not kill and destroy."

"The devil's mission is to hunt, kill, and destroy…ours is to recover, restore, and renew. There are times, though, when it is a matter of your life verses theirs. You *cannot* let the enemy win." The Colonel took her hand as he said, "Sometimes it's a matter of self-defense. You will be able to protect yourself well enough that you may never have to actually kill someone, but that day may come. When it does, I have confidence that God will guide you. We don't take that decision lightly either." He sighed, as he said, "Casey, God has something big for you. We have been protecting you for years. We have fought many battles for you. Our biggest was the other day in the hut. We were finally able to see what we were battling…you did too. Are you really going to tell me you would have had a hard time doing what the angel did?"

Casey thought for a moment before she shook her head.

"If the choice was your life verses that demon's, what would you do? Would you let him kill you? Would you have let him keep this?" He held up the key that hung around her neck. "Or would you have fought him, possibly having to kill him for your very soul?"

Casey had never thought of it that way. The implications of the events surrounding her were massive. The battle was not against flesh and blood. It was against the unseen powers of darkness. Would she be able to fight what she could not see, knowing her very soul could be in jeopardy?

As the Colonel waited for her answer, she looked deeper within herself to find out where the source of her strength lay. The deeper she searched, the more she felt the Spirit fill her. In her mind, there was a vision of a fountain flowing from her heart. Bubbling slowly at first, before it overflowed into her soul, seeping over into her entire body, filling her with His words of power and wisdom.

Words formed in her heart and she spoke them aloud. She looked the Colonel in the eyes as she said, "*"Finally, my brethren, be strong in the Lord, and in the power of His might. Put on the whole armor of God, that you may be able to stand against the wiles of the devil. For we do not wrestle against flesh and blood, but against principalities, against powers, against the rulers of the darkness of this age, against spiritual hosts of wickedness in the heavenly places. Therefore take up the whole armor of God, that you may be able to withstand in the evil day, having done all, to stand.*""

The Colonel nodded, pleased. "Ephesians 6:10-13, good job. See, He *will* help you. You only have to remember Who is in control and Who is in charge. You have to remember Who you are fighting for and what He stands for. The Father will hold you close as He helps you, the Spirit will guide and direct you, and Jesus will walk beside you and never leave you."

Casey smiled as tears ran down her cheeks. She knew he was right. She knew she would be able to do it with God's help. She knew she was in *His* army. Whether she wanted to do actual battle or not – that wasn't an option. The battle had come to her. These men would do their best to help her prepare so she would be able to fight and defend herself. She thanked God for them and for their courage, and asked God to allow her the privilege of not only making them proud, but of hearing God say to her when her race was done, "*Well done, thy good and faithful servant.*"

* * *

A couple of days after the deep conversation with Casey, Fletcher stood by the fire with his arms crossed in frustration while he spoke with Hawk. While Fletcher was only the messenger, Hawk wasn't happy with the message. "I don't know what to tell you, sir. They're looking."

"Tell them to look harder! I have not lost an A.N.G.E.L. in thirty years!"

"I will, sir. They are doing their best. They went over that area as best they could without getting caught. That is dangerously close to ground zero."

Hawk stroked his beard in thought. "There *has* to be evidence one way or the other."

"There was some blood found on the scene, but that was it."

"If they have Stanton and O'Brien, I want to know. We have to get them out if they're being held. Am I hearing you right that no one has *any* clue where they are?"

"They're not on assignment, that's for sure."

"Who isn't on assignment?" the Colonel asked, walking up to the two men. It looked a little heated, so he decided to bail Fletcher out of the conversation.

"We have two A.N.G.E.L.s MIA," Hawk said, crossing his arms in irritation of the Colonel stepping in where he wasn't invited.

Casey overheard the conversation and remembered the dream. She prayed it was wrong, but she had the same feeling of foreboding churning within her stomach from her dream of Keith. The young woman was pretty, and the young man had strong features. Could the conversation going on with Fletcher, Hawk, and the Colonel have something to do with her dream? "Um, I don't mean to step into the middle of a confidential conversation, but, um, I couldn't help but overhear that you have two A.N.G.E.L.s missing?" Casey asked.

Hawk nodded. "We do."

"Was one a female and one a male?"

He looked at her with a furrowed brow as he crossed his arms. "They are."

"Does the female have blond hair? And, the male, does he have reddish-blond hair?" Casey asked.

"Casey, what's going on?" the Colonel asked, feeling uneasy.

"I had another dream the other night," she said, "The last time I had one this strong, it was of Keith."

"And?" Hawk impatiently asked.

Casey shook her head in response.

"What does *that* mean?" Hawk demanded.

"She saw them," Casey explained.

"*Who*?"

"Jackie," Casey said. "She couldn't let them get away."

Hawk narrowed his eyes as he took a step toward her. The Colonel stepped in between them when Hawk's body got tense.

Casey took a deep breath, not wanting to tell him. To her, these dreams were a curse she wished she never experienced.

"What happened to them?" Hawk demanded.

Reading Hawk's body language, Fletcher tried to calm him. "Easy on, mate."

"She killed them," Casey said, nervous by his reaction. "The man gave himself for the woman, in hopes that she could get away. She didn't get away, though. She was killed at the docks while trying to get to the boat."

"Where are they now?" Hawk asked.

She shook her head. "I don't-I don't know."

"You don't know? You somehow know they're dead, but you don't know where they are now? Are you kidding me?"

"She had a dream when we lost Keith too," the Colonel spoke up in her defense.

As Hawk took another step toward her, Mark barreled across the camp from out of nowhere, planting himself in front of Hawk with his arms crossed. "You'd better back it up a step, *mate*," Mark snapped. "I don't like your tone, and I *really* don't like the aggression coming off you. We have a lot of work to do over the next few weeks, and I would rather do it in a peaceful manner."

"Then tell your soon-to-be-bride to keep her mouth shut!" Hawk growled.

Feeling the anger from Mark and Hawk, the Colonel did his best to maintain his own composure. "She's trying to warn you. She's had visions before."

"Tell ya what," Fletcher rested his hand on Hawk's shoulder, "I'll check out her story and let ya know what we find."

Hawk glared at Fletcher. "You'd *better* find Stanton and O'Brien."

"Calm your brumbies, mate. We're not the enemy here."

"Go take a walk and cool down," the Colonel suggested. "I'll see what details I can get out of Casey that will help Fletcher."

Hawk shot daggers at everyone before he spun his heels and took off into the blistering heat of the Outback. The temperatures were brutal. The air was stagnant as the Outback began its shift from spring to summer. The Colonel prayed God would use the time to work on Hawk's heart. He prayed God would prepare Hawk for the possible loss of two of his A.N.G.E.L.s. The Colonel's heart broke for him, knowing what Hawk may face with his team in the upcoming days.

Chapter 3

The English Unification

True to their word, several days after they left for their clan, Ollie, George, and Grace returned to the camp. When they did, they separated Mark and Casey for three days. While Ollie and George worked with Mark on what was about to happen, Grace worked with Casey. It was a time of deep cleansing, while they also looked within themselves to see how they could make their soon-to-be spouse the best person they could be.

Grace and Casey discussed Mark's strengths, weaknesses, and dreams. They also talked about his desires, and his heart. Grace shared with Casey how she and her husband were able to meld together and truly become one in spirit. They had to work at it every day, sometimes forcing themselves to see the good in the other, asking each morning of themselves what they could do for the other one.

On the day of the wedding, Grace and Casey woke up early. Grace left the tent to get buckets of water so Casey could "take clean" again. They operated the same way they did last time, with the exceptions of the oils and the dress.

This time the oils were a mixture. Casey watched as Grace explained the oils. "Dis is you – your essence, your life," she said, as she poured a portion of pink oil into an empty bottle. "Dis is Mr. Mark – his spirit, and willingness t' love and protect you." She poured a portion of blue oil into the bottle with the pink one, turning the oil purple. "As your hearts and souls mix, da color is da color of royalty. Purple means royalty. Your souls are mixing w' da King," she said, referring to God.

She set the bottle on the table, and poured a portion of clear oil into the bottle. "Dis is for your friendship." She turned to Casey and said, "Without dat, dere no basis. It has t' be a basis of friendship, mixed with you, Mr. Mark, and God."

As Casey sat there in her towel, she listened intently to the description. "I understand."

"And dis...dis is da most important one." She excitedly pulled a tiny vial of liquid out from her backpack. "Dis may be da smallest, but is most powerful. It needs t' be added when all da mix is done." She set the precious vial aside, before she took the bottle of already mixed oils and shook it.

When Grace set it back down, Casey watched as the oils intermingled with each other and remembered the story of each one.

"Now," Grace held up the small vial, "Dis is essential. Not gonna work without dis. Smell." She had Casey come over and inhale the oils that were already mixed. They smelled okay, but not quite what she thought they would smell like. "Is okay, no?"

"Yes," Casey said. "It smells good."

"Is good, but needs dis for da fragrance t' be complete," she said, with a knowing smile as she held up the oil she had yet to add.

"What is that?" Casey asked.

She was happy Casey finally asked. In order to add it, it was customary to wait for the bride to ask the question. In order for them to understand, they needed to know all of the elements of a successful marriage.

"Dis is tiniest, but most powerful. With even just a little, it make all da difference in da world. Watch," she said, and only put three drops in it. "One for you, one for Mr. Mark, and one for God." She took the bottle and shook it again before she took the lid off and had

"Wow!" Casey said, amazed, as she sniffed it. Those three little drops of oil turned it from 'good' to one of the most heavenly scents she had ever smelled.

"Is very powerful, no?" Grace asked.

"Yeah. What was that?"

"Is da love of all dree." She smiled. "See, da love makes all da difference. With just a lil' it changes good smell to powerful, no?"

Casey smiled as tears came to her eyes. She fully understood. "Yes."

"You need t' keep dat love," Grace said, handing the vial of oils to Casey that was on a necklace. She placed it around Casey's neck so it rested over her heart. "Dis is for you t' remember."

Casey took off both necklaces, as Grace curiously watched to see what she was doing. Casey finally knew what she needed to do with the key. She took it off the rope, and set it on the table before dripping three drops of the valuable liquid on it. At first, they saw it coat the key. Then, they watched in amazement as it slowly turned the color of a key from gold, to a deep, majestic purple.

"See." Grace smiled. "Love covers all for da King. See? Is purple for royalty. Dat's how you know it from *His* love."

"Well said," Casey agreed, as she put the key on the necklace with the vial, and replaced it on her neck.

"Dat very precious and powerful," she cautioned. "Be careful with both."

"I will."

Grace smiled in satisfaction. She knew Casey understood the priceless value of everything that transpired…not only over the course of the last couple of weeks, but of the core values that would hold their marriage together. Grace had confidence in Mark and Casey to make their marriage last. She knew it was one of faith, as well as a deep love for God and each other. The combination would be unstoppable, provided they stayed focused.

"Is almost time," Grace said. "We need t' finish. Dat is, unless ya wanna get married in dat?" She gestured to the towel wrapped around Casey.

Casey blushed as she looked down at the towel. "Uh, yeah, let's finish."

Grace helped Casey with the oil on the backs of her legs, her back, and her neck, while Casey did the rest of her body. Then Grace went to her backpack and pulled out another sarong. This time it was almost all white. However, along the bottom, about three inches tall and of various widths depending on the picture, were intricate, hand-sewn designs, made with only red thread.

"That is stunning!" Casey said, taken aback.

"All da women in clan put something dey have in high value t' dem. It custom, t' remind da new bride dat da clan is behind her, and also t' remind her of da most valuable."

"Kind of like advice?" Casey asked, as she struggled to follow what she was saying.

She nodded. "Yes, dat it. Advice of what t' hold dear. See, dis mine." She pointed to a cross with an empty tomb next to it.

Casey smiled in understanding. "Beautiful."

"Dis is me mum's. She put a baby here for well-wishes," Grace explained. "Dis is me sister's. She put a hand t' remind you t' be a helping hand t' your husband."

"I love it," Casey said in amazement at the thought put into the pictures. Grace took a few moments to explain each character and who it came from. While Casey did not know the women, and they did not know her, the fact that they still gave her a portion of their heart meant the world to her.

Grace helped Casey put the sarong on, tied with a red cord around her waist. "For da love dat binds you together," she explained. "Leave it on your bed as reminder."

Casey nodded. "I will. This is absolutely beautiful. I never thought I'd ever get married. And never, in my wildest dreams, did I think it would come with so much meaning and beauty."

"God ne'er give anything but da best for His daughter." Grace smiled. "You're a daughter a da King. See, He even showed ya here." She held up the purple key. "You're royalty. Mr. Mark will treat ya like da princess ya are," she said, confidently.

Casey smiled.

"Now, for da finishing touch." Grace had Casey sit down on the cot, and ran some of the oil through her hair before she braided one side of it. Then she braided the other side, before she had them meet in the middle, tying it with a piece of red cord, leaving the rest free-flowing. She took small red and white flowers she picked that morning, and inserted them along the braids.

When she finished, Grace went around to the front of her. "How do dey say...?" She snapped her fingers, trying to remember what Pete called Casey. "Oh yeah! Natural beauty." She grinned. "Beautiful!"

"Thank you." Casey hugged her. "You have made this so special."

"No worries. You my sister, yes?"

"Yes."

"Family look out for family," Grace explained. She had tears of joy in her eyes as she hugged Casey. "You blessed."

"Thank you. So are you."

"Is time."

"Really?" Casey looked at her in confusion. How did she know? No one knocked or anything.

"Da morning of a wedding in our clan, dey wait for da bride. Is custom dat da man get up with da elders at morning light. He prepare da bed with da same oil." She nodded toward the leftover mixture. "You keep for future use."

"Thank you."

"All da men in da camp work with him, preparing him for tonight. Mr. Mark been ready and waiting t' see his bride for dree days. And today, he been ready for hours. Right now, he stand with da elders, waiting t' see you."

Casey took Grace's hands into hers. "This is beautiful! You guys do this for every wedding?"

"Please allow me explain. Our clan, da wedding couple choose four sponsors to guide dem drough dere marriage."

"They help guide the couple, like counselors?"

"Yes." She smiled. "I continue?"

"Please."

"In our clan, we change certain dings so make marriage special. It not just wedding. It joining of two people. It *very* important. Must be prepared. Must have clan behind you t' succeed. Da men here in camp are your clan. Dey will look out for you two."

"I know."

"And, I will raise prays for you two."

"I know. Thank you. You will always be in my prayers as well."

"Thank you. Now, ready?" Grace asked.

"Yes."

She left the tent for a moment, before she came back with a handful of the red and white flowers. She fresh-picked them. "For you," Grace said, handing them to Casey.

"Thank you."

She grinned in excitement. "Dey know you're coming. When da maid goes for da flowers, dey know. Very excited!"

Casey hugged her. The excitement that churned within her for over three days, spilled over into the tears that slowly trickled down her face. Casey's only regret was that her brother, Jack, wasn't able to be there. She knew beyond a shadow of a doubt that he would have approved of the man she chose to marry.

"Since you not have dad, Ollie gonna walk you t' your mate," Grace said, as she went over to the door, letting Ollie in.

As soon as he saw her, a huge smile spread across his face. All one saw were the whites of his teeth. "Beauty!" He shook his head. He turned to Grace and nodded in approval. "Good onya!"

She nodded in appreciation. "Thank you."

He went over to Casey and said, "Mr. Mark tell me you no family."

"That's correct," Casey said.

"You in our clan now," he said. "See." He pointed to the designs at the bottom of her dress. "You, no father. I be."

Casey looked at Grace for an explanation.

"He say he gonna be your dad," Grace clarified. "He my dad too."

"Really?" She looked at her, surprised. She never connected the two of them.

"Will you?" Ollie asked Casey.

"Will I what?"

Grace laughed as she walked over to them. She put her hand on her father's shoulder as she said, "He want to know if you join our family?"

Casey nodded. She wasn't sure she would be able to hold in all the happiness and joy she felt for too much longer. This day was already beyond her wildest dreams.

"Den, daughter," he put his arm out, "Go make family proud. Take care Mr. Mark."

Casey smiled as she looped her arm through his. "I will."

Grace pulled back the curtain, allowing them to walk outside. She quietly followed them as they walked down to the riverbank.

The Colonel was standing beside Mark, and tapped his shoulder when he saw Casey. As soon as he saw her, Mark turned and looked toward her. He watched her come down to them beside the river with a look of pure delight. He shook his head in shock at how beautiful she looked. He couldn't believe that after all of these years, she was going to finally be his. The natural beauty he saw in her soul over all these years, radiated from the essence of her being.

Every portion of the ceremony was symbolic. George made sure he added the elements of God to the traditional ceremony he normally performed within their clan. After a prayer was said for their marriage, George blessed them. Then he nodded toward the Colonel, who pulled two rings out of his pocket and handed them to George. George blessed the rings, symbolizing their unending love for each other, before he handed one to Casey and one to Mark.

Thinly carved, and hand-painted with an identical aboriginal design, the rings were made of solid pieces of wood. George said it was meant to capture the spirit of love between them. They placed the rings on each other's finger and said a vow, pledging their honor, commitment, faithfulness, and allegiance to each other, binding them together forever.

After that, George finally allowed Mark to kiss Casey. Mark took one hand and placed it on her waist, while he placed the other hand on the back of her neck. He pulled her closer to him and whispered, "This is just the beginning." And then kissed her with one of the most tender, gentle kisses he had given her to date.

When the wedding was complete, Grace handed Mark and Casey a bag of food, and the group sent them off into the Outback on their own.

"That's it?" Casey asked, surprised, as they walked away from the others.

He winked with a mischievous smile, and said, "Mmm, not quite." He knew where they were headed. He prepared it over the last few days. While Casey was in the tent with Grace, he and the other guys made a small hut for them to use for a honeymoon. As part of the preparation, he had to not only make the hut, but also made bedding as well. That morning he, George, and Ollie mixed the oils, much the same as Grace and Casey had in the tent. Afterward, he spread it on the covers, allowing it time to dry into the blankets and permeate the hut. He cherished the rituals granted to him by these men. He held dear to his heart everything that was said and done, filing it away for when it would be needed again. These men were strong in the Lord, and shared some of their precious life experience with him. They advised him, counseled him, and directed him as to the many aspects of women. They also took him deep within himself to find what he could do to make her better. He knew what he had to do. He knew that he had to take the strength he knew she possessed, and bring it forward so she knew it was there. He knew with everything that happened in her life so far, that he would have to protect her heart by shielding her mind and body from any further damage. He knew in order to do that, she would have to find the capability within herself to use the power God granted to her as one of His daughters. He was going to have to cultivate and develop those skills in order for her to survive what he knew was coming toward them. He felt it. He knew it was not only going to take everything she had, but also everything the other A.N.G.E.L.s had in them, to come together to fight what was on the horizon. The war wasn't over. They had won the battle, but the war was still yet to come. What battleground the demon would choose was known only to it. All Mark knew, was that he was going to have to teach her to see what was not there, to feel what she could not see, and to anticipate what was ahead.

Casey stared at the inside of the tiny hut in shock. It was small and rustic, but stunning on the inside. The walls were lined with vines of flowers, the bed was made out of brush, covered with blankets, and the red and white blankets were doused with the oils from the ceremony. Casey recognized the heavenly scent as soon as she went inside.

"Wow!" Casey breathed out. That was when she noticed a small cluster of three red candles in the corner. "What are those for?"

"The candles are for the three days we're here," he explained. "We burn one a day. When the last one is out, we have to go back to camp to start our life together."

Casey shook her head in amazement as she began to cry. She couldn't hold it in any longer.

"I know. I feel the same." He sat down on the bed. He turned, lighting the first candle. "It's as if everything is laid out for a purpose."

Casey nodded in agreement, as she looked at the red and white flowers on the vines, which matched those in her hair – the ones that were to symbolize friendship and love.

Mark raised an eyebrow as she stood in front of him. "Um…?"

"What?"

"Well, you look amazing." He smiled. Then, while looking her over from head to toe he asked, "But, um, that key around your neck was supposed to be gold. What happened to it?"

Casey smiled as she held the key in her hand, dangling it from the necklace. She knelt down beside him, and faced him as she kicked her feet out from under her, resting them to the side, and explained, "I took three drops of the oil representing the love of me, you, and God, and put it over the key. Grace and I watched as it turned purple right before our eyes. She said it was the love from The

King that covers all. She also said purple signified royalty, and that's how she knew it was His love."

He smiled as he held the key for a moment. "This day has been...." He shook his head, beside himself.

Casey adored Mark, and in the candlelight, he looked more handsome than normal. She couldn't tell if it was the love emanating from him, or her imagination that made it seem that way, but she prayed it would never go away.

As if he could read her thoughts, he looked up into her eyes and said, "Your soul is absolutely beautiful."

Casey rubbed her thumb on his cheek. She watched as he took her hand into his and kissed it, and then pulled her arm a little closer, kissing her shoulder as he looked up at her.

He took a moment, soaking in what was before him. This gorgeous woman was his wife. He touched the side of her face, and then ran his fingers down her neck all the way to her waist as he inched closer to her. He was having a hard time believing he was going to be able to finally take her in his arms and have her after all of these years. He removed the red cord from around her waist and gently set it aside. He wanted her so badly, that he was having a hard time controlling himself.

Casey leaned over and rested one hand on the side of his face and the other on his neck, looking into his dark brown eyes. Casey gazed into his eyes before she leaned down and gently kissed his neck. He groaned in desire, and pulled her face to his in an explosive kiss as he gently guided her to the bed.

That night was amazing, exciting, and explosive. Casey knew, for as long as she lived that she would never forget a single detail of that day.

Chapter 4

Battle Readiness

The next morning, Casey woke up to Mark holding her. She rolled over and looked up at him. "Morning."

"Morning, my beautiful wife."

"Mmm, that sounds nice."

"I think so too," he said with a grin. "Are you hungry?"

"Um, give me a couple of minutes to wake up, but yeah."

While she looked through her bag for her toothbrush and toothpaste, Mark watched her. She was on her stomach, with the blanket resting at about her waist. His heart broke when he saw her back. He ran his fingers over the scars that still marked her. "Do they hurt?"

"Do what hurt?" she asked. She looked over her shoulder to see him looking at her scars. "Not really. They feel kind of numb around them."

"I'm really sorry I wasn't able to protect you."

She sat up, holding the blanket to her chest. "Mark, you can't hold yourself responsible for that. You were outnumbered."

"It was my job to protect you. While I worked through a lot of the feelings, when I see the scars it reminds me that I was responsible. I feel like I let you and the unit down."

"No, you didn't. You can only do so much." She took his hand into hers. "You are only human."

"But –"

"No buts," she said, cutting him off. "If you are looking for forgiveness, you've got it. If you are looking for me to blame you, you're not going to find it here."

He dropped his head onto his knees, wrapping his arms around them. "It's not that. It's a reminder to me that not only did I let you get caught, but tortured as well."

"God got us out of there."

"Not before you were permanently marked."

"I've worked through it. The marks are always going to be there. They are a reminder to me of the danger out there. They are also a reminder to me that God never leaves His people behind. Sacrifices were made that day to get us out."

"You don't know that. They haven't found them yet."

"Yes. I do. God showed it to me in a dream again the other night. It was the exact same type of I had when I dreamt about Keith. I had it just after my dreamtime. I prayed I was wrong and that it was a product of the dreamtime. I didn't want to see it. I didn't want to be right about this. God showed me the sacrifice that Stanton and O'Brien made on our behalf. I know they are in Heaven with God right now."

"Inadvertently as it may be, if that is the case, it's my fault as well," Mark said.

"No, it's not. Things happen in the world that we may never be able to explain, but I have learned that God allows things for a reason. You told me that."

He shook his head, beside himself.

"If we were never captured, that demon's lair would not have been discovered, right?" Casey asked.

"Right."

"What Satan planned for evil, God used for good."

"But the loss of – I can't even believe I am saying this." He shook his head as he looked up toward the ceiling. "I don't want to acknowledge that they may be gone. I've worked with both of them. Victoria was a beauty, but she was Shawn's. She was as dangerous as she was beautiful. We would jokingly call her a black widow. She would lure them in and get them when they least expected it. Shawn, on the other hand, was passive, which is unusual for a sniper. He was probably the best shot I knew." He shook his head again. "I don't want to talk about them in the past tense."

"It may be a fact that you will have to acknowledge. According to my dream, it's true."

"I'm holding onto hope because they haven't found their bodies yet. I hope they're in hiding until it's clear to come back out."

"Hope's a good thing."

He glanced over at her. "Unless it's a moot point."

"I'm afraid I'm right."

"We'll find out soon enough, but I have a feeling we need to pay more attention to your dreams as time goes on."

"I don't want to. Some of them are scary."

"You've had others?"

"Yes," she admitted.

"What are they?"

"I'm not ready to talk about them yet." She took a deep breath and slowly let it out. "I pray they don't come to fruition."

"God gave those to you for a reason. If they can help us –"

"Then I'll tell you. Until then, I'm keeping them between me and God, with a prayer that they don't come true." If they did, then Casey knew they could be in trouble. The battles that went on in her dreams terrified her. The massive battle between the creatures of the night and the A.N.G.E.L.s of the world in her dreams could mean the end of the A.N.G.E.L.s, and she didn't even want to remotely entertain that thought.

* * *

Over the course of the next three days, Mark and Casey had more in-depth conversations. Mark pressed her for her dreams, but she wouldn't divulge them. She still prayed against the visions she saw while she slept. As a matter of fact, she woke up screaming one night because of them.

When the last day arrived of their three-day honeymoon, Casey confessed that she didn't want to leave their tiny home. Within the hut, she felt protected and safe in Mark's arms. The love they shared over that time provided a strong foundation for their marriage. She knew, however, as the last of the candles went out, it was time to go back and prepare for the battle that loomed ahead.

* * *

For three weeks, the guys trained Casey without mercy. The exercises were painful and brutal. During the training, the guys would say verses, so they would be engrained in her head, allowing her to push through with God's words of encouragement and strength. They would work with her on target practice with a gun, a bow and arrows, knives, and crossbow. They would sharpen her hearing skills by blindfolding her the entire day so she would have to listen to what was around her, as opposed to only using her eyes. They would train her in hand-to-hand combat, balance and agility training, and speed drills, which taught her body to deal with the sudden rush of adrenaline. Eventually they blindfolded her in that as well, so she would use her other senses, instead of looking for the enemy with just her eyes. They wanted her to use all her senses instead of believing only in what she could see. They wanted her to feel the enemy approaching. They wanted her to feel the swings being taken at her. They wanted her to know what the enemy would do before he did…what punches he would throw…even what instrument he may use.

Casey didn't think she had it in her to go as far as she did. However, while she didn't have the full confidence in herself, she had it in the Father, the Spirit, and Jesus. She had faith that They would help, guide, direct, and always keep her within Their reach. She knew she would never be alone. She knew with Their help that she would be able to fight with everything she had.

*　　*　　*

Three weeks into Casey's training, Fletcher dropped off some supplies for the camp. After he emptied the helicopter, Hawk pulled him aside, demanding any news of Stanton and O'Brien.

"We found blood in the two areas where Carter said they were," Fletcher confirmed.

"And their bodies? Have they been found yet?"

"No, sir."

"Then, there is still a chance," Hawk said.

"Until the bodies are found, there is always a chance, but, sir, according to –"

"I *won't* give up hope until I see their bodies."

"We're still searching, sir," Fletcher said, doing his best to avoid the anger he faced during the last conversation with him.

"Don't give up."

"We won't. They wouldn't give up on us."

Hawk patted his shoulder. "Good onya."

"Any other messages, sir?"

"No. Top priority will remain finding Stanton and O'Brien."

"But, sir, there are –"

"Stanton and O'Brien. Am I clear?"

"Yes, sir."

*   *   *

Later that same day, Charlie wandered back into the camp. The group just finished dinner, and they were sitting around the fire, relaxing, while some cleaned their guns from practice that day.

"What're you doing here?" Hawk stood from where he was cleaning his gun. Charlie scared him – no one heard him coming. "Everything okay with your clan?"

Charlie nodded with a smile. "Yes. Okay here too, yes?"

"Yes." Hawk awkwardly stood there, waiting for more. After a minute, he asked, "What is it?"

"I help again," Charlie explained.

"And, how are you gonna do that?" Hawk crossed his arms. "We're healthy."

"Miss Casey need t' learn my ways too," Charlie pointed out.

Mark raised an eyebrow. "What do you mean by that?"

"You no hear me come, yes?" Charlie asked.

The Colonel shook his head. "No, we didn't hear you."

"No hear me before either," Charlie said proudly. "First time I here, yes?"

"You're right, we did not hear ya then either," Hawk agreed.

"I teach," Charlie offered. "I teach all if want."

"Wait a second." Casey put her hand up to stop any more conversations. "Are you telling us that you can teach us to be silent in the woods? More silent than we already are?"

"Yes," Charlie said.

Hawk rubbed his chin in thought. "What *else* can you teach us?" Hawk knew the Aboriginals had ways about them that allowed them to be completely silent when hunting. He knew they had been living off the land for hundreds of years. They could glean a lot from him. He wondered if Charlie was willing to teach them their secrets…and if so, what would it cost them? "And what do you want in return?"

Charlie grinned – the magical question was asked. Everyone anxiously waited for his response. Charlie explained, "I teach you t' see da enemy before he comes. I teach you t' hear with your heart and soul, not with just your ears. I teach you t' hunt and live off da land. I teach you t' be silent and deadly as da enemy – if not more. All I want I return is what Grace has."

Hawk looked at him in confusion. "What do you mean you want what Grace has?"

"When she come back, she has something. I want too."

"What is it?" Hawk asked.

"You teached her," Charlie explained. "I want you teached me."

Mark suddenly realized what Charlie was asking for. "You want Christ."

"He wants…you want Jesus?" the Colonel asked in surprise. While he was pleased, knowing what he had learned about his people the request threw him a bit.

"Yes." Charlie nodded. "She tell me. I want it. I teach you what I know and da ways of da bush, you teach me da ways of Jesus. Deal, no?"

Everyone got a pleased smile on their face, as Hawk shook his hand and said, "You have a deal, mate. Welcome t' *our* clan."

* * *

Charlie was a phenomenal teacher. At the time of his arrival, Casey was already working hard, but he added the other men to the regimen as well. He pushed them. He challenged them. They were well-trained machines before, but Charlie taught them to look deeper. He taught them to be cleverer and more resourceful than they already were. He taught all of them to be able to operate and adapt not only in battle, but also in their natural surroundings, blindfolded the entire time. By the time he finished with them, they could feel a plant with the blindfold on and know if it was a good resource. What the A.N.G.E.L.s taught Casey in military tactics and the Word of God, Charlie taught all of them in nature and working with the unseen. It was an exhilarating experience for her, and one that she would treasure forever.

Also, during his time with them, the others taught Charlie various aspects regarding Jesus, God, and the Holy Spirit. He knew of 'the spirits,' but he needed to know of *The* Spirit – the Holy Spirit. He knew of the 'powerful beings,' but he needed to know of the Almighty Being, the All-powerful God. He knew of the many brave warriors of the past who helped guide, shape, and direct his clan, and consequently all the clans, but he needed to know about the One Warrior who helped guide, shape, and direct the world – Jesus, Son of the Living God. He needed to know that Jesus was the One who came to earth in the form of a man, to show, guide, and direct one in the ways of the Heavenly Father.

*   *   *

The simulations and exercises Charlie ran them through were fierce. They often challenged them beyond what some of them could take – challenging the aggressor as much as the challenger.

Casey stood in the open field, blindfolded. It was her turn to be in the middle as the challenger. They were training for a couple weeks by that point, and between what training the A.N.G.E.L.s gave her and what Charlie taught her, Casey was reasonably sure she could win.

During the fight, the challenger was not allowed to carry a weapon. If one was used, the challenger had to find it on the field – blindfolded. This exercise was also done at night in order to not allow light or shadows to play a part in the success or demise of the challenger.

The Aggressor Challenge was where the guys would pick one aggressor. The remaining A.N.G.E.L.s and Charlie would encourage the aggressor as well as the challenger, until one of them went beyond what they could take. Either one could say, "I give," or the Colonel or Hawk called it, effectively ending the simulation. While neither the aggressor nor the remaining A.N.G.E.L.s were blindfolded, it was still dark, adding a level of difficulty for all involved.

Casey was given fifteen minutes to orient herself before the aggressor was sent in. The aggressor was to be as silent as possible in order to gain the upper hand on the challenger. The challenger's job was to fight as hard as they could, beyond what they thought they could. Charlie and the remaining A.N.G.E.L.s would stand in a circle forming the playing field as they said verses of encouragement. The challenger was not to know who was fighting them until the simulation was over. The reason for this was because Mark, being the biggest, was usually the hardest to beat. If one could beat him, without knowing who he was beating, it was a bigger success. Sometimes if they figured out that they were fighting him, they would give up.

Casey stood there with a blindfold on her eyes for a moment. She took a couple deep breaths to relax. While she had done this before in the weeks past, and had even succeeded a couple of times and failed miserably other times, it was her intention to win this time because it was to be her final simulation.

She silently prayed for strength, courage, and endurance, along with clarity of mind and hearing in order to locate the aggressor. She also prayed for the senses she *could* use to be on high alert in order to assist her in the challenge. "In Jesus' most precious name, I pray…Amen," she whispered as she closed out her prayer.

The silence was almost deafening. She took a deep breath to get a feel for the air around her, which was heavy. She slipped her shoes and socks off, tossing them toward her right. She heard both the shoes *and* the socks as they hit the ground. She was grateful to know that the Father granted her incredible hearing for this challenge.

She swept her feet around her on the ground as she got in a slightly crouched position. If the aggressor came from behind, she could use multiple ways to gain release from that position. However, if she was standing in an upright position her escape would still be possible, but limited.

In her sweep, she found a stick and picked it up to use as a possible weapon. She felt the full length of the stick. It was about an inch in diameter and approximately four-feet long, so she cracked it in half. This did two things: it allowed her to have more control over the stick, and also left a sharp edge on the end, allowing her to use it as a weapon if she needed.

She strained to hear any movement, while continuing to feel around the area in order to create a map in her mind of what was around her. The challenger was taken in blindfolded, so they were not able to see what the playing field looked like. Even though she couldn't see, she inhaled the fresh and earthy smell of leaves and trees. The moist and grainy dirt squished between her toes. Occasionally, she stumbled on the larger rocks mixed with the dirt, making a mental note where they were located. The rocks ranged in size, but for the most part, they were flat. If she had to guess, she would say that they placed her in a dry riverbed. These were found around the Outback that time of year. She knew they had a rather large and overflowing riverbed near the camp. However, in taking walks with Mark, they found several extensions of the river bed to be dry about five miles out of camp, but she wasn't sure which one they used for the field. Come rainy season, all of the beds in the Outback would be full and overflowing, so the timing was perfect.

Casey mapped the area she was in by feeling her way around. She found multiple areas of underbrush until she found a tree. She followed the branches up to the leaves and realized it was a Eucalyptus tree by the scent and the shape of the leaves. She cringed when she stepped on a Twisted Desert Wattle bush. The spikey branches scratched her foot and leg. She quickly pulled away and fell into a Murray's Wattle shrub. She scolded herself as she climbed out of the bush, and dusted the debris from the bush off her clothes…that's when she heard it.

To her left there was the slight roll of a pebble. When she stopped to listen, she detected the aggressor. When a foot sunk into the sand nearby, she spun toward the sound, crouched down with her weapon in her right hand ready for use.

The sound was approximately ten feet away. She knew the A.N.G.E.L. was not blindfolded, so it would be useless to hide behind a tree. By that point his eyes were already adjusted to the darkness.

Another step in the sand. This one was in the pebbles of the riverbed about five feet from Casey. Her heart raced, as she knew the battle was about to begin. By this point, the aggressor already sized-up the situation, deciding his best point of attack. How he was going to come at her was only known to him.

By the sound of his steps, which were about two feet away, he was one of the bigger guys. That could only mean Mark, the Colonel, or Hawk. The others had muscle, but those three were the bigger guys of the two crews.

He was to her right. She felt his presence slide around behind her, so she spun toward him. He jumped away from the stick, startled, which narrowly missed his mid-section. He crunched the twigs of the Twisted Desert Waddle she encountered earlier under him when he landed. His breathing slowed as he calculated his next move, while he brushed off the debris from the bush.

In their training, she knew his first line of defense would be to disarm her. Intently aware of his presence, she silently remained in prayer, hoping to get some sense of what her aggressor was thinking. In her mind, the aggressor was represented by a black figure. She could see the battle in her head. It would be a fine dance for a bit as the aggressor assessed his best plan of attack, and she would have to do her best to thwart his attempts.

In one swift motion, the aggressor leapt into the air and landed on her back, flattening her to the ground, knocking the wind out of her. He held down her wrist with the stick. No matter what he did in the position they were in, she would not release the stick. He had to use his other hand to keep his own balance while she wiggled and squirmed beneath him.

"Isaiah 41:10 – *'So do not fear, for I am with you; do not be dismayed, for I am your God. I will strengthen you and help you; I will uphold you with my righteous right hand,'*" Carson's voice of encouragement rang from approximately fifteen feet in the northern direction of the circle.

Casey took a deep breath and let his words soak into her heart for a moment. She used her aggressor's strength against him and rolled, pushing up before she flipped herself over. She used the momentum to roll both of them over. Now on top of him, she kicked back with her legs and her heel landed near his groin. He released her as he groaned in pain.

Casey sprung up and faced the direction she left him in as she listened, alert to every sound.

"Psalm 18:32-36," Derek's voice came from the southern direction of the circle. "*'It is God who arms me with strength and makes my way perfect. He makes my feet like the feet of a deer; He enables me to stand on the heights. He trains my hands for battle; my arms can bend a bow of bronze. You give me Your shield of victory, and Your right hand sustains me; You stoop down to make me great. You broaden the path beneath me, so that my ankles do not turn.'*"

The A.N.G.E.L.s and Charlie were praying for her. Even her aggressor in this exercise was praying for her, but he also was going to do his best to bring her down. In the challenger exercise, they did not take it easy on each other. The enemy would not take it easy on them in the field, so they were not going to in the exercise.

In paying attention to Derek's voice, Casey missed the motion until a fist land squarely in her kidney. As her body bowed backward in pain, he grabbed her wrist with his hand. Clutching the stick, Casey's fingers give way as her attacker snatched the stick from her hand.

She took that moment to spin around, foot lifted, thrusting it into his stomach. She sent him back at least five feet, as she heard him groan in pain. Casey froze as she stared in the direction she heard her attacker in…*it was Mark*! She took a deep breath to collect her wits. Looking toward Heaven, she said aloud Psalm 30:10, "'*Hear me, Lord, and have mercy on me. Help me, O Lord!*'"

Sensing her panic, the Colonel reminded her of Proverbs 3:5&6, "'*Trust in the Lord with all your heart, and lean not on your own understanding; in all your ways acknowledge Him, and He will make your paths straight.*'"

Casey nodded in acknowledgment, reminding herself that God was the One in control. She took a deep breath. As she slowly let it out, she felt a foot ram her mid-section. When she panicked, she missed hearing him pick himself up off the ground. His kick sent her flying. She felt like a ragdoll sailing through the air a couple of feet. The tree snapped as she slammed into it, landing on the ground with a thud.

Her head was spinning, as she felt Mark's hands pick her up. He wrapped his arms under hers and clasped his hands behind her head. She shook her head to clear it before she lifted her foot and rammed her heel down his calf muscle, landing on the center of his foot. She felt a bone crack and she heard him yell in pain. Several birds scattered into the air, startled. She quickly spun around and kicked him in the head while he was down. She felt sweat from his face splash onto her foot from where she kicked him.

She turned to run before she heard Charlie's voice quote I Corinthians 16:13, and she stopped dead in her tracks. His smooth voice was almost a whisper as she heard him say, "'*Be on the alert, stand firm in your faith, act like men, be strong.*'"

She spun around and listened, hearing Mark pick his body off the ground. She even heard the blood from his mouth drop onto the rock near to where he landed. She heard him wipe the sweat off his face, and then splatter onto the tree behind him.

Casey took a deep breath before she quoted Charlie's verse aloud again, "'*Be on alert, stand firm in your faith, act like men, be strong.*'"

Without knowing for sure where he was, Casey prayed, and then charged in the direction she sensed him to be. It caught him off guard when her shoulder pounded into his abdomen. Her arms wrapped around his body, slamming him into the boulder behind him.

He shoved his hands down on her shoulders and kicked his knee up into her stomach. He then grabbed under her arms, thrashing her side to side until she finally released, and he sent her back through the air again. She landed on the ground, sliding approximately five feet, the pebbles in the dirt cut into her arms and legs.

It was almost too much for her. When she pushed up with her hands, her arms gave out and she dropped back to the ground. When she slammed him into the rock, her hands caught part of the brunt of the hit, and her wrists were telling her that they were not going to cooperate with her anymore.

She prayed silently for strength as the tears poured down her cheeks. She couldn't stop them no matter how hard she tried. There was pain emanating from so many parts of her body that she wanted to give up. That was when she heard Hawk's voice quote I Corinthians 15:58, "'*Therefore, my beloved brothers, be steadfast, immovable, always abounding in the work of the Lord, knowing that in the Lord your labor is not in vain.*'"

His voice was so strong. She used that strength to push up with her hands. She felt them pop and grind under the pressure, but they held. By that point, her blindfold had fallen off. She stood up, hoping to orient her body with some sense of direction. She wavered in her stance as she faced Mark. She could see his heart break in his eyes, even from the ten feet that separated them.

"I have to," he pleaded, hoping she would understand.

"I knew it was you. Don't stop."

"I don't want to hurt you."

"Then you will fail," she said as she sprang forward, knocking him back several feet.

"NO!" he shouted, doing his best to push her off, but she held his hands by the wrists down in the dirt. He grunted, "I don't want to hurt you anymore."

"James 1:4," Casey said, holding him down. "'*Perseverance must finish its work so that you may be mature and complete, not lacking anything.*'"

"Case, please don't make me," he begged.

"You *want* me to fail?"

"No."

Looking him directly in his eyes, she said, "If you do not show me how to fight and win with a guy as strong as you are, *I-will-lose.*"

He took a deep breath to compose himself. He knew she was right, but he didn't want to hurt her anymore, knowing he already did quite a bit of damage.

When they had the meeting before the challenge, the Colonel insisted Mark was to be the aggressor. Mark argued that he couldn't hurt her, but the Colonel said if he didn't, someone else would. What Casey said affirmed the Colonel's words.

"Stop," Charlie called a halt to the exercise. Mark looked up, stunned, as Charlie walked over to Casey. He carefully tilted her head back, bracing her back with his knee as he swiftly replaced the blindfold. He whispered something in her ear, and then returned to his spot in the eastern portion of the circle, leaving her in her position. To Mark's horror, they were still going to make her fight with the blindfold!

He pushed up on Casey, sending her into the air. He heard her groan as she twisted on the ground in pain. Then to his amazement, when he took a step toward her, she froze. *Could she still sense him, even in as much pain as she was in?*

"Hasn't she had enough?" Mark begged.

The Colonel shook his head. "Jackie won't stop. Neither can you."

"That demon is relentless," Derek reminded him. "He's not going to give up just because she's in pain. Don't you think Satan will to send his strongest?"

The pain emitting deep within Mark's soul tore him in two. He looked up at the clarity of the night sky. It astounded him with its beauty. Thousands of stars! And the moon almost seemed to have an aura around it as it lazily hung in the hazy night sky. He put his hands on his hips and sighed, shaking his head. He then crossed his arms as he watched her lying there on the ground, motionless. "All right," he said and walked over to her.

To his surprise, she swung her body around and kicked up, sending him back a couple of steps. Then she jumped up, facing his direction.

What he didn't know, was when Charlie was down near Casey putting the blindfold on her, he whispered, *"Your strength is in God. He will show you how to fight. You inspire us. Keep it up, my sister."*

Casey stood and looked in the direction where she sent Mark. Even though she had a blindfold on, God gave her the sense to see what she could not readily see. She knew she could not beat him with strength. She would have to outsmart him or neither of them would win.

As she walked in a circle facing him, he followed. He matched her step-by-step. She wanted to get behind him, but he continued to circle with her in a fine dance. She was going to have to knock him down in order to do what she felt God wanted her to do.

When she stepped forward, he stepped back. She lunged forward, so he stepped to the side. As she went past him, he punched her in the lower back, sending her to the ground. She quickly scrambled up with strength she did not have. God took that moment to give her a verse of His own. Through the Spirit, He whispered in that still quiet voice, First Chronicles 16:11, "*'Look to the Lord and His strength; seek His face always.'*"

Casey nodded in understanding. She stood up straight as she looked toward Heaven. She could feel the Lord's presence. She took a deep breath before she faced where she knew Mark was standing. He lunged at her, but she sidestepped him at the last second. As soon as he caught himself, she jumped up on his back and got him in a chokehold, bracing her knees on his waist, while she tightened her arms around his neck. He grabbed her arms in an attempt to loosen her hold and backed them into a tree. When that didn't break the hold, he backed them into a boulder. The tree hurt, but the rocks felt as if he punched her from behind. He repeatedly slammed her into the rocks, but she tightened her grip when she felt him struggling for air under her. Then she wrapped her legs around his midsection and squeezed, as she tightened the grip on his neck.

"Casey!" He gasped for air.

"*'I can do all things through Christ who strengthens me,'*" she grunted, quoting Philippians 4:13.

"Mark," Carson called, "Isaiah 40:28-31: *'Have you not known? Have you not heard? The Lord is the everlasting God, the Creator of the ends of the earth. He does not faint or grow weary; His understanding is unsearchable. He gives power to the faint, and to him who has no might, He increases strength. Even youths shall faint and be weary, and young men shall fall exhausted, but they who wait for the Lord shall renew their strength; they shall mount* up with wings like eagles; they shall run and not be weary; they shall walk and not faint.'"*

Mark nodded in understanding as he stood up. He walked forward, struggling to get a breath of air. When he still couldn't get any air, he dropped to the ground on his hands and knees.

"Mark!" Marshall shouted Joshua 1:9 to him, seeing him drop on all fours. "'*Have I not commanded you? Be strong and of a good courage; be not afraid, neither be you dismayed: for the Lord your God is with you wherever you go.*'"

Mark's face was an odd shade of red and purple, and he could feel his pulse pounding in his head. He loved Casey, but he couldn't let her win. She was a girl, and while she was his wife, he would never hear the end of it. He looked up toward Heaven and God, and grunted as he pushed himself up. "'*But they who wait for the Lord shall renew their strength; they shall mount up with wings like eagles.*" Mark groaned, staggering in his steps. "*They shall run and not be weary; they shall walk, and not faint.*'"

He braced one hand on the rock as he swung his body back hard against it. He felt Casey temporarily give up her hold when she lost her breath. He took the second to get a deep breath of air himself. "Give up, Case," he begged.

"No!" she growled. The pain jetted from her back into the rest of her body. She could even feel the throbbing tingle into her fingertips. She was exhausted, but at that point she invested too much and was not going to quit. She envisioned him to be Hunter Morgan while she braced her feet behind her and pushed off from the rock. He fell to the ground, but immediately pushed up with his own hands. She tightly wrapped her legs around him again and tightened her chokehold.

"Case!" he yelled. "I don't want to hurt you!"

"You *will* hurt me if you quit. Imagine if you were Hunter. Would he stop?"

"No."

"Then…" She tightened the hold on his neck, cutting off the circulation at his carotid artery. She felt his pulse in her arm as his heart tried desperately to push the blood through his body in order to deliver the oxygen he needed.

He pushed up and slammed them into the rock again. Casey let out a yell as the rock cut into her back. She angrily tightened her arms and legs. She was not going to let go. If she could beat him, she could beat someone like Hunter. Then someone like Jackie would not have a chance.

Mark slammed them into the rocks as hard as he could. He hit the same place in her back, and she couldn't help but let out a yelp of pain. Her head smacked into the rock this time and she released, dropping to the ground in a daze.

"She's done," the Colonel called the exercise, and the guys ran over to them.

Carson and Grant pulled Mark over to the side to look him over, while Harper and Marshall looked over Casey. Mark rolled his head toward Casey, who was unconscious. "She going to be okay?"

Harper nodded. "Yeah. Give her a bit, mate." He glanced toward Marshall and said, "Get the basket. We need t' get her back t' camp. She took a beating."

"She gave a good beating too," Carson pointed out, as he now had Mark's boot off, and felt around his foot to see if any of the bones were broken in Mark's foot. Meanwhile, Grant checked the rest of Mark's body for any other damage.

"She'll do just fine," the Colonel said, glancing toward Derek who nodded in understanding. They knew there were battles yet to come. They also knew they would be rougher on Casey than even Mark could dish out.

*   *   *

It took the two of them a couple of weeks to recover enough to make the trip out of the Outback. While the others still worked with Mark and Casey, they were gentle with them, allowing their bodies to heal. By the time the six weeks were completed, they were a blended unit, well versed in each other's cultures, beliefs, and ways. Casey was grateful for everything the men poured into her.

Also, by the end of the six weeks, Charlie prayed for Jesus to be his Savior. He already knew a version of everything, but not the in-depth details he learned in his time with the A.N.G.E.L.s. When he was shown the truth, and was able to connect all the intricate little pieces in his head, he knew he couldn't help but ask for Jesus to be his Savior.

They laid their hands on him while he stood in the middle of them and prayed. His prayer was beautiful and exhilarating. Casey loved how his people were in touch with their inner beings, and how they were able to put things into symbols and pictures that even the simplest person could understand.

She was grateful God showed these people and their ways to her. With all of the things that went wrong in her life, as much chaos had ensued – especially in the last couple of months – she was amazed at how well things played out. She knew, however, that this was the calm before the storm. She knew something big was coming. She could feel it. The more she was taught to be in tuned to what was going on around her in nature and in the spirit realm, the more she knew they were headed for trouble.

*   *   *

Mark gently shook her to wake her up. It was about two weeks after the Aggressor Challenge between the two of them. "Casey, honey, you need to wake up."

"No, go away," she groaned, pushing away his hand.

He chuckled. "What's wrong? I know you're not a morning person, but –"

"I don't feel good," she said, cutting him off.

He sat up on his elbow with a furrowed brow of concern. "What do you mean you don't feel good?"

She covered her head with the blanket with one hand, while she held her stomach with the other. "I *mean* I don't feel good."

"*What* doesn't feel good?"

"My stomach and my head."

"Maybe it's because you haven't eaten. I'll go get you some breakfast."

He quickly got dressed before he left the tent, while Casey laid there trying to get her stomach under control. She sometimes got migraines, so this wasn't uncommon, and she knew her head was probably going to hurt for the rest of the day. The nausea, on the other hand, was something she *wasn't* used to, and she didn't like it.

It took several minutes before Mark returned to the tent with a plate of food. "The Colonel said to try and eat this, and he would check on you later."

Casey didn't say anything. She didn't even move. The noises around camp pounded through her core, as the scent of the fish, fried potatoes, and beans infused its way through the camp, making her even sicker. She hadn't eaten anything yet that morning, so she wasn't sure what she would throw up as she lay there. She did her best to stay still and take deep breaths, forcing herself to keep whatever it was down.

"Casey?" Mark set the plate aside and lifted the covers. "What's going on?"

"I don't –" She wretched, and then quickly scrambled to the door, leaning outside the tent in the nick of time. She threw up a putrid yellow substance. What it was, she had no idea, but that made her even sicker, and she threw up a couple more times. The smell sent a tang to her senses, and that made her throw up yet again.

By the time she finished, her head pounded and felt like it was spinning out of control at the same time. She felt like she had a bad case of vertigo, as she rested her head on her arm just inside the tent, mortified. She knew the other guys around camp saw it. She knew there would be vomit she would have to clean later as well. She also wanted to brush her teeth to get that taste out, but she did not dare move.

"Case? Do you feel better?" Mark asked, moving her hair out of the way so he could see her face. He was not used to seeing her in this shape and he did not like it. There was not anything he could do to fix the situation, which made him feel helpless. Being as strong as he was, that was something he was not used to feeling. He kissed her cheek. "Casey?"

She let out a moan, while she lay there motionless with her eyes closed.

"Come on up here and lie down for a little bit. Maybe you'll feel better."

"Nooo." She groaned. "I don't want to move."

"I'm going to go get Harper. Get a pair of pants on while I'm gone," he said, and left the tent.

Casey reached around until she found her pants and slipped them on. Her clothes that survived the torture were her pants, underclothes, socks, and shoes, so some of the guys went through and gave her some of their tank tops and t-shirts to wear until she could get back to the 'real world' and buy some of her own.

Harper poked his head in, as Mark came in and sat down on the other side of her. "G'day, Case. What's going on?"

She moaned in response, feeling like she was going to throw up again.

"Is this hers?" he asked Mark, who nodded. Harper reached over and felt her forehead, and then the side of her face. "What's going on, Casey?"

When Casey looked up at him, her head spun out of control. She quickly sat up and threw up outside of the tent again, while he scrambled to get out of the way.

When she finished, he got a closer look at it. "Hmmm, looks like bile. Did she have her tucker yet?"

Mark shook his head "No. She threw up before she could eat anything."

"Mmm," she moaned, slinking back into the tent. "Please say I'm done?" She leaned back on Mark, who wrapped his arms around her.

"Hmmm." Harper looked at the vomit, and then he climbed back into the tent with them. "How's your head?"

"Hurts."

"You don't have a fever." He glanced back out at the vomit again, before he looked down at her and asked, "Want me t' get you some crackers?"

Casey nodded with her eyes closed, while Mark stroked her hair. While it relaxed her, her body was on edge from throwing up, so even his touch irritated her skin.

"I'll get you some drink too," Harper said as he left the tent.

She nodded.

"Casey, how bad is your headache?" Mark asked after a moment.

"Migraine status."

"I'm sorry. Try to keep something down, okay? We're working on packing the camp to leave in a couple of days. We need you to be strong."

"I'm trying, but…" She shook her head. It was several years since she felt this poorly.

He kissed her head. "Aww, I'm sorry, sweetheart."

"Here ya go. Keep it down and Bob's your uncle. No worries." Harper winked, as he set the crackers and a bottle of water on the blanket next to her. "Just eat slowly."

Casey sighed as she picked up the sleeve of crackers. "You guys really gotta cut that out."

"Cut what out?"

"The Aussie slang."

"Now that would be like us telling you t' cut out your slang. You'd first have t' figure out what part was slang, and then try t' stop it. Sorry, love, you'd have better luck wrestling a croc."

"How's she doing?" Hawk walked over to the tent with the Colonel. They stood slightly behind Harper, who was still crouched near the door.

Harper shook his head. "She couldn't pull the skin off custard."

"What's wrong with her?" Hawk asked.

Harper shrugged. "Buggered if I know."

"Was your father a glassmaker? Give us a gander!"

Harper smiled, as he moved to the side so the Colonel and Hawk could go into the tent.

"What happened, Casey?" The Colonel asked, as she was lying back on Mark with her eyes closed. He had his arm around her, holding her up while continuing to stroke her hair.

"Sick," she said.

"See that. What happened?"

"Don't know. My head's killing me. And while it's starting to settle now, my stomach feels wretched."

The Colonel checked her forehead. "No fever."

"How bad's your head hurt?" Hawk asked.

"Getting better," Casey admitted. "But it was throbbing after I threw up."

"Hmmm…" Hawk rubbed the back of his neck, deep in thought. "Just try t' keep your breakkie down and we'll go from there, eh?"

Casey nodded.

"Sounds good," Mark agreed, so they left, leaving Mark and Casey in the tent. "Can you eat a couple crackers, and then drink some water?"

Casey nodded as she slowly sat up, holding her head. While she gradually ate the sleeve of crackers and drank the water Harper brought her, Mark went ahead and ate the plate of breakfast he had got earlier.

"How are you feeling now?" Mark asked, finishing his breakfast.

Casey finished eating about ten minutes earlier. She watched Mark take each bite of his fish, potatoes, and beans. The smell it emitted was a battle for her to overcome the entire time he ate.

"Better." She nodded, watching him take his last bite, relieved the plate was finally empty so the smell would go away.

"How much better?"

"Better enough to want to brush my teeth."

He chuckled, shaking his head. "All right." He set the tin plate aside. "Do you want to take a bath down at the river, and then see about helping the others?"

"Yeah," she agreed. She grabbed her towels, shampoo, soap, toothbrush, and toothpaste.

He got his belongings before they headed down to the river together. "Still feeling okay?" he asked when they reached the river.

"Yep."

"Good. Go take your bath while I keep a look out."

He stayed up on top of the ridge as she went the rest of the way down to the river. She slipped her clothes off, and quickly slid into the river with the shampoo and soap in hand.

"I can't wait for a real shower," Casey commented, as the water rushed over her body. Mark turned and smiled at her before he turned back around to keep watch. "Can you imagine?" Casey continued. "I can feel the nice, clean, hot water streaming down my body right now."

"You'd better stop," he warned, glancing at her before he looked back toward camp.

"Why?" she asked, shampooing her hair. She kept the water level at her chest, so she would be covered. Although she would never admit it, she would miss taking a bath in the river. The scents and sounds of the various flora and fauna, as the cool breeze washed past her, and the peaceful outdoors could never be replaced. The daily rush of the city would be back in her near future, and she wasn't looking forward to it.

She moaned as she rinsed her hair, running her fingers through to work out the shampoo. When a stone rolled down the hill, she glanced up to see Mark turn to look at her with a look she had come to know very well over the last several weeks. She saw the desire in his eyes and knew he wanted her. She looked at him wide-eyed and blushed. "Sorry."

He smirked, as he leaned on the tree with his hands in his pockets. "No problem. Just hurry up."

Casey smiled, and then dunked her head backwards into the river to rinse the rest of the shampoo out.

"Oh, *please* hurry up!" he groaned, turning back toward camp.

She couldn't help the laugh that escaped her mouth, amused by his behavior. To ease some of the sexual tension, when she finished her bath, she quickly dried off and got dressed, wrapping her long hair in a towel. "Okay." She stood up. "Done."

"Good. I wasn't sure how much more I could take."

Casey gave him a hug. "Go take a cold bath in the river."

She went to take her position by the tree, but he didn't let her go. He leaned down and sniffed the delightful scent of the soap on her soft skin. Then he nuzzled her neck for a few moments, gently kissing it, and then whispered, "Just wait until later."

Casey looked at his eyes. They were drinking in her body as his hands slowly moved over her uncovered skin. "Um, bath," she reminded him.

He pulled her face toward his and strongly kissed her. A moment later he glanced up at her and smiled with a wink. Then he left for the river. While she watched for anyone coming, her mind flooded with memories of Mark and their alone time over the past several weeks.

She periodically glanced down at him while he bathed, with her body feeling warm all over. Mark's body was well cut. She had to take a couple deep breaths to get herself under control. She was relieved when he finished and made his way over to the side of the river to get his clothes.

"Hey Case?" he called, setting his clothes down before he sunk into the river just off the bank.

"What?"

"Come here."

"Not now. Anyone could come and we wouldn't know."

"No, they know we're down here." He boyishly grinned. "Come on. I don't think I'll be able to wait until tonight."

Oh, how she loved his smile – it could melt her heart in a split second. His entire face lit up, and his dark brown eyes twinkled.

Casey looked both ways to make sure no one was coming before she went down to the river. She took off her clothes and hung the towel on a branch before she sunk into the river right in front of him. She looked up to see that he was watching every move she made. He reached over and ran his fingers over her body, drinking her in before he leaned forward and kissed her. The slow sensuality of it sent tingles through her body.

They enjoyed each other for a little while, taking a break from the intense mood around camp while everyone prepared to leave.

*   *   *

"Where ya been, mate?" Carson gave Mark a knowing look when Mark and Casey walked back into camp an hour later, holding hands.

Casey braided her hair when they finished, and Mark carried the towels up from the river. He handed them to her when they walked into camp, so she went over and hung them on the line as her face flushed bright red.

Mark smiled as he glanced at Casey's face. To take the heat off her, he said, "We took a bath so we don't stink like you guys."

Hawk shook his head, chuckling at Casey's face. "Shut your north and south, and go get some more wood for the Nellie McGuire."

"Okayyy, gonna guess that shut your north and south means to shut up, and pretty sure you want me to get wood for the fire, but where does Nellie McGuire fit into that?" Mark asked.

"Just stop bumping your gums and get the wood." Harper said in a sigh, while he continued to stir lunch over the fire.

Mark shrugged, and then headed out to the woods to get some more wood for the fire, leaving Casey in the camp.

"So," the Colonel put his arm over Casey's shoulder, "how are you feeling?"

"Actually, I feel fine. My headache is gone and my stomach is stable."

"Good. How about some tucker?" Harper asked, scooping a bowl of beef stew he made for lunch. He took it over to her. "Think you can keep it down?"

Casey stared at it. It looked good enough, and she knew it tasted good because they had it before. However, the way the carrots, potatoes, and meat blended in the soupy sauce…Casey threw her hand over her mouth, and ran to the edge of camp before it escaped.

"Take that as a no?" Harper glanced up at the Colonel. "Thought she said she was fine."

The Colonel looked over at her with concern as she vomited the crackers and water. "She did," he said.

As Harper watched her throw up her breakfast, Hawk wandered over to the two of them and put his hand on the Colonel's shoulder. He looked at Casey as he asked the Colonel, "Whaddya think? It's been about time enough. Think she's full of paws and claws?"

"Possibly." The Colonel nodded, crossing his arms as he watched her. He wasn't sure how to react. It would fit the timeline, but knowing what they were headed into, he hoped it wouldn't come to fruition for another several months.

"You think?" Harper looked at her as she rested her head on her arm, curled up in the grass, exhausted. He shook his head. "No way."

The Colonel nodded. "It fits. I was only hoping for more time."

"What's going…*Casey*?!" Mark dropped the wood, alarmed that she was lying in the grass and ran over to her. "Casey, look up at me." He turned her head toward him. She went from rosy cheeks a few moments ago, to a ghostly white. "What happened?" he asked her. Casey moaned in response. Mark looked over toward the vomit and shook his head – he knew. He looked up at the Colonel, who nodded.

They knew it was coming. They talked about it one night after everyone else went to bed. The Colonel told Mark that Casey was going to have a baby. While Mark was excited, he was scared, knowing it would paint a bigger target on her. The more they talked about it, the more Mark struggled with his feelings. With the battles coming toward them, adding her in the condition she was going to be in, *and* adding a little one to the mix, made him nervous.

They sat over two hours by the fire that night in prayer. They prayed for safety, and for strength for Casey to make it through and for the health of the baby. They also prayed for themselves and Derek to be strong enough to carry Casey through it all. They prayed for protection from any battles, until she was through the pregnancy. They also prayed God would have mercy on her through the pregnancy, and that it would go smoothly. Then they prayed for the baby's upcoming life itself, that the baby to be a mighty warrior for God. They prayed for protection for the baby's soul until it was strong and wise enough to make a decision to follow Christ. Afterward, they soaked in the love of God before they headed off to bed.

Chapter 5

Coming Storm

Casey felt horrible over the next few days, but as everyone packed the camp, she did her best to help. Because she felt so sickly, she had to stop and rest frequently. After a while, she wondered what kind of virus it was that had a hold of her, and couldn't figure out why no one else was sick. It occurred to her that she could be pregnant, but she didn't want to face that possibility, knowing the storm that was coming their way. A pregnancy would mean she would be more vulnerable than she already felt.

Finally, the guys sat her down one day after lunch. They knew, and had been talking about it, but were concerned by how she would react when they told her. Hawk walked over to Casey and put his arm around her shoulder. Ushering her over to the fire, he said, "We need t' talk t' you, love."

The Colonel, Derek, and Mark sat down with them as well, while the remaining members of camp kept their distance, but held steadfast in prayer, knowing she was going to need it. Mark took her hand into his when he sat down. He had a look of concern and worry on his face.

"What is it?" she asked nervously.

"You've been sick for over a week now," the Colonel started.

Her heart raced. "Do you know what's wrong with me?"

He nodded, as he knelt in front of her and rested his hands on her knees. Derek went behind her and set his hands on her shoulders.

Tears came to her eyes, afraid of the unknown, but it looked serious. Casey had ahold of one of Mark's hands with her left hand, so she grabbed Hawk's hand with her right one. The way they surrounded her terrified her beyond words. "What's wrong with me?" she asked, voice shaking.

Mark leaned over and kissed her cheek. "Casey, I love you."

"Yes. I know that."

"Do you also know you are pregnant?"

The color drained from her face when he confirmed her fears. She dropped her head into her hands as panic surged through her body. "I can't be. We can't have me pregnant."

"Yes, you are," the Colonel calmly said. "You are, you can be, and it's okay. We knew it was coming."

"But..." She shook her head. "We're headed into a storm. We can't bring a baby into this."

"You can do this," the Colonel assured her. "We knew it was coming. This is all part of the plan."

Casey shook her head, beside herself.

Mark rested his free hand on the side of her face and pulled her over to him, resting his forehead on hers. "It's okay, Casey. I'm happy we're going to have a little one of our own." He kissed her head as he said, "We *are* going to have a baby."

"But..." she shook her head, "the battle is ahead. The storms we're heading into...is this safe? I mean, don't get me wrong, I'm happy to be carrying our baby." She looked up into his eyes. "I'm scared for the baby. I'm scared something might happen to it."

"Then we need to pray. Give it to God. Let Him take care of the baby...and you."

"Remember what A.N.G.E.L. stands for?" The Colonel asked.

"Available to Nurture God's Eternal Love," Casey responded, in a shell-shocked daze.

"It's to be available *wherever* and *whenever* He needs us. He knows the plan. He knows what is going to happen and already has the people in place to protect you and the baby. You have to have faith."

Casey nodded in understanding.

"Let's pray for all involved," the Colonel suggested.

All four guys prayed, as Casey sat there in tears. The other four guys in camp slowly made their way over to them, laying their hands on Casey's head and shoulders in prayer for her and the baby, for over two hours. While it gave her comfort, she couldn't stop crying. She was scared for the baby. She stayed away from Angelina so she would be safe – she couldn't give up another one. She couldn't carry this beautiful life inside her in order to hide it so it could live. She couldn't believe God would ask her to do it again. She wanted this baby. She wanted to be able to raise this little one with her husband. She wanted to be able to watch it grow, praying for it every step of the way. She wanted to be a mom.

*   *   *

"You know, some days you're as useful as a screen door on a submarine," Carson snapped at Grant.

He glared at him. "Why are you so argy bargy today?"

"Just get some mother and daughter, will ya?" Carson sighed, while everyone scurried around packing the remainder of camp. "We gotta put this out and pack up the rest of camp."

Grant headed down to the river with a bucket in his hand to get some water to put out the fire.

"Ready?" Mark asked. His and Casey's tent lay on the ground between them, flattened.

She nodded in response, deep in thought about the dream she had that morning. In the dream, Casey was running through the woods in the middle of the night. She had a handcuff on her right wrist, and there was blood running down her arm from the wounds on her wrist. She had no idea where the guys were, or why she would have handcuffs on, but she continued to run. She was grateful Mark woke her out of the nightmare, but she was curious about the dream.

She sighed. She often felt the dreams were a curse. She wasn't sure whether she wanted to know the information they provided or not.

She nodded, so they picked up one end of the tent, and together they walked it to the other end and lay it down. They did this a couple more times before Mark took the long way folded tent and rolled it into a tight roll. When he finished, Casey secured both ends with twine, and then Mark tossed it over to their pile of already folded and packed belongings.

Grant returned with a bucket of water and slowly poured it over the fire to put it out, while others rolled the leftover twine, and the rest finished with their tents and belongings.

"Whew!" Marshall wiped his forehead when they were finally done. "It's hot enough t' boil a monkey's bum."

Casey had to laugh at that one. Some of their phrases were comical, and they weren't holding back on that day.

"I say we go down to the river and jump in," Derek suggested. "We still have an hour before the evac."

"Don't have t' ask *me* twice, mate." Grant grinned. "See ya at the shake n' shiver!" He yelled, and he ran for the river with several others on his heels.

Mark and Casey walked slower than the rest. He took her hand in his as they walked down to the river. "You're looking pretty good today," he commented.

"I'm feeling better, but it still comes in waves," she admitted.

"You seem to be dealing with the idea of the pregnancy better these days."

"I am. I'm scared for the baby though. I can feel what's coming. It's like it's looking for us."

"I know. I've felt it too."

"When we get out of here, are we going to be able to hide the baby deep enough to keep it safe? Or worse yet, keep *me* safe until I can have it?"

"You don't need to worry about that."

"Yes, I do."

"No, you don't. You need to worry about your health, and taking care of yourself and the baby. You let me, God, and the other guys worry about taking care of you."

Casey stopped. He needed to understand what she was feeling. They were walking into a terrible storm. "Mark, you have to feel it."

"I do."

"It's strong! It's as if that demon got stronger or maybe he was joined by others. I don't know. What I *do* know is that we're walking into a tornado. I'm talking an F-5 here."

He looked at her with understanding. He knew. He felt it coming too. He also knew an F-5 tornado was like watching the finger of God run through a town. He had seen an F-5 tornado in person. He knew the damage and devastation it generated, but he had the confidence that the *hand* of God was stronger and that He could protect them from *anything* that came at them.

He rested his hand on the side of her face. Wiping the few tears that escaped, he said, "The hand of God is stronger than anything Satan can dish out. We have *His* army behind us, no matter what. We have to, with everything we have in our beings, pray for strength for His soldiers in battle. They will give their all. We *will* win in the end."

"You don't understand. I can't give up another baby!"

"Why would…? What?" He shook his head in shock. He had no idea where that one came from. "Who said you would have to give up our baby?"

"If I don't, it could be in danger. That's why I stayed away from Angelina. I don't want the baby to have a target painted on it. I want it to be safe."

"Oh, Casey." He wrapped his arms around her and kissed her head. "Our baby isn't going anywhere we don't go. Unfortunately, it's being born in the middle of a war, so we are going to have to keep an extremely close eye on it. Casey, listen, that baby was given to us by God. It's ours. It's not going anywhere. You'll be able to hold it while you feed it. You'll be able to watch it take its first step, get its first tooth. Don't worry, that baby is given to us by God."

"But, can *it* get to it? Will *they* be looking for it?"

"Possibly. But you have to understand this has been planned for a while now. We knew it was coming. There's a plan for this child. God placed that baby within you for a reason. He gave this child specifically to you and me with a purpose. Only God knows at this moment what it is. Maybe it's to continue the fight as a next generation of A.N.G.E.L.s comes up. Maybe the baby will grow to be a mighty evangelist. Whatever His plan is, have faith God will look out for our baby."

Casey wiped the tears from her eyes as she said, "I can't handle losing anyone else in my life. I've already lost so many. I don't think I could handle losing any more."

"Don't say that. You're stronger than this." He lifted her chin so she would look into his eyes. "You are a strong woman. If you think you're about to lose it, I want you to go to a safe place with Jesus. If you can't do it physically, do it in your mind. Let Him hold you close and carry you through it. He *did* lose it all. He knows how you feel. Let God, Jesus, and the Spirit carry you through."

Casey nodded in understanding. She knew she had to get a grip on her feelings. She had the confidence that when God took her through everything, He did to prepare her for what was about to happen. She was terrified, though, knowing everything she had already been through. She held onto her faith that He would never leave her. She knew He would hold her hand, and walk with her until she could stand on her own again. She also recognized that she might have to use her skill of detachment she learned as a firefighter/paramedic, and have to temporarily disconnect from the situation until she could deal with whatever came at them, aware of the fact that she would eventually be able to wade through the coming storm with Jesus at her side and that she would be okay.

After a few moments of collecting herself, Mark and Casey made their way down to the river, soaking in it for a little while by themselves before Mark played around with the others. Casey sat back as she watched them enjoy one last fling in the river as a group. They had gone through a lot over the last few months. They endured, suffered, learned, taught each other new things, and even added a few new family members to the Family of God in the process. She knew it would be hard, but Mark reminded her that they were not in control. They were not guaranteed another tomorrow. They were required to trust God, and that He had a plan. They were to trust He had it all under control, and would never leave them.

After about an hour, the group headed back to camp and organized their belongings into two separate piles. They segregated the American A.N.G.E.L.'s stuff from the others so, it would be easy pull out when they landed.

About an hour after they returned, Fletcher landed the helicopter down near the riverbank. They moved the packed camp to the helicopter landing area and loaded a portion of it, leaving room for Harper and Carson, who were to unload on the other end. When Fletcher returned, they packed the helicopter for two more trips, before they packed the remainder of their belongings, along with Grant and Marshall. When he returned a half hour later, the remainder got in, and they took off. As the helicopter lifted off its landing area, Casey looked down at what had been their home for months. It broke her heart, knowing they were never coming back.

When she looked down, she saw Charlie come out from behind one of the trees, waving at the helicopter. The tears flowed down her cheeks as she waved back. Mark saw who she was waving at and hugged her, realizing how hard it was on her. Granted, most of it was probably hormones, but they were leaving what had been technically Mark and Casey's first home. This was where their baby was conceived. Where they pledged their lives to each other. Where they made good friends. Where Mark and Casey battled inner demons and won. Where Casey was pushed to her limits in physical pain, endurance, and even in mental stamina. Where the group learned to see what was not there, to feel what they could not see, and to anticipate the enemy's movements before he even made them. Where Casey learned how much she *could* endure. Where she learned how much she would need to rely on God for His strength, the Holy Spirit for His guidance, and Jesus for His companionship and example. Where Casey learned just how much power her prayers held. This was where she found herself.

Chapter 6

Into the Unknown

When they arrived to the airfield, there was Caribou DHC-4 on the dirt landing strip. The Caribou could be compared to the U.S.'s C-130. The others already loaded the gear and were inside the belly of the plane waiting for the remainder to arrive.

"Sir," Fletcher said over his shoulder as they were almost to the landing strip, "Just so you have a heads up, Victoria Stanton and Shawn O'Brien were found today."

"What do ya mean by *found*?" Hawk asked.

As Fletcher landed, he said, "They were floating just off the reef in Cairns. They were found four hours ago."

Hawk sat back in his seat, floored. This was the first loss of their crew. While they had lost people they knew before, this was the first time the Australian A.N.G.E.L.s themselves took the hit.

"Sorry, mate," Fletcher said.

Hawk patted him on the shoulder, as he turned to crawl out of the chopper. The rest of the A.N.G.E.L.s took the cue and got out as well, heading toward the plane. The belly of the plane had a flat metal floor for pallet storage, and the sides were lined by cargo-net-backed benches on each side. Their cargo was toward the front, near the cockpit, netted off from the rest of the belly for safety.

"Come back here." Mark pulled Casey toward the front of the plane near the cargo, before they sat down. "You're going to want to relax and breathe. Knowing the way you've been feeling, this might not end well." He put his arm around her in comfort.

Casey rested her head on Mark's shoulder, watching Hawk. His face was stoic. As she watched, she could see him separating himself from his feelings.

Hawk was in agony over the loss of his two A.N.G.E.L.s, but he couldn't show it. He was in charge. He was responsible for the men and women of his squad. He still had to get the crew currently in his custody to safety before he would allow himself to think about the damage this loss was going to do to his squad.

Victoria Stanton was an incredible athlete, and was well versed in the use of hand-to-hand combat, while her partner, Shawn O'Brien, had other strong suits. His strength of character often blended the group together on those hard days. He was also an excellent marksman – probably the best on the squad. The loss of those two would be hard to replace in both their abilities *and* personalities. Hawk wasn't looking forward to telling the rest of his crew about it either.

When everyone was settled, the ramp of the plane rose, as the back portion of the ceiling lowered to meet it half-way, closing them into the belly of the plane. It pulled forward, little by little at first, before it picked up speed, slowly lifting its heavy body off the ground. Casey watched out the small portal windows to see the ground cover get smaller and smaller as the albatross of a plane climbed higher into the air.

Casey had been on plenty of planes over the years in working with the brushfires. She even had the rare opportunity of riding in a couple F-16s and F-17s, thanks to some of Jack's friends. She never did it pregnant though. The motion was hard to take at first, until she resigned herself to getting through it by repeatedly running through her head, "*I am not going to get sick. I am not getting sick,*" until it was the only thought that consumed her mind.

When they finally landed at a Royal Australian Air Force base about forty kilometers north of Perth, Casey didn't remember any of the trip. All she knew was that her body shook and she was dizzy. She was grateful to soon be taking a real shower, and having the opportunity of eating something that didn't have to be cooked over an open fire.

Mark assisted Casey, who was shaky and pale by that point, to one of the waiting Jeeps, and then he helped the others unload the plane. The men and the gear were spread-out among five Jeeps that drove them through the base to an empty barracks used for visiting squadrons.

When she walked in, Casey saw the steel skeleton under the corrugated metal that was the exterior of the barracks. Twenty beds lined up against the wall with ten on each side, along with metal chests at the foot of each bed. While it was practical, it felt cold. She shuddered as she walked to a bunk on the right and collapsed, still shaking. She could smell the bleach they used to wash the sheets, and immediately noticed the lack of fabric softener for the blanket, but she didn't care. All she cared was that she was not in motion. Mark offered to get her dinner, but she didn't want to eat at all. She didn't want to move. She knew they needed help carrying everything into the barracks, but she couldn't move no matter how hard she tried.

After the A.N.G.E.L.s stacked their luggage inside, they took off for meetings, leaving Casey sleeping soundly in the barracks, with two military police at the door of the barracks to stand guard.

*   *   *

Over the next couple days, the crews worked on setting up their future safe house in Mexico. The Colonel, with the help of the computer mastermind of Hawks group, bounced the signal off several satellites and used multiple phantom servers to hack into the various banks that held their money in the United States. He filtered the money into several accounts around the world, which were already set up over a year ago as a backup plan should anything happen, before settling all of the money into a couple accounts in Mexico City, Mexico. The remainder was still a little over one and a half million dollars. They would have plenty to set up what they needed, as well as to live comfortably for several years.

While the guys worked on that, the two remaining women A.N.G.E.L.s from Hawk's team took Casey shopping for clothes.

It was such a relief to get new clothes after using the ones she had for almost three months, washing the two sets of clothing in the dirty river every day after she sweated in them during training.

She purchased a couple of maternity pants and shirts for her to grow into as well while they were out. The women said she would have a hard time finding clothes in Mexico to fit her due to her height. They said the clothes were tailored for the average Mexican woman – who wasn't five-foot-nine. They also got her a pair of dress boots, tennis shoes, and a couple pairs of sandals, mentioning that of no offense to her, but her feet were bigger than the average woman there as well. Casey didn't care. She was happy to have new clothes that fit her and were clean.

*   *   *

A couple of nights after their arrival to the base, Casey had another dream. She wasn't sure where in the world she was, but she saw she was on the side of a mountain. She heard a blood-curdling scream, and looked toward her left through the trees. In the distance, she saw the strangest sight. She saw people fighting with each other. Thing was, it appeared to be men and women fighting black shadows.

That's when she saw it. A woman held a baby in her arms, while a man on the ground held a woman who was in labor. Another woman helped the woman having a baby. Casey squinted to see better, and that's when she noticed the baby being born was not breathing.

A shadowy figure suddenly stood in front of Casey from nowhere. "Are you going to watch, or are you going to fight?"

She froze in fear. The eyes of the creature were glowing, and she could barely see the black wings that hung on its back. She gasped, but nothing else escaped her mouth.

That's when she felt a hand on her shoulder. "You can change your identity, but we will sssssstill find you."

"Casey! Casey, wake up!" Mark shook her to wake her out of her nightmare. She made a terrified moaning noise, as if she wanted to speak, but she couldn't. "Casey, please?"

Casey gasped as she sat upright in her bed. Her heart raced and she breathed heavily. She grabbed Mark's shoulders, looking at his face, praying he wasn't part of the nightmare.

He gently sat on the side of the bed. "Casey, you're safe," he whispered, doing his best not to wake the others. They were going to be leaving the next morning for Mexico.

"I know that," she whispered. "I mean, I think I know that. The dreams I am having are telling me something else, though."

"What are your dreams about? Why won't you tell me?"

"I'm afraid."

"Why?"

"I don't want them to happen."

"I don't know if that will be an option. If we have a heads-up, though, it may be something we can either prevent or prepare for."

"You knew I was pregnant before I did, right?"

"Yes," he admitted.

"How long before?"

"About two weeks."

"Why didn't you tell me then? Why did you let me think for days that I was sick?"

"Because I wasn't one hundred percent sure."

"Well, I'm not one hundred percent sure either. I don't know for sure if these events are going to happen."

"Are they as strong as the dreams of Keith, Victoria, and Shawn?"

"Yes."

"Then?" he asked.

"Then what?"

"Then, why won't you tell me?"

She threw back the covers and got out of bed. "I need air."

Mark grabbed her arm to stop her. "Case, talk to me."

"Not right now."

"Why not?"

"Not now, okay? Just…not now," she said and walked out of the barracks.

The cool night air hit her face as soon as she stepped outside. She needed that. She needed to wake up out of the nightmare, or she may go back into it.

As she walked around, one of the MPs followed her for her safety. She didn't mind. He stayed back enough that she still felt alone with God. She prayed for the long flight tomorrow, and that everything would work according to the plans the Colonel made.

She stopped and sat on a bench, looking up at the night sky. It was a clear night, so she was able to see quite a few stars – not anywhere near the amount she saw in the Outback, but she enjoyed the peacefulness of the early morning nonetheless.

She had confidence in the guys, but the dreams were warnings. She knew despite the peace that currently surrounded them, they were headed into a storm. She felt it grow in strength each day. Her dreams were getting more frequent as well, and she prayed they would all survive the upcoming storms, as she rested her hand on her stomach where she knew their little one was growing.

* * *

The next morning, they did their final packing and loaded up the trucks for the airport. Casey wasn't looking forward to another plane ride, but she didn't have a choice. After digging around, the Australian A.N.G.E.L.s discovered that Jackie and her crew moved their location, but were still in Queensland. The information also stated that Jackie knew Casey was still alive and somewhere in the Outback. That made Hawk and the Colonel nervous, which is why they were sent to Perth in the first place.

The morning they left, Hawk and the Colonel caught Casey up to speed on everything they did over the last few days, while she rested and got ready to go to Mexico. When they explained it all, she knew it was in all of their best interest to get out of Australia as soon as possible.

"Ready?" Mark asked Casey as they got ready to leave.

Casey adjusted the bag on her shoulder. "Not really, but we don't have a choice. We can only be out of the Outback for so long without Jackie finding out where we are."

He kissed her head, attempting to console her. "You'll be fine."

Before they left, Hawk's complete crew and theirs got together, praying for everyone's safety, and for guidance as they navigated the upcoming storm. Then they took off in one of their Jeeps for the international airport, with Hawk driving.

"Here ya go, *Casey English*," the Colonel handed her a passport, ticket, and identity information while they stood in the airport, waiting for their flight.

It was the first time she heard her new last name, and it threw her for a moment. Casey looked at him, pleasantly surprised, as Mark wrapped his arm around her waist.

With a grin on his face, Mark said, "I like that."

"Me too." She smiled. She glanced through the birth certificate, social security card, and passport in her hands. She wasn't sure how he did it, but the Colonel got her an American passport, with stamps from several countries including Australia, in the name of 'Casey Ann English.' The birth certificate wasn't hers though. It was from a different state, with a different set of parents listed. The social security card was a different number as well.

"You only need it to get into the country. Don't worry," the Colonel said, almost reading her thoughts.

"All right," she nodded in understanding. Then a thought struck her. "We're not going back, are we?"

The Colonel shook his head. "We can't."

"Does this mean I've lost all the photos of Jack and my parents and everything in my house?"

The Colonel felt for her. He understood the pain it would cause, but he nodded. "Unfortunately, you can't go back. People know you're missing, and they have an alert out on you. The U.S. and Australia are both looking for you. You came up listed as missing when Jesse went back to work and no one heard from you. There is an open investigation in the U.S., as well as here. When the authorities searched here in Australia, they found your luggage abandoned at a bus station in Queensland. Jackie and her crew have everything tagged, watched, and are waiting for something to happen as well."

"Then, how did you shut the accounts down without triggering anything?"

"It's taken care of, and there is no way they will be able to unwind the trail we made to where the money landed before we can get over there and pull it. We'll shut the accounts down and pull the money as soon as we land. They may have an idea we landed in Mexico, but from that point on they won't be able to track us because we'll use fake ID's and pay for everything in cash."

Casey nodded as she processed the information. Her life as she knew it was permanently changed. She would never see Jesse or the other guys again. She would never be able to replace her photos, or see Jack's or Mac's graves ever again. And she also lost the chance of ever seeing or hearing about Angelina. She rested her hand on her stomach for a moment, grateful for the little one growing inside of her as she looked up and resolutely said, "Let's go."

The Colonel knew she pulled herself out of the situation. He saw the resignation on her face. He saw the determination flash in her eyes to not cry or feel for the things or people lost to her forever. He knew she would be the good soldier she was trained to be. He was proud of her. He hugged her as he said, "It'll be okay. We're here for you."

"I know," she said, and took a deep breath as she stoically looked forward. "Let's go."

Mark took her hand into his as the four made their way through the airport to the unknown future they knew that loomed in front of them.

<u>Chapter 7</u>

Sink or Swim

Casey ran through the dark forest in a pair of dark green shorts and a black t-shirt. Her feet were getting gouged and cut due from the underbrush, while she ran barefoot through the woods. She stopped and leaned against a tree, breathing heavily. The good news for her was that it was a bright moon, which helped her to see around her better.

"Lord, please protect me. Get me out of here," she begged, looking toward Heaven. When she didn't hear anything, she let out a frustrated sigh and continued running. She wasn't sure what she was running toward or running from, but she ran.

She stopped dead in her tracks when the bandana around her wrist fell to the ground. She looked at her wrist, horrified, to see her hand slightly disfigured, and blood dripping from it onto the ground.

Mark jostled Casey to wake her. "Case, we've landed."

"I, uh, thanks," she said grateful to be awake. She looked at her wrist to make sure it was still normal. Relieved, she looked out the window to see they already landed. On the plane, Mark sat beside her, while the Colonel and Derek sat behind them. As she fought to clear the fog in her mind from the deep sleep, they slowly made their way down the aisle of the plane toward the terminal. They would have to get through security and customs before they would be free to head out into Mexico and their new life.

* * *

They were in the hot, stuffy bus for about three hours that day. Casey wasn't sure how much longer she could stand it. This was not her preferred method of travel, and she prayed it would be over soon.

They took the bus after the Colonel shut the accounts down. They only carried one bag of luggage – that was all they were allotted by the Colonel, and each guy carried one bag of money. He said they would get anything else they needed when they settled in their new home.

"Where *exactly* are we?" Casey asked, watching as they passed the stunning landscape around them. It was a combination of forestland and tropical, which changed as they passed from state to state.

"We landed in Mexico City, but we are on our way to Tequisquiapan," Mark said.

"Yeah, okay," Casey rolled her eyes, "that doesn't help me."

Mark chuckled. "We have a couple contacts there. It's smack in the middle of the country."

"Would these contacts happen to be other A.N.G.E.L.s?" she asked.

"Yes. There are only four of them left down here. They have blended into the culture here by doing their work, raising families of their own, *and* their A.N.G.E.L. work on the side. Now, actually *in* Tequis there are only two of them. They're going to help us out…well, mainly you. They're going to work on your language skills, and help us find housing, while we help them out financially with what we have."

"Sounds like a fair trade," she agreed.

"Just so you know, there'll be times where you'll be left alone. Since there are only four of them and three of us, we've joined forces."

"So, you're leaving America unprotected?"

"In a manner of speaking. There are people up there in tuned enough to God to take care of their own, but down here?" He sighed. "They have to battle a false doctrine that has infused its way so deeply into their culture that it's a way of life for them. They are passionate people though, and those who are seeing the truth have picked up their fallen comrade's armor and put it on. There are others who are joining the battle daily, but it's a struggle. The A.N.G.E.L.s here have taken a hit. They have been battered and bruised. Their morale has crashed so many times, that I'm not exactly sure how they recovered. But they keep picking themselves up, dusting themselves off, and run back into the battle head-on." He shook his head in amazement. "Their hearts, courage, strength, resilience, and valor are admirable."

Casey grabbed his hand as she watched him. She saw some of the memories from his past go before his eyes, as if he was watching it happen all over again. "This place brings back a lot of memories." He slowly exhaled as he got his memories under control. "A lot of memories."

* * *

When they arrived in Tequisquiapan, they took a taxi through the town, to a more rural area just outside the town limits. The driving was *definitely* not what Casey was used to. As a matter of fact, she was shocked she didn't see a single accident. People cut others off, made U-turns where they weren't supposed to, and made short cuts where there wasn't supposed to be a cut through, to avoid lights. She wouldn't have believed it if she didn't see it for herself. What was an even bigger shock, was that the police were right there and did nothing about it.

The amount of panhandling and begging being done on the street corners and at the stop lights stunned Casey. While it broke her heart, their creativity was nothing short of amazing. There was everything from jugglers, who sometimes juggled with fire batons, to videos and clothing for sale. People would wash car windows, sell sunglasses, candy, pastries and newspapers. What made her sick though, were the children who should have been in school, but instead were working on the corners in order to raise money for food.

Throughout the city, Casey also saw the pride the people had in their country. The Mexican flag adorned many houses. The architecture was incredible, and the culture was vibrant and full of life. People freely walked down the road, while men worked hard on construction sites or farms. Street tacos were sold on corners, and kids played in school yards that were gated with barbed wire along the top of the tall, iron poles used for fencing. It seemed pride was at a high, but security was at an all-time low.

The history was evident in the country, especially in the downtown areas. Casey wished she had a camera as they toured through the countryside. Mark said she could get one when they were settled. There would be plenty of time to tour around town later. As they drove, he mentioned several features of the downtown district, including old churches and scenic views, along with shopping areas and wineries he knew Casey would appreciate.

When the taxi finally pulled up to a row of houses, they got out. The Colonel paid the driver, while the others went around to the back to retrieve their bags from the trunk. The houses themselves were made of cement, and the windows and doors almost all had bars on them.

Being a firefighter, looking at the houses made Casey nervous. So many fire safety issues jumped out at her, that it terrified her. Crime wise, the houses were well fortified. However, in terms of fire safety they were a nightmare. If a fire broke out within the house, all the exits were barred closed and often locked shut.

The Colonel rang the buzzer at the gate, and they waited only a moment before a small, Mexican woman poked her head out the door. As her eyes adjusted to the bright sunlight, a smile formed on her face. "Colonel!" She squealed, running out of the house, across the concrete area where a small front yard would be, to the door.

A smile filled his face, as he hugged her over the railing that was the door of their fence. "Hello, Claudia."

"Come in. Come in," she excitedly said, opening the gate. She gave them each a hug and a kiss on the cheek as everyone walked by. When she got to Casey, she looked at her for a moment, and then rested her hand on Casey's stomach as she looked up at the

Colonel, who nodded in response. "Oh!" She grinned at Casey. She hugged her as she exclaimed, "¡Que dios te bendiga!"

Casey looked at Mark for help. He translated for her, "She said, 'God bless you' because she knows you're pregnant."

Casey smiled. "Oh, thank you."

She looked from Mark to Casey, before she asked Mark, "Is yours, no?"

He grinned proudly. "Yes."

"Oh! Many congratulations, Marcos!" She squealed, and ran over, giving him another hug. Then she spouted off Spanish so fast, Casey had no idea where the words would break to even begin to sort through them.

Mark nodded and smiled, following every word, speaking Spanish with her as well. They went on for over five minutes before the Colonel gently nudged them into the house. "Where's Juan?" Mark asked Claudia.

"Is working," she said. Then she went on talking with Mark about, what Casey assumed was the baby for a few more minutes before she turned to Casey and said something.

Casey looked blankly at Mark, so he turned and explained to Claudia, "English, please. She doesn't speak Spanish."

She nodded in understanding. "Oh, yes, yes." She went over to Casey and gestured toward the couch as she said, "To be sitting."

Casey raised an eyebrow in question. "Sit down?"

"Yes."

Obviously, learning Spanish was going to have to be high on Casey's list, even if only to talk to her host or hostess.

"Mamá! Mamá!" A little girl of about six came running into the living room from one of the bedrooms. "Is *my* turn, but Juanito said no. Is my turn with the Wii."

"Yes, of course." She nodded. Then she looked up at the others and explained, "She learn English in school. We try to speak English in the house to help in class." Then she looked down at her daughter, and said, "Wait just one minute. You wait. I am talking to them."

"But, Mamá," she whined. "Is *my* turn."

Claudia sighed impatiently. "Juanito, is Cristiana's turn."

"Wait," he called from their bedroom where the Wii was hooked-up.

"Now," Claudia insisted.

"5 minutes?"

"Juanito," she warned.

"Ay, Mamá," he whined.

"Now," she warned again. "What? You want me talking your papá? You no want playing with Wii no more?"

"Yes Mamá," he relented. "Here, Cristiana."

Claudia nodded in appreciation. "Thank you, Juanito."

"I'm going to have to learn Spanish." Casey shook her head, sensing the frustration of Claudia with having to think through her words before she said them.

"You learn," she said confidently. "Children learn you."

"How?" Casey asked.

"Stay with children. They learn you."

"Oh, I don't know about that."

"Yes. They learn Inglés in school. You learn them Inglés, they learn you Español."

"Remember the phrase, ¿Qué es eso?" Mark said to Casey.

"Which is what?" she questioned.

"It means, 'What is that?' It's a game. You ask them, ¿Qué es eso? They will tell you what it is in Spanish, and you tell them in English. Trust me, when Cristiana realizes you are here, she won't leave your side."

Casey nodded in understanding. While she had been in places that spoke Spanish – among other languages – she normally dealt with the hotel personnel, taxi drivers, and the occasional guide who usually spoke some form of English so it wasn't a problem.

"You being hungry?" Claudia asked the group.

"Yes." The Colonel nodded, grateful. "Do you want some help?"

"No, is okay. Siéntate, " she said, going into the kitchen.

"Should I help her?" Case asked Mark.

"No. She told us it was okay and to sit down." He reached down and grabbed Casey's hand to comfort her as he sat on the arm of the couch. He could feel her anxiety and frustration at not being able to understand everything. He knew it would be hard on her, and the hormones of the pregnancy weren't helping either. He knew she was dealing with a lot – the loss of her photos, her belongings…her life.

"Claudia, when is Juan due home?" Derek asked.

"A las cinco y media," she said from the kitchen.

Derek glanced at his watch, which said four-thirty. He nodded. They could wait until Juan got home at five-thirty to discuss their plans.

Claudia went on, talking to Derek, the Colonel, and Mark for the hour, while she worked in the kitchen making something to eat. During the conversation, Casey found out lunch was served between two and four in the afternoon and dinner was served around eight or nine at night. She knew that would take some getting used to as well. Also, through the hour, Claudia stopped a couple more fights with the kids, cleaned up lunch, and began working on dinner.

Juan pulled up at about five-thirty. As soon as the gate closed, the kids put the Wii on pause and ran out of the house with their open arms yelling, "Papá! Papá!"

After he hugged the kids, he came in and shook all of the A.N.G.E.L.'s hands, and then made his way to the kitchen where he hugged and kissed his wife, as he handed her his lunch dishes from work. Juan looked to be about forty years old and around six-foot tall. He had short black hair and dark brown eyes. He spent his day working on a farm just outside of town, so needless to say, he came in filthy.

He got a quick shower before he came in and sat down at the table. "Welcome," he said, looking around the table at everyone. He shook his head and sighed. "Been a long time, friends."

The Colonel nodded in appreciation. "Thank you for your help."

"Hey, you help us, we help you. That was the deal, no?"

"Yep."

"Just so you know, whether you help or not, we would have helped anyway," Juan added.

The Colonel smirked. "Yeah, I know." He loved the Mexican A.N.G.E.L.s and their families. Their hearts were always open, as well as their homes. They were gracious and humble, yet friendly and strong. "We still feel the need to help you and work together."

"My house is your house." Juan gestured out toward his home. He looked around the table one more time until he got to Casey. He looked at her for a few moments before he turned to the Colonel and asked, "She pregnant already, yes?"

The Colonel nodded.

"Um," Casey raised her hand, feeling uncomfortable, "Why does everyone know I'm pregnant?"

"I told you we knew," the Colonel explained. "It's been planned for already."

"How did you guys know before I did?" Casey asked.

"We were informed," the Colonel explained.

"By whom?"

"We don't always know how we know things. We just do. It's not always a still small voice or a dream that tells us…sometimes it's an instinct," Mark clarified.

Casey shook her head. She did not understand. She was not sure she would *ever* understand.

"Remember, you need to see what is not there, feel what you cannot see, and anticipate the enemy's movements before he even knows them," Derek reminded her. "This is one of those instances."

Mark took her hand into his as he said, "Just trust us."

"Oh, I trust you," she said. "The problem is that you guys are telling me future things that are freaking me out. It's like you have some kind of sixth sense."

"No, we have God," Juan clarified. His English was clear, even though it carried a heavy Spanish accent.

"I do too, but I don't know half the things these guys do," she said.

"It is not meant to be scary," Juan pointed out. "It is comforting. We are warned to get out of places before danger strikes. We are sometimes told of coming things, so we plan for them. We talk and work with God. In our prayers and quiet times, thoughts sometimes come to our minds. We have learned to listen to those. Sometimes we are granted a dream or vision while we sleep or pray – we have learned to take those to heart. Sometimes it this small voice deep inside of us, telling us what steps to take – we pay attention to those. Over the years, we learn what is true and what to listen to…as well as what is false, and what to ignore."

"How?"

Juan folded his hands together, resting them on the table in front of him. He knew it would come to Casey in time, but until then, he said, "It takes time and practice."

Casey sat back in her seat and crossed her arms in thought. "So, if I am following what you guys are saying…" She turned to Mark and asked, "When you told me not all of your assignments come from the United States Government, this is what you meant?"

Mark nodded.

She rested her fingers on her chin, running this new information through her head. "Will I be able to do that too?"

The Colonel rested his hand on her shoulder. "You have the skills. You only need to put them into practice. You were taught them in the Outback."

"To see what is not there, to feel what I cannot see, and to anticipate the enemy's movements before he even makes them," she said half to herself, half to them. "So," she looked back up at them, "can all the A.N.G.E.L.s do this?"

Juan nodded. "For the most part, yes."

"Then how do they get killed or hurt? If they know what is coming, how do they get caught?"

"It does not happen *all* the time," Juan pointed out. Casey saw several flashes of A.N.G.E.L.s in the past go across his face in the form of memories. "There are times where we miss it, or we were taken by surprise by the enemy. Despite our best efforts, we are only human. Our enemy is a strong, clever, cunning, shrewd individual, and he has outsmarted and outwitted us many times. His job is to hunt, kill, and destroy. Ours is to rescue, restore, and renew. Do not *ever* take him lightly – that is when he will get you."

Casey nervously looked at him as she placed her hand on her stomach, afraid for both her and the baby. She was worried before, but the dark presence seemed even stronger in this country. She hoped they would all be in tuned enough to keep her and the baby safe, despite the dreams.

Mark put his arm around her shoulder, giving her a gentle squeeze of encouragement. "Relax. We knew the baby was coming. It was already in the plans. God doesn't do surprises. Things may take *us* by surprise, but *nothing* takes *Him* by surprise."

Casey nodded. She had faith in God. She trusted Jesus would never leave her. She prayed she would be able to hear the Spirit if It warned her of incoming trouble.

"Being tired?" Claudia asked, watching Casey.

"Actually, yes I am," she admitted.

"You want sleeping?" She asked, enunciating each word so her Spanish accent didn't jumble her words any worse than they already were.

"Um, no, not yet. Thank you though."

"We're going to have to work on your Spanish," Mark said. "This isn't going to be easy if we don't find a neutral language. Sorry, honey, this is going to be a sink or swim situation – without the option of sinking."

"I know. I've already figured that out," Casey said. "I'm just tired, I think. I hope things will look brighter in the morning."

"Mamá!" Their ten-year-old son Miguel blasted through the front door into the house, excited.

She looked up at him, concern lighting her eyes. "What is it?"

"She said yes!"

Claudia grinned. "Really?"

He ran over and gave her a hug, spinning her around in the air with a grin that went from ear to ear.

"Miguel was nervous about asking a girl, Antonia, to…oh, cómo se dice?" Juan struggled to remember the phrase.

"Asked her to go with him?" the Colonel asked.

Juan nodded. "Yes. That one."

The Colonel looked at him, stunned. "At ten years old?"

"Of course, Colonel. It begins early now." Juan turned toward his son and asked, "She is your girlfriend, no?"

Miguel proudly grinned as he said, "Yes."

"Ahh," Derek sighed, shaking his head, "to be ten again."

"I wouldn't want to go through it again." Mark shook his head. "Going through puberty once was more than enough."

As everyone at the table burst out in laughter, Miguel smiled as well. He understood what they said. While he was young, he was wise. He smiled, looking around the table of people. He recognized all of them except the woman. The men had been in and out over the years, working with his dad. He admired these men. They were strong both physically and mentally. They had a good balance in life though, and added a sense of humor that wasn't always present in the household. With his two younger siblings, it often caused chaos and arguments, not to mention the frequent whining. He came back around to the woman again. She was pretty. She had a natural inner beauty. While she was not gorgeous, her heart, from what he could see in her eyes, was true. She was a Christian – he could see it radiate from her, but she was also sick – he could see that too. "¿Qué pasa con ella?" He nodded toward Casey.

"What did he ask?" Casey looked at Mark.

"He asked what is wrong with you?" Juan interpreted. He turned to Miguel and said, "She is pregnant."

"Ahh." He nodded in understanding, almost studying her. "¿Y el papá?" he asked, looking around the table, pretty sure the dad was among them.

"Marcos." Juan nodded toward Mark. "And, please use English. Is not fair for her."

"No problem." Miguel shrugged. He shook Mark's hand as he said, "Congratulations."

"Thank you," Mark said I appreciation. "And, thank you for speaking English."

"When more difficult, my Inglés not so good." He shook his head. He blushed as he added, "It more a Spanglish."

"We are working with him though," Juan pointed out. "He will be fluent within a couple years."

Miguel rolled his eyes. "Hopefully. They will help in my English class, no?"

Juan patted his son's shoulder. "Lord willing."

Miguel excused himself, "If excuse me, I have homework."

As Casey watched him leave, she said, "He seems like a good kid."

"Yes, he is." Juan smiled, pleased. "All the children are. They are brave, yet stumble in their youth. We have lot of work ahead with them, but worth it, no?"

"Definitely," the Colonel agreed. "Guiding the next generation needs to be of the utmost importance."

"Yes. They are the future."

*   *   *

That night the group discussed what happened with their situation up to that point, and then Juan gave an update as well as to what was going on in their region. He said the battle had gotten a bit fiercer, but still controllable. He was, however, concerned with Casey's safety knowing what happened in Australia. He already notified the other A.N.G.E.L.s in Mexico that the group was on the way, and what he knew about their situation when he met with them.

At about nine-thirty that night, they ate dinner. The time shift in the meals was something Casey would have a hard time getting used to, as well as the late nights.

In the downstairs of the house, Juan and Claudia shared a room, Miguel and Juanito shared a room, and Cristiana had a much smaller room, but she had it to herself. There was also a kitchen and living room downstairs, along with a laundry room located on the back porch. Meanwhile, upstairs there were three other bedrooms and a bathroom – one of the bedrooms was a storage room though. Mark and Casey were going to take one of the bedrooms, leaving the other one for Derek and the Colonel. They were to use the upstairs bathroom at night.

After dinner, Casey was exhausted. She helped Claudia clean up before Claudia sent her to one of the upstairs rooms to go to bed. The cement walls and tile floors made the house feel chilly. Since there was no heating or air conditioning in the homes, it made it difficult to regulate the temperature in the house. The windows were always open to get airflow, but the dust had to be cleaned frequently inside the home, due to all the dirt in the area and the almost continuous wind.

It didn't take Casey long to get changed, brush her teeth, and go to bed. She was so exhausted with all of the travel, along with the events of the day, that as soon as her head hit the pillow she was out.

Chapter 8

Welcome Home

Casey gasped and sat up straight in her bed when she got woken the next morning around seven-thirty by a propane truck's announcement over the loudspeaker of its presence, while it made its way down the street. Mark explained that the trucks drive around all day, and if someone needed the propane, they were to signal the truck. From what Mark explained to Casey, the bottled water was the same. People of other trades went door to door as well. They brought around ice cream, pastries, fresh fruit and vegetables, homemade potato chips, corn on the cob, tamales, fabric for clothing, handmade furniture, and other goods. Mark explained it was because most of the country was so poor, they went door to door to generate more income. While Casey understood, she didn't have an accurate concept of the entire situation.

"Ohhh!" Casey groaned, dropping back onto the bed. She covered her head with a pillow as the truck came by. "Make it stop!"

Mark chuckled, tickled by her morning grumpiness. "It will, when it gets a little further down the road. Don't worry, you'll get used to it."

"Never."

"Come on, I thought you were stronger than this."

"Strength has nothing to do with not being a morning person." She looked at him from under the pillow. "It's the way I'm wired."

"You're not a morning person, and you're not a night person, soooo?"

"I've *never* been a morning person, and I'm not a night person right now because I'm pregnant, and I'm pushing through the day to get to the end. I would love to have an afternoon nap at about three and go to bed at seven."

"Geez," Mark shook his head, laughing, "You sound lazy."

Casey shot him a dirty look.

He looked at her in wide-eyed surprise. "What was that for?"

"You called me lazy."

He pulled the pillow off her face and kissed her forehead. "I said you *sound* lazy. I know you're not."

Casey thought for a moment before she looked up at him and asked, "Are you still going to love me when I get fat?"

"What?" he asked, taken aback. "Where did *that* come from?"

"I'm only going to get fatter. Does the term beached whale paint a pretty enough picture for you?"

"Casey, where is this coming from?" He leaned up on one of his arms, and reached over, resting his hand on the side of her face, rubbing his thumb on her cheek.

She looked at him as tears formed in her eyes. "You're always saying I'm beautiful, and you love cuddling with me and touching me. What's going to happen when I get fat? Am I still going to be attractive to you? Not to mention the fact that I'm thirty-seven years old. I might not lose all the baby weight."

"Casey," he shook his head with a smile. "You are beautiful to me no matter what you look like. It's your heart and soul I'm in love with. It's your gorgeous eyes and brilliant smile I enjoy seeing every day. It's your spirit. I take pleasure in finding out what you're going to come up with next. Don't you understand that?"

Casey nodded, wiping a couple of the tears that fell onto her cheeks.

"Would you love me any less if I was in some horrid accident that left me either disfigured or paralyzed?"

"What? No." She looked at him, stunned he would even ask such a question.

"It's the same thing," he explained. "If you gain too much weight, I might be concerned about your health. However, you are a strong, healthy woman, who I will enjoy seeing get bigger, because then I know our baby, which you're carrying inside of you, is getting bigger and stronger. Make sense?"

"Yeah."

"Good. Then come here and go back to sleep. I'm still tired from the time change and all the travelling we've done. Pretty sure you are too."

She cuddled into him, lying on his chest as he wrapped his arm around her. She listened to the rhythmic beat of his heart and his breathing as it lulled her back to sleep.

When she was almost asleep, he kissed her head, and said, "I love you, Casey. In Spanish, that's te amo."

She kissed his cheek as she whispered, "Te amo, Mark."

* * *

It took the group a couple of days to get their internal time clocks to central Mexico time, which was the main reason Claudia had them upstairs. When they adjusted, Claudia got to work on getting the team acclimated to Mexico itself.

Casey got checked at a local clinic for her pregnancy, and started working on her Spanish with help from Juan's children. She also got a clearer view as to the day-to-day lifestyle of the Mexican people. They were a fun, life-loving people, who had a lot of heart, soul, and passion…but they were also a people who were deeply hurting and financially struggling.

"This one is only three-hundred-and-forty-five-thousand pesos. What do you think?" Mark asked Casey as they walked into a house. The newly built one-level homes were connected in groups of ten, with three sets per side of the street. The gated community had several blocks contained within its gates.

Casey sighed, discouraged. "I *think* it seems cold. They all do."

The houses all had tile flooring, concrete walls and ceilings, and bars on the windows and doors. She shook her head at the idea of it being her home. When she envisioned the house she and Mark would have, this *was not* it.

"Why do you think it seems cold?" the Colonel asked.

Casey took a deep breath, doing her best to control her emotions. They seemed off-kilter at best lately. "When I think of our little one crawling around on a cold tile floor…" She shook her head. Shoving her hands in her jacket pockets, she looked around, disappointed. "When I think of hanging things on the nursery wall, the last thing I think of is having to drill a nail hole in order to hang something. I know they are all basically the same. I just miss the flexibility we had where we used to live, if you know what I mean?"

Mark put his arm over her shoulders and gave her a gentle squeeze. "I do. I guess we are more used to working with what we are given than you are."

Casey looked around the hollow shell of the living room. It was a large room with white tile flooring that went throughout the house. The walls were all white concrete as well. She knew they could paint them whatever color they wanted, but once again there was not a lot of flexibility. Whatever they did at the onset of setting up the home was going to almost have to be permanent. In the living room, she could see that a large table and chairs would fit comfortably, along with a large television and wraparound sofa. There was a large bedroom immediately to the left of the doorway. Then, about halfway through the living room, also to the left, was a small kitchen. The kitchen would definitely be tight, only fitting the appliances and one, maybe two people. At the end of the living room was another large bedroom. While the kitchen was tiny, the three bedrooms, living room, and two bathrooms were of a good size.

Just after the kitchen, still to the left of the living room, was a bathroom. There was tile all over, with two drains on the ground. One was in the walk-in shower, and the other was in the middle of the floor. When Casey asked the realtor about it, she said when Mexican women clean, they dump a lot of water and soap, and then scrub. The drainage helps to stop the overflow from going to the other areas of the house.

"Where is the utility sink?" Casey asked, noticing there wasn't a laundry room.

"Just outside the kitchen is traditionally where the washer is, along with the clothes line. That is also where the sink is."

"In the ally?" Casey looked at her, wide-eyed. "Outside?"

She laughed as she rested her hand on Casey's shoulder. "There is much for you to learn. Your neighbors can help."

"Good news is we only need a pair of scissors to cut the lawn," Mark joked. The lawn in the front was maybe five feet by three feet.

Casey had a look of shell-shock on her face, so the Colonel suggested, "What if we check out the master suite? That will more than likely be your room."

Absentmindedly, Casey followed the others as the realtor ushered them through the doorway off the master bedroom that led out the back of the house. There was an enclosed, walled-in deck of sorts off the bedroom, with a screened door separating the bedroom and the enclosed deck. To Casey it looked odd, but still looked secure.

"Sometimes women hang their laundry in here if there is a chance of rain," the realtor explained. "They also commonly use it for storage since it's a secure area as well."

The area was about ten feet by ten feet, a decent area for laundry. The bedroom itself was approximately fifteen feet by twenty feet, and there was also a master bathroom attached to the bedroom with the same set up as the other one. There was no tub in either, but Casey had yet to see a tub in any of the homes.

"It's a pretty good size and location," Mark commented, interrupting her thoughts. "Just down the road from Juan and Claudia too."

"The bedrooms will give us plenty of personal space," Derek agreed.

The realtor guided them back through the master bedroom, to the final bedroom that was off the living room. It was slightly smaller than the one next to the door, but it was still of a good size.

Concrete and tile. Everywhere Casey looked, she saw concrete, tile, and bars on the windows and doors. It almost felt like a prison to her. While she realized it was for their safety, she still wasn't comfortable with the set up.

"You have decided then?" the realtor asked.

The guys looked at Casey for her answer. There really was nothing she felt she could say. While she understood all the houses were the same, they all still seemed cold to her.

"The benefit of living here is it is a gated community," the realtor pointed out. "Also, if safety is a concern, Querétaro is the second safest state in the country, with Tequisquiapan being among the safer areas in the state. You picked a good place to settle. We have many foreigners who settle here."

Juan studied Casey for a moment before he pulled her to the side and asked, "What is wrong?"

Casey shook her head as she looked down.

Juan lifted her chin. "Casey, what is your worry?"

"It's just not what I would have picked. I know I should be grateful, but –"

"It is a good, sturdy house. Claudia will help."

"I know. There is a lot for me to adjust to, and unfortunately I'm pregnant too."

"Do you like it?"

She shrugged. "I guess it has potential."

"In Mexico, we look for safety and efficiency. A lot of people would love to have home like this. It is large, plenty of room to grow, safe with security gates, never been lived in –"

"I know," she cut him off. "I also know I'll get used to it."

"In time. The others are waiting for an answer. If adjustment is a problem, Claudia and Ana Maria will help. They show you our ways."

"I guess I really don't have much of a choice. I don't mean to sound ungrateful. I just…it's all very different. I…" She looked around with a sigh.

Juan looked at her. He saw her broken heart. He was sure it had to do with leaving everything she ever knew behind her in the United States. He also understood having to adjust to a new culture and country while pregnant wasn't an easy task either. That was a lot for anyone to take. He knew she could handle it, though. He had confidence in her.

She turned toward the others and nodded. "All right."

"You sure?" Mark questioned. He didn't have to be part of the conversation to know her struggles. He saw the look on her face and knew it well. She was suppressing her feelings again. He watched her subdue her feelings a lot lately and that concerned him. What concerned him more, was he knew they would have to leave her in a couple weeks. They would be gone for about three months, but she didn't know about it yet. He knew what it would do to her. He knew what all of this was doing to her. He also knew she was strong, and that she would pull through. He knew she would work it out between her and God later. Even though he knew all of this, he still saw the woman he loved with all of his heart, and his heart broke knowing what all she was facing.

"Yes," she said.

"Wonderful!" The realtor smiled. "Let us go work on the loan –"

The Colonel shook his head. "No loan. We're going to pay in cash."

She smiled, pleased, but slightly taken aback. "Then, we go back to my office." She was thrilled, but she was also not used to people being able to afford paying cash for a new home. It didn't happen too often in her line of work. Payments were often a requirement.

With Juan and Claudia's help, the group also bought furniture, a microwave, refrigerator, household supplies, as well as two used trucks in good condition that were only a couple years old. They were going to share the trucks. When they left for missions, the others would take one truck, leaving the other for Casey in case she needed it while they were gone.

* * *

The day finally arrived where Mark, the Colonel, Derek, Juan, and Raul – the other A.N.G.E.L. in Tequisquiapan – were going to join Mauricio and Rico – the other two A.N.G.E.L.s. One was from up north in Nogales, and the other was from the south in Oaxaca. They took off for a couple of assignments, leaving their families in Tequisquiapan together. The guys felt more comfortable with leaving them all together for an assignment so long, than letting everyone stay separated in their own houses. They were also concerned with how strong the darkness felt around them, and knew the families would be stronger together.

Juan's family – his wife Claudia, and children Miguel (10), Juanito (7), and Cristiana (6), were going to be joined by Rico's family –

his wife Leah, and his two children Maria (7), and Felipe (5). In the meantime, Raul's family – his wife Ana Maria, and children, Anita (14), Carlos (12), Sergio (9), and Antonia (9) (yes, Sergio and Antonia are twins, and yes, that was *the* Antonia that was Miguel's girlfriend), were going to be joined by Mauricio's family – his wife, Ariel, and their two children, Pablo (15), and Pedro (10). They had done this before, and the families were close to each other after working together for so long, so it was not a big deal to cram everyone into the houses.

While Claudia and Ana Maria's homes were crowded, Casey's felt very empty. She would walk to Claudia's house every day since it was only a couple of blocks over so she wouldn't go stir crazy in the house by herself. Ana Maria and Ariel would bring their families over to Claudia's house during the day as well, making the volume in her house high, and it felt continuously in motion. While Casey was not used to all the noise, to her it was nice to see other people. It was a little frustrating though because she didn't know the language. A lot of times, they would talk around her in Spanish, so she would zone out until there was something to do household wise – like cooking, working with the kids, or lending a hand with the cleaning. She knew Spanish would come eventually, but until she learned, it would be frustrating.

While the others talked around the table, Casey would watch television either with the Spanish captions on when they spoke English, or with the English captions on when they spoke Spanish. She also did this at home. It helped her to associate words or phrases with other words. Also, the kids continued to play the game Mark suggested with Casey. At first all of the kids would play, but then the boys would slowly drift off to something more exciting. The girls, on the other hand, were thrilled to teach her Spanish. They were also excited about the baby, and would ask a lot of questions, which she gladly deferred most of them to their mothers for an explanation.

Her Spanish vastly improved, and every once and a while she would listen to conversations in order to see what she could pick up. It was strange, but after a couple of weeks, she started dreaming in Spanish. And, after about six or so weeks, she wouldn't even have to translate to herself before responding. Time was proving to help in this matter.

The longer time went by, the more tired and bigger she got. The women understood why some days she wouldn't go to Claudia's house. The volume and energy wore on her after a couple of days, and she would go home exhausted. Sometimes, she just needed space, peace, and quiet.

The highlight of her day, during that time, was the days when Mark called. He couldn't call often, and when he did, he would have to buy a burn phone to do it, so the same number never came across her phone twice.

"Hey, sweetheart," Mark said when Casey answered her phone.

"Hi! How are things going?"

"Good. Everyone is still accounted for, if that's what you're asking."

She knew he couldn't say much, and that the conversation had to be brief. "How much longer are you guys planning on being gone?"

"Around a month or so. When is your doctor's appointment?"

"It's next Thursday."

He sighed. "I won't make it then."

Her face fell in disappointment. "You know the three-month appointment is when we're supposed to be able to hear the heartbeat."

"I do."

Silence hung in the air for a moment, until she said, "I guess Claudia can go with me."

"That's a really good idea. That way if the doctor doesn't know the word in English, she can translate."

Casey sighed. "I miss you."

"I know. I miss you too. We'll be home soon. Stay safe, okay?"

"I will. Tell the Colonel and Derek I miss them too. The house is scary silent without you guys."

"You still go to Claudia's each day, right?"

"Not every day." She rolled her eyes. "Sometimes that crew is too much."

He chuckled. "I understand. Well, I have to go, but you know I love you."

"I know. I love you too. And, I'm praying for you guys."

"Thank you. We need it," he said before they said their good-byes and hung up.

After the call, Casey wrote the number down. She kept a record of each number, and would compare it before she answered it on the next call. If it was the same number as any of them on the list, she wouldn't answer it. She was glad she wrote them down, too. A couple of times the number was repeated, and if she answered it, there would be no telling who would be on the other end.

*   *   *

The following Thursday Casey went to the clinic for her three-month appointment. Claudia went with her, while the other women watched all the children at Ana Maria's house, which was right down the road from the clinic. Casey was excited, but she wished Mark could have been there to hear the baby's heartbeat. It took the doctor a couple minutes with the Doppler before he was able to find it, but when he did, he was as excited as they were.

The doctor said it was strong, healthy heartbeat, which was one hundred and forty-five beats per minute. On the walk home,

119

Claudia said it was either going to be a boy or a very laid-back girl. She said when the heartbeat was lower than one-hundred-and-fifty, it tended to be a boy, and that above one-hundred-and-fifty tended to be girls.

*   *   *

One night, about two weeks before the guys were due to return, Casey noticed a man walking down the street about the same time every day. She adjusted the time when she walked, but she always saw him. She mentioned it to Claudia, who at first didn't seem concerned, until it had been going on for almost a week. It was then that she decided to start sending Pablo, Pedro, and Miguel to walk her home and make sure she got home safely. She would sometimes send them to get her in the mornings as well. While they got a detailed description, there was not much they could do about it. Casey always knew when he followed her, because the hair on the back of her neck stood on end. She thought about staying with Claudia for safety reasons, but the noise level would be too much, and there were already too many people in the house.

*   *   *

Later that that week, Casey had another dream. She was up on a mountainside with the others. Many people she didn't know were doing some kind of training. Casey was almost nine months pregnant, and had been having labor pains for several days.

While Casey passed water out to those training, a storm formed in the north. Lightning and thunder rolled across the sky as the dark clouds quickly descended around them. That was when she saw it. From the north, there was a group of creatures walking up the mountainside. Casey's heart raced, as the darkness encompassed the area and the hair on her neck stood on end and.

She screamed as she sat upright in her bed, breathing heavily. She glanced at the clock that read 12:36. She had the same dream last week. In order to shake it, she got up to get a glass of chocolate milk.

She warmed it in the microwave before she went over to the window. It was a clear night, and the moonlight was unusually bright. She pulled the curtains back as she took a sip of her milk.

She gasped, almost dropping the milk, as she saw the man that had been tailing her over the last several days. The more she looked at him, the clearer his features seemed to come into focus. That was when she saw it. His eyes shifted to pure black, as she saw the form of a demon. Then he shifted back to normal, before shoving his hands in his pockets and walked away.

*   *   *

The next day, Casey shared the story with the other women. This made an already uncomfortable situation, move toward scary.

Later that night while Casey was at Claudia's, the doorbell buzzed. As if Claudia's house wasn't crowded enough, there were seven Asians standing at the gate. Part of the women went to the door, leaving Leah and Casey in the house. They made sure the children were divided among the upstairs rooms and told them to stay quiet. Things had begun to feel suspicious lately.

Leah and Casey were sitting at the table when the other three ladies brought all seven Asians into the living room. Claudia introduced all of them as the A.N.G.E.L. team from Asia. They spoke broken English, and absolutely no Spanish, so they decided for everyone's sake to mainly speak in English, so everyone had a basic idea what was going on.

They each introduced themselves, starting with all of the males except one.

"I am pleased to meet with you. I am Zon Chi, also known as 'A59.'" He bowed slightly. He looked strong and fit…they all did. They also all had straight, jet-black hair, dark brown eyes, and fair skin. Zon's hair was the longest of the males though, barely touching his shoulders. He had the sides pulled back in a small tie in the back of his head.

"Wish were better times, but happy we being here. I am Qui Nugen, known as 'A56.'" He slightly bowed as well. Qui was the shortest male, but probably the strongest in upper-body strength.

"Pleased to make acquaintance. I am Kim Yong, 'A55.'"

"I am Ming Le, 'A53.' Very humbled to be in your country. Beautiful," the young lady said as she bowed.

"And I am Sing-Li Teng. I am 'A53.'"

"Very happy to meet you. I am Kia Chang, 'A57.'" She bowed. The women were all thin and beautiful, their long hair pulled back in various ways – Ming's was in a French-twist, Sing-Li's was in a bun, and Kia's was in a long braid. They were also respectful and proper in their manners and speech.

"And I am Sun Yun Hueng. I am 'A54,' and I am leader. We lost our honored leader much time ago, sadly. We are here, because we were called. Many more will come. Battle is forming."

"What?" Casey asked, stunned. "It's going to be *here*?"

"Yes. Dark very powerful here. All remaining A.N.G.E.L.s are coming."

"Would that not leave your countries exposed?" Ariel asked. Outside of Casey, Ariel's English was the best.

"No need for concern. Where are A.N.G.E.L.s from here?" he asked.

Casey raised her hand. "I'm one of them, but the others are on a mission. I was recently recruited."

"What number?"

"A7."

He walked over and shook her hand as he bowed. "Very honored to meet you."

"Very honored to meet you, too."

When he looked back up into her eyes, he said, "You new, no?"

"Yes."

"How recruited?"

"My brother was 'A2.' When he died, the remaining four kept me under close guard. Long story short, they needed me as much as I needed them, and we worked closely together for a year or so, until I went through intense training a couple months ago."

"Then, you well trained?"

"Yes sir."

"You not fight, though. You need to wait."

Casey raised an eyebrow at him, while he never took his eyes from hers.

"You are with childs, no?"

"Yes."

"Then, you are the one we here to protect."

"What do you mean?"

"We come," Kia stepped forward, "because the babies are very important. You too. We sent, because darkness grows strong and more powerful here every day. Battle will come. You in danger."

"When the others return?" Sun Yun asked, concerned.

"In couple days," Claudia spoke up. "We together until then."

"And other children? They important and in danger too," Sing-Li pointed out. "Where they?"

The women looked at each other in wide-eyed surprise. How did they know? The children were being completely silent.

"There are many, yes?" Kim asked as he looked around. "They here, yes?"

Claudia nodded, trying to hide her nervousness. Oh, how she was praying for the men to come home. There was too much weird stuff going on, more so than normal.

"Eleven in number, yes?" Qui asked.

Leah nodded. "Yes." She had a feeling to trust them, but what they knew made her nervous as well. While she was used to things happening like this, she could not imagine what it was doing to Casey who only recently stepped into this situation.

Casey put her hand on her stomach, not sure what to think. They said there would be more coming, but they also said the darkness was growing. What kind of battle would this be if the A.N.G.E.L.s of flesh and blood were battling against the unseen powers of darkness? Would there be any element of fairness to it at all?

"Um," Claudia awkwardly stood there for a moment before she asked, "are you hungry?"

"Very. Thank you." Sun Yun nodded in appreciation. "Travel many hours."

"I am sure. Sit, please." She gestured to the table. "Leah, please release children while we get food?"

Leah nodded and headed upstairs, while Ana Maria and Ariel went into the kitchen with Claudia to get them something to eat.

Casey got drinks and set the table. While she was setting the plates down, she asked, "Um, where are you staying?"

As soon as she asked the question, the flurry of activity in the kitchen came to an abrupt halt. That thought had not occurred to the three in the kitchen. Their houses were full. What *were* they going to do?

Kia shrugged. "Do not know. We instructed to come, so we come."

"I have rooms in my house, if you want to stay," Casey offered. "One is the Colonel's and one is Derek's, but I don't think they would mind. The women can sleep in my room with me if they want. You said more were coming, I'm sure we're going to have to live in tight quarters for a bit." Casey thought for a moment before she asked, "How many A.N.G.E.L.s are there?"

"Over years – many lost. Unsure how many left," Kim said, sitting down at the table.

Sun Yun nodded in appreciation. "But we are pleased and gratitude for your offer. Yes, thank you."

Casey smiled, relieved to have someone staying with her. "Good. Then it's settled. You are staying with me, and we will figure the rest out as they get here."

"Here, for you," Ariel said, as she and Ana Maria brought food in that Claudia served up from the kitchen.

Meanwhile, the children slowly came down the stairs to see the new visitors. They looked different to them, so unfortunately they stared for a bit, until Claudia chased them out of the living room into the various bedrooms. The kids were curious. There had been a lot of new people lately. They were beginning to wonder what was going on.

As the group ate at the table, the truck pulled up with the guys. The kids bolted for their dads, relieved they were home. The kids were talking a mile a minute, to the point that even the dads were confused.

When the men walked in, they were shocked to find the Asian A.N.G.E.L.s at the table. They recognized them from past missions they worked on together, but they could not imagine what would bring the entire team here, leaving Asia uncovered.

"Welcome." Juan shook hands with Sun Yun, who he knew to be the leader. All of the men shook hands with their entire team, while a few of the women went and got the others food. Leah and Casey stayed in the living room so there would not be too many people in the kitchen. As it was, people were almost tripping over everyone else. Between the kids, the three teams, and the wives…it was crazy.

Sun Yun explained as best he could, that they were instructed to get there because a battle was looming. The others were coming too, so they were to be prepared.

"Wait a second." Mark put up his hands to stop everyone for a moment. "The battle is going to be *here*?"

Sun Yun nodded. "Yes."

"And, you said the darkness is getting *stronger*?" Derek asked.

"Yes."

"And *all* the A.N.G.E.L.s are coming?" Juan questioned.

"Yes."

"And you have been followed for over a week?" the Colonel asked Casey.

"Yes. It's the same guy. It doesn't matter what time I come here or go home. That's why Ariel's boys and Miguel walk with me," Casey explained.

"And, the kids are the key?" Raul asked, still trying to make sure he understood Sun Yun.

"Yes. The future. Enemy kill future teams," Sun Yun clarified. "Her included." He nodded toward Casey.

"So, is there going to be a literal battle, or a battle of circumstances set up by the other side?" Casey asked.

Mauricio shrugged. "Could be both. The dark sometimes uses flesh and blood people to do work. They possess."

A shudder ran down Casey's spine. Things were getting too scary for her. This was something she *definitely* was not used to. "Just so you know, I asked them to stay at our house," Casey said as she leaned over to Mark. "They said more were coming. I figured Mauricio's and Rico's families were going to probably be hanging out too."

Juan nodded. He was their leader. "Yes, they are."

"We're going to have to find somewhere for the others to stay," Derek said, mulling the logistics of the situation over in his head. "As it is, all the houses are now maxed-out."

"What is maxed-out?" Rico questioned. They had to work through many new terms, but he had never heard that one.

"Full. To the limit," Derek clarified.

He nodded in understanding. Then a thought struck him. "We rent building. We use for sleep and train?"

Juan considered the different aspects of the situation and nodded. "That is a good idea."

Casey raised her hand. "May I ask a question?"

Juan gestured toward her. "Please."

"Well, I know you are used to this, but it's new to me. In saying that…how do you know what you do about us? How do you know there's a battle coming? What did you mean by you were instructed? *How* were you instructed? And, how did you know I was pregnant when I only met you today?" She looked at Sun Yun. He seemed to know the most.

"Ahh, good questions." He nodded in understanding, as he was sitting backwards on one of the kitchen chairs facing the others. "I can answer all at same time."

"Okay." She looked at him, not sure if she wanted the answer, but she'd asked. She decided the more she understood specifically how things worked, the better off she would be.

"Was praying and vision came," he started. "It was of a field. At first, you and your four families were playing and having a picnic." He looked at Juan, Raul, Mauricio, and Rico. "Then you four were added, and you were having babies," he said to Casey, the Colonel, Derek, and Mark. "All playing in the field when a storm came. I saw clouds growing darker in the distance. As it got closer, those from other countries joined, and it went from picnic, to battlefield. One side is all A.N.G.E.L.s, your wives, and your children. On other, creatures of darkness – some in human form." He stopped for a moment, remembering the dream. "Battle was fierce, but we needed all to be there, children included. Fifty total A.N.G.E.L.s there before joined by over five-hundred Heavenly Angels. Some not make it. Was very dangerous. You give birth during battle."

"Oh, no way." Casey shook her head. "Giving birth is hard enough."

Mark chuckled, as he patted her leg. "Shhhhh."

"The babies were strong. The darkness was trying to get to babies and you," he said to Casey. "One in charge wore an angel necklace."

Casey gasped, covering her mouth. *The angel necklace!* "Did it have a gold cross, and the little angel was holding a diamond heart in front of the cross?"

"Yes, that is it." He nodded. Then he narrowed his eyes. "You know this necklace?"

"Yes," Casey said, feeling the color drain from her face as Mark squeezed her hand.

"Then, you know the one wearing it?" Sun Yun asked.

"Yes." Casey nodded. "It was a demon, right?"

"No." He shook his head. "Form was a woman. Demon possessed woman."

Casey closed her eyes and slowly shook her head, dropping it into her hands. With her head down, she asked, "Was the woman tall, blond, thin, and older, but fit?"

"Yes," he said, slightly taken aback. "You know her?"

Casey looked up, feeling shaky at best. "It was Jackie."

Mark shuddered. "The…no way."

"Who is Jackie?" Juan asked.

"She was the woman who tortured me in Australia," Casey said.

"I am sorry," Sun Yun said, as his heart broke for her. "Will be bad."

Casey took a deep breath in an attempt to control her feelings. To know this woman was going to be back to torment her again, terrified her beyond words.

The doorbell buzzed and Casey jumped. Those in the room looked at each other, stunned – it was ten-fifteen at night. The men stood up and walked out together, leaving the women and children inside. The four from Mexico, the four from Asia, and the three from the U.S. all had their weapons in hand as they went outside.

They were back a few minutes later with the crew from Australia – all eight of them.

"G'day Casey." Hawk smiled as he walked in. "We missed ya so much, we thought we'd come for a bit."

"We already know," Casey said, somberly.

"Oh. Well then," he sighed, "Sorry t' be the bearer of bad news, but there's more coming."

She nodded. "We know."

"Maybe introduce?" Ming Le asked, looking around. "Some work with some, but not others."

"Good idea," Carson agreed, as everyone set their bags down.

"Well, I'll start. I'm Danny Hawk, 'A21.' I'm the leader of the Australian group," Hawk said, looking around.

Everyone else went around and introduced each other. After some time of debate, they decided to split all the men from Asia, Australia, and the U.S. between Derek's and the Colonel's rooms, while the two women from Australia and the three from Asia were going to stay in Mark and Casey's room. Mark and Casey decided to sleep in the living room on a mattress with blankets, so they could actually sleep together.

After another hour or so of talking, Raul, Mauricio, and their families went to Raul's house, while the crews from Australia, Asia, and the U.S. rode over to the house in the truck. Most of them were piled in the bed of the truck with their bags, but they didn't seem to mind.

When they got to their house, it was almost comical watching everyone go into the house to get settled. Casey was sure there was a joke in there somewhere. *'What happens when you put together seven Asians, eight Australians, and four Americans into one three-bedroom house?'*

It took them a while, but after everyone finally settled about two hours after they got home, Mark and Casey finally went to bed.

"So, my love…" Mark smiled, wrapping his arms around her and kissing her head. "How are you?"

She cuddled into him. "Freaked out, but okay."

He burst out in laughter, but quickly covered his mouth so he didn't disturb anyone trying to sleep. He cleared his throat before he whispered, "Freaked out, huh?"

"Yeah. I mean, it's wild. Can we dial back the crazy just a bit?"

Mark couldn't help the laughter that escaped that time. "Never quite heard it put that way."

"Well, I mean, right now I'm grateful everyone here can at least speak English so we can communicate. What happens if we get some people who can't?"

"They all can to some extent. That's not going to be a problem. The problem is going to come in the blending of tactics, training, and skills."

"You have all worked together at some point or another, though, right?"

"Well, we've each been with at least a couple of the members of each team at one point or another, but not everyone has met everyone. This will be the first time we will all be together."

Casey thought for a moment before she said, "You know, this is a scary prospect."

"What do you mean?"

"With everyone together, all the A.N.G.E.L.s, realistically, can be taken out at once. If that happens, then who will step-up?"

"The Heavenly Angels won't let that happen," he said confidently. "Besides, we have more power than they do – we have God. We out-strengthen the other side by a long shot. They are only as powerful as their strongest member – which is Satan. If you remember, Satan may have been high up there in the angelic realm, but he *was* only an angel. He has learned some nasty tricks over the years, along with the fine arts of manipulation, distortion, and misrepresentation, so don't underestimate him. He has learned to change facts so they seem accurate. He has learned to distort false doctrine so it seems true. He's learned to misrepresent reality so it seems fraudulent. He has corrupted everything respectable to seem scrupulous. He is the master manipulator – whose mission is to hunt, kill, and destroy. Having said that, he may be good at his job, but the Heavenly realm is better at theirs. They can clear up what seems false, fix what is hurt or broken, and even heal what is shredded. You thought those medicines Pete came up with were good – the stuff the Heavenly Angels can come up with will outdo anything he even remotely can come up with. Our leader is God. We have Jesus and the Holy Spirit on our side. Trust me, the battle may be bloody, but we *will* win the war."

"But will we be alive afterwards?"

"If not here on earth, then yes, in Heaven. That is one of the reasons we don't mind doing what we do. What do we have to lose? We are either alive here on the Earth or are alive up in Heaven, with God and Jesus."

Casey mulled over his words for a while. She knew he was probably almost asleep, but she had to ask him, "Do you think the baby will live through it?"

"I don't know. Only God knows that one. I'm sorry I can't answer that." He wrapped his arms around her as he said, "But once again, if the baby doesn't, it will be in better hands anyway. God will take care of our baby until we can get there."

Casey nodded as she wiped the tears from her eyes. While she understood the words he said, the loss would kill her. In order to focus on what was in front of them, though, she had to push all those thoughts and feeling away. She knew more teams were coming in, and if Sun Yun's vision was accurate, while they already had twenty-three of the A.N.G.E.L.s there, they still had to find housing for the twenty-seven yet to arrive.

Chapter 9

Battleground

Over the course of the next week, the rest of the teams arrived. With fifty total in number, the group seemed small in size, but mighty in power. While the men and women were all from different countries, cultures, and background, some were even countries of a known enemy, they got along very well. They had a unified purpose, which allowed them to stand in battle side by side for the sake of the Lord.

In order to accommodate everyone, the A.N.G.E.L.s rented an empty warehouse. The groups rotated who stayed in American A.N.G.E.L.'s house or the warehouse, so everyone would at least get to enjoy the comforts of an actual home every couple of days, along with a hot shower. However, the Colonel, Derek, Mark, and Casey stayed in their house the entire time. Those in Ana Maria and Claudia's house stayed the same, mainly for the stability of the children with all of the chaos going on around them. As a group, everyone would either eat in the warehouse, or up on the mountain if they were having drills, bringing food from the houses three times a day.

The groups would go out into the mountains for prayer and training each day, with the exception of Sunday – that was their day of rest. Since Casey continued to grow larger with the pregnancy, she was able to participate in the training for the first couple of months, as long as there was no contact, so she could pick up the techniques. She understood it was for the protection of her and the baby.

After she hit her fifth month of the pregnancy, they banned her from training, so Casey joined Claudia, Ana Maria, Leah, and Ariel, who watched the children that would play in a part of the field the others weren't using. They would also set out food for meals, while keeping the water bottles full and cold to drink.

As time passed, the groups blended their cultures, customs, and techniques. There were some disagreements at first, so they decided that one team would take tactical training for a week, before changing to another team for the next week, allowing each team to train in their most used tactics before starting the rotation over again.

This went on for almost six months, until the Asian and Australian group's visas were set to expire in three weeks. Everyone knew by this that the battle was going to occur within the next three weeks. Casey also knew her due date was going to fall in the middle of that as well. It was looking like Sun Yun's vision was slowly coming to fruition, much to Casey's dismay.

Also, during that time, Casey's dreams became more vivid. The dream on the mountainside played over and over in her nightmares, interspersed with the nightmares of her time of torture with Jackie.

Casey sat straight up in their makeshift bed on the floor with a gasp. She was sweating and breathing heavily.

"Hey. Hey. It's okay. You're safe," Mark said, as he sleepily sat up and held her. "You're shaking."

"I...I know. It's coming."

"What's coming?"

"She is."

"Jackie?"

"Yes. I've dreamed about it for weeks. I'm afraid of what is going to happen when she finally catches up with us."

Mark placed both hands on the sides of her face as he focused her on him. "Listen, God is bigger and stronger than Jackie."

"You know as well as I do that it's not really Jackie."

"Whatever is inside of her is nowhere near the strength God has," Mark encouraged. "His power is infinite. Nothing goes on that He doesn't know about. You have to trust He will take care of us."

"I know. And, I do."

"Then trust that He will never let you down."

She nodded in understanding, but she didn't want to go back to sleep with the dream so fresh in her mind. "You need to talk to me for a bit. I can't go back to sleep just yet. Tell me a story."

He slid back under the covers, as she lowered herself back to her pillow as well. "Tell you a story about what?"

"What about the mission you guys went on when we first got here."

"Are you sure you want to know?

"I feel that I need to know. I'm an A.N.G.E.L. now."

He nodded. "True. But I was trying to protect you from the ugly side of this."

"I'm afraid you can't protect me from it. You should have learned that back in Australia."

He cringed at her mentioning his failure in Australia.

"Not to bring up a sore subject, but I'm pretty sure it found me. You can't shield me from this now any more than you could then."

"All right." He sighed as he rolled over, looking up at the ceiling. He intertwined his fingers behind his head with a cluster of memories going through his mind. "We had to help several different people. One was a pastoral family where the pastor was arrested. The intent of those who took him was not to keep him behind bars, but to get him out of the way. It seems in his endeavors to help others; he helped the wrong person. We had to first get him out of jail, and then relocate him and his family to better and safer surroundings."

"Where did you send them?"

"Belize."

"And the next?"

"The daughter was kidnapped. We had to find the daughter while, making sure the rest of the family remained intact. You see, the one daughter was the cause of the other daughter being kidnapped."

"What do you mean?" Casey asked.

"She bragged about her family's money to the wrong person. When her sister was taken, she was uncontrollable and frantic. It took us a bit to calm her down enough to get the information we needed. Then, we had to find the daughter. When we did, we got the entire family and relocated them as well, this time to Venezuela."

"I see."

"There was a third family as well," Mark continued.

"What happened to them?"

"We didn't make it. There was a target on them, but we got there too late. The family was slaughtered by the time we arrived. It was a mess."

"Wow! I'm so sorry."

"As I told you before. Sometimes we get there in time, sometimes we don't." He slowly let out a breath of air as he admitted, "There were a couple more while we were out there."

"I'm afraid to ask."

"It was another kidnapped child."

"What happened to the child?"

"Once we finally found him, he was returned, but he was also found with other children."

"What were they –?"

"They were going to be sold."

The words hung in the air for a moment before Casey shook her head. "I'm sorry, Mark."

"The missions regarding children are the ones that get to me the most. Why would someone hurt an innocent child?"

"What possesses someone to hurt another human being at all?"

"That is a question I want to know the answer to. As a matter of fact, the last one we were out there for was a woman. She was a young American in her mid-twenties. The man she was with was abusing her. He actually beat her up and left her stranded in the middle of nowhere."

"Are you serious?"

"We got her cleaned up and got her across the border with a new identity so he will never find her," Mark said. "We set her up in Utah, and then ducked back into Mexico before anyone noticed."

She rolled onto her side, facing him. "Did you stop in Colorado at all while you were there?"

He glanced over at her, noting the look on her face. "I'm afraid not. We had to get her settled and get back across the border before we were caught."

"I see."

"It breaks my heart what people do to each other. Sometimes it makes me want to go hide all of us under a rock until the world finally ends."

"You know, Chief once said something to us as a group that I will never forget."

"And it pertains to this?" Mark asked.

"Yep."

"Fire away."

"He said, '*We all know emergencies never take a day off. We all know for each one of us claimed, another has to step up to continue taking care of our fellow citizens. Our job is to protect and to serve. Our job is to care for the injured, to help those who need it, and to take down the beast known to us as fire. This beast tries to claim whatever and whomever it can. We all have a call to duty which we have sworn to perform.*' While you guys are not on a fire scene, the same principles apply."

"This is true. So, my beautiful bride, how can we apply this wisdom to *our* situation?"

"Well," she said, taking a moment to get her thoughts in order before she continued, "we've already talked about the idea that all of the A.N.G.E.L.s could be taken out at once. We know God knows everything and already has a plan in place. We also know that for every one of us that is taken, another has to step up to carry on. We all have a duty to perform. God has given each of us a gift to use in performance of that duty as well."

"And we will do it to the best of our ability."

"And if we fall?" she asked.

"Let's take this one step at a time. Only God knows the outcome."

*   *   *

With about a week left for the first visas to expire, everyone was up on the mountainside when Casey had several contractions within ten minutes of each other. She had Braxton-Hicks Contractions for over a month, so she knew the time was close. However, over the last couple of days they were stronger and closer together.

About two hours after their arrival to the field, Casey doubled over in pain. "Ahhhh!" She screamed, as she dropped to her hands and knees breathing heavily. Instead of slowly rising in pain and pressure like the contractions normally did, this one immediately spiked.

Claudia ran over to Casey's side, while Ariel sent Pablo and Pedro to go alert the others and grab Mark. "Casey, can you speak?" Ariel asked, putting her arm around her.

Casey shook her head, unable to talk at that moment. She braced herself with one arm, as she held her stomach with the other.

Claudia knowingly looked up at Ariel and Leah. She was more than familiar enough with the symptoms of the delivery of a baby to recognize the real ones from the false ones.

Ariel knelt in front of Casey and grabbed her face with her hands. "Breathe. Come on, breathe through them."

As the others ran over, Casey let out a yell, finally able to get something out. "Ahhhh!! Ohhh!" she groaned, breathing heavily.

Ariel moved to the side when Mark ran over to Casey in alarm. "Casey!"

She looked up at Mark with tears in her eyes.

"Oh no." He shook his head. "You can't! We're in the middle of nowhere."

"It has begun," Sun Yun said solemnly, and he looked around. The kids were playing in the field, and Casey was in the middle of labor…exactly the same as in his vision. He instinctively searched for the dark forces, knowing they were on their way.

As if he could read Sun Yun's mind, Juan got down on his knees in prayer. He knew the time had come. He knew Sun Yun's vision was correct. As Juan prayed, he glanced at the scene in front of him, soaking it all in. He knew he would never again see a scene this powerful in his lifetime.

The other A.N.G.E.L.s followed suit, one-by-one, dropping to their knees in prayer. They prayed for safety for Casey, the baby, the children, the wives that they had all come to love over the last several months, along with each one of the A.N.G.E.L.s there. They prayed for the incoming Heavenly Angels, praying they would come quickly, and that the battle would be swift. They prayed for strength and for power for everyone to get through safely.

As they prayed, Casey looked up in the distance and saw dark clouds forming due to an incoming storm. "Oh no." Casey shook her head in horror. Mark rolled her so she was lying on him with his arms around her. "Not now!" Casey groaned.

Mark looked up and saw it too. He closed his eyes and began to pray in a language Casey didn't understand. All the voices of the A.N.G.E.L.s prayed in their different languages or in a heavenly language. The Father guided their prayers, as The Spirit came in from the opposite direction of the darkness, like a wall of refreshing, cleansing water in the form of a rain storm, it attempted to meet the evil head-on.

As soon as Casey felt the Spirit's powerful presence, another contraction came. "Ahhhhhhh!" she yelled, gritting her teeth. Then, as if it was all planned and on cue, Casey's water broke.

Claudia, with the help of Ariel and Ana Maria, cleared the table enough to get the tablecloth out from under all the food. She placed it over Casey's legs and removed her shorts and underwear.

Leah gathered the children and took them to a safe distance, while Ariel and Ana Maria emptied water bottles into a bowl so Claudia would have clean water to work with.

Casey felt the glory of God flowing while rain drops slowly transformed to showers. The lightning crackled across the skies and the thunder rolled. Casey instantly knew the Heavenly Angels were on their way.

"Oh! Help me!" Casey cried in pain. She wanted pain medication so badly she couldn't stand it, but she knew medical intervention was nowhere near them. When the contraction finally went down,

Claudia slid a towel under Casey's bottom half. "Mark, I…I can't do this." Casey shook her head.

"Yes, you can," he encouraged. "You're strong. You can do this."

"We're not in a hospital…and there's a battle forming. I can…ahhhhh! I can feel both sides!"

"I help deliver Ana Maria's twins at home. You be fine," Claudia assured her. "Just fine."

"Claudia, I love you, but…ahhhhhh-eeeeeee!" she screamed, squeezing Mark's hands as she tightly shut her eyes, feeling another contraction immediately spike.

"Breathe!" Claudia shouted over the rain.

"No!" Casey growled. "Pain!"

"You can do this," Mark assured her. "You are bringing our child out into the world. Just think…you will be able to hold it, love it, and care for it with the mother's heart I know is in you."

"Ahhhhhh!" Casey screeched, finally able to get out a word. As the contraction went down, she finally let her air out, breathing heavily in an attempt to stop from passing out.

"They are coming," Ariel said, as she glanced over her shoulder. The other A.N.G.E.L.s rose to their feet, and turned to face a group of people hiking up the mountain toward them. The mix was partially human, intermingled with creatures of the night – including physical demons.

"Oh no!" Casey panicked when she saw Jackie leading them. "It's her! Mark! Make this stop!" Casey's body trembled in fear. If it wasn't the extreme pain she was in, it was actually seeing the woman who almost tortured her to death walking toward her while she lay there in an extremely vulnerable position.

"I'm sorry." Mark shook his head. "I am not in control of this."

"Seven centimeters," Claudia mentioned, checking Casey.

"Really? Already?" Mark looked at her in alarm. He had a sudden feeling of overwhelming panic, which was foreign to him. He was used to there being a plan and basically following it, with adjustments that had to be made here and there, but he had no control at all in this situation. There was way too much going on around him for him to focus. Knowing God was the one who *was* in control and had a plan…Mark took a deep breath and closed his eyes in prayer, bracing himself for what was ahead.

"She be in labor for couple days now. This finally reached point today," Claudia explained. "It will not be long."

Casey looked over to see the group walking up the mountain stop about fifty-yards from the others. As the two groups faced each other, the A.N.G.E.L.s continued to stand together, praying aloud, with their hands raised toward Heaven, reaching out to God. Seeing all of the A.N.G.E.L.s from different countries standing together to fight would have been an absolutely spectacular sight to Casey, had she not been in labor. She couldn't stop the tears from flowing, and the pain was a constant. Then, when the contractions came, they were downright excruciating.

Just when Casey didn't think she could take anything else, she heard the demon's voice spew from Jackie's mouth, "Releasssssse her to usss and we will sssstop thissss."

"Never!" The Colonel stood his ground. "She is His. Not yours."

"She'ssss mine!" she hissed. "Ssssssee." She let the angel necklace dangle from her fingers. "I sssstill have a hold of her heart."

"That is just a necklace. That's not her heart. Her heart belongs to The Almighty God," the Colonel declared. "She is *His* daughter."

The Heavenly Angels suddenly appeared among the other Angels. They surrounded each A.N.G.E.L. with their swords ablaze with a Holy Fire. Several also surrounded Casey and those with her, along with the children as well. The fierce determination on the faces of the Heavenly Angels gave Casey comfort. She knew God sent them for protection.

"She'ssss mine," Jackie hissed. "She will always be mine."

"She is not. She is His." The Archangel from the hut in Australia made his way to the front of the pack, where he stood toe to toe with Jackie. "We beat you before. We will beat you again. We have the Almighty One behind us. He will fight for what is His. We also have the power of the saints praying behinds us – not only these, but the others around the world as well. They know we are in a battle, and are down on their knees in prayer for us right now."

"She is only one. Why do you care?" Jackie cocked her head to the side, crossing her arms in amusement.

"Because each one of His children are precious to His heart."

"Yesssss, she *is* preciousssss," she hissed, with a twinkle in her eyes. "Preciousssss."

"Ahhhhhhh!" Casey screamed as a contraction spiked. "Pain! Ahheeeeee!"

"The baby is coming," Claudia said for Mark's benefit.

Casey didn't care what was going on at that moment. All she cared about was making the pain stop.

"Ahhhh, they are coming," Jackie taunted, rubbing her hands together in delight. "They will be mine too."

"They will not!" The Angel declared, "They will be strong men for His army. I know that is why you want them, but they are not yours to take."

The contraction finally began to go down, so Casey did her best to breathe through what was left. "Claudia," she moaned when it was almost gone.

"Yes?" Claudia asked, periodically glancing from the battle lines to Casey.

Casey suddenly sat up and grabbed her legs. She grunted in pain, as she growled, "Need to push."

"No. You were only seven centimeters." Claudia shook her head. "I check." She checked again, and her eyes got wide. She looked down to make sure she felt what she thought she did. "You ten."

"*What*?!" Mark and Casey both asked, stunned.

Jackie laughed a hideous laugh as she crossed her arms. "Delicioussss! Ssssimply delicioussss!" she hissed, then threw back her head, cackling in laughter.

"You are commanded to leave. You are also commanded to leave her and the babies alone," the Angel growled.

"Or *what*?" She put her hands on her hips.

The Angel's eyes blazed, as he said, "You *will* face *His* wrath."

Casey breathed heavily. "Claudia? Ten? Already?" She wasn't paying attention to the battle. She was in too much pain to care what was going on around her. She was focused on getting the baby out.

She nodded. "Yes, I check three times. You ready." She looked over her shoulder at Ariel and Ana Maria, and added, "Get more water ready to clean it off and get me scissors."

"Claudia!" Casey screamed when the contraction spiked again. "Claudia! Ahhhhhheeee!" she screeched, gritting her teeth in agony.

"Push if need," Claudia encouraged. "I ready."

"Face *Hissss* wrath?" Jackie raised an eyebrow. "How am I going to have to face *Hisssss* wrath when He doesn't even bother to show up?"

The Angel's sword suddenly flashed even brighter than it already was. "Leave this place, and these people to do their work."

"Theeessse people," she snubbed her nose, "have been a pain for years. I would not mind taking a couple more while I was at it."

She laughed in pleasure at the thought, and added, "Ohhhh, what a delicioussssss day!"

The Angel narrowed his eyes at Jackie. "You *will* leave this place."

"Ahhhhhh!!" Casey screamed, bearing down to push. The pain and agony was intense.

"Or *what*?" Jackie put her hands on her hips. "The babies are coming," she pointed out, gesturing toward Casey. "They will be mine. Jusssst as shhhe is mine."

"Push Casey," Claudia encouraged. "Come on, you can do it."

"Ahhhhh!" Casey screamed when the contraction went down.

"Next time, keep pushing. Baby come with that one or one after. Very soon," Claudia encouraged.

"By the authority granted to me, by The Lord God Almighty, you are to leave them alone! That woman and the babies are covered by the blood of Jesus. They are *not* yours to touch. Leave them alone or you *will* face His wrath. This is your last and final warning."

"Now!" Casey screamed when the contraction spiked again. "Push now!" Casey grunted through gritted teeth.

"Yes. Push. You can do this," Claudia said confidently. "Almost there. I see head."

Jackie took a couple steps toward Casey, but the Angel stood in her way with his sword less than three inches from her face. Jackie took a step back, glaring at the Angel. "Out of my way, *angel*," Jackie said snidely. "I am going to get *my* babiessss."

"You will not!" The Angel reared his sword back and slashed Jackie through the middle. As Jackie's ashes floated toward the ground, the battle ensued.

Everyone took the cue, as the two sides merged together. Swords clashed, knives slashed, and fists pounded among the shouts of the challenge. There were five Heavenly Angels to each of the A.N.G.E.L.s. There were over four hundred creatures of the night – things nightmares were made of – along with physical beings who were possessed. At current, the sides were well matched in skill and force. Who would be left standing in the end was known only to God Himself.

"Keep pushing," Claudia said to Casey to get her to focus. "Almost here."

"Ahhhhh-eeeeeeee!" Casey screamed, pushing with everything she had.

"A little more."

"Mark!" Casey yelled and pushed again. She pushed for fifteen agonizing minutes, until she finally heard the baby whimper. As the baby's cry quickly built up to a hefty, hearty one, Casey fell back onto Mark, exhausted and in pain.

"Good job, hon." He grinned, and then kissed her head. "He's a beauty."

Casey was almost panting. "Thanks."

Derek glanced to his right, as one of the Heavenly Angels by him fell to the sword of the demon in front of him. Derek yelled as he jumped on the back of the demon, while two other Heavenly Angles took the cue and together attacked the demon who took out their fellow comrade. As Derek tightened his arms around the demon's neck, one Angel took a slice into the demon's arm, and the other Angel plunged his sword into the middle of the demon. The putrid, yellow, puss-filled blood flowed freely as the demon's body dropped to the ground in a heap.

It took Casey several moments before she felt it. Claudia was cleaning the baby when Casey's eyes got bigger. Her heart raced in panic. "Um…Claudia!"

"What?" She looked up at her, seeing her breathe harder again.

"More!" There was a sudden spike of pain, as another contraction headed up. Casey gritted her teeth and arched her back. It hurt too much for her to talk.

"More *what*? Casey?" Claudia asked nervously, crouched beside her. "Is more contractions?"

Casey nodded and grabbed her legs to push. "Yeeeeee-ahhhhhhh!" she screamed when it finally went down.

Claudia shook her head. "No, is after contractions."

"No, it's more than that!" Casey winced in pain. The pain of the contraction only subsided a little, but it never went away.

"Casey, no. Baby is out."

"Claudia, yes!" Casey hissed. Then she shouted, "MORE! They're twins!"

"Twins?" Mark looked at her in shock.

"Si." Claudia nodded, seeing the head of the second baby when it crowned. "Gemelos."

"¿Gemelos?" Ana Maria looked down, stunned.

"Yes, is true." Claudia nodded. "Push Casey. Come on, one more in there."

Casey shook her head as the tears rolled down her cheeks. "Nooo," she groaned. "Too much pain. I'm sorry I didn't tell you. I wanted to make sure they were both born alive."

"You knew there were twins?" He asked, confused and hurt that she didn't tell him.

"I didn't…" she took a deep breath trying to regulate the pain. "I didn't want you to worry."

"Of course I'm going to worry," Mark said. "Why didn't you tell me?"

"Noo," she moaned. "Not now, Mark, please? I can't do this again, Claudia." She shook her head. "I don't have it in me."

Mark had an arm wrapped around her while he gently stroked her hair, praying for strength and endurance for her. "You can do it. I have faith in you."

"I...I...I-eeeeeee!" Casey pushed as hard as she could when the contraction suddenly spiked. She was exhausted and not sure how much more she had in her to push.

"Good! Good! It coming!" Claudia smiled. "Little more! One good push!"

The swords clanged as the men and women fought, while Casey brought the children into the world. Intense chaos continued around them in what should have been a private family moment. The horrific scene must have been terrifying for the other children to watch.

"Now!" Casey screamed as she pushed.

"Little more, Casey. You can do it," Claudia encouraged. "Couple more good pushes, baby come."

"No, I...." Casey shook her head. Her energy was depleted by that point, and she had been in extreme pain for over forty-five minutes. "I can't."

"Have to," Claudia said before she looked up at Casey. Her eyes got wide and she panicked. "Marcos, look at her."

Mark reached around and tapped her cheek. "Casey, you are stronger than this. The kids need you."

"I...." Casey shook her head in an attempt to push the black cloud away that wanted to knock her out.

"Casey Ann English!" Mark shouted, as he lowered her into his arms so he could see her face.

Casey shook her head again to clear it before she rolled her head toward Mark. Everything seemed to be a blur. "Too much."

Claudia shook her head, scared and worried for Casey. "Casey, need other baby. Not good to stay in once baby coming. Be bad for it."

Casey nodded, so Mark repositioned them. He wrapped his arms around her for comfort, even though he felt helpless.

The contraction came like a freight train. There was no stopping it. "Ahhhhhhhhh-eeeeee!" Casey screeched in pain before breathing heavily, unable to talk anymore.

"Push! Baby need to come out!" Claudia yelled at her in her concern for the baby. Claudia knew Casey's past. She knew a loss like this could devastate her beyond what she could handle.

Casey took a deep breath and grabbed her legs. She pushed, grunting in pain. When the contraction went down, she didn't stop pushing. She pushed and pushed, until, "Good! Is here," Claudia said in relief. Then she shook her head as she jostled the baby boy. "Come on, baby." She looked at Mark for help, as tears rolled down her cheeks. "No air. No breathe. I do not know what to do."

Casey put her hands out for her baby. "Give him here." She was beyond exhausted, but her baby needed her, and her paramedic instincts kicked into gear.

Claudia handed the baby to Casey, while Mark held Casey for support. Casey stuck her pinky finger in his mouth, scooping out the gunk that was in it. Then she flipped him over in her arms, with his chin resting in her hand and his body on her arm. She patted him on the back twice before flipping him back over, and breathing into his nose and mouth at the same time, two short breaths. At first, he didn't respond, until she did it two more times. Then he coughed, and a soft cry escaped his mouth.

The panic and adrenaline finally caught up to Casey, and she rested back on Mark while her body shook beyond her control. This was her baby's life. She could still hear the first one screaming his head off while Ariel cleaned him. Casey gently flipped the baby currently in her arms so he faced her. "Good job." Casey smiled, looking down at him.

"Good job." Mark kissed her head. "I knew you could do it."

"I cut now…yes?" Claudia asked, reaching for the baby. Casey handed him to Claudia, feeling utterly drained.

"I need…" Mark turned toward the battle to see the A.N.G.E.L.s winning. The ratio now seemed to be one Heavenly Angel along with one human A.N.G.E.L., to one demon. He could hear the military cadence of a snare drum in his ears from several areas in the field, as he also heard his fellow A.N.G.E.L.s join in a song of praise to God.

"No, you need stay. She need you," Claudia told him, as she got up with the baby in her arms. "You want to go to hospital for checking?"

Casey nodded. The fact that the second one needed resuscitated terrified her beyond words. She wanted to make sure he was okay.

"I call ambulance already," Ana Maria explained.

Mark looked toward Heaven and saw the clouds begin to part. "The God of Angel Armies is always by my side," he prayed. "He is the one who is, who was, and who is to come – the Almighty One! He will never leave us, nor forsake us. He stands beside us today as we fight. Father, I pray for those brothers and sisters who are fighting at this moment. I pray You will give them the strength to win. I pray You will put Your hands of protection around them. I pray You will keep all of us safe. I give You every believer in this field, from the men and women, to the children, to the newborns. Thy will be done."

Casey glanced around the field in front of them, watching as the evil, dark forces, ran down the hill away from them. As the Heavenly Angels chased them, more dark forces came in from behind. Casey let out a scream when she saw them heading toward the children and Leah.

The Angels still near Casey turned and streaked toward the children, while the other half chased after the retreating army. Demons and Angels were flying past them at high rates of speed, while the Heavenly Angels fought to keep everyone protected.

"Go, Mark. Help them," Casey said, feeling Mark wanting to go.

"Are you sure? If you need me –"

"You were here when I needed you," Casey cut him off. "Now, they need you. Go."

"I love you." Mark kissed her head. He gave her a hug before he gently slid out from under her, and ran to join the A.N.G.E.L.s when they ran past him toward the children. Now that Casey was taken care of, he needed to take care of the others. The A.N.G.E.L.s were not going to give the dark side an inch.

All Casey could do was helplessly watch while the battle dragged on for almost two hours. The A.N.G.E.L.s were beaten, battered, and beyond exhausted. They fought hard, until suddenly there was a loud clap of thunder that shook the entire mountain. The words boomed from above, "IT IS FINISHED."

In an instant, what was left of the dark armies fell to the ground, dissolving into piles of ash. There was a brief silence as everyone looked around, stunned. Then, as quickly as the storm clouds came, they dissipated, and the sun shone brightly around them.

"What happened?" Hawk asked the Heavenly angel standing beside him.

"He said it was finished," the angel matter-of-factly replied.

"For the moment, for a month, for a year, forever…what?" the Colonel asked the one next to him.

"He said it was finished," he echoed the other angel's response.

"Let's just assume that means for now and we'll get more information later," Derek said. "I am okay with that."

Casey took that moment to take a good look around. Much to her relief, all of the human A.N.G.E.L.s were still alive. They were badly beaten, but they all made it through. Casey, the babies, the children, the wives, and the A.N.G.E.L.s had all survived the attack.

The angel from Casey's dreamtime walked to her. He knelt beside her, battle wounds coating his body. He placed the angel necklace in her hand. "*Now*, it is finished. You will be free to live in Christ." Then he looked her in the eyes, as he rested his hand on the side of her face. "What is free in Christ, is free indeed. You have been freed by The Lord God Almighty. He is your protector. He will keep you and your children safe."

Casey closed her hand around the cross necklace, as a whisper of gratitude barely escaped her lips.

The angel placed his hand on her forehead, while he held the hand with the angel cross necklace, and said, "God bless you, daughter of The King. Your children will rejoice in His name and will follow Him all the days of their lives. Teach and train them well," he said, and stood up.

She watched as he, along with all the Heavenly angels took off, straight into the sky in streaks of light. They looked like bolts of lightning streaking toward the sky. It was almost like watching a reverse meteor shower.

As soon as they were out of sight, the ambulance pulled up and loaded Casey and the babies. They drove them to the hospital, with her holding one baby on one side and the other on the other side – both boys were sound asleep, oblivious to the battle that surrounded their birth. Casey took their cue and rested until they got to the hospital, where she was finally able to go to sleep, relieved they all were, in fact, safe and sound.

Chapter 10

Life Lessons

After several hours of deliberation, Mark and Casey finally decided on Jonathon Mark English and Jesse Allen English. Jonathon was the older of the two, with Jesse being the one Casey had to revive. Of course, Jonathon was named after her brother Jack and Jesse was named after Jesse from the fire department. The Mark and Allen were Mark's first and middle names.

After the doctor checked them out, he said both babies were healthy. He said they were 'strong little guys any parent would be proud of.' He stated the reason Jesse had to be revived, was because his cord wrapped around his neck during the birth.

Casey felt blessed to have both boys. She knew God would take care of them and she was excited to see what God had in store for them.

*   *   *

The A.N.G.E.L.s from around the world got together for a night of celebration when Casey was released from the hospital. The celebration lasted late into the morning hours as they all discussed missions past and memories of former A.N.G.E.L.s. There was a lot of laughter, encouragement, along with tears shed for those lost to them.

Around mid-night, Casey couldn't hold it in anymore, and asked, "With all of the stories shared, it seems to me that there is going to be a problem here within the next several years."

"Which is?" Hawk asked.

"Well, I know I'm new to this, but if people pass and no one steps up to take their place, won't the A.N.G.E.L.s die off? And if so, won't the balance of power shift? Wouldn't it be pertinent to work on building the teams *now* instead of waiting to see what happens?"

A dumbfounded silence hung in the air.

"I'm just saying," Casey continued. "The darkness didn't have to kill us off on the mountain. At this rate, they only have to wait until we die. Not to seem morbid or anything, but realistically that isn't going to be very long into their timeline. Has anyone thought of rebuilding the teams, and starting the ones that have completely died? Those are the regions that need them the most, yes?"

"This is true," Sun Yun, an A.N.G.E.L. from Asia, agreed.

"We know God knows everything and already has a plan in place. We also know that for every one of us taken, another has to step up to carry on. We all know we have a call to duty we have sworn to perform, but what happens if we don't take the initiative and train new people?"

"Then we die," the Colonel said somberly. "And the A.N.G.E.L.s die with us."

*   *   *

Over the next couple of days, the A.N.G.E.L.s discussed how to rebuild the teams, especially those units who no longer existed. As a group, they brainstormed and prayed, asking God for direction.

By the time the teams left for their prospective areas, they were excited about what possibilities the future held for the A.N.G.E.L.s. They each had some ideas on how to grow their teams. And those near the areas whose teams were non-existent, had ideas on how to get them started again.

*   *   *

Over the next two years, they would periodically hear from other A.N.G.E.L.s through the world. It was an encouragement to hear about the growth of the teams. Casey was excited to hear that the Australian group picked up Charlie, along with a couple of his friends – who he was able to lead to the Lord as well.

Also during that time, the babies grew. Casey had to admit the stress levels reached major proportions throughout the twenty-four months. However, with Derek, Mark, and the Colonel's, along with Claudia and Anna-Marie's help when the men went on missions, she survived it. The boys were identical. They had Mark's blond hair and build, along with Casey's green eyes. Their facial features were a good mix of both of them, though. They were solid, stocky little guys. While Jonathon was more outgoing and open, Jesse was quieter and kept things more to himself – which was a complete opposite of their namesakes. Even though they were complete opposites, they were extremely close to each other.

There were many memories granted along the path – one's Casey cherished and held close to her heart.

"Your turn," Mark sleepily jostled Casey when he heard Jonathan whimpering.

Casey slowly got up and glanced at the clock – five o'clock in the morning. The babies were about eight months old by that point. Casey thought sure they would be able to sleep through the night by this point. The schedule was wearing thin on her.

"You know as soon as one goes, the other one will take off," Mark hinted for Casey to hurry up.

She took a deep breath and nodded, before sliding on her slippers and robe, and padded out to the kitchen. She put their formula into the microwave. By that point, making bottles was almost mechanical. She would do them both before grabbing two clean diapers and the wipes, and then heading back into the bedroom.

At that point, Mark would have the first one awake – which was usually Jonathan – in his arms, ready to go. Casey would have to go wake Jesse to feed him. It was easier when everyone was awake, because then they could cry and Mark and Casey wouldn't feel bad if they woke someone.

As much as she dreaded waking up at five in the morning, she enjoyed the quiet time they had with the boys. Seeing their little, but growing bodies, in Mark's large hands, melted her heart every time. He would even change the diaper of whichever baby he fed when they finished with their bottle.

In listening to the wives of the other A.N.G.E.L.s tell her multiple times that their husbands didn't do a thing to help out, Casey knew she was blessed beyond measure. The women explained their husbands stated they worked so their wife could stay home and care for the children. While she understood what they were saying, she was grateful Mark didn't share in their theory. Mark helping the way he did, allowed the boys to bond with him in a way they may not have been able to had he followed in the other husband's footsteps.

As time went on, Casey enjoyed the privilege of raising those two strapping young men. They watched them get their first teeth, get their first haircut, touch their first animal, hear them speak their first words – Jonathon's was 'papa', while Jesse's was 'mama.' They even got to help them take their first steps.

"Okay, we'll do Jonathan first," Mark said with Jonathan in his arms, while Jesse was playing on the rug in the middle of the floor with a baby jungle gym.

Mark and Casey sat with their feet together, but their legs straight, facing each other. "Okay little buddy, it's time to begin to spread your wings." Mark kissed his head.

"Are you sure you want to do that?" the Colonel asked as he walked into the living room from the kitchen with a yogurt in hand.

"Yeah, why not?" He looked up at him, confused. Jonathan stood wobbly in front of Mark, with him holding Jonathan under his arms.

"They are contained for now. Once you help them walk, it could get dangerous. Nothing will be sacred."

"Yeah, you could be chasing one, while the other one will run the opposite way and get in trouble," Derek pointed out.

"I would *assume* with four adults keeping an eye out, that they shouldn't be able to get into *too* much trouble," Casey said, as she looked from the Colonel to Derek.

"Uhhh, I don't think our opinion is going to matter in this case." Derek pointed toward Jonathan, who decided he was tired of waiting and took his first steps by himself. He stood between Mark and Casey with a proud grin on his face.

"Ohhhh, look at you!" Casey clapped. She put her hands out. "Come here, sweetheart."

Everyone watched, as he swayed a bit before he bravely took another step. With how sturdy he was, he went to fall, but then found his balance. Then he looked up at Casey with a grin again, while the tears slowly fell down her cheeks.

Mark shook his head with tears in his eyes as well. "Wow," was all he could get out.

The Colonel crouched beside him, dipped his spoon into his yogurt and put it out for Jonathan. "You, my man, deserve a treat for that."

Jonathon happily took the smooth tasting strawberry yogurt reward before he reached toward the Colonel's cup.

The Colonel stood. "Not yet. We need a little more from you. When you're done, if it's all right with your mommy and daddy, I'll give you some while your brother works for *his* reward."

"For right now, why don't you go give mommy a hug," Derek suggested, watching him from the couch.

Jonathan turned toward Casey and took a step. This time he fell on all fours.

"Why didn't you catch him?" Mark looked at her, slightly irritated.

"Watch," Casey said, keeping an eye on Jonathan.

At first, Jonathan had a pouty look on his face. He looked up at her as if he was going to cry.

"You're okay. Try again," Casey encouraged.

He looked around for a moment, deep in thought. Then he reached over and pushed himself up with his hands, using Casey's leg for a brace. She turned him so he faced her before she put her arms out once again for him to walk toward her.

He reached for her hands before he practically stumbled the last three steps into her arms. Cheers erupted from the men as she hugged her little boy.

"Great job!" She smiled in encouragement. She looked down at him, while he looked at her with a grin. "We are proud of you. Want to go see daddy now?"

He looked toward Mark for a moment before he turned toward the Colonel, who still had the yogurt in his hands.

Mark smirked as he got off the ground. "I think he wants yogurt." He picked Jonathan up into his arms, and said, "Great job, little buddy. We're very proud of you. You want some yogurt now?"

"Papa," Jonathan said, slapping his hands on Mark's cheeks.

"Yes, I am your daddy.

"Papa!" He giggled.

"Here, this is too cute for me to break up. I'll go get some more." The Colonel smirked, as he went to give Mark the yogurt. "I know when I'm outnumbered."

"Actually, why don't you go ahead and give him his yogurt. I want to help Jesse too," Mark said, and passed Jonathan over to the Colonel. With Jonathan on the Colonel's lap, he fed him the yogurt. Mark sat back down with Casey, with their feet touching and legs extended. "Next?" He nodded toward Jesse, who was on the floor behind Casey.

She reached over and tickled Jesse's tummy. "Looks like it's your turn." He giggled, and smacked one of his toys on the jungle gym.

His eyes danced, as he watched the toy swing over him. "No, need to do some work, little one," Casey encouraged. She moved his jungle gym over. As soon as she did, his bottom lip trembled and he looked up at her. "No, no, none of that." When she picked him up, he wrapped his arms around her neck and rested his head on her shoulder.

Mark crossed his arms with a smirk. "Oh, he's good."

"He's not getting away with it." Casey shook her head. "I'm letting him *think* he got out of exercise for the moment."

"Since we're taking a break, can I ask why you let Jonathan fall and didn't help him back up?" Mark asked.

Casey rubbed Jesse's back. "A couple reasons. One thing to keep in mind is that children learn their reactions from their parents. If a child falls, or does something, they look toward their parents. If they panic, the child will panic. If they make it seem like no big deal, then the child will follow suit."

"Interesting." Mark nodded in understanding. "Never thought about it that way."

"The second portion is a bit more of a life lesson."

"Oh really?" Derek raised an eyebrow.

"Yep. God, like a parent, sometimes allows us to fall so we know how to pick ourselves up. If He caught us every time before we landed, we wouldn't know how to get up on our own when we stumble. We also would not know how strong we really are, and how much we can take. Just like children, we are stronger than we think. When we get pampered by life, what do we do when we fall? We look to someone else to help us up."

Mark looked at her with a hint of surprise. "Wow, I'm impressed."

While she continued to talk, she set Jesse down on his feet with her hands under his arms. "When we're allowed to walk on our own, with The Father watching of course, we can do things we never thought we could." Jesse took a couple of steps with Casey's hands still under him. "Even if we fall," she said, and removed her hands, "we know He is still watching over us."

Jesse took another step, and then promptly fell on his bum. He looked toward Casey, who gestured for him to get up. He then looked to Mark for help.

"You can do it," Mark encouraged.

"Here," Derek got up and went into the kitchen. He pulled out the jar of baby food bananas. He grabbed a spoon before he went back into the living room. He then crouched down next to Mark and opened the lid. As soon as he did, Jesse's head snapped up toward Derek. "Yep, it's your favorite." Derek winked with a smile, as he took a bite of the bananas. Casey wrinkled her nose at it, knowing the flavor of it was less than desirable – especially for Derek, who hated bananas.

Jesse's bottom lip trembled again as if he were going to cry.

Derek shook his head, taking another bite. "Nope, need to come and get it before I finish it."

"Taking one for the team, eh?" the Colonel chuckled, as Derek's face slightly flinched on the second one.

Derek forced a smile again as he looked at Jesse. With a sweet tone to his voice so Jesse wouldn't understand, he explained, "It was a bit chunky."

Jesse pushed to get himself off the ground, but his legs were tangled, so Casey readjusted them. "Now try," she encouraged, positioning his feet on the ground. She looked toward Mark and winked as she said, "Sometimes we just need a little encouragement and an adjustment, before we get the courage to stand firm."

Jesse pushed himself up using Casey's leg. He stood there, he wavered for a few moments before he looked at the valued reward in Derek's hands. "You can do it," Derek cheered him on. "Come on, little buddy. It's waiting for you."

Jesse looked from Casey to Mark for a moment deciding what to do.

When he looked back toward Derek, Derek said, "They're not going to help you. If you want it, you have to work for it like Jonathan did."

Jesse looked toward Jonathan, who was sitting comfortably on the Colonel's lap indulging in his yogurt, before he took a determined step forward.

"Grab him!" Casey scrambled forward, but thankfully Mark caught him before he landed face-first on the ground.

"What happened to letting him fall?" Mark asked, scooping him off the ground.

"Not to the point that he gets a bloody nose. Watch his trajectory and make an educated decision on those that will be a helpful fall, or those that will be a detrimental to progress fall." Casey took a breath, calming her nerves before she said, "Put him back where he was when he went to fall, and let him try it again."

"How do you know which one is good and which one will hinder?" Mark asked, setting Jesse upright again.

"How can I explain this?" Casey silently prayed for clarity. "If you almost drowned when you were young, you would be terrified of water from that point on, right?"

"Right," Mark said.

"And rightly so," Derek added.

"But," Casey continued, "if you went to swim, and you slipped under the water, maybe even hundreds of times before you learned to swim, but came back up, you would not be afraid of water, right?"

"More than likely not." Mark shook his head, as Jesse stood there debating in his head whether he was going to go forward.

"The difference here is when Jonathan fell the first time, he had the cushion of his bum, so it was like him slipping under the water. When Jesse went to fall the second time, potentially it would have scarred him, and he would never have wanted to try it again. Now he also knows if he goes to fall too hard, he can count on his dad to catch him," she pointed out.

"Interesting." Mark nodded in understanding as he kept an eye on Jesse.

Jesse debated one more time before he turned toward Mark again, and took another step forward. "You can do it." Mark smiled with his hands out toward Jesse. "Only a couple more steps."

Jesse took three more strong steps before Mark took him into his arms and hugged him. Jesse hugged him for a moment, and then he remembered the bananas in Derek's hands and reached toward Derek.

Mark chuckled, handing Jesse over to Derek. "Yeah, I see how you are."

Derek took him over to the couch and set him on his lap, feeding him the bananas. "Good job, little buddy."

The Colonel chuckled regarding Derek's aversion to bananas. "At least you didn't say, better you than me."

"Hey, I'll make the sacrifice for my nephew." He shrugged. "It could have been worse."

"You're just lucky he doesn't like sweet potatoes or green beans as much as he likes bananas," Mark said, helping Casey off the floor with a hug.

"Thank the Lord for small favors," Derek said in a sigh.

<u>Chapter 11</u>

The Flu

One day, while Casey was getting everyone's breakfast ready, the boys were in their highchairs and the men were watching the news…she felt it! She covered her mouth as she ran for the bathroom.

"Casey?" Mark looked up from where he was sitting on the couch. He shut the stove off and went into the bathroom with Casey. "Oh wow." He shook his head as he crossed his arms. "Are you okay?"

"I don't…" Casey shook her head. She threw up a couple more times. "Oh, yuck." She shuddered, resting her head on the side of the toilet bowl.

Mark crouched next to Casey, and moved her hair out of her face. "What's wrong?"

"I don't know. I suddenly felt sick."

"Maybe you should go lay down for a bit. I'll finish breakfast."

Casey nodded, so he helped her back to their bedroom to lie down. Her head spun out of control, so she curled up on the bed with her eyes closed and eventually drifted off to sleep.

*   *   *

Throughout the next few weeks, she was sick off and on. The men were all worried, so she finally went to the doctor.

"So," the doctor said, leaning back in his chair, "¿Qué pasa? What brings you here today?" They picked a doctor who was bi-lingual, so Casey knew for sure he understood what she was telling him, and vice-versa.

"Over the last several weeks, I've had the flu. I've been throwing up, really tired, and even sometimes dizzy. I know it's going around and I –"

He cut her off, "Could you be pregnant?"

"Doctor," she looked at him like he was crazy, "I'm thirty-nine years old. I'm a mother of two-year-old twins. If it wasn't the stress keeping me from getting pregnant, it would be my age. Isn't menopause right around the corner?"

"We will see," he said with a knowing smile. He wrote a couple of things down on the chart as he asked questions, "When was your last menstrual period?"

"I don't remember. A couple of months ago, I guess. It's been messed up since the twins were born."

"And, are you and your husband sexually active?"

She blushed. "We are."

"Once a week? Once a month?"

"At least a couple times a week."

"Have you been using any form of birth control?"

"No. Like I said, we've been getting up there in age. Mark is even older than I am. We really didn't think it was needed."

He chuckled, shaking his head. He cleared his throat before he said, "I am going to have blood drawn for a test. I think your flu is pregnancy."

Casey looked at him in wide-eyed shock. "No way. Doc, give me a break here! I have two-year-old twin boys! I'm thirty-nine! That means I'll be forty when it's born."

He laughed. "Baby doesn't care. Just wait. Nurse will be here in a few minutes to take blood. I will call you tomorrow with results, yes?"

"Yes." Casey nodded. She wasn't sure how to take this news. *She was almost forty after all!* She could not imagine this would be safe. Not to mention the fact that they would have three children, three and under.

The nurse went in and took a vial of blood before Casey was allowed to leave. She went home, still confused as to how she felt. If she was pregnant, then it would be a relief because she wouldn't have something worse, but on the flip-side, would she be able to carry this child safely? But, then again, she felt it would be wonderful to give Mark another baby of theirs.

When she got home, the men were watching the soccer game on the TV, while the twins were asleep in Mark and Casey's room where their cribs were. She had another horrid thought. *Where would they put them all?* Casey shook her head and sighed.

"What is it?" Mark asked, looking at her as she stood in the doorway shaking her head with her arms crossed.

"Um, you're going to think this is funny, but...." She looked up and started crying out of frustration.

"What?" He stood up, scared. He went over and put his hands on her arms, looking her right in the eyes. "What did he say?"

"Mark," she shook her head, tears running down her cheeks, "I might be pregnant."

"*What*?!" They all three looked at her, stunned, as Derek and the Colonel stood up in shock.

"I know! Trust me." Casey shook her head again. "He'll call tomorrow with the results."

Mark stood there, visibly rattled. "You *are* serious."

All she could do was nod, tears streaming down her face. The emotions of the last hour finally caught up with her.

"Come here. Sit down." Mark ushered her over to the couch, while Derek slowly sat back down in his chair, and the Colonel sat down on the other end of the couch. "Tell me *exactly* what he said."

"Well, he asked me what I was feeling and I told him. Then he asked me if I could be pregnant. Mark, I'm too old to be pregnant, right?"

"You? I'm forty-two!" He shook his head. "Kind of thought those little guys retired by now."

Casey would have laughed if she wasn't so confused. "I mean, I'm happy if I am, because then it'll mean there's nothing else wrong with me, but…." Her voice faded.

He nodded in understanding. "Yeah."

"And, where are we going to put them all? We kind of have a full house as it is."

"We can add a second floor to the existing house. They do it all the time here." Mark shrugged. "That's not a problem. We'll get the help of the other guys."

"Actually, that would be appreciated," Derek said. "With the little guys, it's been kind of loud at night. If I have a vote, put the Colonel and me upstairs with our own bathroom, and you guys take over all three rooms down here."

The Colonel nodded. "I agree. Then you can have your room back."

"There, problem solved," Mark smiled, satisfied, doing his best to keep her calm, even though he felt like he was going to throw up.

"But —"

"I knew there was another one of those there," Mark said.

"But, will I be able to safely deliver this little thing? I'm not young anymore. Having the twins at thirty-seven was pushing it. I can't imagine what this is going to do to me to deliver at forty."

"I'm sure they'll keep a close eye on you. We'll just pray, and let God handle you and the baby."

"And, what if it's twins again?"

Mark's heart skipped a beat in fear at the thought. "Um, let's not go there right now. We'll plan for one at the moment." As much as Mark loved the boys, two sets of twins scared him to death. It was hard enough going through it once…he couldn't imagine going through it twice.

"What are the others going to say?"

"I'm sure they'll be happy for us. Yes, we got started a little late, but think about it – we have a full family, along with the love of our lives."

Casey hugged him. She wanted to know everything would work out. "So, this is okay?"

"Yes." He held her close, as he glanced at Derek and the Colonel. They had the same concern on their faces Mark was feeling, but they didn't want her to see it. They didn't want to worry her, seeing the shape she was already in.

"God doesn't make mistakes," Derek encouraged. "If this baby was meant to be, then God will protect you *and* it."

Casey nodded, wiping the tears off her face.

The Colonel rested his hand on Casey's shoulder. "We'll be here too. Don't worry,"

Casey nodded in response. That was all she could do at the moment. She was an emotional mess. And she would probably stay that way until the doctor called the next day.

*   *   *

The men, along with Mexican A.N.G.E.L.s – who were at that point all located within a couple of miles of each other – got together the next day at their house to make a plan to add two more bedrooms upstairs along with another bathroom. Regardless if Casey was pregnant or not, the twins needed a room, so they were going to do it anyway.

167

That afternoon, Casey was making lunch when the phone rang. She glanced nervously over at Mark, who looked up as the guys were drawing out the plans in the living room.

"You want me to get it?" Mark asked.

Casey nodded. She was nervous and struggled inside as to which way to react.

"Bueno," Mark answered the phone in their bedroom. "Yes, this is Mark, her husband…Yes, I understand…Of course…Thank you for your help…Yes…God bless you too. Thank you," he said, and hung up.

As he walked back into the living room no one moved. The men sat silently on the couch and chairs, watching Mark go into the kitchen. He turned the stove off, before he took each of her hands into his, facing him. "I love you with all my heart," he said, and kissed her lips, as the twins watched from their high chairs just outside the kitchen.

"But…?" she asked, looking into his eyes. She could tell by the look on his face there was more. However, she wasn't sure what the answer was by looking at him.

"But we *are* going to have another one."

Casey stared at him. The color drained from her face and her heart raced. By the look on his face, she was not sure how he felt. He rested his hands on the sides of her face, as she rested hers on his wrists. She looked into his eyes while the tears overflowed onto her cheeks.

"I love you. I love that we will have another gift from God made from the two of us," he said. "I love that we will have another chance to influence this little angel for the Lord. I am happy. I hope you are too." He wiped her tears away with his thumbs.

"I am, but –"

"But?"

"It's going to be stressful for a while. We will have three, three and under," Casey stressed, hoping he would understand her heart.

"I understand that. However, I'm pretty sure we have some uncles in there who will lend us a hand," he said, looking over her shoulder to the others in the living room for help.

"That, and the women and children. They help with these two. They help with the next one. Family sticks together," Juan reassured her.

"And, I already told you we're not going anywhere," the Colonel added.

Derek winked. "Yep. As long as I have one of the upstairs bedrooms to escape the rug rats once and a while, I'll enjoy uncle status, with the option of handing them back at the end of the day."

Casey had to laugh at that one.

"It's going to be okay, Casey." Mark smiled. "You are going to be okay. Our family is only getting another one." He put his arm around her shoulder as he turned her around to face the others. "They're behind us. Things are settling. The twins are growing. Little Jonathon and Jesse are looking forward to another playmate. Granted, we are probably going to have to take the little thing into protective custody for a while until we are sure they won't accidently hurt it. Know that they are all surrounded by love. They can't help but pass that on to this one." He rested his other hand on her stomach.

"Okay." She nodded. Then she turned to look at him. "Just so you know, I'm getting fixed at the birth so this doesn't happen again."

"I don't have a problem with that. Look at this as a blessing, not a curse."

"I am." She placed her hand over his. "This little angel was meant to be here."

"With us," Mark added.

"With us," Casey agreed.

*   *   *

Throughout the next three months, they stayed with Juan and Claudia, while the guys tore apart part of the house, and rebuilt and added an upstairs. They took out part of the living room to add the staircase. Since they were doing that, they also shrunk one of the bedrooms toward the back of the house, to make more room for a dining room area. They didn't have a table as of yet, but knew when they did, it was going to have to be an eight-seat table, due to the seven of them. The back bedroom was cut down by a third, but Casey didn't mind, because she knew it would only be for one child. Meanwhile, upstairs they built two bedrooms, and in the space left, they had a laundry room and a bathroom. Casey was impressed they not only got it all up there, but also got it all done over the course of only three months.

By the time they finished, the group was more than ready to move back into their home. While they appreciated the openness of Juan and Claudia to let them stay there, they wanted their own space.

When they got in there, though, they had a lot of cleaning to do. The deal was that the guys would do all the lifting and moving of furniture, as long as Casey washed everything down. They wanted to make sure everything was spotless before setting it in a clean room.

In order to do that, Casey headed upstairs first. She scrubbed the entire floor, while the guys watched and fed the twins. Then, she went downstairs to the Colonel's room first, and, as she cleaned things, they moved it upstairs. Next were Derek's belongings, followed by their bathroom.

After that was finished, she went down and thoroughly scrubbed their former rooms. When she finished, she scrubbed all the living room furniture and the appliances in the kitchen. The guys moved all the furniture into one of the bedrooms, as she washed them to keep them clean before she scrubbed down the living room itself. Then they moved the refrigerator and microwave stand into the living room so Casey could get into the kitchen. She scrubbed the floors, the cupboards – even the boxes and bags of food and the dishes – the counters, and even her cookbooks. The dust was thick, but everything was clean when they finished.

After that, the guys took off to go buy a table and chairs. Casey trusted Mark's sense of style. They usually agreed about everything anyway.

By the time they returned, Casey had the twins fed and bathed, and was playing with them on the rug in the living room. All of their floors were tile, so they had a huge area rug in the middle of the living room area to play with the boys.

Casey scooped up the twins and set them in their high chairs in the kitchen to get them out of the way. When the guys brought in the table and chairs, she had to admit she was impressed. It was a cherry wood set, but they even thought about the little ones and made sure the corners were rounded. The table itself was rectangular, with three chairs on either side, and a chair on each end. It was a stunning set. It also fit perfectly in the space they set aside for it.

Casey smiled, pleased. "It's beautiful."

"Glad you like it," Mark kissed her cheek, "because it's heavy, and we're not taking it back." He hugged her from behind as he rested his chin on her shoulder.

"We also worked on something else while we were at it," the Colonel commented.

"Oh yeah, what's that?"

He nodded toward the door. "Go look."

When Casey looked outside, she was surprised to see two twin bed sets in the back of the truck as well. "Um?" She turned toward Mark in question.

"They're two. Don't you think we should work on them getting into their own bed? Since they're getting their own room, kind of a two-for-one thing," he said, hopeful.

She thought about it for a long moment, while Mark held his breath. She finally looked at him and said, "You're right. If we do it now, they should be settled enough by the time the baby is born."

"That's what I was thinking."

"Not to mention that we wouldn't have to set up both cribs again," Derek added. "We know we'll have to set one of them up for the new little one, but this way it's *only* one."

"And we can get the boys used to giving their bed to the baby," Casey said, thinking through all the aspects. "Good thinking, guys."

Mark sighed in relief, as did the other two. They were a little nervous about making this big of a decision without talking to her first. When it came to the kids, Mark and Casey talked about everything so they were on the same page. It worked for them, and they even caught the boys already trying to play them against each other. They also caught them using Derek and the Colonel, so communication was a high priority in the house.

The first couple of weeks of the twins adjusting to the bed were rough – mostly with Jonathon rather than Jesse. Jonathon was one of those kids who just went, and went, *and went*…until he crashed. Once he was asleep, though, he was out. Jesse, on the other hand, drifted off to sleep, but he was a light sleeper so they had to be careful with him.

After the first couple of weeks, things began to smooth out, and they set a routine for the boys so they went down easier. Casey was pleasantly surprised things were going so well. The boys were sleeping in their own room. They were successful in their potty training, and were dry for over a month by the time her due date came around. She had also let them help decorate the baby's room, so they felt they were a part of it. And at night, they would say a prayer for the baby while they each had a hand on her stomach. Then they would say goodnight, and kiss her belly before they went to bed. Casey was sure it made them feel good knowing they were protecting the baby with their prayers.

If they didn't get a chance to say their prayers though, it was rough. If Casey was out, for example, and they had to go down without her home, the guys had a hard time getting them to stay in bed. After a couple times of this, the group talked about it and came up with a plan to alleviate the issue. They had Mark, the Colonel, or Derek put them to bed during the last month, so the boys got used to the guys putting them down. That way, when she was in the hospital, the boys wouldn't be a problem to put down for naps or bedtime. The boys would say their prayer, and give their kisses before heading into the room, where one of the guys would read them two stories before tucking them in for their nap or bed for the night. When they were tucked in, the guys would take their hands and pray with them. They would also alternate whose turn it was to go first, so one boy wasn't always waiting for the other.

They did their best to keep things as fair and balanced as possible, keeping in mind the differences between the boys. Where that came mostly into play was when it came to discipline. They both had their time-out chairs, but Jonathon had a little more of an outspoken temper, while Jesse's was more of an undercurrent. Jesse was the one Casey would have to keep an eye on. While Jonathon blatantly disobeyed, Jesse did it almost without anyone knowing he was doing it.

However, when it came to getting their feelings out, Jonathon would yell and scream, while she had Jesse sit down and color. She had him pick out a color for what he was feeling, and he would scribble it on the paper. This allowed Casey to see what he was feeling, even if he could not verbalize it. They had a color code to his feelings: blue meant sad; red meant mad; yellow meant happy; purple was upset; while green meant he was troubled by something his brother either did, or got to do, that he didn't. There were also colors for the adults. Orange meant he wanted his dad, pink meant he wanted to spend time with Casey, while the Colonel's color was teal, and Derek's was light blue when he wanted to spend time with them. In the meantime, with Jonathon, he was allowed to say whatever he wanted, as long as he talked about it. While he was good at verbalizing his feelings, he needed to get control of his temper.

*   *   *

Finally, her due date arrived…and went. She was so disappointed. She was uncomfortable, and more than ready to have the baby. So, a week after the baby's due date, Mark and Casey talked to the doctor about it. He said since she was three centimeters, they would go ahead and induce in the morning if she didn't start on her own. In doing it via induction, it allowed them to prepare Derek, the Colonel, and the boys. The two guys were going to stay at the house to tag team the twins. This worked out pretty well since Jonathon was close to the Colonel, and Jesse was close to Derek. They could each take custody of one of the twins, and the boys would be comfortable as well.

That morning they took a bag for Casey, along with one for Mark since he was going to be staying with Casey the entire time in the hospital. Their theory was that the boys would probably pitch a bigger fit if Mark came and went, rather than if he just stayed, and they all came home at once.

When they arrived at the hospital, the nurse came into the room for information and asked some questions regarding the pregnancy. Then, she hooked up the IV, along with adding the Pitocin – which would begin the induction. She also asked Casey if she wanted an epidural, to which Casey promptly responded 'absolutely!' Casey didn't have any medication with the twins, and the doctor said an induction is a harder delivery. He said it was faster, but he said the contractions were harder.

Casey was worried, but blessed by an easy delivery. She didn't feel a lot of the contractions due to the epidural, so when it came time to push, that was her hardest struggle. However, in looking at the delivery of the twins, the doctor knew the baby was going to come fast, so he was ready.

By the time the epidural kicked-in, with the medicine at its fullest effect, the delivery was in full gear, which didn't leave time for it to wean when it came time to push. The baby came into the world in only two hours. Casey was grateful when she finally heard the baby cry, and heard the doctor say, "It's a girl!" He held her up for them to see the little thing crying loudly. Poor thing just wanted to be warm.

The month prior to delivery, they set-up the hysterectomy to take place the day after the birth so she would have a day to recover before having the surgery. She wanted it done while she was in the hospital so she would be able to heal from all of it at one time.

Mark shook his head, smiling, as he held the baby in his arms. "She's absolutely beautiful, Case." She looked so tiny next to his huge body. It reminded her of when he was holding the twins. It amazed her how gentle he was with them.

He leaned down so Casey could look at her. "What are we going to name her?" She asked.

"Oh no." The doctor shook his head and sighed, remembering the last time. "You have not decided yet?"

Mark shook his head. "Not yet. We've been a bit busy to think of names."

"Let me know when decide," the doctor said, as he worked on getting the placenta and afterbirth out by pushing on, and manipulating her stomach.

"What do you think?" Mark asked.

"Well, we could keep the 'J' idea, and name her Jillian, Jennifer, or maybe Joy?" Casey suggested.

"Or we could go with something completely different."

"This is going to be another day-long debate, yes?" The doctor smirked, as he placed everything into a bowl the nurse had waiting.

Mark chuckled. "Possibly."

Casey shook her head. "No, I want to go into the surgery knowing she has a name."

"Then, what do you think?" Mark asked, as the nurse took the baby away from him to take to the nursery to clean her up, get her measurements, etc. He sat down on the side of the bed. "Any ideas?"

"Well, I'd say Jacqueline, after Jack, but it gives me flashbacks of *her*."

"Yeah." Mark shuddered. "Let's not do that one."

"What are the Colonel and Derek's middle names?"

"Um…" Mark looked up, thinking. "The Colonel's is Matthew, and Derek's is, um…oh, yeah. Derek's is Thomas."

"Hmmm, those are of no help."

"Well, yours is Ann. We could do something with that."

Casey shook her head. "Naaa, that's too common here."

"Your daughter is a beautiful angel whatever name you give. You are proud, yes?" The doctor said, coming back from cleaning up and washing his hands. "They move you to your new room shortly. Good job." He shook Mark and Casey's hands.

"And tomorrow we are taking care of the other issue, right?" Casey asked, hopeful.

"Oh yes." He nodded with a smile. "No need to worry. They will come get you at seven in the morning. You will be out by nine at latest."

Casey smiled and shook his hand as well. "Thanks."

Mark smiled when it hit him. "Angel!"

"What?" Casey asked.

"Angel. She's our little angel. What about Angelina Christine, to remember Angelina?" He asked, hoping Casey would understand that it was not meant to hurt her, but an honor.

The more she thought about it, the more she liked it. She looked like an Angelina Christine, so she nodded. "I like it."

"Really?"

"I do," Casey agreed. "It fits her."

"So, her name Angelina Christine English, yes?" The doctor asked, looking at both of them.

"Yes," they said at the same time.

"Sounds good." Doc nodded in approval. "I will see you in morning."

Through the day, they were able to relax as they filled out the paperwork regarding the baby and the surgery for the next day. While Casey was a little nervous to know he was actually going to be cutting her open, she knew she would rather get all the pain over at once, and she trusted in God to keep her safe.

Chapter 12

R and R

The next couple of months were quite an adjustment. While Casey recovered from the delivery and the surgery, she looked out as best she could for little Angelina. Her brothers loved her dearly, but they didn't know their own strength, so one of the adults had to be around her at all times. Since Casey couldn't move around much at first, the guys gave her custody of Angelina while they tag teamed the twins – who were giving them a hard time for the first several months with all of the attention given to Angelina.

With the addition of the little one, it added a bit more chaos to a sometimes already crazy house. There were many nights where Mark and Casey were up at all hours, not only in feeding her, but with the boys and their night terrors or them having to go to the bathroom. Casey was thankful the Colonel and Derek were upstairs so they could get some decent sleep. At least they knew *someone* was getting sleep in the house.

Finally, about six months after she was born, Angelina's schedule settled, and the boys finally adjusted, making things manageable around the house.

Mark looked up at the others, as they sat around the table one night for dinner, while Angelina was asleep on the couch in her carrier. "All right."

"All right, what?" Casey asked, nervously. "Or do I not want to know?"

"Well, I think it's time we planned our first family vacation. We've adjusted. We've gotten the boys through the tough part." At the mention of them, they looked up with a smile, so he winked at them. "So, before Angelina heads into the rough stuff, I think we should go. Also, I do believe our four-year anniversary is coming up here in a couple weeks." He looked over at Casey.

Casey nodded, still not too sure about the idea, but she wanted to support Mark.

"So, is this for you guys or us too?" Derek asked, trying to follow Mark's line of thinking.

"You are our family," Mark pointed out. "We don't go anywhere without you. That's a given."

"Well then," he sat back in his chair with a smile, resting his arm over Jesse's chair, which was right beside his, "Where are we going, '*Dad*'?"

"Well, I was thinking," Mark started, as a grin of excitement formed on his face, "Mexico has some absolutely wonderful places to go. There are beautiful beaches all over. However," he held his hand up to stop the Colonel who went to open his mouth, "the more I thought about it, the more I liked the idea of going to the Yucatan Peninsula area. Cancun is close to there, and so are the Mayan Ruins. We could go all over up there. What do you say…two weeks?" He asked, looking around the table in anticipation. "When we get back, we can look around for work too, since our money's going to be low by then."

"Ahhhh," Derek sighed. "The reprieve is over, eh?"

"Yep. Sorry, man. We're actually going to have to work for our money now."

"Well, we worked for it before, but we've exhausted it," the Colonel pointed out. "We knew it was going to happen sometime."

"So, is that a yes? One last fling, so to speak?" Mark asked, looking around the table.

Everyone nodded in agreement.

"Sounds like fun," Derek said. "Of course, taking these little guys into the water is where the adventure is going to be."

"No." Casey shook her head. "They'll play in their rafts, while one of us holds Angelina. That's an easy one."

"Then, we're in agreement?" Mark asked. As everyone nodded again, his grin got bigger. He pulled out an itinerary along with bus tickets, and passed them around the table. They couldn't go by plane, since legally they were not supposed to be there. They were working on it, but not everything had gone through yet.

As he passed the information around, the excitement grew. The hotels and some tours were even booked. All they had to do was pack, show up, and enjoy. It sounded like a blessing and a relief!

*   *   *

Getting to the hotel by bus wasn't as bad as Casey thought it would be. The boys slept almost the entire way, and once she fed Angelina she was out for the rest of the trip as well.

The scenery on the drive was stunning. That was one of the things Casey loved about Mexico. Funny thing was that one could almost tell when they changed states, because the terrain slowly shifted as well. It seemed like each state had a type of terrain all their own.

When they arrived, they settled into their hotel rooms. The Colonel and Derek had an adjoining room with the others. In Mark and Casey's room, there were two queen-sized beds. This allowed the twins to have one bed, and Mark and Casey to have the other one, leaving Angelina in the portable crib. The Colonel and Derek's room was identical to Mark and Casey's, and was adjoined to their room by a door.

"Okay, here's the deal," the Colonel said, when he and Derek walked into their room at about seven that night. "We have decided to let you two go out on a date for the dinners while we're on vacation."

"And in return?" Mark questioned the generosity of his teammates.

Derek shook his head. "Nothing. We've been through a lot over the last four to five years. We don't mind watching the little tikes.

Even Angel over there is getting easier to feed. Just so you know, though, you will owe us big time if she fills her diaper," he warned. "Those are just wrong!" He shuddered, as everyone laughed at him.

"We look at it this way," the Colonel said, leaning on the doorway between the rooms with his arms folded, "the last time you two had any decent amount of time alone together was about four years ago when you guys went off for those three days. Since then it's been a roller-coaster, which we're used to, but in a marriage, you need some time."

"And you are not going to get it after we go back either," Derek pointed out. "You've got three little ones now, along with adding work to it. Time is going to be precious."

"That's incredibly sensitive and generous of you guys! Thank you!" Casey smiled in excitement.

"Enjoy it while you can, eh?" Derek ruffled Jesse's hair as he clung to Derek's leg. "It's going to be few and far between for the next ten years at least."

"That's true." Casey nodded, looking at her little ones.

*   *   *

That night, Mark and Casey enjoyed a wonderful dinner along with a walk on the beach. Casey was looking forward to the dinners they were going to share, along with the walks on the beach for the next two weeks to come. She knew she would treasure those moments when it was just the two of them for the next several years until the little ones grew.

Over the first week, as a group they enjoyed several tours, as well as taking a couple days for the ruins themselves. Mark got Casey a camera a couple of years ago, much to her delight, and she was having a great time with it on the trip. She captured not only all of the beautiful scenery, but the ruins, the people, the culture, along with some great moments with the kids and guys as well. She enjoyed watching the boys running around everywhere, experiencing new things left and right. Angel even had fun discovering grass. Multiple times throughout their trip, Casey reflected back to when she was sitting in the lake watching the children and their parents while she camped with the fire department. It seemed that while she thought there was no way she was ever going to have a family, God had a different plan…and for that, she was grateful.

"Um, we've got company." Derek leaned over to the Colonel as they, along with Mark and Casey, watched the kids play for a little bit at the ruins. It was at about the middle of week two.

The Colonel scanned the area. "Are you sure?"

"I've been keeping my eyes out for a couple days, since I started seeing them at more than one place. I wanted to be sure before I told you and set off any alarms."

"Where?" Mark asked, looking around.

Derek walked in front of Casey and Mark. With his arms crossed, he said, "There's a blond-haired man and a brunette who are together, along with a Latino woman and dark, reddish-brown haired man. They are over my left shoulder, facing the pyramid."

They looked over, to see the blond man mostly blocked by the reddish-brown haired man, as the women stood in front of them.

"You sure?" Casey squinted to get a better look at them. They were in the shadow of the pyramid and the afternoon sunlight was shining in Casey's eyes. Even in shielding her eyes, she couldn't get a clear view of them.

"Would I tell you if I wasn't?" Derek looked at her, taken aback she would think otherwise. "Just keep an eye out. I don't think they're dangerous, but I *have* seen them watching us multiple times."

Mark nodded, memorizing as much of them as he could see for future reference. He knew he would get a better look another time.

In her nervousness, Casey leaned down and picked Angel up, much to her dismay. Angel grabbed a couple handfuls of the grass on the way up, not wanting to let go.

Mark chuckled as he slowly, but gently peeled it out of her hands. When it was out, he cleaned her hands with a wet-wipe. After he finished, he called the boys, who came over right away. They held onto Mark's hands and the group walked away, with the Colonel and Derek keeping an eye on their 'company.'

*   *   *

The rest of the day, Casey paid closer attention to her surroundings. Even though she saw them a couple more times, despite her best efforts, she still wasn't able to get a good look at them. It was a little frustrating, because they seemed like they were familiar to her, but she couldn't tell if it was from an Air Force base, from all her traveling, or from any of the places she worked.

That night, the Colonel and Derek watched the kids, while Mark and Casey took off for dinner. They went to one of the local restaurants recommended to them by the receptionist at the hotel. She said not a lot of tourists would know about it unless they asked a local, but the locals loved it.

When they went into the restaurant, Casey immediately noticed the low lighting and the wonderful scent of fresh-made Mexican food. The decorations were traditional of the ethnic culture and customs. There were tables and booths, along with high-back wood seats. The restaurant looked to be around twenty to thirty years old. Casey was impressed when the waitress took their order within minutes of them being seated.

"Well, my bride." Mark took one of Casey's hands when the waitress left. She brought them their drinks, along with chips and salsa. "How do you like our second honeymoon?"

"I love it." Casey's face lit up. "And having the kids, Derek, and the Colonel here makes it that much nicer. I also like that we have our time alone at night. I have to admit that I'm going to miss this when we go back."

"Yeah, me too, but we do get our bedroom to ourselves again. Who says we can't have dates of our own when the kids go to bed at night?"

"Sounds like a great idea." Casey smiled as she thought about it. Then she watched as Mark's eyes drifted from her, to right behind her, as he watched someone approach the table. She turned to see where he was looking. A gasp escaped as she covered her mouth.

"Ya know, I said to myself, 'that looks like her, but it can't be. She's presumed dead. That can't be her, with what looks like children and a husband,'" Jesse McFadden said, standing right beside their table with his arms crossed, looking down at her.

"Jesse!" Casey about choked on her drink as her face went pale.

"So, I said to Rob and Jessie, 'Guys, doesn't that woman look a lot like Casey Carter?' And, you know what they said?"

Casey shook her head, not sure what to say. Glimpses she saw of the group went through her head, and realized one was Jesse, one was his girlfriend, Carol-Anne, and the other two were Jessie Martes and Rob Katz from the fire department. She sat there in shock as her worlds collided right before her eyes.

"They said they didn't think so, because the two boys looked like they were yours, and they didn't look like they could be any more than three or four years old, which, coincidently, was when you disappeared. So, in order for that to be true, you would have had to meet this gentleman before then." Jesse leaned on the table with his hands, looking at Mark. Then he turned back to Casey and continued, "Then there's the lovely little lady. The new one, who can't be any more than a year, but who looks like the spitting image of you. You guys looked like a happy little family, along with your bodyguards there," he added. "So, I said to myself, 'self, she wouldn't do that. Because if all of that was true, then: a) she would have had to keep the relationship she had with him secret from you

– which I didn't think we had any; b) I couldn't figure out why she would have disappeared the way she did, in the middle of the night; and c) why she wouldn't have made a *single* phone call over the course of the last *four years* to let me know she was okay.' So, when we saw you walking down the street to this place, we followed you. The others are at a table over in the corner. Would you like to go say hello, oh re-incarnated one?" he asked, glancing at a table across the restaurant before he looked back down at Casey.

Mark cleared his throat before he reached up and turned Jesse's chin toward him. With as big as Mark was, Jesse didn't want to start anything with him, even as angry as he was. "I'll answer that for her," Mark said.

Jesse stood tall, with his arms crossed. "By all means, go ahead."

"Will you sit down first, so the scene you are generating will look less conspicuous? I will even sit on the same side as she is, so you can have this side by yourself if it will make you more comfortable."

He nodded, so Mark moved to Casey's side of the booth, blocking her in. Jesse sat down on the other side, with his hands rested in front of him on the table.

"You see, it's tricky," Mark started.

"Oh, please try to clear this up," Jesse snapped, crossing his arms in irritation.

"Due to her brother's past connections, she was being hunted down by some not-so-nice people."

Jesse suddenly sat up and narrowed his eyes at him. "I *know* you," he said, realizing who was sitting across from him.

He nodded. "Yes, you do."

"Where's your accent?"

"It was false."

"You're Colby. And the other guy, Clinton, your brother? He was…he's here too, isn't he? He is one of her body guards."

"In actuality, he is. I am her husband, but the guy you know as Clinton is one of her bodyguards, and so is the other guy."

"Explain! *Immediately*!" he growled, as the anger flashed in his eyes.

"You need to calm down, or you're going to blow it," Mark warned.

"Blow *what*?"

"She's a protected witness," Mark explained. "In order to protect her, we had to hide her deep, and also keep a couple guys on her."

"Is this true?" Jesse asked Casey.

In a manner of speaking, yes, it was true, so she nodded.

"Anyway, you guys were drugged in Australia. When we found out, we pulled her to keep her safe."

"Is that what happened? I thought it was bad food."

"The drugs were in the soda. Does this make any sense to you?"

"In a way," he said, lining up things in his mind. "So," he turned to Casey and asked, "Are those *your* kids?"

Casey nodded.

"And yours?" he asked Mark.

"Yes," Mark said.

Jesse sat back in his seat, studying them for a moment before he asked, "Do I get to know their names?"

Mark thought it was a reasonable request, so he gave him the information. "The twins are Jonathon Mark and Jesse Allen, and the little girl is Angelina Christine."

"Really?" He looked up at her in surprise.

"Yes. You were never far from my thoughts. Jonathon was named after one of my brothers, Jack, while the other was named after my other brother, you," Casey explained. "Their middle names are his first and middle name." She nodded toward Mark.

"I see." Jesse rested his chin on his hand, deep in thought. "So, is that why I was never able to find a store called 'Leighton Western Wear' in Colorado…or in the U.S. for that matter?"

"Yes," Mark said.

Jesse thought for a moment as he leaned on the table. He could see how everything lined up, so he asked, "You're safe here?"

"Yes, she is. We've been watching you guys watching us for a couple days now, but we weren't sure who you were," Mark explained. "You were never close enough to make a positive ID."

"And, are you happy?" he asked her.

Casey reached over and held Mark's hand. "Very."

He shook his head, unsure where to go from there. "What do I tell *them*?" he asked, nodding toward the table. "I don't want to put her in danger. If Jessie or Rob figure out that she's really here, it'll fly through the company."

"That's true," Mark agreed, contemplating the situation. "We can't let them know."

"But I'm sitting here talking to you. What do I tell them?"

Mark thought about it for a couple minutes before he shrugged. "We tell them the truth."

"But –" Jesse and Casey both objected at the same time.

"We don't tell them *everything*," Mark rolled his eyes, cutting the, off. "Come on, work with me here. We only tell them that she is in the witness protection program. We don't tell them anything else…for safety reasons."

Jesse thought for a moment before he nodded in agreement. He and Mark headed over toward the other table, where Mark sat down with them to explain the situation.

While he was gone, the waitress delivered Mark's and Casey's meals, so Casey lightly snacked on it until Mark could get back. Her stomach was in knots as she wondered how the conversation was going. After a few minutes, her nerves couldn't handle it anymore and she had to go to the bathroom. She signaled to Mark where she was going, as she headed toward the bathroom. He nodded before turning back toward what looked like a heated conversation.

When Casey was washing her hands, two men walked into the bathroom. "Um, wrong restroom," Casey said, drying her hands as she kept an eye on them.

In one swift motion, one of the men wrapped his arm around her neck, while he covered her mouth to squelch her screams. Meanwhile the other one injected something into Casey's arm.

As the black cloud took over, she felt herself being slid into a burlap bag that tied at the top before being flipped over the shoulder of one of the guys. They took her out through the kitchen, which was adjacent to the bathrooms. They said something about linens when they went out the back door.

She knew she needed more help than ever. Not only were Mark and Casey alone at the time, but Mark didn't even have anything to go on. To him, it must have looked like Casey just disappeared. She knew her only hope was that they would send for some sort of ransom.

Chapter 13

The Great Escape

When Casey gained consciousness, she was blindfolded and handcuffed with her hands above her, around a thin metal pole, while she hung helplessly below. Even though her hands fell asleep, she was almost afraid to move. With not being able to see anything, she had no idea if someone was standing right in front of her, or anywhere near her.

As she sat there, she listened. She used what she learned about seeing what was not there, and feeling what she could not see, so she could anticipate the enemy's movements. That's when she remembered God's words from Joshua 1:9, *"Have I not commanded you? Be strong and of a good courage; be not afraid, neither be you dismayed: for the Lord your God is with you wherever you go."*

"I know, and thank you," Casey whispered to the Lord. Then she listened, but only heard noises one would hear in an industrial plant. She did her best to tell if there was anything she could smell. It smelled musty, yet she smelled a cleaner of some kind as well. She also knew she was sitting on concrete, so she was going to assume it was a business. She heard washers and dryers in the distance. *Could it be a laundry company of some kind?* It was then she remembered the guys told the kitchen people something about linens. It had to be a laundry service of some kind – maybe an industrial one? Casey wished she stayed conscious in the transition. It would have given her a clue as to what was going on around her.

She listened, but didn't hear evidence of any other humans in the immediate area. So, she slowly stood, continuously on alert to any noise. She didn't want to get taken by surprise. When she was in a semi-standing position, she leaned her head back near her hand and slid the blindfold up. That way she could still see, but if she needed to, she could drop it back into place.

Much to her relief, there was no one around. She didn't hear any voices or movements of any kind either, so she kept that in mind while she cautiously scanned the area.

She discovered a camera down the hall facing a larger room, but nothing near her. She looked for any doors or any windows for a potential escape route. She noted the couple of windows toward the top of the building as a possible exit. Since she was in a hallway that was about two stories tall, she would have to use the fire escape ladders located inside the building to gain access to the windows. It would be a possibility, but she couldn't figure out how she would get down once she was outside.

Proverbs 3:5&6 ran through her mind, "*Trust in the Lord with all your heart, and lean not on your own understanding; in all your ways acknowledge Him, and He will make your paths straight.*"

"I trust you," she whispered, looking toward Heaven. "Please don't leave me."

Isaiah 41:10 then went through her mind, "*So do not fear, for I am with you; do not be dismayed, for I am your God. I will strengthen you and help you; I will uphold you with my righteous right hand.*"

She nodded in understanding. "Okay, here we go." She looked at the pole she was handcuffed to. It was about an inch and a half piping, probably used as a water pipe. In looking at it, there were portions she may be able to get loose if she tried hard enough.

She slid the blindfold back down and sunk to her knees in prayer. She hung from the pole with her knees about three inches off the ground, feeling sick to her stomach. She needed help to get out of there, but the only help she could foresee was going to be from God.

While she prayed, she heard a couple men talking in the distance. When they came closer, she pretended to still be unconscious. One of them jerked her head back by her hair, but she stayed limp. When she didn't respond, he swore in Spanish, and the pair walked toward the room where Casey heard the washer and dryers. She waited a few minutes to make sure they were gone, before she stood back up and lifted the blindfold again. She knew if she was going to get out of there, she had to do it while they thought she was still unconscious.

She studied the pole for the weakest point. That's when she saw one portion was already dented, so she quietly slid down there. She put her feet on the wall and placed all her weight on her wrists. It hurt, but nothing compared to what Jackie did to her…and she wasn't about to voluntarily go through that again without a fight.

She pushed her feet with all her might, while she yanked the opposite direction with her hands to the point that her wrists were bleeding. When she saw the blood drop, she stopped and looked at her wrists. *The blood may make it slippery enough, that…*she looked down at her hand. It took a bit of gymnastics to do it, but she got her foot up and slammed it into her thumb until she finally heard it snap. She groaned and writhed in pain for a few moments, breathing through until it was tolerable.

Casey purposely broke her thumb in order to slip her hand out. She quietly groaned in pain for a couple more moments, struggling to compose herself. Then she pushed her thumb into her hand. She seethed in agony for a several more minutes, praying God would keep the men away long enough for her to get free.

She pulled and tugged until her left hand finally dragged out of the handcuff, enabling her to be released from the pole. She used the blindfold to tie the loose cuff around the wrist that still had the other one on it so it wouldn't dangle or jingle. Then she looked both ways and ran for the ladder that would take her up the stairs. She jumped and reached for the ladder. Grasping onto the bottom rung, she pulled herself up. Her adrenaline kicked-in, so she didn't feel the pain anymore. She stayed focused on the window at the top of the ladder that would be her escape, her freedom.

She was halfway up when the rattle of the metal ladder brought the two men running from the laundry room. One of them fired his gun at the steps above Casey.

"Bájate!" One of them ordered.

Casey stopped dead in her tracks. They wanted her to go back down.

"Bájate ya!" He ordered again.

Casey slowly climbed back down the stairs while they kept their guns trained on her. She didn't want to, but if she was going to have any chance at all of getting out, she had to somehow get rid of them to do so.

"Please help me, Father," Casey whispered, slowly making her way to the bottom.

In response, she remembered the verse in First Corinthians 16:13, *"Be on the alert, stand firm in your faith, act like men, be strong."*

"I will," she whispered.

When she reached the bottom, one of them jerked her off the ladder. He wrapped his arms around her body, as the other one reached up and snatched the necklace off her neck. It had the angel and cross pennant, the key, and the tiny vial of liquid on it.

Casey shook her head, beside herself, while the man held it up in the air cackling in laughter. She snapped her head and glared at him. He kept laughing, which made her even angrier. She couldn't take it anymore, so she took a deep breath, kicked her legs up, and kicked him in the face. It sent him back several steps into the wall, where he fell to the ground. When she came back down, she took all her weight and ran her foot down the leg of the guy holding her, landing square in the middle of his foot. She heard him groan in pain. She also heard and felt the crunch of the bones in his foot shatter. He momentarily let her go. When he did, she spun around and kicked him in the head. It stunned him, so she used the moment to grab his gun from his belt. She took the gun and aimed it at him. He looked up at her and rammed himself into her midsection. He hit her so hard, it knocked the wind out of her as they went to the ground. He grabbed her wrists and aimed the gun toward the wall while he tried to gain control of Casey.

Casey took a second and slammed her knee into his groin. When he curled up in pain, she scrambled to her feet and aimed the gun at him. With the gun between them, the man leapt toward her. In a split second, the gun went off as he stood right in front of her.

She gasped as she looked down at the gun and then back up at him, in shock. She saw blood pour from his nose and mouth, as he stared at her, wide-eyed. She shot him directly in the heart. She shuddered at the gurgling noise he made before he collapsed to the ground in front of her, lifeless.

Casey stood there staring at the dead man with the smoking gun in her hand. A man whose life she had just taken. She shook her head, beside herself. She was a life-fixer, a paramedic…not a killer! Suddenly, she felt the arms of the man she slammed into the wall wrap around her. She gasped in surprise.

Something told her to look down. When she did, she saw the necklace dangling from his hand. As his hands and arms tightened around her, it cut off her air. She glanced at the gun, knowing it was her only option. As she prayed for forgiveness, she turned it toward the man and shot him in the stomach.

When he released her, he took a step back. She spun around and closed her eyes before she fired at his head. She wasn't going to give him a third shot at her.

The blood was immense as it splattered on the wall behind him. His body crumpled onto the floor, and Casey waited only a moment before she ran and snatched her necklace, slipping it into her pocket. She tucked the gun into the back of her shorts, and jumped for the metal stairs. She quickly glided up the staircase to the window. When she got to the top, she unlatched the window and slid it to the side to open it.

She slipped out and stood up, happy to be breathing fresh air. She took one last look at the two dead bodies she'd left behind, before using one of the fingers of her left hand to slide the window closed. She didn't want to see what she did anymore. She wanted to forget it, and get back to her husband and babies.

As she maneuvered the building, her thoughts drifted. She couldn't believe she had to take a life, let alone two. She struggled with the fact that she made a conscious decision to look into a man's eyes and fired a gun at his head. The Colonel was right, when it was her life versus his, she found the strength to pull the trigger. She knew she would eventually have to find the strength to work through her thoughts and feelings, and also knew it would be an act of God for her to navigate it successfully. For the moment, though, she needed to get herself out of there in case there were any more people around.

In getting out of the building, it led her to her next problem. She had to figure out where to go from there. The roof was about two feet above her head. The other option was the drainpipe, located about ten feet to her left.

"Seriously?" She looked to the Heavens. As she prayed through both options, she decided the drainpipe was the better of the two because she wouldn't have to climb. Her thumb was going to cause some problems for her in climbing, so she prayed she wouldn't have to climb anywhere else before she could get to safety.

Casey looked for the cameras. There was one on each corner of the roof, but they were facing out toward the parking lots, so she slowly made her way over to the drainpipe. Casey sighed, shaking her head. "I'm too old for this."

She looked at the drainpipe, placing her bare feet on either side of the pipe. They took her shoes and socks off while she was unconscious, leaving her in her dark green shorts and black t-shirt. She was grateful for the dark clothes, but really wished she had her tennis shoes.

She shimmied down the drainpipe, using her feet to hold most of the burden, taking the load off her hands. She would move her feet down, lock them into a secure position before sliding her hands down, slowly inching her way downward toward the ground.

When she reached the bottom, she looked around. Making a mental note as to where the cameras were positioned, she closed her eyes for a moment in prayer for direction. When she opened them, she saw the tree line. It was dark enough outside that if they came after her, they wouldn't be able to see her. So, she checked the cameras one more time, confident she could land herself between them.

As she stood there, First Chronicles 16:11 came to mind, *"Look to the Lord and His strength; seek His face always."*

"I'm trying, Lord. Please guide my feet to safety. Please give me strength to make it to where I need to go to get home to my husband and babies."

Then, she took a deep breath and ran with all her might. When she got to the trees, she turned to see if anyone saw or heard her. Since she didn't see a sign of anyone else, she took off deeper into the woods. While she knew she wasn't safe by herself, she also knew if she could somehow get to another business of some kind or a home, she could get help.

She ran for what seemed like hours, afraid to stop. Her feet were bleeding from the tree roots and underbrush. She also had multiple cuts on her arms and legs from tree branches. After a while, she didn't even feel them…she just kept running.

"Lord, give me strength," she begged. Her body was shaking, and she didn't think she had it in her, but she used her training and pushed beyond what she thought was possible.

Finally, after four or five hours, she felt safe enough to rest. She leaned against a tree, looking around, breathing heavily. She had no idea where she was. Last she knew she was in the Yucatan Peninsula. However, by that point, she could be anywhere. She didn't have any money or direction. The one thing in her favor was that over the years she had become fluent in Spanish, so she would be able to explain what happened to her to get the help she needed if she ran into the right person.

"Okay, Father, which way?" Casey asked, looking toward Heaven. "Where do I go?"

She waited for a few moments, but didn't hear anything…absolutely nothing…so she continued in the direction she was headed. "The Teacher is always quiet during the test, huh?" she said to the Lord. "Okay, I'm going this way. Please provide help somewhere?"

When she thought sure she was going to pass out, she saw a gas station. She knew she looked a mess, but she needed help.

It was still dark, so there were very few people around. Even in the middle of the night the heat and humidity made everything sticky. She heard the crickets chirping, along with the men at the gas station talking loudly while they drank.

She snuck around to the bathroom and slipped in. She cleaned her feet and wrists, re-wrapping the one with the handcuff so it looked like she had a bandana around her wrist. When she scrubbed her feet, the pain came back with a vengeance, and they bled all over the sink. Casey shook her head in frustration before she left the bathroom. Mexico at night was dangerous. She knew whatever her next move was, it would have to be a careful one.

She saw a phone next to the OXXO – the local convenient store. As usual, there was no phone book. She growled out of aggravation and looked toward Heaven. "A little help here?"

When she looked back down, she saw two men watching the pumps, while a woman was inside the OXXO. At night they close the doors, so if one bought anything it would be passed through a small window, for safety of the worker.

Casey opted for the woman, so she went over and knocked on the door. When she came over, Casey greeted her before she asked her in Spanish where exactly she was.

The woman looked at her suspiciously for a few moments. She decided Casey might be okay to talk, so she told Casey she was in Veracruz.

Casey thought through the mental map of Mexico, realizing that Veracruz was west of Yucatan, but right in the middle of Yucatan and Tequisquiapan. She tried to think about what to tell her. Realizing the truth was her best option, she finally explained what happened to her. Casey showed the woman her hands and feet, and asked her for help. The woman looked around to make sure no one else was around, and that it wasn't a robbery attempt, before she finally let her in, locking the doors behind them.

She had Casey sit on the floor behind the counter to get a better look at her injuries, while Casey told her where she needed to go, and asked if she could have access to a phone. Casey knew she could call Mark, since she knew his cell number. It took the woman a few moments before she finally agreed.

Mark let it ring, probably because he didn't recognize the number. She called again. This time he answered after the third ring, before it was about to go to voicemail. "Bueno," he answered.

"Mark?"

"Casey?" He asked, relieved and nervous at the same time. She heard him call the others so they could listen. "What happened to you? Where are you?"

"According to the lady next to me, I'm in Veracruz. As far as what happened to me, I was kidnapped from the restaurant. Are you guys close enough to come get me?"

He sighed. They were still in Yucatan and they had all three children with them. It was over three days since they had heard from her, and were about to leave. They didn't have a thing to go by and were afraid for her, but they had to get the children to safety.

"It's four o'clock in the morning. It's going to take us several hours to get there. Where can you go while you wait?"

Casey asked the clerk what she thought she should do. When the woman shrugged, Casey suggested, "I could call the police and have them take me to the station."

"No," he said firmly. "That might not be safe. Is there a way you can stay there until we can get there? Can you stay in the shadows around, so no one will get suspicious?"

"I can, but I don't know if the people who took me will find me before you do."

"How far away from them are you?"

"About five hours, running on foot."

"What direction?"

"I don't know for sure. I just ran."

"All right." He let out a frustrated grunt. "Okay. We can only go as fast as the vehicle will take us. You don't have any money either, do you?"

"No."

"Let me talk to the clerk," he finally said.

When the woman got on the phone, they spoke solely in Spanish. Mark explained what Casey said was true, that she was kidnapped, and that they were on their way to come get her. He asked if there was any way for her to help Casey get to a local hotel where he would call for a room for her. She said her mother was coming to pick her up in an hour, so that she could drop Casey off then. While he had her on the phone, he got her number at the store, the number of a local hotel, and exactly what town in Veracruz they were in. Then they hung up.

He called back about twenty minutes later, giving the woman the name of the hotel holding Casey's reservation, which he reserved on Juan's debit card. He also told her there would be a monetary award for her silence regarding this situation. All she had to do was give him her first name, and he would leave it at the hotel in the form of a message the next morning. She did, and then they hung up. All she had to do was hide Casey for the next forty-five minutes until her mother came.

*   *   *

Thankfully, her mother was on time, and there were only two or three customers before she was off work. She had Casey wait in the car with her mom, while she changed shifts with the morning person.

When the girl got to the car, she explained everything Mark and Casey told her, especially in regards to keeping silent about Casey or where they were to take her. Then her mother drove Casey to the hotel without question. If there was money involved, she was all for it.

Casey got checked in easily enough. The office itself was closed, so they had to conduct their business at the window. The night manager explained he and Mark spoke, and that Mark would come and sign for the room at checkout, but until then the room was being held with a debit card number. Since they were at a window, he couldn't see Casey's feet, so to him, Casey seemed like one of the many other girls he had seen come through on a daily basis.

Before she left, Casey asked him if he had any hydrogen peroxide. He thought it was a strange request, but he got it for her anyway. Casey explained she cut her wrist and wanted to make sure it was clean. She avoided letting him see her left hand. It had a broken thumb injury that was over six hours old, and the wrist, along with that part of the hand, was sliced-up from the handcuffs.

Casey went to her room, which was on the third story facing out toward the road. Mark did that for safety purposes, it was the standard whenever they stayed in a hotel. When she got to the room, she took a long, hot shower. She watched as the dirt coated the bottom of the tub, oozing down the drain. She scrubbed her hair three times before adding any conditioner to it. She also scrubbed every inch of her body she could. When she got to her wrists, she washed the blindfold in the water, and then she set it outside of the shower to dry. Afterward, she let the water run over her wrists. While the right one still had the cuff attached, the left one looked worse by far. In looking at her hand, she knew she would to have to re-break it to set it. She cringed at the thought of it, but relieved that it was the worst of her injuries.

When she finished, she scrubbed the tub, and then sat down to clean her feet. She only used soap and her hands to do so since the bottoms of them were so tender. It took her over forty minutes in the shower, but when she finished, she was clean. She took a deep breath as she looked over at the hydrogen peroxide. She sat on the side of the tub wrapped in a towel, with her feet still in the tub. She cringed as she poured hydrogen peroxide over her feet. She took long, deep breaths, as the stinging was instantaneous upon contact with the bottom of her feet. She gritted her teeth and groaned as she watched the foam form around the many cuts and gouges in her feet. She pounded her good hand on the side of the tub, unable to handle the pain.

Finally, after about twenty minutes, she dabbed the bottom of her feet with a clean towel. She turned so her feet were out of the tub, resting on a clean towel on the floor. Then she turned and got down on her knees. She held her right wrist over the tub and then poured a portion of the peroxide over the wounds. She almost screamed, but bit her lip to stop herself as it instantly foamed. The pain of doing it that way was excruciating, but she knew it was the fastest way to get them clean. After the pain calmed down, she poured it over her left wrist. She dropped her head on her right arm, breathing through the pain. She thought for sure she was going to pass out before it was over.

Just when she didn't think she could take any more, the pain finally calmed down on all the wounds, but it was still high. She waited about fifteen more minutes, before she slowly and gingerly made her way to the bed and collapsed…relieved to be on a bed, clean, and alone. It didn't take long before she gratefully passed out.

*   *   *

Casey got woken up several hours later by a knock on the door. It was two short, followed by three more. She waited a minute before she heard two short, followed by one more. She knew it was Mark and the Colonel, so she slowly swung her feet around the bed and stood up. As soon as she did, she fell to her knees in immense pain. It was as if someone sliced her feet with a knife as soon as she stepped on them.

She proceeded to crawl to the door, getting there as fast as she could, gritting her teeth in pain and agony. When she was almost there, she heard two short knocks followed by three more again. She pulled herself up into a chair, slightly pulling the curtain back to see the Colonel standing right in front of the window. Both he and Mark had concerned looks on their faces. The Colonel knocked again, two short, followed by one more, so Casey reached over and unlocked the door. She then opened the latch, while she stayed on the chair wrapped only in a towel. She was in so much pain, though, she didn't care what she had on, she was grateful they were there.

"Casey." Mark looked down at her, shaking his head. He knelt down and picked her up. As he moved her over to the bed, the Colonel stopped him. While the Colonel locked the door, Mark stood in the middle of the room with Casey in his arms. "What?" Mark asked.

The Colonel went over and showed Mark Casey's feet in the mirror. He shook his head, beside himself, and then set her down on the bed. "Casey?" He knelt beside her.

"Can you…?" She asked, holding up her right hand with the handcuff on it.

"I got it," the Colonel said, taking out a small packet of tools. He sat on the side of the bed and rested her hand on his lap. When he looked at her left hand, he shook his head. "What happened?"

"To what?" Mark went around to the other side of the bed. He took the blanket and spread it over her body, pulling her arm out so he could look at her hand. "This looks broken." The more he looked at it, the more events lined up in his head as to what Casey did. He looked from her right hand to her left. "Did you break this yourself?" He asked. Casey nodded. "To get out of those?" He nodded toward the handcuffs. Casey nodded again. "Oh Case." He shook his head, beating himself up inside for not protecting her. She was his responsibility at the time, and his alone. He dropped the ball…*again.*

"You're free." The Colonel slipped the handcuff off her wrist and shook his head at the shredded mess of her skin.

Mark brought the Colonel back to the situation. "We need to get her out of here. Derek's meeting us at home, but –"

"Yeah," the Colonel agreed. "You need to get dressed. We've rented a car. It's right outside."

Casey nodded as she slowly sat up. "My feet," she moaned. They finally stopped burning and downgraded to continuous pulsating, stabbing pain.

"I know, but we have to do it. Can you go to the bathroom to get dressed?" Mark asked.

Casey looked from her feet, to him, nervously, so he picked her up and carried her to the bathroom. He set her on the toilet lid and grabbed the blindfold to wrap her wrists when she finished.

It took her several minutes to get her clothes on. Afterward, she called to Mark for help. He carried her back to the bed and set her down. He took off his shoes and socks and gingerly put his socks over her feet in order to cover them from any other infections. He figured they were only worn for several hours during the drive, so he decided they were clean enough. Then he took the blindfold and tore it in half, wrapping her right wrist with half of it. Then he looked at her left hand and shook his head.

"Want me to do that?" the Colonel asked, not sure who it would cause more pain to in order to re-break it – Mark or Casey.

"Yeah." Mark nodded. He took a pen by the phone and stripped it of its insides. He brought it over and knelt beside her on the floor, while the Colonel sat on the side of the bed.

"I'm not going to lie to you, this is going to hurt," the Colonel said, felling around her hand to figure out where it needed to be broken. He did this many times over the years. While he hated it, he knew it would be better for her in the end. "Ready?"

Casey slowly shook her head before she nodded. She held her breath, bracing for impact.

"On three. One…two..." he said, and cracked her thumb, snapping the bones in not one, not two, but in three different areas. As he did, Casey gritted her teeth and squeezed Mark's hand with her right hand while she tightly shut her eyes.

"Breathe," Mark coaxed. "Come on. You need to breathe or you're going to pass out. Breathe Casey."

"Maybe it'll be better for her if she passes out," the Colonel commented. He took the pen shell from Mark and used it as a splint, resting her hand on his lap as he strapped the pen shell to her hand using the other half of the blindfold. "There," he said, satisfied. Then he looked up at Casey and said, "You *do* need to breathe, Casey."

"I..." Casey groaned. "It hurts!"

"I know," he said, compassionately looking down at her. "You have to suck it up though. We have to get out of here. You did good about getting away, now we have to get you to safety. Can you let Mark carry you to the car so I can check you out of the room? We used Juan's card to reserve the room. I have to pay in cash so he can get it back and leave your friend from the OXXO her gift for helping you."

Casey nodded, so Mark wrapped her in a sheet and carried her out of the room. When they were out of the room, the Colonel went around and cleaned up. It didn't take long for him to find the gun on the dresser. He pulled the magazine, noticing there were four bullets missing. "Oh Casey." If they were missing, and Casey was the one with the gun, he could only imagine where the other four bullets went since she didn't have any in her. "You did it, didn't you," he sighed, shaking his head again. He slipped the gun into the back of his pants and tugged his shirt over it, making a mental note to mention it later to Mark.

After that, if there was any blood anywhere in the room, he cleaned it with the towel that already had blood on it. He then grabbed a clean towel and cleaned off any areas that would potentially have any fingerprints before he threw both towels, along with the hydrogen peroxide, into a trash bag, and grabbed the bag, taking it out with him. He, of course, used his shirt to open the door so there would be no fingerprints. Then he headed down to the car and tossed the bag to Mark to burn later before, heading into the office to sign for the room and leave the money for the clerk from OXXO. He was back a couple minutes later. "Let's go," he sighed, glancing back at Casey.

Casey lay down on the back seat, resting her head on Mark's jacket with her eyes closed, hoping to go to sleep quickly. There were several areas of her body that were pulsating in pain, and she wanted it to stop so she could rest.

"Is she asleep?" Mark asked, as he pulled out of the hotel.

"Yeah," he sighed, shaking his head, "Poor girl."

"She got away, though." Mark proudly smiled. "I can't wait to hear how."

"Well, at the very least, she had to break her thumb to get it out of handcuffs. I give her credit on that one. She also had to use this," he said, pulling the gun out from behind him.

Mark glanced down at it before returning his eyes to the road. "How many?"

"There are four missing."

Mark sighed, shaking his head. "I wonder who did it *and* I want to know why. We haven't heard from anyone trying to get to her in over three years, until…" He suddenly sat up in his seat, alarmed.

"What?"

"I wonder…" he said, thinking. Then he shook his head. "No, he wouldn't do that."

"Jesse?"

"Yeah."

"What if it wasn't Jesse? What if it was one of the other three? And what if it wasn't *actually* them inside of them? What if they weren't in control of their actions?"

"You're thinking an Unnatural?"

"Maybe."

"Well then," Mark sat up, a little more on edge, "we'll keep a closer eye on the family from now on."

The Colonel sighed. "I remember when it was only one of them we had to keep safe. Now there are four."

"But look at them." Mark shook his head, smiling. "They're adorable…all of them."

The Colonel rested his chin on his hand, as he propped his elbow on the door. "I envy you some days, brother. You have a beautiful wife, along with three loving, adorable children. I'm just glad to be a part of it as well."

"It comes with a high price, though. We are not in a particularly safe country. And, we can't go back to America because we know her face is publicized there. She's still missing as far as they are concerned."

"And I don't think Australia is a safe place either. I'm not sure where Jackie's crew ended up after her demise."

"Europe is big," Mark suggested.

"No, they would have to potentially learn yet *another* language. I don't want to put them through that. What if…what if we sneak back into America? It's been four years. Her looks might have changed enough that if we're in a different state we may blend in."

"You think?" Mark asked.

"We can definitely make better money."

"Colonel, it's not about the money."

"But can we go to work, leaving them alone during the day, potentially putting them in danger? For all we know, it might have been a random act at the restaurant, or it might not have," the Colonel pointed out.

"Point well taken." Mark shook his head and sighed. "All I wanted was to give us a vacation."

"And, it was good and much needed. We have enough left in stash that you don't have to work for right now. You stay home, watching them, while Derek and I go to work."

"What's Derek going to say about that?"

"He'll be happy they will be protected. You know us – safety is number one. This is *your* family. In an indirect way we are too, but they are *your* flesh and blood and your *wife*. You have first precedence in any considerations. You have the most to lose."

Mark nodded in understanding. As Casey drifted the rest of the way back to sleep, she was relieved to know Mark was going to be home with them. She felt a sense of relief to know he was the one who would to look after them when they returned.

Chapter 14

Pandora's Box

"Bájate ya!" The man yelled as Casey was halfway up the stairs.

She looked toward the window and debated before she climbed back down. She knew she would have to get rid of them before she could escape, and hopefully before anyone else showed.

When she got to the bottom of the staircase, one man got his arm around her body, while the other one stood in front of her. He reached up and snatched the necklace off her neck, laughing. She took one look at him, holding not only the angel necklace and the vial, but also the key, and got angry. She knew she was responsible for those things. There was no way she was going to let him keep them. She took a second before she swung her legs up. Using the strength of the other man holding her to brace herself, she kicked the man holding the necklace back against the wall.

As soon as she came down, she took her foot and slammed down on the foot of the man holding her. She slid her foot down his calf muscle, landing square on his foot. She even felt the bones crunch under her weight.

He momentarily let go, and she kicked him in the head. Within an instant, a struggle ensued over the gun. This went on for several moments before they were both on their feet, and the gun was between them. In a split second, it went off.

Casey looked up to see the blood running down his face, and then he collapsed. She stared at him in horror for a moment before the guy she originally kicked, grabbed her from behind. She gasped in surprise. Then she looked down to see the necklace still dangling from his hand as his arms tighten around her, cutting off her air. She glanced at the gun, knowing it was her only option. As she prayed for forgiveness, she turned it toward the man and shot him in the stomach.

He took a step back as he released her, so she spun around and fired directly at his head. She wasn't going to give him a third shot at her.

Casey watched in sheer terror as the blood spattered on the wall behind him before it ran down the wall in streaks. She looked from the gun to the wall again…and screamed!

"Casey! Casey!" Mark yelled at her while he tried his best to wake her. "Case!"

Casey gasped as her eyes flew open.

Just then, there was a knock on the door, so Mark got up and let the Colonel and Derek in. "Another one, huh?" the Colonel looked over at Casey, who was still breathing heavily as she sat on the bed.

Mark nodded, watching her with his arms crossed, not sure what to do about the nightmares.

"Well, before she begins to wake the little ones, let's work through this," he sat on the bed with Derek and Mark.

Casey sat up to make room for them. She dropped her head in her hands, still shaking from the vivid nightmare.

Mark wrapped his arms around her and pulled her over to him. He kissed her head, and said, "Shhh, you need to calm down, honey. You're safe. You're home."

The Colonel studied her for a few moments. He saw the visions going through her mind once again. "Casey, we need to talk. You've had nightmares every night for a week. And, anytime any of us asks you about what happened, you shut down and brush us off."

Casey's mind swirled with the visions from the nightmare, along with the feelings of sheer terror, horror, and guilt.

"I found the gun in the room," he said, and watched Casey for her reaction.

Casey looked up at him, wide-eyed, as her heart pounded feverishly within her chest. *Did he know what she did?*

"There were four bullets missing. Tell us what happened, Case," the Colonel pleaded.

Casey shook her head as the tears rolled down her cheeks. How could she tell them she took a life…actually *two* of them? They would never look at her the same.

"We love you, Casey." Derek rested his hand on her knee. "You're not going to tell us anything we haven't already done ourselves. There is absolutely nothing you could tell us that will make us think any less of you. We've seen what you're capable of. We know what we trained you to do. We also know your heart," he said, calmly. "We know that whatever you had to do, you did in self-defense."

"How many were there?" Mark asked.

Casey looked up at him, terrified out of her mind. She half expected them to walk into the room in the shape she left them in.

Mark reached down and lifted her chin as he asked again, "How many were there?"

Casey's lip trembled. She didn't want to say out loud what she did. That would make it real.

"We love you," Mark said. "God loves you. He was with you there, and is still with you here."

Casey shook her head. How could God still stand by her after what she did?

"Rest assured, God was there," the Colonel added. "Jesus was standing there right beside you the entire time."

"How many were there?" Mark asked again. He figured if he started with simple questions, he would be able to pull more information later. It would at least give them a start to the puzzle.

"Two," Casey quietly replied.

"What did she say?" Derek asked. He thought he heard her say something, but it was so quiet he wasn't sure.

"She said two," Mark said, not taking his eyes off hers. He clarified, "There were two people?"

Casey nodded.

"Were they men or women?"

Casey looked down, tears flowing freely down her cheeks. Mark didn't let her go, so she was forced to look in his eyes. He kept his one arm around her, and his other hand on her chin. He faced her toward him as he looked deep into her eyes, struggling to understand what happened.

"Were they men or women, Casey?" the Colonel asked again. He knew what Mark was doing. If they could get enough information to piece things together, it might help her to say it all out loud.

Casey fought to keep her emotions under control. "Men."

"There were two men?" Derek confirmed.

Casey nodded.

"Case, there were four bullets missing," the Colonel pointed out. "Where are they?"

Casey vigorously shook her head. She didn't want to say it. How could she tell them she took two lives? She was a life-saver, not a life-taker!

"Where did the four bullets go?" Mark asked, still not taking his eyes off hers. If he could get her to trust him, to get lost in his eyes, he knew he could pull the information he needed.

Casey shook her head again.

"Casey, where are they?" Derek pressed. "There were two men. Are they both dead now?"

Casey jerked her head from Mark's hand as she spun toward Derek in horror! Her heart raced…her palms were sweaty…her face was flushed…and she practically felt her pulse pounding through her head!

Derek and the Colonel both looked at her wide-eyed for a moment, before Derek moved closer to her. He put both hands on the sides of her face, as he firmly, yet securely asked, "Did you kill those two men?"

Casey vehemently shook her head. She couldn't think. She couldn't focus. She knew what happened, but she was having a hard time believing it was true.

"Casey Ann English." Mark turned her face toward his, as Derek moved back to his spot on the bed. Casey was losing it and he knew it. He grabbed her face and kissed her with as much love as he could. If he could get her sidetracked, he knew he could get her to focus.

Casey took a moment before she kissed him back. After a moment, the man she shot in the head flashed through her mind as she heard the echo of the gunshot. She gasped as she pulled back. She stared at the wall, where she could faintly see the blood and chunks of flesh running down it. She gulped as her face went deathly pale.

"Look at me, Casey!" Mark yelled with his hands on the sides of her face. He tried to look in her eyes, but he knew she wasn't there. He dropped his head, shaking it. He used everything he could think of to bring her through this. He wasn't sure where to go from there, so he looked at the Colonel for help. He hadn't felt this helpless since Australia.

The Colonel shook his head, unable to give Mark any answers. He dealt with this kind of thing before, being in the military, but in dealing with it he was working by a different set of rules. Those were military people. Those were people who were trained to kill the enemy. While she was trained to defend and possibly kill the enemy as well, it was well engrained in her to heal. He knew it would be a struggle if she ever had to take a life, but knowing she did, and that it was possibly two…knowing how much she struggled during training about taking a life, he wasn't sure where to go either.

Derek looked at her, knowing she was in the middle of flashbacks. He saw it in her eyes multiple times throughout the week. He prayed for her, not sure which way to go. He had no idea how to pull out what happened. He knew though, if she could verbalize it, she might be able to begin to work through it.

He glanced toward Heaven with a silent prayer before he moved in front of her, beside Mark. He sat between her and the wall. "Casey," he took her hands into his, "we need you to come back to us from wherever you are. Your children need you. Your husband needs you."

Casey slowly shook her head, staring at the wall in a daze.

"What do you see?" He asked.

Casey didn't say a word. She just stared at the wall behind his head in shock.

He glanced at the wall, praying for intervention from God. He prayed God would allow him to see what she saw, so he could understand…that's when he saw it. He looked from the wall, to her, wide-eyed.

"What?" the Colonel asked, looking at Derek's ashen face. He looked at the wall, stunned, as he saw blood pouring down it with chunks of flesh splattered on it as well. "God, please help her," he whispered, knowing the vision was from God, put there to help the three of them get through to Casey…to understand.

"What is it?" Mark asked, looking up at the Colonel. He followed his line of sight over to the wall, where he saw what everyone else saw. He shook his head as his heart broke into pieces. He knew at that moment what she did. He dropped his head into his hands, doing his best to control the tears that formed at the brims of his eyes. He knew her heart. He knew her soul. He knew if she'd killed, it was a choice between her life or theirs…but he also knew if she made that choice, there was a struggle going on deep inside her.

"Casey," Derek cupped her face in his hands as he pointed it directly toward him. "I see it, Casey."

Casey looked at him, horrified. She could tell by the look on his face that he knew what she did.

"I see the blood on the wall," he said, calmly. "I know you killed those two men, didn't you?"

Her tears flowed in a steady stream as she looked up at him. Her body was shaking while the adrenaline coursed through her. She slowly nodded in response. She knew what she did. She also knew they needed to know.

"I need you say it," Derek coaxed. "I need you to admit it."

"I...." She shook her head. She couldn't say it aloud.

"You killed those two men, but it was in self-defense wasn't it? It was your life or theirs, right?"

Casey nodded.

"Case, there are four bullets missing, but only two men dead. You need to tell us what happened to those four bullets. I'm going to say numbers one to four, and I want you to tell me, in one word, where they landed. Can you do that?" Derek pushed. If he could get her to talk through it, even if it was only one word at a time, then it was a step in the right direction.

Casey gulped. She took a deep breath before she nodded. They needed to know.

"Okay, here we go," Derek said. "One?"

"Staircase," Casey said.

"It hit the staircase?"

Casey nodded.

"Who was on the staircase? You or the men?"

"Me."

He breathed a sigh of relief she was going to respond. "Good. So, the first bullet hit the staircase you were on?"

"Yes."

"We are going to work on that for a moment. As soon as I say another number, though, you need to give me one word for where it went, okay?"

Casey nodded.

"Okay, you were on the staircase. Were you trying to escape?"

"Yes."

"So, that was after you got out of the handcuffs, right?"

"Yes."

"Where was the staircase headed?"

"Up," she said, as the tension in her body eased, and the splatter on the wall slightly faded. "There were windows at the top of the staircase I would be able to crawl out of."

"So, that's how you were going to get out?"

"Yes, but they stopped me."

"By shooting at the staircase?"

"Yes."

Mark took one of her hands into his, relieved she was talking. He continued to pray for her, knowing they were only at the beginning. He knew she was going to need the backup as Derek moved further into the story.

The Colonel took her other hand into his, praying for wisdom and guidance for Derek. He knew Derek was moving with the help of The Spirit. He knew he was going to need the prayers of the guys if Casey and Derek were going to make it through this.

"I was about halfway up the stairs," Casey said, concentrating on Derek's face. If she stayed focused on his eyes, then she wouldn't look at the wall and see the blood.

"So, let me see if I have it, okay?" Derek asked.

Casey nodded.

"You broke your thumb, therefore releasing yourself from the handcuffs, and ran over to a staircase?"

"The staircase was metal and went up the wall to the windows at the top – kind of like a fire escape," Casey explained.

"Good job," he encouraged. "What else can you tell me about the building?"

"It was concrete, like a warehouse. It was a laundry service of some kind, I think."

"Good. Can you tell me how you got there?"

"Um, when Mark and Jesse went to the table, the waitress brought over our food," Casey said, not looking away from his eyes. There was something comforting in them that she needed at that moment. Her body began to relax as she went on, "After a few minutes, I had to go to the bathroom. I signaled to Mark where I was going as I went through the dining room of the restaurant."

"Good. Keep going," Derek coaxed.

"After I went to the bathroom, I was washing my hands when two men walked in."

"Into the women's bathroom?"

"Yeah. I told them they were in the wrong one. They didn't say anything though. One of them wrapped his arm around my neck and his other hand over my mouth to muffle my screams. Then the other one injected something into my arm."

"Do you know what it was?"

"No, but it knocked me unconscious."

"Can you remember anything at all between the bathroom and waking up?" Derek asked.

"I remember them putting me in a burlap bag and carrying me through the kitchen. They said something about linens to the staff as they went through."

Derek nodded in approval. "Good job. Making progress. What happened next?"

"I woke up blindfolded and handcuffed to a water pipe. My hands were around it and I was under it – that I could feel. I sat there for a few moments, trying to hear and feel what I could since I couldn't see anything."

"Good," Derek encouraged. "What did you hear and feel?"

"I felt concrete, so I knew I was in an industrial building."

"Can you close your eyes for me so you can feel yourself there? That way maybe you can give me some details you forgot."

"No!" Casey shook her head, wide-eyed. There was something comforting about his eyes and she didn't want to look away.

"Okay. Concentrate on me," Derek said. "Take a deep breath. I want you to get back to where you were a few moments ago. You were starting to relax."

Casey took a couple deep breaths before she nodded for him to continue.

"Okay, you felt concrete. What else did you hear and feel?"

"I smelled cleaner and heard the washers and dryers, so I knew it was a laundry place of some sort."

The Colonel looked up at Mark, who was looking directly at him. They both were taking mental notes of the details.

"Good," Derek said. "What else can you tell me? Give me as many details as you can."

"It smelled musty, like I was in a basement. I didn't hear anybody, so leaned up and moved my blindfold with my hand so I could see."

"What did you see? As many details as possible."

"The building was made of brick – they were big bricks. They were painted white. There was a black iron staircase that led up to the windows that ran along the top of the building. I had to jump to get to the ladder to start climbing though, because it was about seven feet off the ground. It looked like a fire escape."

"Okay, good job. Keep going," Derek encouraged. He knew he would have to go slowly with her to get as many details as possible if they were going to find out who did this and why.

"I looked around for any cameras. There was one pointed at a big room where I heard the washers and dryers."

"So, there was only one camera in the basement?"

"It really wasn't a basement. It was a section of the building. There was only one camera that I saw, though," Casey said.

"Okay. What else?"

"I was handcuffed to what looked like a water pipe. I looked at it to see where the weakest point was, hoping I could break it to get my hands free."

"Good. Is that what you did?"

"No. I heard the men, so I lowered my blindfold back down and went limp on purpose."

"So, they thought you were unconscious?"

"Yeah. They came up to me and jerked my head back by my hair. Then they left me, thinking I was still unconscious."

"Good job. That was smart. Then what happened?"

"When I couldn't hear them anymore, I pulled up the blindfold again. I knew if I was going to get away, I had to do it then. I looked at the pipe and saw an area already dented, so I figured that was my best shot. I braced my foot on the wall and pushed with everything I had, pulling on my wrists to slip them out of the handcuffs."

Derek cringed at the thought of the damage that would cause. He glanced down at her wrists before he looked back up at her. "Did it work?"

Mark rubbed the wrist and hand of her left hand – the one he had. His heart was breaking, but he continued to pray, knowing at that moment that was the only thing he could do to help.

Casey shook her head, not looking away from Derek's eyes.

He looked at her for a moment before he had a look of realization go across his face. "That's when you broke your thumb, wasn't it?" Derek asked.

"It wasn't working. I even tried using the blood that was coming from my wrists to slip my hands out, but it didn't work. I figured if I broke my thumb, that I should be able to slide my hand out using the blood."

"Oh wow, Casey. Um, okay, so, then what did you do?"

"I had broken my thumb a couple of times before by playing volleyball in high school, so I didn't think it would take too much to do it again. I used my left hand, knowing my right was stronger, and if anything came up, I would need it. I took a moment, and then kicked my thumb until I broke it. Then I pushed it into my hand, probably breaking it in a couple more places, but I was able to get my hand out. I took the blindfold and wrapped the handcuff along with my right wrist so the cuffs wouldn't dangle and make any noise."

"Good thinking. Then what happened?"

"I went over to the staircase, jumped up to it, and began climbing. I was able to get about halfway up when the two men came out. When they saw me climbing, they fired at the stairs."

"That was the first one, right?"

"Right."

"Was that the second one, too?"

Casey shook her head as her heart raced once again. Panic set in at what was coming up in the storyline.

Derek put his hands on her shoulders, making sure to keep his eyes in line with hers. "Deep breaths. C'mon, you can do this. Take a couple of deep, cleansing breaths for me."

Casey nodded as she took a couple of breaths, slowly letting them out to help her relax.

Derek knew they were heading into where the memory block was – he could feel it. He knew the next steps he took had to be with caution. He continued to pray for clarity and for the words to say in order to guide her in the right direction. "Okay, you're on the stairs and they just fired at you. What did you do?"

"I knew, um..." Casey shook her head to clear it from the visions that were doing their best to overtake her mind.

"Focus for me," Derek said. "You're on the stairs. What did you do?"

"I knew I had to get rid of them before I could get away, so I climbed back down." Casey struggled to breathe slowly, but she felt like she was suffocating. Feeling trapped, she looked around the room for a way out.

"You're not there, Casey. You're in your bedroom. I'm here, the Colonel's here, and your husband, Mark, is right here. You need to breathe slower for me. You're going to pass out if you don't. Trust me. You are safe. We are not going to hurt you. Look at me," Derek said as he leaned closer to her. "*Look-at-me, Casey.*"

Casey concentrated on his face, taking deep breaths.

"Good. Now, you climbed back down, and then what happened?"

"When I got down, um, one of them grabbed a hold of me, while the other one stood in front of me. He ripped the necklace off my neck." She reached up for the necklace to make sure it was still there.

Derek smiled, trying to set her at ease. "It's there. So, what happened next?"

"I was mad."

"I'll bet."

"I was responsible. I was mad that I was going to lose them again. And when I looked up at him, he started laughing. That made me even madder."

"What did you do?"

"I leaned back on the guy who was holding me and kicked the guy who took my necklace in the stomach. He went back into the wall and hit the ground."

Derek nodded in approval. "Good job."

"When I came back down, I took my foot down the leg of the guy who was holding me. When I landed on his foot, I felt it break under my weight."

"Impressive."

"He let me go for a moment, and when he did, I turned and kicked him in the head. While he was dazed, I grabbed his gun from his belt and aimed it at him."

"Good job. Now, is it time to ask for another number?"

"Not yet."

"Okay, then what happened?"

"He was angry and rammed himself into me, sending us both into the ground. He, um…" Casey shook her head, fighting within herself, knowing what was coming.

"What did he do?"

"He grabbed my wrists, pointing the gun toward the wall."

"Okay. So, you guys were fighting over the gun. Then what happened?"

Casey's body shook and tears came to her eyes, knowing what was ahead. She didn't want to say it. If she did, she would have to own up to what she did.

"Two," Derek said, understanding what was coming.

Casey shook her head as the tears flowed down her cheeks. She glanced at the wall behind Derek, only to see the blood getting darker.

"No, look at *me*." Derek turned her chin toward him. He leaned closer so he was in her face. He, a little more forcefully said, "Two."

Mark didn't like how close Derek was getting or the tone of his voice, but he knew it needed to be done. Even though every bone in his body wanted to jump in and save her from what he knew was coming, he forced himself to continue in prayer, relying on God to get her through.

"Two," Derek said, getting louder. "Where is it?"

Casey glanced from the wall, back to Derek, and said, "In him."

"How?"

Casey closed her eyes as she saw it play in her head over again. She shuddered and then explained, "I, um, slammed my knee into his groin and he curled up in pain, so I got to my feet and aimed the gun at him."

"Good girl. What happened next, Casey?" Derek asked.

Casey shook her head, looking down. Her body shook as the tears streamed down her face.

He lifted her chin so she continued to face him. "What happened next?" He asked a little more forcefully.

"I can't. Please don't make me!" she begged. "Please!"

"Two," he said sternly.

"Please don't!" she pleaded. "Please!"

"Two!" he said, getting loud.

"He, um…" She shook her head as she looked down.

He jerked her chin up, facing directly into his eyes. At that point he was less than three inches from her face and growled, "*Two*!"

"He jumped at me! I didn't have a choice!"

"I know you didn't!" Derek shouted. "Two!"

"There was nothing I could do!"

"Two!" he yelled, grabbing her wrists, pulling her hands from Mark and the Colonel.

She shook her head as she sobbed. "I shot him! He jumped at me and I shot him! I did it! I took a life! I didn't even try to save him!"

He let out a deep breath of air as he pulled her toward him and hugged her. "I know," Derek said quietly. "It's okay. I already knew it."

She looked up at him, her body trembling in fear. "You don't understand. I took a man's life and didn't even *try* to help him!"

"I know," he said, resting his hands on her shoulders, looking directly into her eyes. "It's okay. It was either him or you."

Casey shook her head, beside herself.

"Three," Derek said, trying to get her to focus again.

She got her hands free and dropped her head onto her hands, shaking it. "I can't."

Mark was getting upset at Derek. He felt Derek was pushing too much. He moved closer to Casey, resting his hand on her back as he glared at Derek. Derek shook his head, meaning for Mark not to do anything. Mark looked over at the Colonel for help.

The Colonel watched the whole thing spill out in front of him. While he understood Mark's position, he also understood Derek not only knew what he was doing, but was also doing it right. He shook his head for Mark to do nothing.

Mark sighed, dropping his head onto Casey's shoulder. He was upset and once again in a helpless position regarding Casey. All he could do was sit there and watch her fall apart as he prayed. He prayed it wouldn't get too much worse before she got though the darkness of that night.

"Three," Derek said again, down near her face. He gently lifted her chin up toward him and asked, "What happened after you shot the first man? Where was the second man?"

Casey felt like she was going to vomit. She looked at Derek, almost begging for him to understand what she was trying to tell him. "Do you understand that the blood was pouring from his nose and mouth? He was standing right in front of me, staring at me, as his life drained from him…and I did *nothing*! *I* was the one who shot him and I just stood there watching him die!"

"Casey, what happened next?" Derek asked.

Casey took a deep breath as she watched it play right in front of her like a horror movie. "He, um, dropped to the ground."

"He was dead, right?"

Casey grabbed her stomach and closed her eyes as she rocked on the bed.

"Okay, one was in the staircase, two was the first dead man. Where did three and four go?"

Casey's body shook with fear. She was having a hard time focusing on anything. To her, the room felt like it was closing in on her. She was almost too scared to think.

"Where are they, Case?" Derek insisted.

Casey looked up at him like a scared child. He had no idea what he was asking her to tell him.

"Where was the second man?"

Casey stopped rocking and stared at him wide-eyed, frozen.

He saw where she was, so he put both of his hands on the sides of her face and demanded, "*Where-was-the-second-man*?"

"He, um, grabbed me from behind while I still held the gun."

"You know for sure it was him?"

"Yes. I saw the necklace hanging in his hand."

"Okay, then what happened?"

Casey shook her head. She didn't want to say what was coming.

"What happened, Case?"

The suffocating feeling was coming back as she struggled to get air. "He was cutting my air off! He was squeezing me too tight!"

"What did you do?"

Casey grabbed Derek's arms, slightly shaking him. He had to understand. He had to know. "I couldn't breathe! All I saw was the necklace and…and I couldn't breathe! He was holding me too tight!"

Derek looked at her, slightly surprised at the abrupt turn in her disposition. He knew he was walking into the worst part. He knew he had to move with strength and courage, but along the same lines, with caution. This was the pivotal point.

"I couldn't get any air! Do you understand me? No air! I was suffocating!" Casey said.

Derek looked up toward Heaven, asked for forgiveness from God, before he took his arms and flipped her hands off him. He grabbed her wrists and pulled her toward him. His eyes were angry as he shouted, "*What-did-you-do*?!"

"I couldn't help it! It was my only choice!" Casey yelled back, struggling to get free of his grip.

Mark jumped back against the headboard in shock as Derek jerked Casey out from under him and got into her face. He couldn't believe Derek, the man he had come to love and respect as a brother, was being so physical with his wife. He had to put a stop to this…now!

The Colonel saw the look flash across Mark's face, and he jumped at him to stop him from attacking Derek. As the Colonel went across the bed, Derek pulled Casey off the bed. He used only a little force to keep her under his control, as he put her up against the wall. The walls were cement, so he didn't want to hurt her. As it was, he knew he and Mark were more than likely going to get into it when this was finished. However, this was a crucial moment and he didn't want to lose the momentum. *"What did you do*?!" Derek growled as he got in Casey's face.

"I had to!"

"Had to *what*?"

Mark and the Colonel struggled on the bed while Derek yelled at Casey. "Let him do it!" the Colonel said, getting into Mark's face. "She has been stuffing her feelings since this started, and now it is as if Pandora's Box has been opened. Let him."

"That's my wife!" Mark growled in anger.

"Do I need to make it an order?" the Colonel snapped.

"Had to *what*?" Derek demanded from Casey.

She shook her head as the tears poured in an uncontrollable torrent. She was pinned against the wall. She had nowhere she to go. She had to tell him. "I shot him! Ok? I shot him!"

"Where? Three! C'mon, where is it, Casey?"

Casey squirmed under Derek. "In the stomach! I shot him in the stomach!"

"Then what?"

"He let me go and I aimed it at him again."

"Where?"

"Please don't," she begged as she fought to get away from him.

"Where is it?" Derek pushed. "Where is four?"

"Please don't!"

The Colonel slammed Mark against the headboard, before Mark jumped back at him and they fell off the other side of the bed in a struggle. The Colonel finally got him flipped onto his stomach. Then he grabbed Mark's arm and pulled up on it. He got down near Mark's ear, and sternly, but quietly said, "Let it go. It needs to go forward. Derek is the one who needs to do it. He's right there. We'll pick up the pieces when he's done."

"You'll have to pick up the pieces of *him* when *I'm* done!" Mark roared.

"Four!" Derek shouted. His face was red. Casey couldn't tell if it was because he was angry or just emotional, but at that moment all she could think of was where the fourth bullet went. "*Four*!" He yelled.

"Head!" Casey screamed as she shut her eyes in fear. She didn't want to answer him, but she didn't have a choice. He wasn't going to stop.

Derek looked at Casey wide-eyed for a moment before he took a step back. Releasing her, he suddenly realized exactly what it was he saw on the wall.

Casey slid down to the floor in a sobbing mess, as she crossed her arms in front of her. She couldn't believe she said it out loud. She saw the shock on Derek's face and felt the shame within herself.

As the Colonel got off Mark, Mark scrambled over to Casey. He glared at Derek while he scooped her up in his arms. She looked so broken and defeated.

"I had to, man." Derek shook his head, beside himself. He knew it was bad, but he had no idea it was *that* bad. He dropped his head into his hands as he sat on the side of the bed.

The Colonel got off the floor to see Mark set her down on the bed. Then Mark climbed onto the other side of her and carefully held her as he stroked her hair. It broke the Colonel's heart, but he knew Derek had to do it. He felt for Mark, but he knew it had to be done. He knew she had to say it out loud in order to work through it.

Derek knew he had to talk to her some more, but he didn't want to. The Spirit was pressuring him to press on, but he resisted. As it was, he knew Mark was probably about ready to pummel him. "I can't," he said, looking up toward Heaven. After several moments, he finally relented. Sitting on the side of the bed, he took Casey's hands into his. She looked like a scared cat as she lay there, shaking, with the tears pouring down her cheeks. "Head?" He asked.

Casey nodded. It was all she could do at that moment.

"He stood up and you shot him in the head?"

"Derek, stop it!" Mark snapped.

"Let him," the Colonel said, sternly. He didn't like it any more than Mark did, but he knew it had to be done or they would have to deal with nightmares again and again.

Mark looked up at the Colonel, stunned. *How could he let Derek continue?*

"He stood up and you shot him in the head, right?" Derek asked Casey again.

She nodded.

"You need to verbally answer my question," Derek pressed.

She shook her head. She didn't want to answer him aloud.

"If you don't, we'll end up back against the wall again," Derek threatened as he tightened his grip on her hands.

Casey looked down at her hands, and then back up at him in surprise. He was actually hurting her.

Mark glared at him. How *dare* he threaten her! She was his wife. "If you don't back down, *I'll* be the one slamming *you* against the wall!"

The Colonel felt the immediate tension and said to Mark, "Mark, come over here."

"No." He looked at him in defiance.

"That's an order!"

"That's my wife!"

"*Now,* Captain!"

Mark sighed, shaking his head. He slipped out from under her and went over to the Colonel. In one swift motion, much to Mark's surprise, the Colonel grabbed his wrist and whipped it behind his back, slamming him into the wall. "You've got five minutes, Cruise! Make it good."

"Yes, sir," Derek nodded. Then he shook his head, forcing himself to forget what he just saw. He pulled Casey closer to him and got into her face, "Four!"

"No!" Casey shook her head. "No! Please!"

"Four!" he pushed. He was limited on time, so he wasn't messing around. As it was, there was probably going to be another fight between the three men when it was finished. He had to push her through the rest of the story.

"Colonel!" Mark growled as he struggled to get free of him.

"*Four!*" Derek shouted. He looked so angry to Casey.

"I shot him again," Casey confessed. "I-I didn't have a choice. He was going to get me!"

"Where?" Derek asked.

"I…"

"*Where*?" He demanded.

"I shot him in the head!" Casey yelled through her tears. "I shot him in the head! Right in front of me. I looked him in the eyes and shot him in the head. I did it on purpose." She sobbed.

He nodded in satisfaction. "Good."

Casey looked at him, horrified. "How can you say that's good?"

"Because if you didn't, you wouldn't be sitting here. Your children would be without a mother. Your husband would be without a wife. The Colonel and I would have lost another sister. Don't you get it?" He backed up as he loosened his grip on her, satisfied he had what he needed. Now all he had to do was clean up the mess. "If you didn't shoot to kill, those men would have killed you or done worse. You wouldn't be sitting here. Do *you* understand that?" When she didn't answer, he moved back, giving her space to breathe before he asked, "What happened next?"

"Don't you get it? *I shot two men*! *I killed them*! I looked the second one right in the eyes and shot him in the head! I'm a life-saver, not a life-taker. I don't kill."

He gently took her hands into his. With his voice full of compassion, he said, "Don't *you* understand? If you didn't kill them, you wouldn't be sitting here. You mean more to us than you know. Your life is valuable and priceless. You are an A.N.G.E.L.! You are on our squad. You don't think each one of the A.N.G.E.L.s has had to take a life?"

Casey thought for a moment before she nodded.

"You don't think Jack had to take lives?"

She wiped the tears off her face as she started to calm down. "I'm sure he did."

"If the choice would have been those two men or your children, what would you do?"

"I'd do it again," she said, quietly.

"Then, why do you think *your* life is any less valuable?"

As his words sunk-in, her heart softened.

"You were taken through that training for a reason. It wasn't for the battle on the mountainside. It was for the battle you just went through. You had to use your training to get through it. You're probably going to have more flashbacks. What you went through was traumatic. Trust me when I say that we've all had our share. You've heard some of the stories of the other A.N.G.E.L.s who have passed, but you only know a small portion of our stories."

She wiped the dried tears off her face. "I know."

"Okay, you're more calmed down. Can you tell me what happened after you shot him in the head? Skip the details of what the scene looked like. Tell me how you got away."

Casey knew she could handle that part. "I went over and grabbed my necklace from the man and put it in my pocket. I didn't want to lose it again."

"Good thinking."

"I put the gun in the back of my shorts and jumped for the stairs. I didn't know if anyone else was around, so I didn't want to chance going into one of the other rooms." He nodded in understanding, so she continued, "I got up the stairs and went out the window. I looked around to see if I could figure out how to get down. I was close to the roof, but with my broken thumb I didn't want to climb, so I went down the drainpipe to the ground. They took my shoes and socks off, so I was barefoot."

"And you climbed down the drainpipe barefoot?" Derek asked in amazement.

"Yeah."

The Colonel got near Mark's ear, satisfied things calmed down enough to let him go, and said, "Now, I'm going to let you go and you're going to go to your wife. We'll deal with the feelings later, got it?"

With his face smashed against the wall, Mark's response was a simple nod. He was furious – too angry to talk at the moment. As the Colonel let him go, he rubbed his shoulder. He went over and sat on the bed beside Casey. Even though Casey seemed calmer, Mark kept in mind that he was going to have to deal with Derek and the Colonel later. There was no way he could let that one slide.

"So, then what happened?" Derek asked Casey.

"I looked for cameras, and there was one on each of the corners of the roof. I looked around until I saw a tree line. I was pretty sure I would be able to make it, and that I could get between the two cameras, so I ran. I ran for hours, not sure if there was anyone near me or coming after me."

"Is that when you ran to the gas station?" the Colonel asked, sitting on the side of the bed. He made sure to keep some distance between him and Mark. He knew Mark was angry and he had a right to be. He was concerned about what was going to happen when this was over.

"Yes," she said.

"Is that the rest of the story?" Derek asked.

"Yes. I got to the hotel, thanks to the OXXO clerk, and got checked in. I took a long shower. Then after my shower, I poured hydrogen peroxide on the wounds."

"Oh! Ouch!" Derek cringed. "That had to hurt."

"It did, but not as bad as when the Colonel had to re-break my hand in three places to set it."

Derek looked over his shoulder at him. "Oh, man, Colonel."

"Trust me. I know." The Colonel sighed, shaking his head. "I didn't want to, but the other option was English doing it. I wasn't sure who that would hurt worse…him or her."

Mark didn't say anything. He was still fuming. While everyone else seemed to be relaxing, he was still angry by the way it was handled.

Derek set his hand on her shoulder as he said, "You're calmed down now. Do you think you can get some sleep? You've got some rug rats to care for in the morning. They don't care that you've been up for half the night."

"Yeah," Casey said, as she started to feel the weight lift from carrying the stress. She was exhausted, so she leaned her head over onto Mark's shoulder. It was then that she felt it. She looked up at him.

Mark looked down at her. "What?"

"What is…why are you so angry?"

He shook his head, not saying a word.

"Tell me, please?"

"No, I want you to go to sleep." He pulled her toward him, stroking his fingers through her hair. He gently guided her head onto his lap as he continued to run his fingers through her hair. "Go to sleep, my love."

Casey tried to resist, but she couldn't. Everything finally caught up to her. The many sleepless nights she had over the last week, the emotional spikes she had that night, combined with Mark stroking her hair, she could only hold on so long. As she went to sleep, her body relaxed to the point that she went limp. Everything around her felt like a dream.

"She asleep?" Mark asked.

Derek nodded. "Yep, good job."

Mark glared at him, furious, and Derek looked at him, wide-eyed. "While I understand why you had to push her," Mark said, "I am struggling with the way you did it."

"It was the only way I could get her to respond. Come on, man," Derek pleaded, "we've done it before."

"Not to her."

"She was blocking it. You know that's not healthy."

"I know, but you were abusive…and *you*," he glared at the Colonel, "*you* were abusive with *me*. You guys are both lucky she's fallen asleep on me or I'd take you both out."

The Colonel smiled. "I'm sure you would, but you have to admit she actually said it. While the way he did it was rough, it needed to be done that way. I prayed for him the entire time."

"You don't seriously think I enjoyed that. Do you?" Derek looked at him, taken aback by Mark's reaction. "That killed me just as much as it killed you. I've been in charge of her as long as you have, buddy. We are all close here. She's like a sister to me. Trust me, I was fighting with the Spirit, knowing what He wanted me to do. There's no way I would do that if I didn't have to. It was the only way to get through to her."

Mark shook his head, still angry.

"She's been through a lot. Do you really want her nightmares to continue?" the Colonel asked.

He shook his head. He couldn't believe the Colonel would even ask that question.

"Neither do we. We're not done either. While I'm pretty sure this is the worst of it, we will still have to deal with the fallout. She's in the middle of Post-Traumatic Stress right now. We need to walk her through this, holding her hand. We might have to get rough again, not that we enjoy it. He's right. It was the only way she was going to respond. When he pushed, she gave information."

"She's not a criminal. She didn't need to get slammed up against the wall," Mark argued.

"Yes, I did," Derek said, and then looked up at him. Mark snapped his head toward him, appalled. "I needed to put her back there…maybe not right there, but I needed her to have the same feelings. She needed to feel like she didn't have a choice."

It made sense, but the way he did it was where Mark was having the problem.

"And you weren't cooperating," the Colonel added. "I didn't have a choice either."

Mark looked over at him, stunned.

"I know you," the Colonel continued. "Derek and I know both of you very well. We are all going to need to walk her through this, but you're going to have to back down if we get in her face again. She has to face this in order to walk through it. If you have to go into another room, fine. I can't guarantee that next time will be any easier. I will promise you that she won't be seriously injured, though. We are trying to heal her heart and soul, not scare her even worse."

"I understand that," Mark said, "I am having a problem with the way you did it."

"And we will do it again if we have to," Derek said, very seriously. "Think through what just happened. The only time I got in her face is when she needed to push through. She had to push through the worst until she could tell me how she got away. It's like watching a scary movie. You have to watch all the terrifying parts to get to the end to see how they got away, right?"

"Right," Mark agreed.

"Well, she got away. She needed to tell us the whole story, and she may have to do it several times before she realizes that she can jump to the part where you're carrying her out of the hotel room and she's safe."

"We don't envy you in this. You have got a lot of work ahead of you. We do too. It's going to take a little while," the Colonel continued. "I'm sure between the three of us we can handle it, though. Have faith, brother. Come on, I know it's in you. Think of the times we had to pull Jack through some things, or Keith. Think about Ariel. Do you want her to stay in the same mode Ariel was in?"

"But she's not." Mark shook his head, confused. "Those are two different situations. That's like comparing apples to oranges."

"No, it's not. Ariel lost her love. She stuffed her feelings to the point that all she wanted to do was escape them. Casey was headed that way. While she may not have a death wish, once she starts stuffing feelings this big, she may do it in other areas, systematically shutting herself down. Are you really going to tell me that you didn't see Ariel shutting down?"

"She did," Mark admitted.

"Do you want Casey to do that?"

"No."

"Then, are you going to work with us or against us?" Derek asked.

"You have to decide now. We are not going to apologize for what we did," the Colonel moved closer toward Mark.

Mark thought for a moment as he picked her up and cradled her in his arms. He looked down at her. As he rested his hand on the side of her face, he shook his head and sighed, "I just love her so much." He looked up at the Colonel and Derek. "What was going on was killing me inside. While my heart broke for her, I was trying to deal with the anger in the way you guys were doing it."

The Colonel nodded in understanding. "We know. It was killing us too."

"I wanted to stop multiple times," Derek added, "but the Spirit wouldn't let me. God knows better than we do. We have to trust Him."

"I do!" Mark said, almost offended.

"I do too." Derek moved closer toward Mark. He knew they were going to have to pray.

The Colonel rested one hand on Casey's head, and his other one on Mark's head. "Then trust where He's guiding us."

"What are you doing?" Mark looked at him. He looked over at Derek, who laid one hand on the other side of Casey's head, and his other on the side of Mark's head.

"We are going to let God guide us," the Colonel said.

Derek closed his eyes. "We need to pray for both of you."

Both of the men prayed quietly at first before their volume got louder. After a moment, Mark joined them. As their voices blended together, the Spirit filled the room. It felt like a cool shower, trying to wash away all the bad feelings that swirled through the room.

It was at that moment, that Casey knew it might take a while, but between God, The Spirit, Jesus, the Colonel, Derek, and Mark, Casey would be able to work through this and still stay sane in the process.

Chapter 15

The Next Generation

It took Casey a couple of months to completely recover from what happened to her. She had many more nightmares throughout that time. Each time, the Colonel, Derek, and Mark walked her through it over and over again, healing her heart and mind. All three of the guys worked with Casey in processing through having to take a life. To her, that was the hardest part of the entire ordeal. There were many times where she had to explain in detail exactly what happened, pushing through to the end to where she was safe.

Together they sorted through the details in an attempt to figure out where Casey was held. Unfortunately, the information she gave was not a lot to go on. The Colonel and Derek even went back to the OXXO. They backtracked to see what they could find. While they were able to locate the laundry, it functioned as a normal laundry service. So, once again they were back to square one in figuring out exactly why she was taken.

The thing is, people are kidnapped all of the time in Mexico and held for ransom. More times than not, the people are not returned in the shape they were taken, and sometimes they are killed. With that thought in mind, the guys discussed it, and decided they were happy Casey was home. They were going to stay on high alert from that point forward, especially when it came to Casey and the children.

After several long discussions on the logistics of how the family was going to work, Derek agreed with the Colonel's assessment of the situation. Derek and the Colonel talked to Juan, and were able to work with him on the farm while Mark stayed home with Casey and the kids. It was a little hard on Mark, allowing the other two to provide financially for the family. There were days he had to force himself to stay focused on them. He relished the fact that he *could* spend as much time as he did with the kids. He knew not many fathers had an opportunity like that, so he didn't take it lightly. His issue was watching the Colonel and Derek leave every morning, knowing they were working in the hot sun all day, only to come home exhausted…while he stayed home with the family.

*   *   *

"What's wrong?" Casey asked, sitting on the couch next to Mark while the kids took a nap.

"Sometimes it bothers me that I have to stay home while the Colonel and Derek go to work," he admitted.

"There's a reason for that."

"I understand that, but I have to admit I sometimes miss the excitement of going on missions."

"You guys still go on them."

"Not anywhere near as frequently," he pointed out. "Please don't take this the wrong way, but I sometimes feel like a babysitter."

Casey sat back in her seat, mulling his words through her mind for a few moments before she asked, "If we lived in the U.S., would you still have to babysit us?"

"Not as much. If we were there, the Colonel, Derek, and I could shift around a little more easily. The dark is stronger here. We have to be more alert."

"Then, why don't we move back to the U.S.?"

"Because you are still a 'missing person' in the United States."

"I understand that, but if I don't work, I won't be on radar."

"I don't know." He shook his head. "Maybe in the future, but not now."

"I understand."

"You're in thinking mode again, aren't you?" he smirked, as she sat on the couch biting her nails – a nervous habit of hers.

"Yeah."

"What about? Care to share?"

"Well, since things have finally slowed down, and I have been able to get a grip on my nightmares, a lot of random thoughts have been coming to mind."

"Like?" he pressed.

"Well, for example, Jack. While we lost our parents, God still left me with stability in him. Jack was an anchor for me when I needed him. And, in working with you guys, I now have the confidence of knowing that you guys were a stability factor for him."

"Yep. We tend to keep each other up when things get rough."

"Then there's Mac. He taught me it was okay to give my heart to another after what life threw at me – and for that I'm grateful. I might not have allowed you in if he didn't. And, while I miss him, I know he is in a much better place, same as Jack."

"It's sometimes rough finding the balance of missing them, verses being happy for them to be in the presence of God."

"Exactly." She sighed. "Then there was Jesse and Tommy. They were like brothers to me, but they each had their own strengths. Jesse could make me laugh in even the roughest of times, while Tommy helped me find my strength when I needed to dig down deep for it."

"That's true."

"Then there's you guys."

"What about us?"

"Well, at first I couldn't figure out why I had to have that training from the Outback, especially after I gave birth during the actual battle."

"Yeah, I can imagine that was a bit frustrating for you."

"But it was necessary. After all, I needed it when those men took me from you guys. When they did, I didn't have you guys to protect me. I was on my own. Up until that point, I knew you guys were still in the shadows somewhere ready to jump in if need be. In the long-run, God took all of my 'anchors' away, and it was just me and Him. He helped me get out of there. He gave me the strength and courage to do what needed to be done."

"It was a strength you had in you all of the time – you just didn't know it. We knew it was there. We've watched God develop it within you through the years. And after the Aggressor Challenge with me, I knew you could take on anything you put your mind to," Mark said. "You gave me quite a beating."

Casey shuddered as she remembered the challenge where she had to fight Mark in the deep Outback.

"I knew at that moment that you would be able to do it."

"At that point, I wasn't one hundred percent sure of myself, but I was sure of God."

"That's where you needed to have your confidence, and He didn't let you down, did he?"

"No. He didn't."

"And He won't. You're one of His."

"And for that I'm thankful."

He looked over at her and still saw concern on her face. "What's wrong?"

"Well, I can't help thinking about Hunter."

"What *about* him?"

"Well, the devil is like a roaring lion, seeking whom he may devour."

He shook his head in confusion. "You've got a bit of a jump on me regarding your thoughts. I'm not seeing the connection."

"How do I explain this?" She thought for a moment before she said, "Hunter was gorgeous."

"I'll have to take your word for it."

"What I mean is that he was gorgeous on the outside, but on the inside he was evil. I didn't know that until it was almost too late."

"Unfortunately, that's how it works. If evil looked as scary as it actually is, no one would fall for it," Mark pointed out. "Satan makes evil look good."

"That he does." She sighed. "I guess my concern is not so much for me, but for the kids."

Mark glanced toward their rooms. "We'll train them the same way we trained you."

"Can we teach them quick enough, though?"

"Meaning?"

"Meaning, can we train them before he can get his claws into them? Can we be good enough parents to those three?"

"There is a verse in Proverbs that says, *"Train a child in the way he should go, and when he is old, he shall not depart from it."* We do the best we can, pray over them, and leave them in God's hands."

"I can't help in being selfish in this area. After everything I've been through, I don't want anything to happen to them."

"We can only do what we can do."

"And you can only do what you can do," Casey said, bringing the conversation back around.

"What does that mean?"

"God has you leading this family for a reason. He gave the Colonel and Derek the idea to leave you with us for a reason. It's up to you to find out what that is. I think the best place to start is with the kids."

He chuckled as he shook his head. "Okay, how did you get to be so smart?"

"Hanging around you guys, I guess." She smirked. "Don't worry. Things will work out."

"Trust God and let Him lead, huh?"

"Yep. He hasn't let us down yet."

*   *   *

The good news was that the family was close to each other, and as the years went by, they only got closer. Yes, they had their struggles – one of the big ones was getting the twins through the younger ages with Angel on their heels. She did live up to her name though, and was an absolute joy. Every day, she looked more and more like Casey. She had her build, and definitely her looks, much to Mark's delight. She also had Casey's demeanor and love for helping others.

While Mark loved the all children the same, he found the fine balance of loving them to their strengths. Jonathon was an excellent athlete, joining soccer early and keeping it even into high school. Jesse was more into art. He was an exceptional artist. His drawings topped a lot of the school competitions, and all the competitors were incredible. Mark struggled to believe they were only in high school. Angel was more into academics – with math and science as her strong suits. While she was more scholastic in her educational endeavors, she was also very popular and played a little soccer herself. She didn't top it like Jonathon, but she did play well enough to be on the team. She said she enjoyed playing, and enjoyed the camaraderie of her teammates. While Jonathon did enjoy his teammates as well, he was in it for the competition aspect and excelled at it.

Mark and Casey were proud of their children. Not only were they successful in their strengths, they were also active in church and in church activities. They were also proud in the way they conducted themselves, and in their thought processes. The children of the other A.N.G.E.L.s influenced them greatly growing up, making them almost more mature than they were supposed to be at their age. The older children took them under their wings, keeping them out of trouble and giving them advice when they needed it. Casey was grateful for the closeness they all shared, and enjoyed the many adventures they had over the next several years. While the guys never left them alone, they still took off for missions. Mark told Casey about some of them, which sometimes involved the blending of some of the other A.N.G.E.L. teams again. It was good to hear about the others they had come to love and admire when they were in Mexico. She was happy to know the ones she had heard about were still alive.

Also, over the course of time, Casey watched as all seven men would take all of the A.N.G.E.L.'s children up to the mountain and train them. They split them up into groups. Pablo and Anita were one; Carlos, Pedro, Miguel, Antonia, and Sergio were another; with Juanito, Cristiana, Maria, and Felipe in the third; leaving Jonathon, Jesse, and Angel in the fourth.

Basically, as soon as they could hold a bow and arrow, the children started training. Some of it was physical strength, some was marksmanship, some of it was mental and emotional, and some of it involved learning to see and feel the unseen.

Casey watched over the years as the children went from being good, to being good enough to go on some missions. The rule stood that they weren't allowed to go until they turned eighteen. Once they turned eighteen, if they wanted to, they were entered into a pool to see who would go with the guys – the choice was theirs to be entered or not. Only one younger was allowed to go on each trip out until they were twenty-one, then it was strictly voluntary.

While most were terrified on their first couple of missions, they began to relax as they learned to let the Spirit guide them, and over time it became easier for them.

Following their progress over the years, Casey saw where Jack had done a lot of the same things with her. She even taught the games Jack played with her to the guys, who in turn used them on the kids. It was exciting to see the strength the kids held. She knew they would be used for the good of God's Kingdom. She knew God would also be looking out for them.

As Casey watched them in the field, she couldn't help but dwell on the battles over the years…the big one being right there on the hill they trained on. Had Satan won that battle and gotten a hold of Casey and the boys, then Angel wouldn't be there and the unit wouldn't be three stronger.

Casey also didn't think the training would have been initiated either. Mark was the one who came up with the idea as he saw the kids growing. He talked to the guys about his idea, so while they were gone or working, he would take the older kids up to the mountain. Of course, Casey and the kids would go with him, and the kids watched what was going on. After a while, the boys mimicked what they were doing, which triggered Mark's line of thinking even further and the four groups were formed. As the younger ones came up, they were stronger than the older children, because they had been watching and learning all along. It was as if it were second nature to them. It didn't take the older ones long to catch up either. They already had the Spiritual strength instilled in them from the beginning. They only needed to add the physical strength and the techniques.

Casey thoroughly enjoyed watching the Mexican-American teams build from four and three, to a combined twenty-one by the time Angel hit twenty-one. While it was an obvious strengthening of the team, it was the way it was done that struck her. The verse in Proverbs that says, *"Train up a child in the way he should go, and when he is old, he shall not depart from it,"* continuously ran through her mind. They were training the children. They not only trained them in regards to the real world, but they also trained them in the Spiritual/Heavenly ways as well.

The kids were strong, formidable opponents of the dark forces. The kids not only fought battles on missions, they were doing it daily in school, and with their friends outside of school as well. They were all leaders within their own right. They all were zealous for the rights of others, including in leading them toward God. They were fierce, powerful challengers to the adversary, who was going to have to think twice before coming against any of them.

During a lot of their group prayers, and even some of the ones Casey caught her own children having at home, she heard them praying for revival. They loved the people of Mexico. They prayed for those whose hearts were true to the Lord, to bring others to the truth of who He is, and what He stands for. She heard them praying for strength for themselves, to stand up for what was right, and for guidance of the Spirit in keeping them safe.

While she was in her own quiet times with the Father, Casey prayed for the same things. She also prayed for the other A.N.G.E.L.s who she knew existed around the world. She prayed for reinforcements for them, knowing they were all coming up in age. She asked that in the same way the Mexican-American team increased, that God would enlarge the other units, especially the ones that only had one or had become extinct over the years. She prayed for others to step-up and carry the torch. It reminded her of what her Chief said many years before, *"We all know for each one of us claimed, another has to step up to continue taking care of our fellow citizens. Our job is to protect and to serve. Our job is to care for the injured, to help those who need it."* While she understood he was referring to firefighters, she often applied this to her daily life as an A.N.G.E.L. For each Christian that falls, someone needs to pick up their armor and continue the fight. In First Peter 5:8, it says, *"Be sober, be vigilant; because your adversary the devil, as a roaring lion, walketh about, seeking whom he may devour."*

The A.N.G.E.L.s passed onto their children the gift of being able to see what was not there, to feel what they could not see, and to anticipate the enemy's movements before he even made them. They passed down their skills to the next generation, so when they could no longer do it, the younger would take over. She prayed the others around the world were doing the same, or that God may even push others forward into those areas where the units were either extinct or dwindling. While she may never know for sure whether that prayer would be answered, she knew in her heart that the Heavenly Angels were still around, and she prayed for strength and power for them as well.

The more she thought about it, the more she wondered just how many A.N.G.E.L.s *were* around, whether the physical or Angelic. People might walk right by one and not even know it. In Hebrews 13:2, it reads *"Do not forget to show hospitality to strangers, for by so doing some people have shown hospitality to angels without knowing it."*

One might not know who they are just by looking at them. People might not even see their work, but they have to trust they are there. God will not leave His people alone. Rest assured, that there are, in fact, Angels Among Us.

<u>Epilogue</u>

As a group, the Mexican A.N.G.E.L.s and American A.N.G.E.L.s had a meeting, discussing the future of their teams. Since Angelina graduated college, she was set to begin her Master's Degree in Anthropology at the University of Nevada in Reno in the fall. Jonathon finished his degree for Physical Therapy last year, graduating from Texas A&M. Jesse also finished his schooling for Graphic Arts last year at Texas A&M as well and both of them had been doing internships to gain experience in their selected fields. The question came up about the status of the teams. They decided since the children were older, that the Mexican unit was at a viable size, which would free the American A.N.G.E.L.s to return to America and begin rebuilding their unit as well.

The American A.N.G.E.L.s looked around and decided since Angelina would be going to college there, that the family would relocate to Reno, Nevada to make their start and rebuild their lives. The move was to take place in a week.

Derek and the Colonel were packing their rooms, while Jonathan and Jesse were out gathering boxes. Mark and Casey were packing the kitchen when twenty-three-year-old Angelina walked in and leaned against the wall.

"Have you finished packing your room?" Casey asked, shoving the wrapped plates into the box.

"Yeah," she said, trying to decide how to ask the next question.

Mark could never get over how much Angelina looked identical to Casey at her age. She also had a lot of the same habits and mannerisms Casey did as well. He knew by her actions that she was hiding something or wanted to talk. He crossed his arms as he leaned on the counter. "What is it?"

"Well, I was done with my room, so I started on the storage area off the master bedroom."

"Oh, good!" Casey smiled. "We'll get the packing done in no time with initiative like that."

Mark's heart skipped a beat at the mention of the storage area. "Um," he nervously cleared his throat, "you, uh, started packing the storage area?"

She nervously bit her nails and admitted, "Yeah."

Casey narrowed her eyes as she studied Angelina's body language. "Is there something you found?"

"Yeah. Just a minute."

"Oh, boy." Mark sighed, looking up toward the ceiling, praying she didn't find what he thought she found.

Angelina went into the storage area and picked up a locked metal box that was approximately three feet in length, two feet wide, and two feet tall. When she took it into the kitchen, Casey gasped, covering her mouth in shock, and Mark groaned.

Angelina asked, "What's in the strong box?"

Joel 1:3 - Tell it to your children, and let your children tell it to their children, and their children to the next generation.

Books in the Holy Flame Trilogy.

 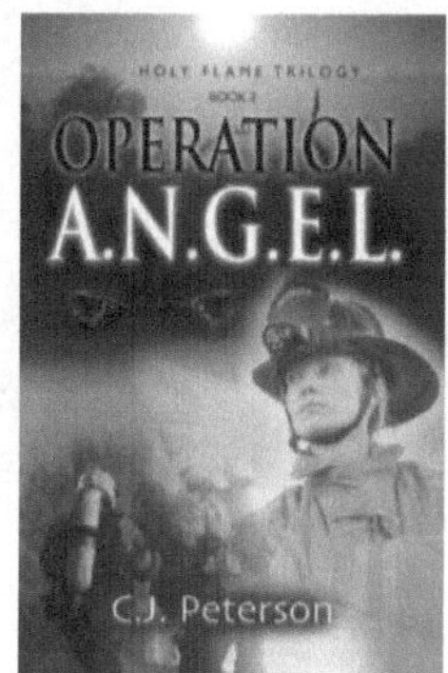 

See what the other A.N.G.E.L.s have been assigned -

Books in the Grace Restored Series

 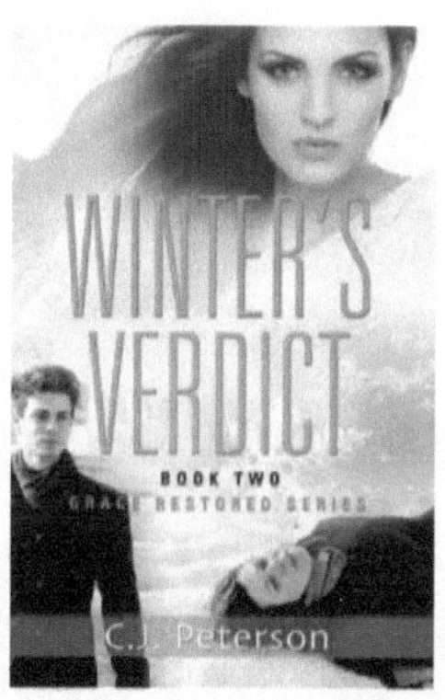 

The next generation is taking over. In the Award-Winning
Divine Legacy Series.